SHIELD OF THE SUMMER PRINCE

Book Two of the World of Ruin

Erik Scott de Bie

DRAGON
MOON
PRESS

SHIELD OF THE SUMMER PRINCE

Book Two of the World of Ruin

Erik Scott de Bie

"The World of Ruin:
A dying world—an inevitable end.
Much and many have been lost,
All must pass to Ruin."

Shadow of the Winter King
Copyright ©2016 Erik Scott de Bie
Cover art © 2016 Aleta Rafton
Map created by Cory Gelnett

p ISBN 13 978-1-897492-96-3
e ISBN 13 978-1-897492-97-0

Printed and bound in the United States

www.dragonmoonpress.com

Dedication

For you, my readers—for believing in this story as much as I do.

Acknowledgments

The hard work of many hands has gone into the World of Ruin series. None of this would have come to pass without my parents, Lynne and Scott. Some years ago, they read a draft of what eventually evolved into the World of Ruin. They gave an honest account, and the result is centuries better. Many thanks also to Gwen Gades and Gabrielle Harbowy, for trusting me and putting together such a beautiful product. Thanks always to my friends and writing colleagues, for inspiration, camaraderie, and the occasional kick in the pants when I needed it. And thanks to my wife, for talking it all through, putting up with my excited rambling, and pushing me to write the best book I could.

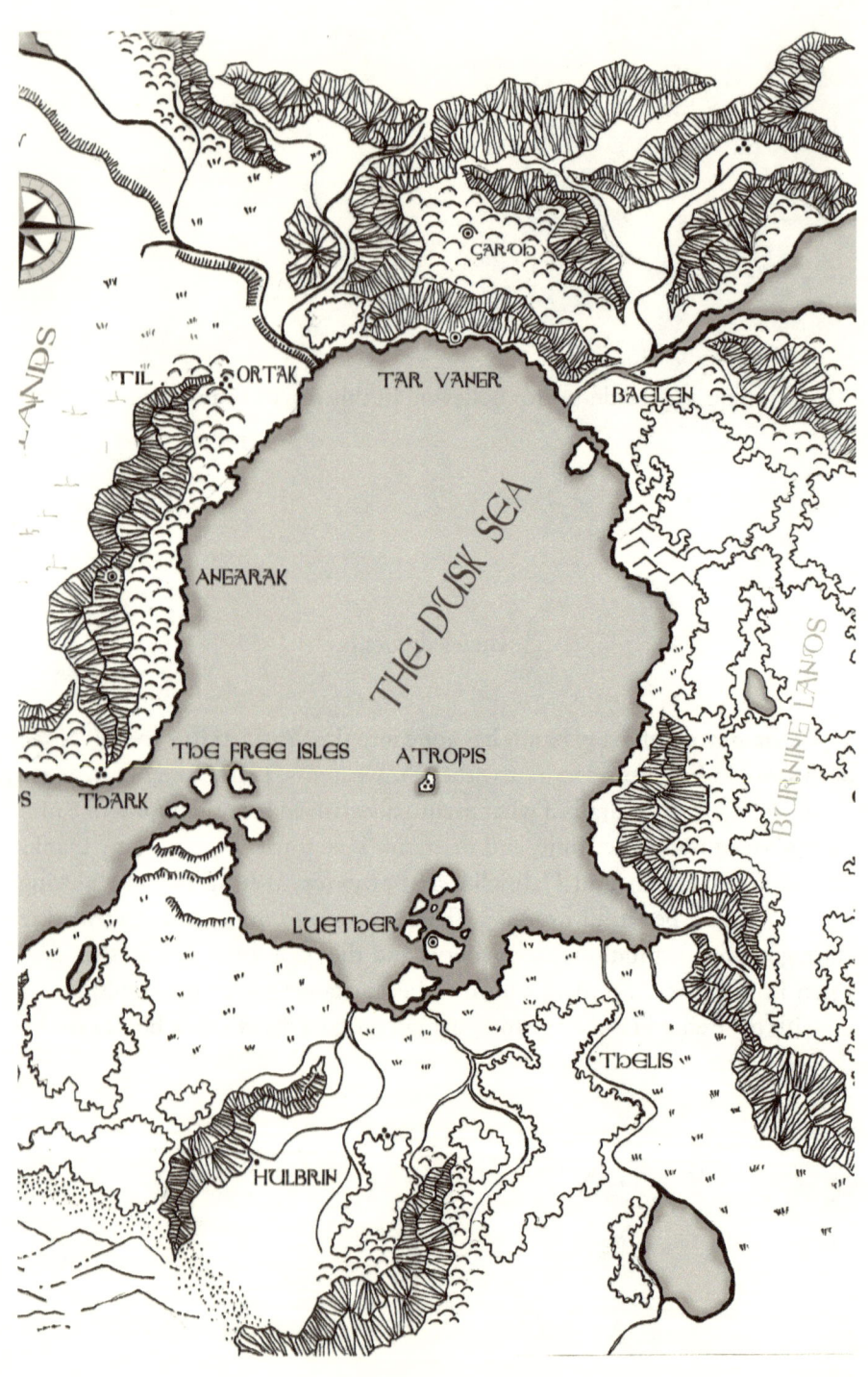

GAROD

TIL

ORTAK

TAR VANER

BAELEN

THE DUSK SEA

ANGARAK

THE FREE ISLES

ATROPIS

THARK

BURNING LANDS

LUETHER

THELIS

HULBRIN

PROLOGUE

THE CROWN PRINCE OF the Summer City walked through the swirling white at the top of the world, and all eyes followed his path.

As he stepped off the lift, snow crunched like fingerbones beneath his footfalls, and his breath steamed up into the frigid morning air. At this height, the vicious winds tore at his clothes, fraying the scarf that extended out of his hood. He wiped his mouth to clear away the frost that had collected in his red beard. Burn and *rot*, it was cold. Until just a few days ago, he had never even *seen* snow, and he didn't like it one bit.

Garin Ravalis, the Fox of Luether and heir-apparent of a lost city, hated this, but he knew it had to be done. What choice did he have?

"Carriage, Syr?" the lift operator asked. "I can call you one."

"Call me what you like, but no, thanks." Garin ran his fingers through his hair, making the rings on three fingers of his right hand twinkle in the thin sunlight. "I'll walk."

"What? In this snow?" The woman looked at him like his head had just fallen off.

Garin gave her a helpless smile and set off toward the castle.

Stone buildings with spiraling glass buttresses rose around him, their tiled roofs dripping with snow melt to form icicles longer than any man's sword. He made sure to give them a wide berth, though neither did he want to risk through the middle of the roads, where the snow mingled with the greasy leavings of mage-powered wagons. He walked a narrow balance through the snow piled on the lanes, trying not to slip with every step. He could feel the tingling burn even through the thick leather.

High-City was packed today with citizens who wanted to see the king's grand unveiling. Other than Ravalis functionaries, no one had been able to get in or out since the incident on Ruin's Night, and no one had seen the Summer King. But today, Lan held court, and he had invited any who wished to see him to come. This was remarkable, as some insisted the king was dead or gravely injured and could not appear. Garin had also heard the base rumors about the nature of his wounds. Perhaps this was Lan's attempt to lay all that to rest.

A flurry had descended upon Tar Vangr's High-City at the start of the new year, and not one of snow. The streets of the silver-white city ran red and blue with the cloaks of Ravalis soldiers patrolling at all hours. By order of the Summer King, the armed men enforced a curfew that began before the sun set and ended only after it was nearly at its peak. Citizens on the street had to deal with their harassment. As he walked, Garin saw six occasions where soldiers demanded bribes from vendors to keep their stands open, twice in quick succession with the same merchant. Down in Low-City, it was worse, he knew: blood ran in the streets and battered citizens were often left exposed in the burning snow. This succession had been anything but peaceful, and to have a pale face under the rule of the new King Ravalis was a mistake many in the city had tragically made.

Garin had assessed the risks of his current course of action: that Lan knew of his role in aiding Regel and Ovelia, and would have him executed for treason immediately. He wondered if he would even be able to approach the palace without being detained. He'd considered pretending to be dead and fleeing the city—Alcarin had certainly supported that idea—but ultimately, confronting his cousin was his only course. He had no loyalty to the Winter Throne, only to his greater mission, and for that, he'd need Lan's aid. By the laws of justice, he should be marching into the palace to slay his cousin. Face darkening, he remembered Ovelia's bloody face as she limped out of Lan's room. But justice would have to wait.

Soon enough, Garin came to Serra Way, the main road of Tar Vangr's High-City, and he saw to his dismay that Ravalis machinery had cleared all but a light dusting of snow from the wide boulevard.

Looking down, Garin saw the void through the cloudy mage-glass beneath his feet, and it loosened his grasp on his balance. He'd never much liked Luether's High-City either, preferring to spend his time down with the common people, but at least there the distance was not so great—only a hundred paces or so. In Tar Vangr, one false step would send him on a thousand foot journey to the polluted slums below.

"No choice, remember?" He smiled up at the ancient monument that named the avenue: a scarred, winged warrior, her hair streaming wild behind her. "I wish you were here, too, Angel Serris."

He set out, cutting his way through the sea of bundled people.

Walking through High-City was only the first hurdle. Another day, Garin would have powdered his distinctive dark cheeks and worn a plain cloak to hide his red hair, but today's purpose required that he approach the palace openly. The thick snow filled his boots, and his feet were wet within half a block, but he trudged on. Almost every native winterborn in the street glared at him, though plenty of soldiers took note of his rich cloak and cast him curious glances. Though this was not his city, he was a Prince of the Blood of Ravalis, and that still carried weight.

He sympathized with the Vangryur: he didn't want his Blood in this city either. Not that he could leave, with the ports closed while dusters searched every ship. Reports said all the conspirators involved in the coup were dead, but Garin knew for a fact the reports were more wishful than accurate. The very fact that the search continued gave the lie to the palace's claims, and Garin knew Regel—at least—was still alive. When the old assassin had left, his eyes had gleamed with such resolve that not a thousand fully armed ornithopters could stay him.

"Ruin's eye slip past you, Regel," Garin murmured. "May it slip past us all."

He paused at the steps of the palace of Tar Vangr and looked up at the great iron doors that had welcomed hundreds to a celebration on Ruin's Night just a few days ago. To see them now, dark and hulking and laced with frost, Garin could hardly imagine they had opened in centuries. Mist swirled into the morning air, tracing the ancient stone and dancing through the deep carvings. The building was undeniably beautiful in its eternal solidity—like the palace of Luether. In the City of Pyres, however, those wisps of mist would be flame and smoke. His city burned, and no one else could save it.

The masses of people huddled outside the great doors, Garin realized, without exception, shared a common theme. Snow-streaked white faces. Worn coats and shoes. Emaciated bodies. These were Tar Vangr's disenfranchised: the poor and powerless had gathered here to hope for a word from their king. And considering that it had been a band of loyalists to the old regime who had so grievously wounded Lan and nearly toppled his kingdom, Garin did not expect these folk would get what they wanted. It was so like looking out upon his own people—the brutalized lowborn of Luether—that his heart swelled and his blood warmed in sympathetic anger.

As he stood there, the massive doors ground slowly open, and a dozen Dustblades trooped out, their armor and weapons crackling with ensorcelled dust magic. Called "dusters" for their traditional gray cloaks, they symbolized the strength of the Ravalis, and the message was not lost on Garin. Swift retribution would meet any unrest fomented in this place. They gazed at the prince without pity, and Garin knew they would kill him in a heartbeat if so commanded. This was not promising.

9

Between them emerged a comparatively tiny figure, one Garin recognized at a distance as Roderk, an orderly in service to his cousin Lan. Garin had always had a keen memory for names and facts—it came in handy on his particular path. The fat little man, cheeks rosy from the warmth inside the castle, immediately shivered and wrapped his arms around himself. He had apparently forgotten a coat. Garin couldn't help but shake his head.

"Y-Y-Your Highness," he said, teeth chattering. "Your visit is un-un-unexpected, but welcome. Won't you—?"

Cries of alarm drifted on the wind from above. Garin looked up in time to see a huge black rock crashing toward him. He wanted to stagger aside, but his body was too slow. The hunk of stone shattered into the snow not a dozen steps away, and a storm of glass shards stabbed down around it like thrown blades. One came close enough to nail the fringe of his cloak into the snow. The glass studded the space between him and Roderk, who staggered back with a wail.

Garin looked up, the wind catching his hood and billowing it wide. Far above, at the apex of the great palace at the height of the mountain, crews and even an ornithopter worked to clear the rubble and glass of the shattered window that had once protected the throne room. The massive battle on Ruin's Night had laid waste to the Palace of Tar Vangr, and the city still showed the scar.

Garin became aware of many eyes watching him—winterborn locals and summersworn soldiers alike. They stood in silence, judging him and wondering. He gave them all a smile and a wave, picked his way between the fragments of rock and mage-glass, and leisurely made his way up the steps as though he hadn't almost died horribly only a breath before. He strode right past Roderk, who could only sputter and look confused. Murmurs rose among the gathered throng, and he hoped they were in praise of his courage, rather than astonishment at his madness.

Garin slipped through the great doors—still ajar from when the servant had come out—and instantly felt the mighty warmth on his face. The great palace of Tar Vangr was sweltering inside, as though someone had transported them to the wild jungles of Echvar. His nose clogged and sweat beaded all along his noble brow and the strong contours of his face. He could not show discomfort, however, and the primary reason sat at the end of the vast open Revelry Hall, past a sea of people in red and blue.

"Cousin," a voice intoned, bouncing off the clever acoustic architecture. Garin could not see the speaker through the packed hall. "This surprise is so very…pleasant."

Every face turned to look at him: Ravalis soldiers, local power brokers, powdered servants, rich advisors, summerblooded folk laying their entreaties before the king. Most of the faces had the dark complexion of the southern lands, and those who bore the paler coloration of the north wore Ravalis colors of crimson and azure. Courtiers and supports of the Summer King. They all looked tired and dirty, and Garin saw no friendly faces here. A few curious stares, but most held open contempt.

"Leave us," the king said to the gathered assemblage. "My cousin and I have words to share."

The horde of folk shivered like a living beast and started to stretch in various directions. People broke away, heading toward various exits from the vast hall. They shuffled and muttered, obviously just as weary and broken down at the masses huddled outside the great doors. Unlike them, however, these folk had warm homes to go to, plenty to eat, and pleasurable company awaiting them. They cleared the path between Garin and the dais, upon which the Ravalis had announced their unquestioned dominance of Tar Vangr on Ruin's Night, only hours before Demetrus's death. With an unsettled shiver, Garin noted the massive reddish stain on the stone from where Lan had personally executed Kiereth Yaela, a prominent nobleman in the city and leader of his opposition on the council. The act had terrified them into obedience, and Garin admitted it was doing a fair job on him as well.

In short order, he and the king were alone in the hall, save for a few gray-cloaked dusters who remained at a discreet distance from the dais. That, and the bent figure of Vhaerynn the Necromancer, who hovered behind the throne. Alas, Demetrus's old advisor had survived Ruin's Night, and Lan retained his services. Garin had watched Vhaerynn take a shattering course through a window, torn apart in a storm of deadly scything shards, but the sorcerer didn't bear so much as a scratch. Blood magic, no doubt. Garin knew enough about the foul stuff to stay as far away as possible.

"Come closer," the king said.

Garin swallowed his uncertainty. The king hadn't had him killed before he even stepped through the doors, but that did not mean he would not lash out later. If Garin would get what he needed from his cousin, he would have to play along.

Lan Ravalis, the Bear of Luether, King of Tar Vangr the last mage-city of Calatan, sat in the massive basalt throne his father Demetrus—his father and Garin's uncle—had sat only days before. The cousins had not seen one another since that fateful night, and Lan did not look well at all. As Garin approached, he could see clearly that Lan's hair had grown long and haggard and his face wan. He wore plentiful rouge, but Garin could see the facial bruises beneath it. Sweat beaded Lan's forehead, and his slouch showed that he clearly favored his midsection. He wore a thickly lined golden robe, open at the chest to reveal the massive bear's head tattooed there. His impressive stature seemed to have sucked in upon itself, making him lean and vicious, and his kingly robes hung loosely around his wiry frame. A scabbarded sword with a crimson-banded handle leaned against the side of the throne, its hilt fashioned after the semblance of a dragon. Garin could tell the presence of the sword was meant to intimidate him, but the knowledge failed to negate the effect.

"Cousin," Lan said. "You've not called on me for days, nor has there been any word. We are relieved to see you alive and—" He trailed off, wincing at some inner pain.

Vhaerynn filled in: "Intact."

"And you, cousin." Garin bowed. Words farther from the truth, he could not have spoken. "You had the throne brought down. I can't imagine how many ornithopters that took."

"Is this what you brought me?" Lan asked. "Pleasantries? Idle converse, while great events transpire around us? While the realm prepares for war?"

Lan had begun that way, then blamed Garin for responding in kind. Typical of him.

"While the *realm* prepares for war." Garin nodded to the sword. "I see *you* are prepared, though I might recommend that special power armor I built for you." He nodded to Lan's shrinking body. "The people I saw outside your gates seemed more interested in food. How has the crop been?"

"Ah yes." Lan leaned forward suddenly, such that Garin flinched. "I am aware of your little show for the smallborn: walking the streets on foot, like a beleaguered hero for a lost cause. Tell me, did it unfold to your liking? This inspiring demonstration of your resolve?"

"I wouldn't have minded some applause," Garin said.

When Lan didn't laugh, however, Garin's ease withered into anxiety. The king's stern demeanor and hard face barely sealed a nigh-boiling cauldron of rage. It would not do to upset him. Indeed, his eyes even now were starting to gleam with anger, and Garin worried he'd gone too far.

"Apologies, cousin," Garin said. "A poor jest. These are difficult times."

Lan opened his mouth to speak, but at that moment Vhaerynn leaned in to whisper to him. There was a pause as the old man's lips rustled against Lan's ear. Unless his eyes deceived him, he thought he saw a pale pink mist float through the air between the men—a trace of Vhaerynn's blood magic. Finally,

Lan nodded and waved in a dismissive fashion, clearing the air.

"Difficult times in need of a hero," Vhaerynn said, his voice quaking with age.

"And so you present yourself, cousin," Lan said. "Do not think you are so subtle."

"Was I aiming for subtlety?" Garin shrugged. "My mistake."

The king leaned back in the throne, which looked too big for his lanky body. Having seen his massive cousin march off to war alongside Dustblades and Ironclads and look comfortable doing so, Garin would never have thought anything would dwarf him. Sitting there, face drawn and eyes stormy, Lan seemed to have aged a dozen summers in the last ten days. Considering how much blood Garin had seen in his chambers on Ruin's Night, perhaps he should be impressed Lan could speak to him at all.

"I know why you've come *now*," Lan said. "But why not before? This is a time when all the Blood of Ravalis should flow together. Tar Vangr grows dangerous, despite my best efforts.

"So welcoming," Garin said. "As I recall, when your father summoned me, you had a few choice words for the occasion. Did you want me within a thousand leagues of your city then?"

"Answer my question." Lan glowered. "Why wait until now? Why not send word?"

Garin had expected this query. "I might ask the same," he said. "There was no word from the palace—no reason to suspect any of our Blood yet flowed. I could not rely upon our spy network, as the king—your father, I mean—had not yet invested me with the powers of the Shroud. Coming to the palace or sending word might have been a death sentence for me if someone else ruled, and so I made subtle inquiries but did not show myself. Not until you announced your unveiling today."

This was true in part, though the parts Garin omitted were significant and would surely brand him a traitor. What mattered was whether Lan bought into the story as he told it.

"I am to believe you've heard nothing of me?" Lan said. "Of my…injury."

"Whatever do you mean, cousin?" Garin took care to seem oblivious. "Are you unwell?"

"Do not play games." Lan leaned forward to put his face almost to Garin's own. "I know what they call me in the gutters and the whorehouses you love to frequent. You have heard the names."

Garin's easy expression slipped. The darkness stirred deep inside him—that familiar companion who'd always been with him. "I…I don't know what you mean, cousin."

The king glared at him, eyes slowly narrowing, and Garin's hands began to tremble, the way they had since he was a child. His cousin had always been the bully, able to terrify him through will alone. Fear mingled with shame inside him, and he almost blurted out the truth, and burn the consequences.

Vhaerynn coughed quite loudly. "I dare say, Prince, had I worn your boots, I might have done much the same."

The words broke the tension between the cousins, and when Lan swept his gaze to the blood sorcerer, Garin felt as though the king had lifted a heavy cloak from his shoulders. When he looked back, Lan's face had grown stormy once more, any momentary focus lost in the chaos inside his head. He reclined in the massive black throne. "Still, cousin," he said. "Such timidity is unlike the Blood Ravalis. I should have expected more boldness."

Garin bowed, suitably chastened. "Apologies, cousin."

"It is of no matter." Lan looked to Vhaerynn. "Summon my council. I would have words for all."

The necromancer nodded and spread his arms. Garin felt his veins and arteries grow warm, and the sensation was unnervingly pleasant. Around them, the doors opened to Revelry Hall, and men with the dark faces of summerborn filtered back in. It reminded him why he distrusted magic. If Vhaerynn had a sample of Garin's blood, who could guess what the sorcerer could make him do? Unsettling.

And yet, Vhaerynn had aided him just then, challenging the king at a vital moment. What game did the necromancer play? Garin privately suspected him of meddling in the affairs of succession, and perhaps Vhaerynn did not support Lan as stolidly as it seemed. Could Garin claim his loyalty? Regardless, Vhaerynn's craggy face offered no hints.

There were half a dozen Ravalis heirs in attendance, mostly lesser cousins and their wives safely distant from the throne. Garin recognized only a few of the faces: some the deep brown of the summerblood, many blended with the paler winterborn. They varied in age from beardless youths to grown men and women, and two of them even had tattooed animals on their chests in the Luethaar style. Having been away for nearly so long, he barely knew them, and some hadn't even been born before he'd last seen his family. Garin knew Parthis Ravalis, the Stallion of Luether, more by the horse tattooed on his chest than his face. Standing beside him was a younger Ravalis he did not know—a boy probably not even born before the fall of Luether—who had a partially completed hunting dog of some sort on his chest. It was a reunion of strangers, and Garin did not feel at all soothed. They gathered around Garin, so that Lan was addressing a large group of his kin.

14

He recognized Lan's wife, at least: Laegra Vargaen, a woman rough hewn of sandstone. Her hair had gone mostly white in the few days since Garin had seen her last. She looked as if she'd not slept since. Laegra went to stand behind the throne, edging away from Vhaerynn on the other side. Garin felt a pang of sympathy for her: he'd never felt comfortable knowing that beast had a woman to torment.

Lan waved. "As you can see, the Ravalis yet stand strong. This day, we will venture without these walls and call our city back to order. Show them a king yet sits upon the throne of Tar Vangr. Unless—" He sat taller on the throne, and looked at his fist. "Unless any of you mean to challenge me."

This, Garin had not expected. He looked around at the horde of Ravalis, most of whom were staring at him expectantly. So that was Lan's plan: call him out, force him to speak, and thus assert dominance. Like always.

"Certainly not I, cousin," Garin said. "I care nothing for Tar Vangr."

"Come now." Lan smiled, and it was not a pleasant expression on his bruised visage. "You may not want the Winter Throne, but what of the Summer? If you sat the Winter Throne, you'd have all her forces at your command to march forth to reclaim your father's throne. Is this not your wish?"

No doubt Lan had meant to trap him and make him look a fool, but perhaps Garin could use this situation to his advantage. He turned in a circle to address his gathered kin.

"What need have I to do so?" Garin asked. "My cousin sits upon the throne. He will give me that which I need to liberate the city of our fathers."

Lan looked momentarily startled, then laughed uproariously: "Think you so? What a child you are, cousin, to think it so simple. I can assure you, I mean nothing of the kind."

"No?" Garin didn't back down. He looked his cousin straight in the eye. "You are certain?"

"I am king," Lan said. "I have spoken."

That drew a few unsettled murmurs among the assembled Ravalis. Emboldened, Garin pressed upon his cousin. "Tell me, if you will," he said. "What could be so important that it will stay you from the objective my uncle—your father—spent years pursuing? Why stop now? Why not honor his legacy?"

Vhaerynn nodded to Lan. "His Majesty is still recovering and might not—"

"I will speak for myself, Necromancer." Lan's face had grown ruddy with anger. "I have no fonder wish than to destroy the monsters who stole our beloved homeland out from under us. But the demands of the throne come first. I will launch no ships and field no troops in a war with Luether until the last threat to my reign is extinguished."

Garin had the wherewithal to look confused. "Threat, cousin? What do you mean?"

Vhaerynn opened his mouth to offer a warning, but Lan ignored him.

"The assassin who came to kill me," the king said. "Semana Denerre."

Murmurs spread through the room. "Then the rumors are true." Behind his back, Garin touched the only ring on his left hand for strength. "And the Denerre princess lives."

Lan shrugged. "She lived on Ruin's Night, that much I can attest. She and the treacherous Regel Oathbreaker, Lord of Tears, and Ovelia Dracaris the Bloodbreaker. Whether she truly was the lost princess or no, she bore significant power and posed a true threat to the crown and the city entire. I will make no move until I have her gape-mouthed head on a pike above my gates."

Uneasy rumblings met the dark words, and no surprise. No doubt many of the folk assembled had heard wild rumors, but not until this day had anyone confirmed them, let alone the king himself. And by the look in Lan's eyes, he had not meant to reveal that information just yet. And thus did Garin assert *his* superiority over Lan: that of the mind, the only advantage he'd ever had over his larger, braver cousin.

"That is wise, cousin," Garin said. "Is it also why Ravalis soldiers storm into every house in the city? Because you fear she remains in Tar Vangr?"

Lan looked long and hard at him, not amused in the slightest to be dancing to Garin's tune. "I fear no little girl, no matter how mighty her powers," he said. "But perhaps you believe otherwise? That I tremble in my throne and hesitate to march because I am a coward? Perhaps you think you could do better." He raised one finger to point directly at Garin. "What of it, cousin? Would you stand against me? Me, the rightful King of Tar Vangr?"

He had issued the challenge to Garin, whether he had a gauntlet to throw or not. Garin had hoped it would not fall to this. He had not come prepared to fight Lan, and even if he defeated his cousin, he did not know what would happen next. All of his plans would fall to ruin. Dark despair rose up inside, telling him that to run was pointless and to stand was death. He could not win. Could not do this.

Perhaps he should tell Lan the truth—put all his knives on the table and be done with it. But...

"*Half* a king of Tar Vangr," said a voice behind Garin. "And not the half the women want."

Immediately, Lan fixed his smoldering attention on this pompous lordling. "Who dares?" he asked. "Come forward."

16

It was the lad with the half-finished tattoo on his chest. Fine musculature and impressive conditioning marked him as a warrior, but he was still hardly a man grown. Parthis Ravalis watched him with paternal pride, and Garin realized the lad must be his son. He put up his arms to gather support.

"I am Arat Ravalis, son of Parthis, eighth in line for the throne, and I say I should be seventh," the boy said. "Look at you, cousin. You can barely stand! Ruin's Night was a fool's jape, after you and the old mad king slaughtered the head of the Vangryur council. Is that rulership? Fear and gloating? No wonder what happened to you, after you took the Bloodbreaker into your bed—"

Laegra abruptly made a strangled cry, drawing the attention of all. It seemed Lan had not apprised her of that detail of Ruin's Night. She glared at her husband, then fled the chamber. The gathered Ravalis whispered to one another.

"Silence," Lan said, and the hall was once more still. "Continue, cousin Arat."

The boy stepped closer to him, climbing the steps of the dais. "Unmanned and unmade," he said. "We've all heard the stories, about the Dracaris sword-swallower. We know as well as you that mere pieces of a king sit upon the throne. And even if you should rule, what then? The Dracaris bitch has killed many kings to come."

Lan laid his fingers over the hilt of the sword leaning at the side of the throne. "Speak plainly, cousin. What are you saying?"

Arat smiled cruelly and put his hand to the hilt of the sword at his belt. "How are we to know you can even rut a woman, much less sire heirs? Should the Blood of Summer die with your manhood?"

"So." The king's voice was low, and his eyes cold. "Do you challenge me?"

Silence filled the hall as Arat raised his chin. "For the good of House Ravalis," he said. "I offer you challenge, Eunuch King. Accept—"

Lan moved faster than Garin could credit. He propelled himself forward, unsheathing the sword in a flurry of crimson shadows, and lunged across with a rising slash to rip out Arat Ravalis's throat. The lordling stared, startled. Blood welled instead of words, and he gurgled for breath.

"Challenge accepted," Lan said, and kicked the boy down off the dais.

The hall erupted in cries of alarm and terror. Parthis shoved through the gathered Ravalis lords to cradle the shuddering body of his son, openly weeping. Lan stood over them all, sweat livid on his flushed face.

"Else?" Lan asked loudly, brandishing the bloody sword leaking crimson shadows. "Another challenge?" When no one came forth, he flicked blood off the flamed blade, then turned to Vhaerynn. "Clear this rabble. We've a busy day."

The necromancer put his hands together, and Garin could feel his blood heat up. Abruptly, Parthis gave a cry and fell back. As the onlookers watched in horror, the corpse of Arat stood up, head lolling to one side, and strode rapidly away from the throne. Parthis tried to restrain it, but the blood magic was too strong. As Garin watched, it hurried out of the palace, spilling blood onto the swirling snow, and strode right off the edge of High-City. Then it was lost to the winds of winter.

The hall had fallen deathly silent, and the gathered Ravalis looked up at Lan in a chorus of shock, outrage, and terror. The folk outside were even more confused and frightened. The king merely chuckled and limped back to the throne, his left hand hovering over his midsection. Garin noted the massive sweat stains on his robe. That display had been impressive but taxing.

"Begone," Lan said to them all. "I'll have words for you on the morrow. Oh, and not you, Garin. For you, there is more."

The hall was quickly emptied once more, and Garin found himself waiting on the king's pleasure. Lan waved, and Vhaerynn presented him with a goblet of wine so thick and red it looked like blood. There was no wine for Garin, of course. Anger at being so snubbed let him stop wavering on his feet.

"What will you have of me, Majesty?" Garin asked.

"You came here to a purpose," Lan said to Garin. "I've made them forget all about your little display walking here. It seems unkingly to make you walk all that way back without what you came for. But before we get to that, I've a command for you." He sat heavily in the throne and idly twirled the sword against the ground, making a skittering sound. "I assume you know this sword."

"Draca, the bloodsword of Blood Dracaris. I know it by the blade and the hilt." Garin glanced at the sword with its red-tinged steel, trailing shadows as it spun. "More than that, I know of its power to show its wielder the near future. You knew that boy would attack you. The sword warned you."

Lan made a face. "Nothing of the sort," he said. "I killed him because he insulted me. I needed no magic to know how to do it. This sword is merely a fine blade in my hand. No." He lifted the sword on his two hands and held it out to Garin. "I want you to study this sword. Find a way to control its magic and—more importantly—duplicate it."

"Duplicate it." Garin took the sword reverently and turned it over in his hands. Crimson shadows leaked around Draca's hilt. "This is a relic of the World of Wonders. I doubt any thaumaturgy can match the beauty of its enchantment."

"It had better," Lan said. "Imagine, a company of Dustblades who cannot be taken unawares, who always know how to move—how to kill." He smiled as if delighted at the thought. Then his face fell to seriousness once more. "Do not fail me, or the crown can make life quite uncomfortable for you."

Garin nodded. That had been Lan's threat to control him for years, and it was almost comforting to see he still relied upon it. "Fantastic," he said. "I shall keep you apprised of my progress."

"Progress?" Lan narrowed his eyes. "What do you mean?"

"I am returning to Luether, post haste," he said. "I will reclaim the city before your army can mobilize to march against it."

"Oh you *will*." Lan raised an eyebrow. "And you expect me to agree to this course?"

"Yes. Either I will succeed, and your armies will have an easy time of it, or I will fail, and you can avenge me. Either way, I'm going." Garin raised the sword. "And I'm taking this with me."

He expected Lan to say no, that his show of boldness would only infuriate his cousin, but the king surprised him with a dismissive nod. "Take the sword. Study it in the homeland of our fathers," Lan said. "You have until midsummer before our armies march. I'll have no further need of you then."

Garin was surprised Lan had agreed so quickly, but he smiled all the same. "My thanks for the confidence," he said, even as the darkness inside clawed at him. "I shall make you proud."

"That," Lan said, "I highly doubt."

~

When his lesser kin were gone and the great doors were shut behind Garin, Lan finally allowed himself a rueful smile.

"You are pleased, Majesty?" Vhaerynn asked.

"Why not?" Lan's smile widened. "I got to make my point, prune another dead branch from the Ravalis tree, and defeat my cousin at his own game."

"I'm not sure that's what happened, Majesty."

Lan looked over to Vhaerynn—his haggard old face looking so disapproving—and his smile slipped slightly. "Garin has always thought himself better than the rest of us because of his cleverness, and now I will show him just how wrong he is," he said. "He thinks he outwitted me and deprived me of that sword, but he does not see that I am already a dozen steps ahead."

He stood, and immediate pain ripped through his midsection. He caught the arm of the throne to brace himself and looked up at Vhaerynn balefully. The blood sorcerer kept his bemused look a little too long, and Lan saw it. Or perhaps Vhaerynn had intended him to see it. Lan felt warmth in his belly growing to burning rage. Vhaerynn was looking at him the way Garin did—the way his brainless, unworthy kin always had: down, as at a worm underfoot.

19

Lan Ravalis was no worm but a bear, and bears were the most dangerous when defending themselves. He would see them all dead before this was over. But first.

"Vhaerynn," he said. "Are you my servant?"

"Of course, Majesty." The blood sorcerer bowed low, but Lan could see the hesitation in his movements, the pause before real deference. He was like Garin, and thought himself above the king.

Lan straightened before the throne, ignoring the pain, and raised his chin. "Kneel before me."

Irritation flashed through Vhaerynn's eyes, which only encouraged Lan. "Majesty?"

"Come now, sorcerer," he said. "You could kneel when you were half dead and broken. Surely you can do it now."

The necromancer looked around the hall, which seemed voluminous in its emptiness. He would find no support there. He had no choice but to submit. Slowly, he stepped toward the king, then sank to one knee. Lan cupped Vhaerynn's chin in his hand and lifted the old man's eyes to his own.

"No more will you call me Majesty," he said. "Master. Do you understand? *Master*."

Vhaerynn glared up at him with indescribable hatred. Red veins crept into his aged eyes: the wrath of his necromantic powers. Then he nodded, slowly. "Yes, Master."

"There's a good boy." Lan patted his cheek. "Attend me in an hour. We have business below."

He strode out of the room, trying not to limp, and he could feel Vhaerynn's smoldering rage the whole way. It made him feel inestimably better.

ACT ONE: EMBERS

A WOMAN'S SHRIEK RESOUNDED through the narrow corridor between the
walls, making Garin gasp despite his best efforts. He had a knack for
keeping quiet, but that cry had been so loud and sudden—

"Quiet!" Lan jabbed him in the side with one meaty fist. "They'll hear."

This might only have been the little lordling's fourteenth summer, but
Lan had always been stronger than his age allowed. Bigger than his peers too,
particularly compared to his spindly cousin. Lan always muddled through the
earliest parts of their training sessions and perked up when they got to the
sparring, where he relished pounding the sweat and blood from Garin.

In the dim alchemical candlelight, Garin could see his own pain reflected in
Lan's eyes, and the bully lad grinned wider. Nothing provoked him like seeing
weakness. He was an unpredictable, volatile substance, one that demanded
to be carefully handled. No stranger to the laboratory, Garin found even the
most explosive chemics more comforting than his cousin.

His other cousin Paeter, however...He was different.

"Quiet, both of you." Paeter's cool assurance defused a conflict before it
happened. His older cousin, beautiful and unassuming in the shadows, took
the pipe from his mouth and gestured to the spyholes that allowed them to
peer into the guest chamber. "You're missing the show."

Lan's hunger took a new path, and he shoved Garin aside in his haste to peer
through the slits at the princess and her handmaiden. Garin rubbed at his ribs.

"One of the bitches had a nightmare," Lan said in an excited whisper.
"She's thrashing about, kicking off her coverlets...Summer's fire, she's naked!"

"Which one?" Garin asked, his stomach churning. "The princess, or—"

"Yes, have a care," Paeter said. "That's my betrothed you're describing so
lasciviously."

"It's just the mongrel, Paet," Lan said. "Fire, but her tits are huge! I'd love
to squeeze those around my cock."

21

"Let me see," Paeter said.

He rose with the grace of a cat and crossed to the spyholes. Lan stepped aside deferentially, the way he did for no one but his older brother. Even Crown Prince Garin, son of King Cassian who sat upon the throne, did not merit anything approaching the respect Lan paid Paeter. The eldest prince knelt down to peer through, and Garin was uncomfortably aware of his strong hand on his thigh. It made his skin tingle, and he did his best to suppress a shiver. Good thing it was dark, or either of his cousins might have noticed the swelling in his breeches. Lan's eyes glittered in the light of the single candle, but he was clearly too occupied imagining rutting Ovelia Dracaris's chest to look at the cousin he loathed.

Lan's disrespect hardly seemed odd—indeed, Garin had known it all his life. His father Cassian might rule Luether, but that did not mean Garin would necessarily ascend the throne after him. Of old, Luether law passed the throne to the one who earned it; of the scions of their Blood, Garin hardly ranked himself first in merit. Paeter, Cassian's nephew and Garin's elder by a full decade, was not even the most worthy of the Ravalis youth. He chased his older brother Strevon, a born warrior and already the victor of a dozen bloody duels. In part to distract Paeter from the throne, Cassian had brokered a marriage to Lenalin Denerre, that a Ravalis scion might rule the northern mage-city one day.

Young Garin and Lan were more of a match: of an age, the last of their respective fathers' children, and neither much exceeded the other in valor or deed. They had grown up together as boys, but rather than being a brother to Garin, Lan never passed up the chance to insult of needle his cousin.

All these thoughts Garin used to distract himself, but he found his mind drifting back to Paeter's noble face, his perfect musculature, his hands...one of which was on his leg. And it was not there by accident, Garin realized, or merely for support. Idly, Paeter's fingers curled against Garin's breeches, brushing the inside of his leg in a way that was very, *very* distracting.

"Eh, I've seen bigger," Paeter said. "Here. Garin." Paeter's voice—half-croon, half-whisper—made Garin's name a thing of poetry. "Have a look."

Lan immediately started forward, but Paeter stopped him with a look. "Why him? Little bugger doesn't even care—" But Paeter's narrowed eyes cut him off.

"Go on." Paeter lifted his hand from Garin's thigh to put it on his shoulder. "Have a good look."

Garin drew in a breath by reflex and peered through the spyholes. The fit seemed to have passed, and both girls were awake in the chamber.

Sure enough, Ovelia Dracaris sat on the bed, her golden body revealed in all its sweaty glory as she panted and shivered in the wake of a nightmare. She must not have worn any clothes to bed, for only a blanket clutched to her breasts kept her from being nude. Having seen six and ten summers, she was a girl on the verge of womanhood, simultaneously youthful and mature compared to Garin. She sat with her back to him, exposing a beautiful red dragon partially inked into her skin—there was work still to be done around the wings and talons, but he could definitely tell what the tattoo was meant to be.

Princess Lenalin sat beside Ovelia, wrapped in a sleeping gown and looking just as modest as she had the day they arrived. Her silvery blonde hair perfectly matched her light complexion and her vivid blue-purple eyes held wisdom beyond her youth. She was older than her companion—perhaps by two summers—and more tightly controlled, a noble daughter from toe to crown. She had one hand on Ovelia's upper arm while her other hand stroked the handmaiden's hair, and she whispered in soothing tones in the woman's ear.

Both were beautiful—Ovelia in an earthly, sexual way, Lenalin a pristine, perfect statue—and neither stirred Garin at all. He could appreciate them in an aesthetic way, but they did not shake his heart or warm his core the way Paeter did.

"The same nightmare?" Lenalin asked. "About the fire?"

Ovelia nodded, making a few sweat-slick strands of her crimson hair fall in her face. Lenalin immediately brushed them back behind first one ear, then the other.

"It doesn't mean anything," she said. "It's just nerves. You're worried about me—about these summerbloods consuming me. And I told you, I'm well."

Ovelia did not look convinced, but Garin could not be sure which part she doubted: the interpretation of the dream or Lenalin's assurances.

"I am sorry, Lena," Ovelia said. "I don't mean to be a burden. And you need your rest. This meeting is about you, not your stupid, lowborn squire."

Squire, was it? Gain knew a little about the winterborn tradition of the master and the squire, closer in many ways than parent and child, or lover and beloved. The Tar Vangryur had no tradition of marriage or family, outside of Bloods—the master and squire was the closest they came.

Lenalin smiled wearily. "Hardly lowborn, and hardly stupid," she said. "You mustn't say such things. These summerbloods will pounce on any sign of weakness like sharks."

"Sharks don't pounce, Lena," Ovelia said.

"If you say so." Lenalin moved closer to Ovelia, sliding her arm around the handmaiden's waist. She brushed aside another lock of hair and touched her nose to Ovelia's. "We're safe. Here together."

Ovelia's body relaxed—Garin could see it in the muscles of her back and in her relaxing fists on the bed. She opened to the princess like a flower greeting the dawn: not changed, but not the same either. Garin could hear his heart thudding in his throat. Could they not hear it too?

Then something happened Garin did not quite understand: Lenalin pressed her lips to Ovelia's, and they kissed. It was tentative at first, but they kissed again with a degree of warmth that far exceeded that of the closest friends. Garin watched as they melted into each other, perfectly suited and fulfilled.

"Stop hoarding it," Lan said in a whine. "I want to see."

Paeter clicked his tongue at his little brother. "What do you see?" he asked softly.

He rested his hand on Garin's neck, making every tiny hair awake and rise. The prince felt his lower parts stir and willed himself not to tremble. He held his breath.

"Something good, I wager," Lan said. "He's all warm."

This…This was not something Lan or even Paeter could understand. This was sacred.

Somehow, he had to stop them from seeing.

He pulled away from the spyholes, but in the process he made sure to kick over Paeter's scabbarded sword leaning against the wall near his foot. The weapon hit the floor with a loud clatter: muted slightly by the fine leather, but deafening in the relative silence of the Luether night. The girls could not have failed to hear that.

"Clumsy burner!" Lan shot at him.

Paeter pushed Garin aside and looked in the spyhole. "Burn and rot," he said. "Follow." Then he reclaimed his sword and hurried toward the exit from the secret passage.

Garin made to scramble after him, but Lan checked him into the wall as he barreled past. Garin's hip smashed hard into the stone, and he staggered, face close to the spy holes. He could glimpse movement in the room. He caught a flash of Ovelia's red hair and the gleam of naked steel. His stomach clenched with terrified excitement.

Lan rushed out the door and pulled it mostly shut after him. Without Paeter's alchemical candle, Garin could barely see the thin crack of dim light that marked the edge of the door. He scrambled for it, fingers searching, and he caught the edge. Garin staggered out into the corridor and pulled the secret door closed with the faint rustle of stone against stone.

Then he turned, face streaked with sweat, and found himself staring at an opening door and the hard hazel eyes of Ovelia Dracaris, daughter of Norlest, who was First Shield to Orbrin Denerre, the Winter King. And from the

24

dangerous expression on her face, he thought her just as forbidding as her infamous father. She wore a thin night gown and held a scabbarded sword, ready to draw at need. Lenalin could not be seen behind her, but Garin knew she was watching.

Ovelia narrowed her eyes. "What is the meaning of this?" she asked. "Any of you? Speak."

He'd never been this close to Ovelia, and Garin could not stop thinking Lan's label for her—mongrel—did not fit. She bore the blood of both worlds, of Summer and of Winter, like a bridge between the dark-skinned boys in their loose fitting shirts and the strange, light-haired princess of the icy northland. There was something noble about her countenance and carriage that far exceeded her station: lowborn, albeit descended from a kingly Blood. He found that he liked her immediately, even if she was a breath away from drawing steel on him.

Lan did not take as kindly to Ovelia's stance or her tone. "You dare rebuke us, we princes of the realm?" He sneered. "I'll not answer to a common slattern."

Ovelia did not like that, nor did she back down even slightly. She scrutinized each of them in turn. "I see no princes," she said. "Only three fool boys stealing about where they should not be."

Lan's face was growing redder with each heartbeat. "Where we should not be?" he said. "It's our castle. You and your lady are the ones who should not—"

With a hiss of steel on leather, Ovelia drew her sword, and its appearance cut everyone short. Hers was no ordinary blade either, flames like waves leaving marks in the sand and gleaming with a deep crimson as of inner fire. Even as they watched, it began to leak reddish mist, forming vague shapes like men on a battlefield. It was too big for her hand, but not by much. In two or three summers, she would look every bit the warrior her father was.

Lan's eyes went wide at the drawn steel. "You mad whore," he said. "You would threaten the children of your hosts? You—"

"Calm, brother," came Paeter's voice, just as Princess Lenalin appeared and put a hand on Ovelia's neck to soothe her. The synchronicity of their intercessions was so tight, Garin could hardly believe it a coincidence. Their respective effects upon their younger charges were equally notable: Lan immediately backed down, looking chastened but still angry, while Ovelia visibly relaxed and sheathed the shadow-burning sword. Again, Garin saw that level of intimacy he hadn't thought possible.

He turned his attention to the sword. "That's Draca," he said. "Your father lets you carry that?"

"He does not *let me* do anything, little boy," Ovelia said.

"Lia!" Lenalin gave her a disapproving look.

Her handmaid pacified for the moment, Lenalin turned toward them with an easy smile. Her manner was far more diplomatic than Ovelia's. It was obvious she came from royalty. In particular, she eyed Paeter. The two had met, Garin knew, but only briefly and under close supervision.

"What, may I ask," Lenalin said, "brings such handsome young men of the Ravalis to our chambers at this late hour of night? And with all of us so little attired."

For a moment, they were simply five young people unobserved in a dark corridor, two of them women wearing little more than shifts, three of them men dressed only in knee-length leggings and loose shirts. The awkwardness of the situation stole words for a moment. Garin saw an intrigued shadow on Paeter's face. The way he was staring at the young women—at Lenalin, yes, but equally at Ovelia—made Garin uneasy. Then his sculpted face lit with the warm confidence that was so familiar to its features.

"Not late, my lady, but early," Paeter said, seizing control once more. "In Luether, we reckon our days from the moon's zenith, but only the bravest and best of us take advantage of the early hours. We came, in fact, to invite you to make just such an attempt. After all, you're leaving on the morrow, but you have yet to experience all the City of Flame has to offer." He extended his hand. "Won't you come with us, Winter Princess?"

"She's not going anywhere." Ovelia narrowed her eyes at Lan. "Especially not with you."

Lan screwed up his face in anger. "I'd like to see you stop us."

Lenalin focused on Paeter to the exclusion of all others, while Ovelia locked glares with Lan. Garin was left to observe the two silent duels unfolding: one of command, one of nerve. Paeter sought to bend all to his whim, Lenalin asserted her own control, Ovelia had no fear of Lan, and he in turn hungered to crush her insolent will. He had a sudden vision of the four of them, much older, carrying out much the same dance.

"Please come with us, my ladies," Garin said. "The world is by and large a trying, sorry place. 'Twould be a shame for such beautiful young people as we not to enjoy the very best moments it has to offer. Let us be your guides."

The tension drained away, and all eyes turned to him. Lan looked vaguely annoyed, but no longer did he rage at Ovelia—instead, his antipathy had settled back to Garin. Lenalin looked surprised and perhaps a little impressed. Paeter winked to convey his approval. Only Ovelia seemed unconvinced.

"The five of us?" she asked. "Out in the street alone? Without protection?"

"We have you, Princess's Shield. And Garin. " Paeter put his hand on

Garin's shoulder. "After all, my silver-tongued cousin here is the Crown Prince of Luether, beloved by all his people. What other chaperone do we need?"

∼

Less than an hour later, they were sitting in the outdoor common area of the Crimson Swan, a low-coin tavern and brothel that Paeter loved and of which Garin was quite fond. He had to like an establishment that put up a figurehead such as the Swan's: a nude woman, reclining to bare her voluptuous and exaggerated body, her lips open wide and inviting as she held her winged arms crossed behind her head. He appreciated the craft that had gone into shaping her engorged assets and the way the flaking red paint on her wings looked like blood from a murder she had just committed. It was just so ridiculous—and so very against Luether's stodgy expectations of dignified men and chaste women—that he couldn't help but love it.

Packed even mere hours before dawn, the wine garden itself was like a paradise for those who defied expectation in the name of love and pleasure. Surrounded by blooming flowers in cracked clay pots, men and women danced, bodies pressed tight, or lay lazily against one another and drank, whispering erotic secrets and making promises. Desire charged the very air, making the world giddy and blurring the night. Rarely was the sex blatant. Toward the back of the garden, under the eaves of the Swan, a chubby lordling bounced a woman on his lap, her blouse undone and her hair coming loose from its scarf. Just a few tables to Garin's left sat Chorun of Blood Ruvee, a dark-haired lordling of an age with his cousin Paeter. He nodded to Garin, smiling dazedly, his hand between the legs of a woman who sat beside him.

Garin's noble party did what it could to avoid drawing attention. Since his twentieth summer, Paeter had openly patronized all manner of drinking dives and brothels in Luether, but neither Garin nor Lan had yet come of age, and so they went unannounced, wearing light cloaks to hide their distinctive visages and the tattoos that marked their chests. Also, it would not do for the princes of Luether to take the Winter Princess to a house of such reputation as the Swan. He could just hardly imagine the scandal.

For her part, Lenalin had needed little convincing to tie her distinctive silvery hair back under a scarf, and a swipe of grease hid the sheen of her pale skin. She seemed to enjoy being disguised, as though throwing off her responsibilities was something she had often experienced. Now she was dancing and drinking with Paeter, every bit the loose-moral lass she appeared to be. Even Lan had abandoned his sneers and lewd remarks for a lighter mood. Garin found the stealthy inversion of what was proper and dignified very exciting, and he played his part to the fullest.

Indeed, if they hadn't brought Ovelia along, Garin might have lost himself in the night.

Of all of them, Ovelia proved the only one ill-at-ease in the tavern. The mostly darkness deepened her dusky skin, making her look like a native girl, but her body language called her anything but comfortable. She sat at the edge of the party, watching Lenalin with exacting precision, ignoring any lordling who attempted to address her. Eventually, even the drunkest ones gave up, and she sat alone, surrounded by an aura of general disgust.

He moved over to sit beside her and waved over the serving woman. "My lady?" he said. "Offer you a fine libation on this fine night?"

"No." Ovelia's watered wine still sat in front of her, mostly untouched.

They sat in silence for a moment, listening to the music and the laughter of the dancers. Lenalin had obviously had a great deal to drink, and she took up dancing with others beside Paeter: Lan, Garin himself, and other fellows from the wine garden. Every time another man touched Lenalin, Ovelia's jaw tightened slightly. Garin well understood why, but perhaps he could distract Ovelia and lighten her glower. After all, the City of Flame was no place for a beautiful woman to be sad.

"I am sorry, my lady," Garin said. "Where is my gallantry? Would you like to dance?"

Garin's apology jarred her out of her focus on Lenalin. They were of an age, she and the prince, though perhaps she had seen one more season than he. She looked at him, then looked away. "Not a lady," she said. Her expression soured at something new she had seen.

Garin followed Ovelia's gaze to Chorun, who had laid his head back and trembled as his whore—who had moved under the table to return the favor—worked on his blade. In a flash of thought, Garin saw Paeter in the place of Chorun and himself instead of the whore under the table. Garin ordinarily kept his mind free of such scandalous things, but something about the night: the drink, the dancing, seeing the kiss…It unlocked something within Garin, something that cared little for social convention, and less for concealing his own desires. Before this night, he'd thought his desires perverse, but what he'd seen in the guest chamber had changed him. If only he had some way to thank Ovelia for that—one that didn't involve telling her his secret, or that the three boys had been spying on her naked. He couldn't quite decide which would be worse.

As though she could hear his thoughts, Ovelia made a derisive sound in her throat, and Garin's skin stretched tightly over his bones. "I'm sorry you had to see that, Lady," he said. "Such a disgusting display. I assure you, a man of dignity and discretion knows better how to conceal his activities."

Ovelia turned her hazel eyes on him. "Not disgusting," she said. "Inexplicable."

"Ah." Garin was intrigued. "If you do not object, then let us discuss this quandary. Sex. In public. They seem to be enjoying it. Why shouldn't a man and a woman do as they like?"

"That's not why *she's* doing it."

Ovelia indicated the woman near the back, whose moans had grown more frequent, but she wore a bored expression. Finally he was done, and she just looked relieved. Immediately she began interrogating him about coin.

"Prostitution is common in Luether," Garin said. "Is it not so in Tar Vangr?"

"Certainly. But that isn't what I mean."

Ovelia indicated the woman under the table, who had redoubled her efforts. Chorun shuddered and spent himself in her mouth, and she cleaned him before slithering up into the seat beside him. She made to kiss him, only for him to pull away, his triumphant expression falling a little at the thought. The woman looked for a heartbeat as though he had struck her, then took up her goblet and drained it at one go. Garin realized with a shock that she was not a prostitute as he had assumed, but an heiress—Lady Nysa of the Blood of Martagen, wed to a noble of some lesser blood Garin didn't remember—and that made the tableau especially unsettling.

"I find it inexplicable that any city values some of its own so little." Ovelia looked back to Garin. "Do all men in your city care nothing for the pleasure of their lovers?"

It was such an odd question it took Garin by surprise. He hesitated before answering. "I never thought of it that way."

"I suppose not." She went back to staring at Lenalin.

Garin opened his mouth to explain—to assert that Ovelia was being harsh and unfair and two trysts in the wine garden at a house of low reputation was not enough to condemn an entire city—but the words wouldn't come. Men had always ruled Luether. He did not know of a single woman who had sat in a position of power over any Blood in the mage-city in his lifetime. They still told stories of treacherous Queen Vulta, the slattern witch who had seduced the great heroes of Luether's early days and almost destroyed the city, and it was still a mark against the Blood Vultara that they could trace their ancestry to her. The man was always in command, the woman always subservient to his will, and any man who had the temerity to desire another man...That was an affront to Luether itself.

Ovelia gazed upon Lenalin with palpable concern, and Garin thought he understood a little better. She loved Lenalin and wanted her to be happy, even if it meant leaving her behind.

"I love this city," Garin said. "Every part of it, from Kirthmin's rise to the majestic walks of High-City to the darkness of Tuerine to the filth in the gutter. It is flawed, but it can be redeemed. Not all of it is meant for me—not even most of it—but it's mine all the same. It will be for everyone."

Ovelia looked at him curiously, then smiled slightly. "You'll have to do better than that, Your Highness."

"What?" Garin pressed his hand to his chest. "To convince you of my own magnificence?"

"To win me over," Ovelia said. "Impressive words are breaths shaped into what others want them to be. If you would be a good king, then be a good king. Don't simply tell me what I want to hear."

"And why would I care what you want to hear?" Garin asked, a little more heat in his voice but a smile on his face. "You think I'm saying these things only for you?"

"Who can say?" Ovelia drank a sip of her wine. "Perhaps you want to see my breasts again."

"I knew it," Garin said with a little smirk. "They say the Blood of Dracaris cannot be caught unawares. You knew we were watching."

"I do *now*."

For a second, Ovelia's eyes glittered dangerously, but ten she smiled. That made Garin grin wider. He found no end to how much Ovelia intrigued him.

"Thank you but no, my lady," he said. "Though I assure you, yours is a most exquisite body that any man would be blessed to see."

She had no reply, but when she went back to scrutinizing Lenalin, her expression seemed lighter.

Like Paeter, Lenalin seemed to stand above her fellows, as though cut of purer material than they. Since her older brother Althar had died in a duel three summers past, Lenalin was the only daughter of the Orbrin Denerre and thus the heir of Tar Vangr. After centuries of feuding between Ravalis and Denerre, her marriage to Paeter would finally end the division and secure an alliance between the last mage-cities of Calatan.

"Do you fancy her?" Ovelia asked at his side.

"What?" The direct question had come so abruptly it startled him. "Perish the suggestion. I should rebuke your impertinence."

"But you won't," Ovelia said. "I can tell what kind of man you are."

Interesting. "What makes you think I...*fancy* the Princess?"

"I see you looking at her," Ovelia said. "I'll wager you could bond with her instead of Paeter—the word is *marry*, right? If you wanted. You're the Crown Prince."

She certainly had a way of getting to the point. "No," he said. He made a point to avoid looking at Paeter's finely muscled back. The two were dancing obscenely close together, so Ovelia's mistake had been a natural one. Garin hated himself for the odd reactions of his body. "She is...very beautiful, your princess. Like a nymph sculpted of ice and snow."

"She is." Ovelia didn't sound happy about the admission. Her shoulders slumped a little, and she sighed deeply.

Understanding of a kind passed between them at that moment, and Garin realized what he had seen in the guest chamber. It had not been the comforting touch of close friends, but something more—or at least, it had been to Ovelia. Paeter had told Lan and Garin that sometimes among the winterborn, women lay with women or men with men, but he had always assumed that was perversion for coin. His cousin had certainly phrased it in those terms, and Lan had near vomited at the mere mention of two men lying together. But what Garin had seen in that chamber had been real, and it stirred his heart—opened his mind to fresh possibilities.

Their earlier flirtation fell away, and Ovelia and Garin sat, enthusiasm slowly ebbing, as the night wore on until finally brightness kissed the horizon, signaling an end to the evening's festivities.

"Well." Garin rose, a bit shaky with the wine, and offered his hand to Ovelia. "We should be getting back. The dusters will be up and about soon, and if your princess is discovered to have vanished in the night, it could provoke a war between our two great mage-cities."

"Fair enough."

Ovelia accepted his hand to rise, then crossed to where Paeter and Lenalin had collapsed, lolling amongst other lordlings in the wine garden. Paeter was mumbled incoherently as Garin pulled him to his feet. Lenalin seemed the same, but Garin got the distinct impression the princess was putting on a show. Lan was the least appealing, as when he awoke from his stupor he glared and grumbled angrily all around.

An unmarked carriage was summoned, clattering and steaming in the morning haze, and Paeter led the way into its cool confines. Lenalin immediately went back to sleep, leaning her head against Paeter's shoulder. Ovelia climbed in immediately after her, leaving only one seat available. Lan glared at Garin and immediately made to step into the carriage, but the Crown Prince held him back. There was simply no way he was leaving a partially drunk Lenalin and Ovelia alone with his cousins.

"Royal privilege," he said, leaving Lan befuddled outside the carriage. Ultimately, Lan rode atop the carriage, grumbling the whole way back to the palace.

In retrospect, perhaps Garin had made the wrong choice. He and Ovelia sat across from Paeter and Lenalin, who snoozed contentedly beside each other. However their bodies seemed to fit together, they did not seem right for one another. Perhaps it was because Ovelia loved Lenalin, and Garin loved Paeter. In a way, Ovelia and he were the same: hopelessly in love with folk they could not have. It was incredibly awkward, and it only became more so near the end of the journey, when Paeter started whispering in Lenalin's ear, and she giggled. He repeatedly attempted to woo her with poetry and erotic insinuations. Lenalin deflected him every time with a consistency Garin admired.

They escorted the women through the secret passages back to their rooms, where they saw guards had not yet been posted, and bid them good morn. Paeter attempted to kiss Lenalin, but she turned aside seemingly by accident so his lips could only brush her cheek. Lan murmured something gruff and probably offensive, then took his leave.

Garin and Ovelia shared a moment at the door to the guest chambers.

"Farewell," he said, bowing over her hand without kissing it. "'Twas an honor to spend a night with you, my fair lady of two worlds." He looked up into her eyes. "Care for her. Be happy for her."

Ovelia nodded, though her eyes were troubled. "I would prefer you as a match for her, you know," she said.

Garin nodded. "Alas, that is simply not to be."

He bowed and returned to his sumptuous chambers, where he collapsed onto his bed and stared up at the engraved ceiling. Of all that had transpired in the last hours, he could think of little but Paeter: dancing, smiling, wooing Lenalin. Had he his way, she would be in his bed right now, and their marriage would be consummated before they spoke the words. Why could Garin not have something like that?

But, remembering the love that had passed between Lenalin and Ovelia, perhaps he could.

He slipped a hand down his breeches, but realized he was too drunk. Instead, he lay back on his bed and gazed up at the ceiling, wishing and wondering. Darkness coiled beneath his hope, threatening to swallow it as it always did. As it always had, since he was just a boy.

Garin had almost nodded off when a discreet knock at the door plucked his attention. He sat upright, every nerve suddenly alert. Weariness fled his body, and he didn't feel any of the many goblets of wine in his belly.

"Who—?" He swallowed. "Who knocks?"

No words. The tap came again, more insistent this time.

Why no reply? A romantic mystery unfolded in Garin's head, blooming from that one question as from a seed. Whoever stood without could not speak, for fear of being heard and known. He—Garin knew for certain the visitor was a man—was not supposed to be here, and dire consequences would befall if his presence was revealed. An illicit liaison, in the early hours of the morn, before they two would be observed…

Garin slid from the bed and almost stumbled over himself. His feet felt too small, and they refused to go where he needed them for balance. The world felt like a dream, as though he yet slept. His head felt blurry and he became acutely aware of how the night had left him: stinking of sweat and wine, confused and in desperate need of sleep. His racing heart, however, would not let him rest. It was a kind of desperate madness, the fear and hesitation boiling inside until they exploded forth.

"This is not a dream," he said, without knowing who heard. "Do not let this be a dream."

He put a shaking hand on the handle of the door and pulled it open, Paeter's name all but spilling from his lips. Then he stopped short, caught in a moment of paralyzing confusion. "I don't—"

Lan Ravalis blasted Garin in the face with a vicious right cross that sent him staggering back to his backside and one knee. His vision swam and his face pulsed in pain, but instinct kicked in and he got up his hands to block the next punch. Lan's third blow—a hook—sent him to the floor. Garin knew he had already lost: his only chance when they sparred was not to let Lan touch him. He tried to get up, head spinning, but Lan kicked him in the stomach, blowing all the air out of his body.

"I see how you look at my brother, little girl." Lan strode casually around him. "You think I don't, but I do."

"I don't know what—" Garin's words exploded in a rush when Lan smashed him across the face with one fist. He coughed and drooled blood onto the floor.

Lan grasped Garin's bloody shirt, pulled him to one knee, and put Garin's face to his own. Garin could taste the alcohol on Lan's breath, and the unnatural closeness made him shiver. It was awful.

"You better stop," Lan said. "I don't care if you are the Crown Prince. I'll rip your stupid little cock right off. You hear me, little girl? You understand?"

Lan closed his fingers tight around Garin's throat. The prince fought and struggled, but that only made Lan squeeze harder. Bright lights appeared at the edges of his vision. Finally, Garin nodded.

"Good. That's a good little girl." Lan released him, and he collapsed, gagging, to the floor. The bigger boy stood over him, smiling as though he'd just eaten a particularly good meal. "Now, little girl. If you want a cock to suck..." His fingers fell to his laces.

Through all the pain and humiliation, Garin understood something clear about Lan then. It was control that he wanted, and always would. He looked away and sniffed blood back into his nose. "No."

"No?" Lan drew his blade out of its sheath and massaged it. "Are you sure, little girl?"

Garin swallowed blood and mucus in his throat and nodded. His bones ached.

"Good," Lan said again. "Next time, I'll make that choice for you." He laced up his breeches and walked out, leaving his cousin panting for breath and shivering

ONE

In her dream, there is fire.

It flows before her: a coursing sea of flame so hot it defies color.

It pulses like a living thing, breathing in the same air and expelling smoke. It burns with no perceivable fuel, no limit, and no ending.

She stretches out her hand, fingers splayed wide, and she can feel the heat as she reaches for it. The flames react to her touch, swirling around her fingers. It makes her skin tingle but it does not burn.

Her dragon awakes, and she can feel it writhe upon her back. The world unravels around her.

She stands on the precipice, between the World of Ruin and another— one of chaos and destruction but also rebirth.

She presses, just a little bit harder. Not because she wants to, but because she has to.

She has no choice.

She never has.

The fire erupts around her, roaring across her skin, burning her crimson hair to ash. Her golden skin crisps black and she screams in agony and joy.

She wakes into hot darkness.

⤳

THE WIND TORE AT Garin's bright red hair as the lift swept down through the drifting snows, and he pulled his cowl tighter against the chill. Draca was warm in its scabbard thrust through his belt, and he grasped it tight for comfort and reassurance. His heart was thudding hard and fast—it had hardly slowed since he'd left the palace. He could barely believe he had walked out of there alive.

People had looked at him differently on the walk back to the lift. They had regarded him with something like respect—almost awe. And while none stepped forward voluntarily to follow him along his dangerous path, it was a start.

The lift spiraled down into Low-City and ground to a halt on rusted rails grimy with snowfall. He nodded his thanks to the lift operator and stepped off into the grime. The Narfire deep below warmed the cobbled streets just enough to turn the snow into muddy slush that made his toes tingle as he trod through. Over the last few days, his boots had grown ragged, scarred and pitted from the acidic chemicals of Ruin's rain. Tar Vangryur leather was tough but ugly: he'd have to get some new footwear soon.

Most of the people who lived down here thought the rain some sort of magical legacy of the ruining of the world, but the alchemist in Garin knew better. The World of Wonders had already polluted itself with the filth that magic produced, and the World of Ruin was no different. If folk stopped using magic, the rain would gradually go back to being simple water. Not that it would ever come to pass. The World of Ruin had become utterly dependent upon magic to survive, and even if another course presented itself...Well, that was a quest for another day.

Garin slogged through the mud past the charred ruins of the Burned Man tavern. Lan had been swift in his retribution against the Circle of Tears for their involvement in Ruin's Night, but the Tears had abandoned this place long before any soldier arrived. Lan had burned it to the ground, leaving only a gutted wreck to offer a warning to any other treacherous elements in Low-City. Meanwhile, the soldiers of Ravalis hunted for anyone who bore the teardrop tattoo of the Circle, until now without success.

If only they knew where to look.

It was a bit of cleverness Garin highly respected.

Cloak pulled tight around himself against the cold and any prying eyes, Garin slipped past the destroyed building, then around into the alley nearby. He leaned against the burned out wall, loosened his breeches strings, and relieved himself against the stone. He hadn't wanted to risk wetting himself in Lan's presence, so he hadn't had a drop to drink since the previous day. Thus, he didn't have much water to make, and the pissing lasted only a five-count or so. It gave him, however, plenty of time to make sure no one was following or watching him. After spending most of his life as an insurgent in barbarian-ruled Luether, ducking Ravalis seekers seemed a pleasant vacation.

He tied up, then slipped not into the street but rather the burned out foundations of the tavern. He pushed aside a blackened beam and lifted up a rain-scarred iron plate to reveal steps leading down. He descended, taking care to lower the plate back over the access point. Darkness settled over him, enriched with the mingled scents of cool earth, ash, and sizzling rain. The approach was still awkward to him, but the shadows leaking around Draca's hilt cast the narrow space in a dull red haze. It had once been a root cellar and larder, and still held the broken remains of empty casks and crates of withered stalks that had once been herbs and now moldering root vegetables.

He stepped up to one of the walls and traced his fingers along the seam a few fingers in from the corner. Two hands down, he came to a catch, a mechanism in the wall clicked, and a door slid open.

Electricity sizzled in the cool darkness, and two deep brown eyes peered at him over the point of a drawn caster. That glare said, in no uncertain terms, that Garin's life was forfeit if he stepped wrongly.

"Summer lasts a season," he said, "but Winter endures."

The caster lingered a moment, wavering where it pointed at his face, then abruptly lowered. Its wielder wrapped Garin in a fierce hug and pressed warm lips to his. They stood in the dark together, embracing and taking reassurance in one another.

"Thank the Fire," he said, and kissed Garin again. "You were away so long, I feared—"

"Squire, my squire." Garin smiled brilliantly. "The snows were deep, and I did take it into my fool head to walk through them personally."

"I told you they would be," Alcarin said. "Didn't I tell you?"

"You did." Garin kissed him again, and felt Alcarin's hand at his belt. "Well, you're in a rush."

Alcarin gave him a coy look. "Is this what I think it is?" He touched Draca's hilt.

"Oh indeed," he said. "I thought it would be harder to get away from my cousin, but he gave it to me. Granted, that was to do the impossible, but you know my Blood. We never settle for the easy path." He stretched his weary feet. "Is Nacacia here? It's time we talked. You know the theme."

Alcarin nodded gravely. He took his master's hand. "Follow me."

Together they moved through the surprisingly spacious confines of the Burned Man's basement, a network of fortified rooms with innumerable, closely guarded connections to Low-City above. The complex had once been part of the city's sewers and was kept particularly well heated by the Narfire forges that burned not a hundred feet below. Garin felt quite comfortable in the warmth, but the crowded winterborn working in the rooms sweated. He saw dozens of pale faces, many marked with the eyedrop tattoo of the Circle of Tears. If the Ravalis only knew that their quarry remained where they had been before, only ten paces lower, it would have made their city-wide search much shorter.

Garin had never seen the lair of the Circle so busy as at mealtime. Vidia the baker supervised two others whose names Garin did not know as they carved out tureens of thick black bread and ladled stew into them. The Circle's operatives would be out in the city at all hours of the night, discerning information however they could, but the sun rising to its zenith marked the time they would gather for a briefing with the Lord of Tears or his designee. Until a few days ago, that had been Regel the Oathbreaker or his Squire, Serris. But now that one was fled and the other dead, that left the fierce Nacacia in charge.

It could be worse. Garin could hear Nacacia barking orders throughout the tunnels, and he had to smile. Considering the former winter knight's assertiveness, no other Tear could have stepped up in the chaos after Ruin's Night.

He found Nacacia in the central command room, standing at the head of a circular table covered over with a great yellowing map of Tar Vangr and its environs held down by thick leather-bound books and—at one corner—a dagger that nailed it into place. The gathered Tears were listening as Nacacia spoke at length on the movements of the Ravalis in the city, and which businesses required protection. Nacacia looked up when Garin came in and weighed both him and Alcarin in an instant. She was a warrior born and trained, her eyes always moving and her hand never far from her blade. Garin did not relish what he had to say to her this day.

"You're not dead," she said. "Must have gone well."

"Direct as always, my dear," Garin said. "And might I say, the candlelight and shadows flatter you quite nicely. They give you a certain…ambiguity quite fetching in a rebel leader."

Nacacia looked entirely unmoved by his flattery. "Shame," she said. "If the usurper had killed you, I would never have had to hear that."

Alcarin snickered at his side, and Garin elbowed him in the ribs.

"You wound me, lady." Garin put his hand to his heart. "Truly, I am wounded."

Around the table stood several Tears he did not know and two he did. Daren, who wore a fresh scar from a run in with Ravalis soldiers two nights past, stood at Nacacia's side, and the way she avoided looking at him told Garin they had put their relationship on hold during this new era. Also he saw Erim, a beautiful young man who seemed to go nowhere these days without the little girl Sarelle trailing in his wake or riding on his shoulders. Erim had taken the news of Serris's death very hard indeed, but he had risen to the challenge of fatherhood and claimed the newly dubbed Sarelle as his own. She was the last he had of his sometime-lover Serris, and he doted on her like the dutiful father he was not. Such a bright child, with her big wide eyes and winter-dark hair. She never failed to smile at Garin when she saw him, and no matter how bleak his day had passed, he smiled back.

Erim was a fine lad, one who possessed great skills in the bedchamber, but there was no way Sarelle was his daughter. Not, of course, that it was Garin's secret to tell.

"I shall come straight to the point." Garin unbuckled Draca from his belt, unsheathed it, and laid the blade on the table. Crimson shadows bled from the wavy steel. "I am leaving forthwith."

Silence greeted his pronouncement. The Tears assembled around the table exchanged looks, and finally Nacacia fixed her measuring gaze on Garin. "Good," she said.

"You really don't need me," Garin said, his mouth racing. "Under yon dangerous lady's capable leadership, you should do perfectly well, and I've built those alchemical weapons for any conflict you have with the—wait. You said *good*." He furrowed his brow. "You won't try to stop me? Not even an insincere protest?"

Nacacia glanced left and right. "We need the room," she said.

The assembled Tears filed out. As they went, they offered Garin words of encouragement and congratulations, as well as assurances that they would pass perfectly well without him. Alcarin wore a sly expression that spoke volumes, and Garin suspected his squire knew something he did not. A glance from Nacacia sent He would have to punish the knave for this transgression, and already had a few amusements in mind. When he was alone with Nacacia, he put on his brightest, most charming smile.

"What would you have of me, beauteous lady?" he asked.

Again, she ignored his courtly posturing. "It is time for you to go," she said. "Your movements are watched. Just today, in the hour it took you to return from the palace, the Tear I had following you had to evade two different Ravalis spies and throw a third off your trail."

"If you say so." Garin shrugged. "Myself, I saw none, and I'm quite adept at subtlety."

"Not today, you weren't," Nacacia said. "The Lord of Tears warned us you had a penchant for drama: marching through the snow to drum up support for your cause. How many do you think looked upon you and saw anything other than a madman with no respect for his own well-being?"

"I trod through the snow on foot like any of ten thousand people of this city," Garin said. "There are as many poor and disaffected people in this city as in mine own. Who am I to ride, while they walk?"

"Save your speeches." Nacacia's words were irritated, but her eyes sparkled. She was pleased, even if she could not show it. "You may have the Lord of Tears's blessing, but you are still a Ravalis, and we cannot fully trust you. Half the Tears in this place want to hand you to the king for a proscription reward. The sooner you are quit of Tar Vangr, the sooner we can get back to our work."

"And that is?" Garin asked.

Nacacia's expression turned dour once more. "Killing your kin."

Garin suppressed a shudder. He could spend hours arguing over a different, better way, but in truth, it was not his concern. Lan and his father Demetrus before him had built a kingdom on the basis of fear and brutal oppression. They had taken a great gift—the chance to rule Tar Vangr and mold its destiny—and pissed it away by making enemies not just of the Circle of Tears but all native Vangryur. Garin had been fighting to liberate his own city for two decades, and he could already see that Tar Vangr was headed for a similar fall. He would never actively harm one of his Blood, but at this point he did not think he could save them either.

"So you will not help me." Garin sighed and leaned on his hands on the table. "I came to Tar Vangr hoping that my uncle would lend me troops for my cause, but he died. I threw in my lot with the Lord of Tears, but he is fled. I went to my cousin, but he is mad with paranoia. Now I come to you, and you refuse me as well. It seems it shall be Alcarin and I, alone against a city full of barbarians."

Now Nacacia's mouth quirked up at the side. "I wouldn't say *alone*."

At that, a shadow stirred in the darkness behind Nacacia—someone Garin hadn't noticed before. This unnerved him, because his keen eyes rarely missed anything. The hidden woman unfolded from the darkness like a ghost, her footsteps silent. The crimson cloth wrapped around her scarred eyes clashed sharply with her golden skin, and the crimson hair that flowed around her head seemed to burn in the candlelight. Her lips were set rigidly in a determined grimace.

"Not alone," she said.

"By the Fire," Garin said.

She reached for the sword, and her fingers searched the table top for a heartbeat before she found it. Her hand closed around the ruddy leather grip, and the sword blazed to new life and heat. Shadows poured from the blade, painting a new world around them that Garin could not quite grasp. It was the future and the past, secrets lurking just past his perception.

"I'm coming with you," Ovelia Dracaris said.

TWO

Beneath the Palace of Tar Vangr

THE WALLS SHUDDERED WITH the moans of the damned, reverberating through his mind like the dull hum of bell that never quite died away. He had become an expert on the sounds of misery: the ragged groan that resonated from a gut wound, the chattering of chipped teeth, supplications for mercy that became screams of agony right on cue. He knew his fellow prisoners not by name, but by pain. They were his constant companions, and the only comfort he had in this horrid place.

Tithian Davargorn had no choice but to love the suffering of others.

He knew his jailors as well. A hunched man with a perpetual scowl checked in on him periodically, mostly to heave a pail of disgusting liquid at his face. It did not taste like water, but it was wet and kept him functioning. He was ravenous for food, but hunger hadn't killed him yet. The man with the knives he had never seen, but he knew him by the screams he evoked, and he recognized the distinctive sound of metal parting flesh and skin being drawn back. A bulbously fat woman there was also, who he recognized not by sight but by the smell of moldering flesh that preceded her wherever she went. She had an unmistakable laugh as well: wheezing and wet, like she was heaving for breath with a blade in her mouth.

Davargorn hung naked and alone in the pitch darkness, in the center of a cylindrical chamber, his feet never quite touching the ground. His arms stretched out in either direction and up, making him a hanging Y that could spin slowly in a circle. For another man, the sensory deprivation but for the cries of his fellow prisoners would have been enough to drive him mad, but with his devil eye, he could see perfectly fine. He stared at the scored steel walls, rusting and moldering from the inside out. He saw movement outside his cell door every so often, and it reminded him that not all the world was in prison and in pain. It motivated him to move: draw his legs to his chest, pull himself up by one arm and then the other. Anything to keep his body from deteriorating. It was a constant war at which he might have handily won, if not for the necromancer.

Those were the only moments Davargorn truly felt fear.

41

Occasionally, Vhaerynn would visit and stand there in the shadows, not bothering to hide. Davargorn had learned days ago not to let on that he could see him. Even the slightest hint that Davargorn detected the necromancer returned searing pain all through his body. His blood boiled and crawled, his body ripping itself apart. Somehow, seeing his assailant made it worse. Vhaerynn never spoke, let alone asked him a question: he simply stood, stared, and eventually used blood magic to torture Davargorn for a time before he left. The young man hung gasping in the chains afterward, waiting for his magical gifts to heal him. At first, it had taken only moments, but now it seemed to take hours. He could not flex his muscles during the healing, and eventually he had to rely constantly on his magic.

Through it all, Davargorn would not cry out in pain. He would not give Vhaerynn the satisfaction of breaking him.

On the fifth day or perhaps the tenth—Davargorn had no way of keeping time—his cell door slid open as far as it would go, grinding to a halt perhaps a hand out from the wall. He saw it out of the corner of his eye, but offered no reaction. Let Vhaerynn think him asleep. Perhaps if he came close enough...

"This is the one?" a voice asked.

"Think so," said another. "Can't see a thing in here."

The words seemed strange to Davargorn's ears, spoken in a foreign tongue long lost to him. How long had passed since he had heard words?

A light flared in the darkness, blinding in its sudden brightness. When his mismatched eyes adjusted to the dazzle, he saw two Ravalis guardsmen standing before him. They wore the red and blue tabards of palace guards, rather than the drab, earth-colored woolens Davargorn had seen the jailors wear. He wondered why these men had come, but more importantly, he saw an opportunity. They did not know him like the jailors did. They would not know his capabilities.

Did he have the strength? This might be his only chance.

"Check him," said one of the soldiers. "The king will want to be sure."

The king. Davargorn wondered what Demetrus wanted to do with him. Execute him for treason?

"*You* check him," said the other. "I heard he done killed dozens of our mates. I'm not going anywhere near him."

"Piss-blind coward." One of the soldiers, a southerner with very dark skin whose twisted scowl matched his oft-broken nose, drew close to squint into Davargorn's face. "Raise the light, will you?" he said to his companion, who held the lantern. "We need to be sure."

The other man, a stocky warrior inclined to fat with a bristling red beard grumbled something and did as his companion asked. The lantern illumined the dripping, empty stone chamber, as well as the winch near the wall that held Davargorn's chains in place.

Just a pace closer. Davargorn turned his face subtly so the man had to lean in if he wanted to see. This the soldier did, seeming quite oblivious.

"That's him," said the scowling one. "I think—"

Davargorn pulled up his legs and wrapped them around the soldier's neck, locking his head between his thighs. The man flinched and tried to squirm free, but Davargorn held on. The other man was drawing his caster, eyes wide.

"Listen." Davargorn spoke as clearly and calmly as he could, though his words came out ragged and weak. He hadn't spoken in days, and his own voice sounded strange to his ears. "What is your name?"

"I...I don't have one," said the fat soldier. His eyes were wide as dinner plates.

Davargorn cleared his throat. "I am Tithian Davargorn, squire of Mask the Sorcerer," he said. "I swear on his name, if you let me down, I will release your ally and yourself. And then I shall leave this place without violence." The captive soldier was struggling, sputtering to speak but failing. He made a gasping "kuff" sound, but that was all. "Do not, and I shall snap his neck, and then I shall kill you, and I'll leave anyway."

The intimidated soldier nodded, shaking all over. It made his body giggle. "I have your word?"

"My word."

The soldier crossed hesitantly to the winch and pulled the lever to release it. The chains suddenly slack, Davargorn began to fall. He curled tightly around his captive, hands at his belt, and used the force of his weight to bear the man to the ground. There, he jerked his legs to the side hard and fast, breaking the soldier's neck with an audible snap.

Without hesitation, Davargorn raised the caster he'd just taken from the shuddering corpse's belt and shot the fat soldier through the belly, blasting right through his armor and into the wall behind him. The man had been sucking in air for a scream, but now it blew out of him in a gasping rush. He sank to a sitting position, his useless legs twitching, and his caster clattered to the floor. He looked on with betrayed confusion as Davargorn casually recharged the caster for another shot.

"But...your master," the soldier said in gasps. "You swore...on his name..."

"My master," Davargorn said, "is a woman."

He fired, and the fat soldier's head exploded across the wall.

❧

The boy was fast. Brutal. Merciless. All as the hunter had expected and hoped.

He came staggering out of the old world cell, none too certain on his feet. And why should he be otherwise? He had spent nearly ten days suspended from chains. It would take him some time to learn how to walk once more, let alone run.

The hunter had endured far worse.

Compared to over twenty summers of imprisonment, the last ten days had been truly remarkable. The hunter had known nothing of these halls at first, but over time they had become a home. They were a stalking ground waiting for the hunter's confident steps, on the dozen or so occasions when a guard had faltered in his duty and the hunter had sprung free. True, there was never an escape from the tunnels beneath the world—not that the hunter had ever found, before capture—but one could dwell in this place for days on end until starvation necessitated surrender.

And now this deformed boy—this Tithian—was proving just as capable. The hunter had not found such sport in nearly a decade.

Tithian ventured down the hall, and the hunter followed. No more than a shadow, no less than skulking death. Wild, untamed, and thirsty for vengeance.

～

Davargorn stumbled along, concentrating on putting one foot in front of the other with something like consistency. He'd kept his body limber and strong during his long imprisonment, but after so long off his feet, walking felt as unnatural as speaking had. His club foot impaired him, never quite able to reach as far ahead of the other so that he moved at diminished speed, but at least he moved. Runes in the walls lit his path, but only partly—he relied mostly on his devil eye for guidance.

He carried both guards' casters, the one near a full charge, the other with enough dust magic for one or two more bolts. Their blades would serve better, though they had carried only awkward, heavy cleavers, better for butchering hogs or chopping vegetables than artfully opening a man's flesh. Davargorn had taken both, of course, but he had to get hold of a proper falcat or some other sword as soon as he could. Around him, prisoners moaned and screamed for mercy, or banged soundlessly on the inside of mirror-steel windows in high security chambers. Davargorn ignored them all, limping on to a chorus of the doomed.

Walking became easier as he maneuvered around long dry pipes and over corroded iron plating, and eventually he carried himself on sure steps. Then he was running. His healing magic had sustained him in the dungeon, and now that hope had returned, it rekindled and healed his wounds. For a surety, the blessing was diminished. His lungs heaved, and his every breath came dry and ragged. Sweat ran down his face, dripping into his eyes, but he did not care. He lived, and he would find freedom once more.

The tunnels wound and twisted, moved up or cleaved down, just as he remembered from that awful night when Regel had betrayed him. Led him down here to find only a corpse where he needed to find Mask. *Semana*, he corrected himself. Once she'd removed her mask and thus dispelled their secret, she had become Semana. Somehow, it did not seem right to think of her that way, even if it was her true face. It had been, anyway—he did not know if she was living or dead, and did that really matter? She had denied him. Turned him out. Betrayed him. Even after he'd given his life for her ten times over.

It was the Ravalis. Her quest for revenge. If not for them, they would be happy again.

The Ravalis had taken everything from him, and now he lived only to destroy them.

He came to a junction of three passages and chose one at random. So long as Davargorn kept moving forward, it seemed possible—even likely—that he would eventually come across more Ravalis to slaughter. The crude blades seemed well suited to such work, and he would relish the blood and screams of any man who fell under his knife. The two guards in his chamber had died too quickly. He intended to make the third suffer. And the fourth. And the fifth. He would kill as many as he could before they finally killed him.

Davargorn heard a scuffling sound behind him, leaped forward, and came up with a caster drawn and leveled at the darkness behind him. His hand trembled, but he tried to keep it steady, breathing only as he had need. He waited for what seemed like an eternity, but nothing presented itself. Finally, he lowered the caster and moved on—slower this time. Cautious.

As he turned around corners and scooted under low ceilings, he occasionally heard noises that suggested he had a tail: a slight whisper of footfalls, the thin rasp of breathing. If Davargorn were to look over his shoulder, he knew he would see nothing and only give away his suspicions. Instead, he pressed forward, seeking a likely ambush spot.

He came at length to a spot he remembered from his first visit to these passages: a length of hall where geologic forces had shifted the rock between the upper floor and lower one at chest height, and he could either scuttle under and drop down into the lower hall, or climb up and wedge himself into the upper corridor. He glanced over his shoulder—nothing—and tossed one of the useless blades clattering down the lower corridor, then swung himself up with little more than a hiss of air to scramble into the upper corridor. There he lay, caster ready, and waited. Only his dead white eye peered over the edge, so that he could see in the darkness behind him.

He waited.

And waited.

When Davargorn had almost given up, finally he saw it: a thin limbed creature seemingly made of bone and sinew, covered over with thin flesh. It moved like shadows, hardly separate from the darkness. His devil eye couldn't see the hunter at all, and it was only through the faint light of the runes on the wall that he could make the shape out. A mortal human, he thought, but he could not be certain. It slipped through the corridor with an astonishing grace that he could not easily credit. A true hunter.

Slowly, he brought the caster to bear, hardly seeming to move it at all. If the hunter saw the weapon's faint glow, all would be lost. Surely he would die rather than defeat such a remarkable creature. He brought the sights down upon its torso, aiming for the center mass where even if the hunter dodged, a shot would still prove fatal or at least crippling. Slowly—carefully—he squeezed the trigger.

The caster clicked but did not fire. Its charge had burned out.

Yellow eyes like those of a wolf burned up at him for an instant, and then the hunter was gone. Davargorn brought up his second caster, but to no avail. His quarry had vanished.

It had been his one shot, and he had missed.

He dashed the useless caster to the ground and pushed himself to his feet, which was much harder than he had expected. Through his magic, he'd survived so long without food, but he was on his last reserves of energy. His body trembled, and he could practically feel it eating itself out of a desire to live. He staggered, dizzy and confused.

The echo of clanging chains sped him along his path, and he tried not to think of Mask's body—Semana—hanging dead in a pit. He bit back a snarl that threatened to become a sob and pressed on.

THREE

THUNK.

The sand bag shuddered under a heavy punch, but she could not see it.

Ovelia *felt* the bag move—heard the faint creak of the chain as it swayed back and forth, gradually diminishing in its swing until it hung mostly still. She exploded forward and hit it again, this time with a left jab and a right cross, and it trembled under the strain. The chain links sang in protest.

Thunk. Thunk. Clang.

Something warm and familiar entered the room, and she felt soothed in its presence.

She smelled the dust drifting around her, shaken off the bag like water from a dog and arisen from the creaking floor. She knew where the bag would move, and lined up her hook to catch it perfectly. The bag shook back and forth. The chain links creaked. She loosed a combination that made the chain groan. Her innards churned and she ignored it.

Thunk-thunk, thunk. Clang.

She had hit the practice bag over and over for at least an hour, and she could still see it no clearer than when she had started. That aspect of the world was gone to her, and all that remained was darkness and shadow. She could smell it, feel it, taste it, and hear it, but not see it.

It would have to be enough.

"I know you're there." Ovelia stood up straight. "It's impolite to steal upon a blind woman."

Behind her, leaning against the cold brick wall of the sewer beneath the remains of the Burned Man, Garin cleared his throat. "Remarkable trick," he said. "I thought you couldn't see."

"Very little." Ovelia rubbed at the crimson blindfold around her useless eyes. "Then again, I can't help but smell that awful perfume you wear," she said. "Alcarin has a little of it on him too, obviously, but you're practically drowning in it." She held out a hand. "Towel."

He tossed her a thick sheaf of cloth, with which she wiped away the sweat that slaked her neck and scalp. Her muscles felt warm, but her body trembled slightly underneath. Sweetsoul withdrawl took a long time, and it would grow worse before it got better. She tried to push the itch down deep in her belly.

"You've been talking with Alcarin, have you?" Garin asked.

"I wouldn't say talking. But he has been watching me when he thinks I don't know." Ovelia turned back to the bag and struck twice more, making it sway. "I don't think he likes me much."

Garin moved toward the faucet and poured a beaker of water. "Alcarin is particular."

"How do you explain"—Ovelia grunted as she launched a withering cross that made the bag shudder—"*you*, then?"

"I see your mood is intact." Garin chuckled. When he spoke again, though, his words were soft and full of purpose. "How are you feeling, since Ruin's Night?"

Ovelia hit the bag once more, making it sway, and expelled a slow breath. She had dreaded this question. She felt...disconnected. Not like the woman she had ever been. She had become something colder, like a shadow of herself. At times, if she didn't have the gnawing longing for sweetsoul, she wondered if she would forget she yet lived. She had lost something she could not seem to find within herself, even as the exertion warmed her. But she could not tell Garin that.

She dreamed persistently of fire, but she could not tell him that either.

"I am well," she said. "The Tears want me gone, particularly Nacacia." She struck the bag with a *thump*, and threw a few jabs. "I cannot blame her. I brought the Ravalis upon them and it was my quest that saw their best agent slain." She thought of Serris's glower—of her burning eyes and scar as she pointed a caster at Ovelia's face. She understood that anger, and she mourned Serris's death. "The only one in the Circle who can stand me is her child, Sarelle. Odd to give one so young a name, but we should honor Serris's final words. She certainly earned the right." She punched again and again.

Garin had gone very quiet, and Ovelia paused in her training to consider him. She wondered as to his expression, which she could not see. When he finally spoke, he sounded serious.

"I admire your spirit," he said. "But you don't have to come with me to Luether. When you made your vow to me, that was before certain circumstances..." He sighed. "Well, here we are. I cannot in good conscience take a blind woman into battle where she will get herself killed. Or worse— get *me* killed."

Ovelia flexed her arms, which burned with soothing exertion. After the weakness brought on by the thaldrin that had purged the sweetsoul from her system, and after so many days and nights abed, it felt good to use her body as it was intended. Physical activity almost made her forget. She struck the bag a few more times, listening to the heavy *thunk* and resultant ring of the chain above. She wiped sweat from her brow and turned to face where she thought he was standing. Abruptly he spoke from behind her, however, and she flinched.

"You don't seem to be hitting it that hard," Garin said. "I see Tears come practice down here, and they make the thing dance like a leaf in the wind. You barely move it."

"Good."

Ovelia poured all her strength into a right cross, and the bag shivered but barely swayed.

"Brawling is about control, not strength," she said. "Accuracy."

She struck again, and the bag quaked but barely moved. The chain, however, shrieked.

"Project your strength through your foe—strike at his weakness, and break him."

She jabbed and stepped forward with a hook. *Thu-thunk!* The bag hardly seemed to move, but the chain above snapped off, and the bag toppled away in a cascade of sand. It fell to the floor, deflating as it poured out its guts on the cold stone. The grains made a sifting sound like waves rolling over the beach.

"Land the perfect strike," Ovelia said, "and a good warrior will stagger, a novice fall senseless."

She could not see his expression, but she recognized Garin's impressed exhalation. She imagined his wan smile.

"A clever trick. But can you do that to a living target?" Garin put up his hands, balled tightly into fists. "What if I attacked you—right here, right now? Could you defend yourself?"

She regarded him without seeing him for a moment, sensing his posture—his tense muscles. He was testing her. She stepped away from the hanging bag and put up her hands.

He launched a slow jab at her, and she slapped it aside easily. "I trained to fight without my sight," she said. "And you are anything but a pugilist."

"True enough." Garin launched a combination, which Ovelia managed to block with her arms and shoulder. "I learned fisticuffs from my cousins—mostly when they were beating me."

Ovelia listened for the creak of leather, felt the air displacing around his jabs. When their bodies connected, she felt Garin moving and knew how to block the next attack. As he increased in speed, she managed two out of five blocks, but suffered a hit on the other three strikes. The princeling was better than he let on. Ovelia had to reassess.

"You've adapted well." Garin drew back and swiped at his sweaty forehead. Ovelia could hear his lungs heaving. "But what if I had a blade?"

Now she recognized that air of familiarity. "You *do* have a blade," Ovelia said. "But you left it"—she pointed to the faucet—"over there."

Again, she heard rather than saw his smile. "So I do and did," Garin said. "But before—"

Ovelia crossed immediately to the small table beside the faucet. Her fingers brushed the sword's hilt, and she felt the magic within respond to her touch. She would have known Draca's presence anywhere: the warm leather handle that fit her hand perfectly, the perfect balance from pommel to tip so that it felt almost weightless in her hand, the undulating blade that whistled through the air and ground hard against a foe's weapon.

The flamed blade was the bloodsword of her father Norlest, and his father before him, and the ancestors of the Blood Dracaris dating back twenty generations—six hundred years or more—to High General Lewr Dracaris, the first of their line. Lover to a betrayed Empress and foe to the first Blood King, she had meted out justice for an atrocity that rocked Calatan. If not for Lewr's valor, the Empire would have fallen that day, but it persevered, and she became Queen Regent over a new renaissance at the heart of the World of Ruin.

As soon as Ovelia picked it up, Draca leaked shadows and her world expanded. It took her breath away—she, who had dwelled in darkness for days, could suddenly *see* after a fashion. She perceived Draca's shadows— saw the warning magic that leaked from the blade to tell her of the now and the future. Now that she did not have eyes to distract her, she could perceive all that it was telling her through her other senses. She was suddenly aware of exactly where Garin stood, and what he was doing—arms crossed, pondering—even five paces distant. And she sensed a man she had not detected before, leaning against the stone entrance. How she had not felt his palpable anxiety, she could not say.

"You're testing me," Ovelia said. "But you're not the one I need to impress." She gestured with the pommel of Draca. "He is."

Alcarin cleared his throat at the sewer tunnel opening. "That's right, Lady Dracaris," he said. "You can defeat a helpless target that can barely fight back—and a sand bag, too."

"Oh, very clever," Garin said under his breath.

"But what about a man with a sword?" Alcarin asked. "You know, one who can *see*."

"Calm yourself, squire." Garin stepped toward Alcarin. "Now's not—"

"It passes well," Ovelia said over his objections. "You're leaving on the morrow. If I'm to go with you, I need Alcarin to accept me. And for that, I need to defeat him. Is that right, lad?"

The youth nodded, which she dimly saw through Draca's shadows, then added: "Yes."

"At least use practice blades." Garin pressed two blunted swords into Alcarin's chest. "No sense in either of you getting hurt in this wall-pissing contest of yours."

"You speak as though she has some sort of chance." Alcarin tested one of the practice swords. "There's no glory in defeating a woman who can't fight back, but I'll do it. For you, Garin."

"I'm so flattered." Garin's jest was wry, but Ovelia could almost feel his bemused little smile. He expected something far different.

Tempting as it was, Ovelia uncurled her fingers from Draca's hilt and let the sword lie on the table. Deprived of its magic, her vision dimmed to a world of vague shadows once more. She held out a hand, and after a brief pause, Alcarin tossed her one of the swords. She bobbled it and the blade clattered loudly to the grimy floor. The awkward silence in the room was palpable as Ovelia stooped, picked it up, and assumed a defensive posture.

"Shouldn't you attack first?" Alcarin said. "How are you hoping to defend? You can't even see."

Ovelia said nothing, only held the sword in a high, hanging grip. Regel had taught her this, for when she had no shield to block high attacks. Alcarin could not charge her, lest he risk being impaled on the sword, and she could easily slash down at any low move he made. Like a shield, the blade formed an impenetrable barrier he would have to engage one way or another. She couldn't see him coming, but she would *feel* him.

And hear him as well. Alcarin's slippered feet hissed on the stone floor, and Ovelia felt the air stir. She turned aside, shifting her blocking sword, and his strike caught it near the hilt. If she hadn't moved, that would have slipped past her guard and smashed her forearm. With Alcarin's blade against hers, she could feel his body moving, but he disengaged too quickly. He danced away, blade scything through the air. Testing its weight. He was young and impatient but not an idiot.

"Easy enough," Alcarin said. "You didn't react to me. You just shifted your defense. I could have attacked at any angle."

"But you attacked at *that* one," Garin said in an observational tone.

Ovelia slowed her breathing, preparing herself. She moved away from the faucet, deeper into the chamber, and assumed the same defensive posture as before. She could almost *hear* Alcarin's self-confident smirk. The youth would try a different technique this time, and Ovelia had less of a guess as to which. She focused.

51

He struck again, faster and better. Ovelia heard the hesitation in his breath, the footsteps, his silk pantaloons rustling. She stepped into the attack and brought up her sword, backed by one hand halfway up the blade. Alcarin hit hard with an overhand slash, and she held him back, muscles tense. Much stronger than the boy, Ovelia could have thrown him back, but that wasn't what she wanted.

The lessening pressure meant he would withdraw, so she pressed harder, holding their blades together. Alcarin grunted in frustration and tried to twist away, but she felt him moving and followed. He pulled left to disengage, but she matched him step for step. His breathing was so fast, his movements erratic, that she might as well have seen him.

Ovelia had already won, and Alcarin did not know it.

The youth moved faster, swaying back and forth and trying everything he could to escape, but to no avail. Ovelia stayed on him, attached as surely as if she was grappling him. He was like a fly caught in her web, which she rapidly spun around him. It was only a matter of time before panic took him: she could feel it building in his movements, in the tension in his sword. He was done.

"Yield," she said.

Ovelia pushed him back against a wall and pinned his sword high. He dropped his left hand from the pommel and grabbed at her, but she pressed her forearm against his throat, eliciting a surprised gag. He slapped at her, but she barely felt the stinging blows.

"Fire's *sake*, Allie," Garin said. "Yield. She's won."

Alcarin sputtered and fought, but she could feel him weakening. The practice sword clattered from his hands to the floor. Finally, he relaxed entirely, and Ovelia couldn't be certain if he'd surrendered or lost consciousness. She eased two steps back, and Alcarin slumped against the wall, gasping for breath.

"I took no pleasure in that," she said to her coughing opponent. She turned to Garin, who had approached to within two paces behind her. "Enough?"

"Quite," Garin said. Draca burned as he held it out toward her. "Sorry I doubted you."

She touched it, and abruptly the world returned in shadows. The bloodsword's magic swelled around her, painting her ruddy vision with images both present and future. She could not see as mortals did, but rather further. *Beyond.*

Behind her, shadows materialized and swelled. Alcarin was on his feet, lunging toward her. He held no sword—that was a tool of a man. The fury within him was something uncivilized. She could hear him growling, low in his throat. Enraged. He had become a feral animal.

She stepped aside and caught his fist as it passed her head, rustling her thick red hair. Then she bent forward and down, using Alcarin's momentum to hurl him over and onto his back at her feet. She looked down at him, a bleary, startled outline—but also one that promised retribution at a later date.

"No." She left Draca in Garin's hands. "I will not go where I will endanger you." She nodded to Alcarin, then walked toward the exit from the practice room. "Or where I am unwelcome."

Back in darkness, she felt her way along the stone corridor, her fingers trembling against the slick. She felt so tired—her arms and legs almost like dead flesh—and realized that she'd been pushing herself so hard for so long. It wasn't wise, this soon after her sick bed, but she was tired of feeling tired. The hunger for sweetsoul gripped her with a hollow, ravenous need.

Ovelia had to get out and *do* something, but she had no set course. She had pushed Regel away, then Semana, and now Garin. What was she trying to do?

Footsteps resounded on the stone behind her, thunderous in her sharp ears. She turned, fists raised, but she recognized Garin's scent. He put Draca in her hands, and the world burned into focus around her. They were alone in the corridor, standing close like confidantes. He trusted her, even where he shouldn't. He put his hands on her shoulders.

"Come with me," he said. She could feel Garin's strength—his certainty in his path. "You and I—we will be the embers that spark a revolution. We will take back this world."

Ovelia paused. "And Alcarin," she said.

"And him, of course," Garin said. "Though he's all mine."

He meant it as a joke, but Ovelia didn't laugh. She considered him a long time, listening to his heart beat. Through her blindness, she saw shadows gathering around them, dozens of enemies with blades and casters drawn. Garin couldn't see them, of course: they were only vague shapes she perceived through the magic in her bloodsword. If he did this, those slayers would surround him at all times. He would be walking to his death, but he was so certain of his course that even such an assurance would not dissuade him. But if she went with him…

Ovelia hugged the sheathed Draca to her chest and walked off without a word.

FOUR

THE CORRIDORS BECAME A blur, and Davargorn no longer cared about being pursued. He just had to keep moving. Useless caster discarded, he fumbled his way through the darkness with a knife in one hand, its edge clinking off the stone. His devil eye picked up his path clearly enough, but he needed the walls for support.

No exit. No Ravalis to murder. No escape. Why had he bothered to break free of his cell, if he would find nothing?

His blood tingled, heating up in his veins, but he ignored the sensation. Had he not been so exhausted, he might have recognized the familiar feeling.

Davargorn turned a corner into a crossing room with three other corridor entrances and pulled up short. Vhaerynn stood before him like a mountain of darkness, his black robe flowing down to pool at his feet. Only his withered, pale face shone above the black, and the hint of the golden dagger on a chain around his left wrist. His red eyes seemed old and dead, but still full of baleful heat. The necromancer could see in the darkness just as well as the devil eye could.

Vhaerynn's sudden appearance startled Davargorn, making him hesitate a fraction of a second. He drew his borrowed caster in a heartbeat, but it was too late. Vhaerynn stepped forward, blackness trailing, and raised his right hand. In response, Davargorn floated up into the air, arms and legs pulled wide by invisible hands. He opened his mouth to shout in rage, but the words would not come.

The necromancer looked up at him and smiled. "Ah-ah," he said. "You've been—"

A shadow detached itself from behind Vhaerynn and struck at him with a glinting weapon. The necromancer staggered, and caught himself on his arms on the floor with an audible pop. His attacker followed, raising the discarded caster high to smash down on him again, alternating with a blade made of a sharpened shard of metal. A blurring assault of strikes followed, and Davargorn was in awe.

The magic slipped from Davargorn, and he found himself floundering on the ground. He snatched up the caster where it had fallen, but the hunter leaped onto him next, batting the weapon aside with a single expert blow. Davargorn raised his blade and cut high while his attacker cut low.

Davargorn paused, his steel at the hunter's throat. The sharpened metal had paused just above the sort spot in his ribs where a single upward thrust would spit his heart. He felt it prodding his bare skin.

Bright yellow eyes bore into his own, and he saw the features surrounding them for the first time. The dark-skinned woman had patches of short black hair, her scalp riddled with tiny scars from a blunt razor. Her noble features and sharp nose depicted a history of violence all its own, marked with the legacy of a hundred small breaks and bruises. Her hand looked odd gripping the blade, and he realized that she was missing at least one finger. Her body was wiry and much scarred, obviously as underfed as his own but well-maintained. Like him, she wore nothing—for who would need clothing in the dark parts of the world?—but her carriage turned her nakedness to strength, not weakness.

She stared at him hungrily, conveying the full force of her threat with just her wolf's eyes, and he stared right back with the same ferocity. Poised on the brink of killing one another, they fought in their minds rather than with their bodies, each trying to overcome the other. They were of a kind, and they recognized that in one another. Perhaps that was why they had hesitated to deal the deathblow.

Then she smiled, and he saw that someone had filed her teeth to sharp points. Probably her.

"Enough," said a commanding voice. "I see I have chosen well."

Torches flared, dazzling Davargorn. He stumbled back, the sun dancing in his vision and his devil eye blinded once more. The woman, whoever she was, instantly tried to flee, only to pull up short before the spiked morningstars of two Dustblades in crackling power armor who appeared out of the corridor. Suddenly a dozen soldiers surrounded them, the thaumaturgy of their arms and armor filling the room with the stench of magic. Half a dozen casters sighted on him. Davargorn brandished his cleaver, but he knew it would do little good. Behind the Dustblades, someone made a mewling, terrified sound, which matched Davargorn's own feeling. This was a trap, and he had limped right into it.

"Tithian Davargorn. Alistra. Welcome." A man approached behind the ranks of Dustblades, and Davargorn realized where he had heard that voice before. Lan Ravalis strode forward, a silver diadem upon his head, clad in his golden power armor—the same harness he had worn the night Mask had attacked him. The same night...

"The Diadem of Winter," said a husky woman's voice, and at first Davargorn was confused. Then he remembered the hunter was a woman, and that she was the one who had spoken. She must be this Alistra that Lan had addressed. "So Father is dead, then? Did you finally kill him yourself?"

Lan made a tiny, mirthless sound, then stepped forward and smashed a fist into the side of her head. Alistra slashed at him at the same time, but her metal shard barely scratched his ensorcelled armor. She fell to the floor, where she drooled blood onto the broken iron plating.

"Huh." Alistra smiled broadly "Huh ha *ha!* You still hit like a little virgin girl."

Lan's face curled back in a grimace, and he kicked Alistra in the stomach, sending her rolling into the far wall. As if provoked by the sudden violence, a terrified wail echoed through the chamber, but Davargorn had made no sound, and from the looks of her, Alistra would die before she cried out in pain.

"Did I say you could speak, whore?" Lan looked to his guards. "Restrain her."

"I see your weakness, Little Bear," Alistra said as the Dustblades grasped her arms and legs. "You don't look so well—certainly not strong enough to hit a whore without that armor."

The king drew up tall, but Davargorn could see what Alistra meant. Lan trembled—so faintly only a trained eye might notice—and sweat lay thick on his neck and hair, even though the dungeons were bitter cold. He could barely stand.

"Tithian Davargorn," Lan said. "I wish I could say it's a pleasure to see you again."

"Mutual." Davargorn tensed as though to spring, but he knew the dusters would just put him down again. "So you are the king now. *Blessings.*"

He made the last word bitter indeed, but Lan did not seem to notice. He prodded Vhaerynn's bleeding body with his boot. The necromancer loosed a dry rumble of breath. "For the Fire's sake. How many times did you strike him?" Lan glared at Alistra, who smiled wetly through bloody teeth, then beckoned forward one of his dusters.

Davargorn watched as the duster drew forward a whimpering, hooded man who was the source of the piteous sounds he had heard before. Just a prisoner, malnourished and emaciated, bristling with gray-black hair and missing a few fingers and toes. A broken man—worthless but nonetheless still a man.

Lan looked down at the hunched man, who was at least two hands shorter. "Bow to your king," he said, pointing with one hand at the floor.

The prisoner, his will broken, did exactly that. He threw himself at Lan's feet, wailing and pleading in some language Davargorn did not know, and clawed at the king's blue and red cape.

Face twisted in a grimace of distaste, Lan reached out with one hand, making magic fumes leak out from around his fingers. The golden dagger on its chain rose into the air, pulling Vhaerynn's limp hand with it. Lan's magic put the blade where he could grasp the handle, and he immediately plunged it into the prisoner's throat. The oblivious man gasped, projecting a swell of blood, and then his skin turned gray and flaked off before Davargorn's eyes. Lan released the dagger, and the eroding man collapsed atop Vhaerynn, his life's energy leaking into the necromancer. The golden dagger, fallen next to one withered hand, gleamed in the light of the dusters' lanterns. More than one of the assembled men uttered a groan of dismay, and Davargorn could tell that the display unnerved them.

He chanced a glance over at Alistra, who was watching the demise of the hapless prisoner with unrestrained pleasure—even desire. She sensed Davargorn's scrutiny and smiled at him with her shark's mouth, and he had to suppress a shudder as he looked away.

Suddenly, the old man grasped the dagger's hilt. His decrepit lungs breathed in a gout of air, and he coughed and sputtered. The withered corpse turned to ash upon him, and he stood up, a mess of blood and gore. "Apologies, Master," he said to Lan. "She caught me by surprise, it seems."

"So it seems." Lan dusted some prisoner off his boots. He gestured to the Dustblades. "That is all for now. Leave us. See that no one leaves this place."

The soldiers glanced at one another uncertainly.

"Do you defy me?" Lan grimaced. "I'm more than capable of handling one stupid whore, and Vhaerynn can kill the ugly one at a glance. Or shall I have him demonstrate his powers for you?"

That caught them. The soldiers filed out, though they cast warning glances back at Alistra and Davargorn. The naked woman smiled at them and made lewd gestures.

When they were out of ear shot, Davargorn cleared his throat. "Thank you for that," he said. "It will make killing you much easier. King or no, sorcerer or no, I *will* kill you."

The threat was empty—Davargorn could barely control his own body, much less fight Vhaerynn and Lan both. And the king's widening smile said he knew that.

"Spare your breath." Lan gestured to Alistra. "Allow me to introduce you: this vicious bitch is my half-sister, Alistra. Don't worry." He held up a hand. "She's not in any danger of inheriting the throne. The line of succession has no place for a merciless, psychotic murderer."

"I wonder why *you're* king," Davargorn said under his breath, but again, the words rang hollow.

"She has her uses, however," Lan said.

"I'm so flattered." Alistra cupped her breasts and stuck out her tongue. "Won't you tell him about the ways you used to *use* me, little brother?"

Lan looked vaguely ill. "You're embarrassing yourself." He turned once more to Davargorn. "You are needed—and you, Alistra, for a quest of national importance."

"Oh? You need an heir for your rule and can't bring yourself to rut a woman? Do you need me to pop out a princeling?" Alistra sized up Davargorn at a glance. "You want the ugly boy to rut me while you watch, brother? I won't mind. Please yourself while I make him squeal."

"She jests, boy," Lan said. "Her womb is as dry and shriveled as the rest of her corpse of a body. Not bearing children as is her duty was one of the sins that threw her in a lightless hole."

"Your brother threw me in here," Alistra said. "Or have you forgotten? How is Paeter, anyway? A whore bit off his cock yet?"

Lan smiled through gritted teeth. "But she has a valuable talent. Vhaerynn."

The necromancer looked at the king warily, and Davargorn perceived that they differed in this. Lan must have advanced this scheme, and Vhaerynn disagreed. He'd gone along with the throne's commands, of course, but Davargorn could not help remembering back to the words that had passed between Vhaerynn and himself in the tunnels on Ruin's Night.

"Let there be an end to it," Vhaerynn had said. *"An end to Summer and to Winter. Let the Blood that rules the World of Ruin be that of* real *power."*

He didn't seem powerful now. In fact, for all his might and control, he caved to Lan's wishes like a broken slave. What had the king done to him?

As Davargorn watched, the necromancer reached into the folds of his robes and drew out a battered, blackened iron gauntlet, its fingers barbed like talons. He handed it to Lan, who donned it readily and flexed it toward Davargorn. Only then did he recognize the terrible contraption.

"Silver Fire," he said. "That's Mask's gauntlet. What are you doing—*No!*"

Without pause, the king turned the claw on Alistra—the woman he had called sister—and fire roared from it like a rushing river through a cracked dam. It struck her fully, and she vanished into the flames, limbs contorting and mouth wide in a soundless scream. Davargorn cried out and fought, but Vhaerynn's magic tightened and he could not move. He could only watch in helpless horror.

Then the fire relented, leaving behind thick black smoke that filled the chamber. Davargorn coughed and shut his eyes as tight as he could against the necromancer's control. He struggled, heart hammering in his chest. He would be next. The mad king would execute *him* next.

"Ease your mind, slayer," Lan said. "I told you my sister served a purpose."

His armor whirred, and wind swept through the chamber, blowing the smoke away. In its place stood Alistra. All her body hair had burned away, soot blackened her dark skin, but otherwise she seemed unbroken. She was heaving for breath but unhurt.

"You rutting blade-sucker," she said to Lan with a sneer. "You couldn't have just *told* him?"

Lan smiled, making him look both handsome and monstrous. "I have a sense of drama."

"Rut you." Alistra took a menacing step toward him, but Lan held up the talons menacingly to keep her at bay. Perhaps the magic hadn't touched her, but those blades certainly could.

"I don't understand," Davargorn said. "How is she not dead?"

"My sister is dead to *magic*," Lan said. "It passes through her and cannot harm her. She is the perfect assassin to send after my foolish cousin, now that he has that damned sword back."

Alistra crossed her arms. "Explain."

"War, dear sister," Lan said. "War."

He gestured to Vhaerynn, who cleared his throat with a sound like hawking spittle. "Tar Vangr will march against Luether at Midsummer. It will require that long to field enough soldiers for the invasion," the Necromancer said. "In the meantime, you will follow the Fox of Luether to the summerlands. There—"

"Little cousin Garin?" Alistra smiled gleefully, an expression made very threatening by her filed teeth. "I've always wanted to see what that simpering man-lover tasted like."

"Yes," Lan said. "You will follow my cousin on his pointless quest to Luether. There he will die and become a martyr for our cause. My soldiers will be marching not as conquerors but as liberators."

"He's yet in Tar Vangr, yes?" Davargorn asked. "Why not kill him here? It seems simpler."

"And end his just cause before he has a chance be useful? No." Lan smiled. "My little cousin is to have the time I promised—to cause as much damage to Luether and Pervast as he can before midsummer. Keep the barbarians off balance. Slay their forces. Sabotage their apparatus. Whatever he will do to harm Pervast, you will see to it that he does it—to pave the way for my forces. If he dies in the attempt, so much the better. Luether needs a martyr" He smiled. "If not, then *you* will kill him at Midsummer, and Tar Vangr will march to avenge him."

"Why would I do anything for you?" Davargorn asked. "You killed my master. Semana."

Davargorn glanced at Vhaerynn to gauge his reaction. The necromancer offered only the slightest narrowing of the eyes.

"You want to kill Ravalis, do you not?" Lan asked. "Here I am sending you after one. Armed with my best weapon at your side. And you will be rewarded handsomely when you succeed."

"That's not enough," Davargorn said. "I think I'll kill you, your sorcerer, all your men, and *then* I'll kill your cousin." He glanced at Alistra. "And your crazy sister."

"Then do it for the simplest of reasons," Lan said. "Do as I command, or die. Your choice.

Davargorn nodded, but not to the king's offer. He understood. Vhaerynn hadn't told Lan what he'd said to Davargorn—about Semana being alive. That seemed to confirm that there was another angle here the necromancer was yet playing.

"Wait," Alistra said. "Queer little cousin Garin is trying to redeem Luether? By himself? Ha!"

"Not by himself," Vhaerynn said.

"Ovelia Dracaris is with him." Lan smiled. "The Bloodbreaker."

That made Davargorn's blood go cold. The Ravalis might have driven Semana's cause, but it was the Bloodbreaker who had started this whole terrible business. Ovelia was the one who had humiliated him, defeating him so easily in Luether. And after that, she had turned Semana against him. Of all the people Davargorn hated, he reserved the most vehemence for her.

"Very well," Davargorn said. "If I'm to kill them, I'll need my weapons."

Lan's smile widened. "Done."

He pounded his fist against the wall, and two dusters came back in, bearing bundles of leathers and steel. One of the men dumped his bundle at Davargorn's feet with a derisive sniff, then purposefully turned his back and walked away. The other more gingerly set down his burden in front of Alistra—a leather harness similar to Davargorn's and some smallclothes. The duster's eyes lingered on Alistra's naked body, and when she glared a challenge at him, he shrank back a step in surprise.

"You there," Lan said, and the soldier stood suddenly to attention. "Do you have a name?"

"Erdris, your Majesty," he said. "You—you named me after the battle of Echvar ten summers past. I took an arrow meant for you."

"Ah, yes, Erdris—a good name." Lan's eyes hardened and he raised his chin imperiously. "A name you no longer deserve if you would suffer a woman to insult you with her eyes."

Erdris stared at him, wide-eyed, like a deer that has just seen the hunter. "Sorry, Majesty, I—"

"Don't apologize to *me*," Lan said. "Apologize to yourself. Strike her. Beat her. Mount her in front of me—I don't care. Be a burning *man*."

Erdris was visibly sweating and his fingers curled and uncurled into fists as he stood, caught in indecision. He looked to Alistra, who had ignored her discarded equipments in favor of staring at Erdris. Still naked, she shifted her weight to one foot, crossed her arms, and gave him a fake smile as if daring him to touch her.

For his part, Davargorn pulled up his breeches, then settled back to watch the drama unfold. He knew how it would end, but precisely what Alistra would do captivated him.

Ultimately, Lan's goading combined with Alistra's defiance proved more than enough for Erdris. The duster stood up to his full height, swelled his chest, and headed toward her, picking up speed as he went. She seemed to shrink a little as he approached, dwarfed by his size and crackling power armor. Indeed, when Erdris reached for her, Alistra pulled away as though frightened. But Davargorn had spent the last five winters in the presence of a destroyer in a frail body. He saw the situation very differently.

So skillfully that it looked casual, Alistra slipped aside and grasped Erdris's wrist. She stepped into him, ducked low, and flipped him over to the floor hard enough to blow all the air from his lungs. Before Erdris could draw a fresh breath, Alistra knelt on his neck, exerting just enough pressure that he coughed and sputtered. Still holding Erdris's wrist over her head, his arm taut to the breaking point, She flexed, and Erdris's arm popped out of its socket, wrenching a muted shriek from the choking man. Alistra looked up at Lan with smoldering eyes.

The king shrugged. "Is that all?" he asked.

Alistra's defiant smile returned. "No."

She twisted her leg, and Erdris's neck broke with a wet crunch. His legs twitched madly as his body fought its way down into death. Casually, Alistra climbed off the duster and claimed the clothes he had brought her. She hummed a jaunty tune as she dressed, pulling on the garments with such obvious relish it made Davargorn wonder how long it had been since she'd had proper clothing. His cheeks felt a touch warm, and he looked away to give her privacy. The king glared at them both, outwardly impassive, but his eyes had narrowed against an angry storm. Davargorn was pleased.

"So what now?" Davargorn asked as he finished buckling on his armor, breaking the silence between brother and sister. "We board a skyship? A mage-caravel?"

"An ornithopter is charged and waiting for you, along with coin and more resources as you might require." Lan gestured idly to his vizier. "And you'll be taking Vhaerynn along as well."

The old man looked at him, startled. "Me, Master?"

"He will supervise this important mission and see to it you do not wander from the path." Lan looked at the necromancer sharply. "Or do you not agree?"

Vhaerynn bowed his head, evoking the first of Lan's arrogant smiles that pleased Davargorn.

"Good." Davargorn lifted the two sheathed falcata the dusters had left. Their balance was acceptable. "But when this is over, I'll return for you. And no necromancer will keep my blades at bay."

Lan shrugged. "Ruin smile upon you, then."

Alistra cleared her throat behind Davargorn. She had donned a hauberk of dark leather with leggings to match. A small axe rode either hip, and Davargorn saw the hilts of daggers poking up from the mouths of her boots. Clothed and armored, she looked more than ready to kill a hundred Ravalis.

"And what if he succeeds?" Alistra asked.

Lan waved. "He will not."

"But what if he does?" Alistra stretched. "What if he redeems Luether and places himself newly upon the throne, ushering in an era of peace and hope?"

Lan narrowed his eyes. When he spoke, his words were cold and sharp.

"Make sure he does not."

FIVE

A S THE LAST RAVALIS patrol swept the Avenger before its departure, Garin reminded himself for the fifth time to stop tapping his foot. It was a nervous habit he'd never liked in himself.

Dustblades in red and blue tabards had searched the docked ship at least a dozen times since Ruin's Night, and found no sign of a long-lost princess or a grizzled court assassin. All they had succeeded in doing thus far was to delay the small army of landed people and desperate traders who depended upon Luethaar silver and gold to maintain their lifestyle. It was among these that Garin Ravalis had insinuated himself, along with his two "slaves" to make the trip south. Those impatient to get on the ship stood in a milling crowd, waiting while Dustblades searched the skyship and made some cursory effort to check them personally. Garin's party had passed this inspection easily enough.

Under pressure from wealthy merchants whose goods sat gathering dust in High-City storehouses when they could be bringing southern coin northward, King Lan had grudgingly freed up the *Avenger* for travel once more, though the crown strictly forbade pleasure jaunting for the foreseeable future. Normally, the pools and divans on the *Avenger*'s deck would be full of glistening flesh and laughter, but now they stood bare and empty. Relations with Luether had long been in decline, and Garin knew haste was the matter of the day. He had only a limited time, and any delay could cost him dearly.

"*Until Midsummer,*" Lan had said. "*Then our armies march. I'll have no need of you then.*"

Winter had already begun to pass. Ruin's Night marked the darkest night, but Dark Solstice had been the longest. The days grew longer, the nights shorter—an inevitable march toward Midsummer.

Alcarin laid his hand on Garin's wrist. "Master," he said.

Garin realized he had been tapping again. He smiled at Alcarin, who wore the simple roughspun, unassuming clothes of a slave. His squire always seemed to know when he needed reassurance. Garin adjusted his alchemist's cloak with its many pockets and buckles. Traveling in noble regalia of Ravalis red and blue had never been his preference, and now it would only draw the wrong sort of attention.

"I just want to move," he said. "We only have until Midsummer."

Alcarin nodded. "It makes sense," he said. "Take the spring to build a fleet of warships, set sail when the weather clears, and land on the southern archipelago ready to fight. Half a winter, a spring, and half a summer. Leaves a tiny stretch of time to spark a revolution."

"And throw down a usurper." Garin gritted his teeth at the thought of Lord Peritis, his bulbous body and diseased mind festering like a sore at the heart of Luether. The Ruin King should have just destroyed the city, but instead he kept up the illusion of civilization, to enrich himself and torture the people with hope. Garin would set it right…if only they could get moving.

"Disaster."

They both looked over at Ovelia, and Garin noted for the second time how extraordinary her transformation had been. Where only an hour before had stood a proud, bronze-skinned woman entering her fifth decade of life, now hunched a weathered crone, well past her eightieth winter, with stringy gray hair, wrinkled skin, and a white linen blindfold. Ovelia might one day look like that as a venerable elder, but just now it was the result of cunning make-up. Garin wondered if any of them would ever be that old.

"What did you say, old woman?" Alcarin's voice was clipped. Still fuming about his humiliation at her hands, it seemed. He called her that regardless, but her current guise made it bemusing.

"Disaster." Even Ovelia's voice crackled like that of an aged creature. "Vangryur are ill-suited to fighting in the heat. Lan will lose more men and women than he can imagine."

"Men." Garin and Ovelia both looked at Alcarin, who cleared his throat and added: "Only men. Luethaar women do not march to war."

"Well, *our* women do." Ovelia shook her head. "If Lan sends only half the army, he is doomed."

"Or he knows something we do not," Garin said. "That he bears some great weapon that he believes will make the difference."

Alcarin's eyes widened. "Like what?"

Garin shook his head. "I wasn't in Tar Vangr long enough to see them for myself, but the Narfire forges beneath the city have been working non-stop for almost a year," he said. "The nameless call it Lan's attempt to make the Winter City more like Luether, but I think there's more to it." He touched the warpick at his belt, feeling its magic roil, ready for release.

Two of the searchers hurried off the *Avenger*, shouting something to one another, and the three had to move apart for a moment to avoid them. The two men shoved their way through the crowd, and Alcarin snuggled up to Garin once more. Ovelia leaned subtly toward them.

"Dust magic?" Alcarin bit his lip. "You think he's building war machines."

"That would not surprise me," Ovelia said. "Regel and I faced an entire squad of Dustblades with gleaming power armor before Dark Solstice. When was the last time you saw anything new with that sort of power? Or anything *new* at all?"

Garin looked down from the spiraling height to the bleary rooftops of Low-City, three hundred paces below. Even at this distance, he could see steam rising from the evaporating snowfall. Every so often, a gust of wintry wind caught the steam, and he could taste the sourness in the air. Low-City had become nearly as warm in the depth of winter as at the height of summer. Below the streets, the forges roared, churning out…what?

It was not his problem. He had to focus on Luether or all of this would be for naught.

Finally Hyldir, captain of the *Avenger*—a stout woman with hair the color of an old caster barrel and a dubious expression to match—appeared on the dock and waved. Apparently, the search was nearing its conclusion. Garin released a relieved breath and started forward, only to find himself barred by a pair of Ravalis soldiers. They seemed to have appeared out of the wintry dusk itself, their gray cloaks hiding them against the overcast sky. The maces that hung from their belts hummed with what he judged to be sonic thaumaturgy, and they wore light power armor. The three of them could defeat these men without trouble, but it would make quite the scene.

"May I help you, gentlesyrs?" Garin asked.

"Hold," one of the Dustblades said, in a gruff voice that brooked no argument. "We've orders to detain anyone who resists." The other one put his hand on the handle of his mace.

Garin's mind raced. Had his cousin anticipated their plan? He thought he had bought them time with the ruse about Draca. What if—?

"That will be enough, soldier," said a commanding voice behind Garin. The Dustblades snapped to attention, then stepped away.

Amongst a retinue of a score of Dustblades, King Lan stood before them in his grand golden regalia, his customized power armor of red gold shining in the rising sun, his sword and shield polished and near to hand as though he meant to march to war on the instant. Beneath his elegantly sculpted red hair, he wore the traditional cosmetic enhancements of the Ravalis kings of old: gold dust powder to brighten his face, blue kohl to shadow his eyes, and blood red to outline his lips. Garin had seen his brother just the previous day, so he knew well what that rouge was hiding. Also, he noted that Lan had neglected to wear the Diadem of Winter—doubtless it would not match the rest of his glorious ensemble.

All those assembled bowed, some quicker than others. Climbing smoothly down to one knee, Garin tried not to look at Alcarin or Ovelia and thus draw attention to them. His companions stood two paces away near his luggage, looking like nameless slaves. Lan recognized Garin, but perhaps he would not realize the others were with him. Finding Alcarin would be a scandal, but Ovelia? Death for certain.

Fortunately, the king's eye passed only briefly over Garin as he searched the rest of the crowd.

"The rise of a new king is always a hard time," Lan declared as he walked through the clearing in the crowd. "But that is no excuse for relieving ourselves of our responsibilities to be good, loyal citizens of Tar Vangr." He turned on his heel and looked directly at Garin. "Alas, some among you have not learned that lesson."

Did he know? Had Nacacia betrayed them, seeking to remove Garin more permanently rather than allow him to leave the city? He could feel Alcarin edging closer to him, and he made a staying motion with his hand under the hem of his cloak. He hoped Lan and his soldiers would not see it. He realized Ovelia was holding his squire back, one hand on his wrist.

"I shall show you all what becomes of traitors under my rule." Lan crossed his hands behind the small of his back and raised his chin. "Bring them before me."

Garin tensed, ready to move, but no attack came. Instead, the Dustblades pulled three people—a mewling steward, an unmoving brute of a man, and a struggling, snarling woman—from the *Avenger's* deck. They had common faces and wore the white livery of *Avenger* crew. The steward was a reedy man Garin had met on his previous voyage on the *Avenger*. He kept trying to plead with the Dustblades in incoherent rambles that grew more insistent as they approached. The big man shivered in the soldiers' hands, showing clear signs of having been stuck with a thaumaturgical blade that shocked the fight right out of him. The woman clawed and fought against her captors, earning a good left hook to the side of the head for her trouble. That left her stunned and quiescent. The Dustblades shoved the three to their knees before the king, in a space that the crowd cleared near the edge of the platform.

Wind whipping at his hair, Lan stood over them imperiously. "These three nameless smallfolk—"

"I have a name, your Majesty!" cried the steward, panting. "I have…a name."

The king paused in his recitation and looked down at the gangly man on his knees. "My apologies," Lan said. "By all means. Tell us your name."

The man's mouth opened and exploded into a shower of blood and tooth fragments as Lan punched him with his powered gauntlet. The force knocked the man reeling on his knees, and the king followed up with a hook that snapped his neck with a vicious crack. He slumped to the mage-glass beneath their feet, quivering and choking on the blood pouring from his face.

Garin trembled with the rising urge to intervene. He glimpsed Alcarin staring at him, terrified for him and of what he might do. Ovelia stared at the mage-glass platform beneath their feet. The familiar darkness rose up inside Garin and he willed it away. That was not him. He still lived. Luether awaited him, desperately in need.

Flicking blood and spit off his gauntlets, Lan turned to the others. The woman stared up at the king in defiance that was quickly bleeding away into panic, and the big man groaned and looked as though he would vomit in a matter of moments.

"You have been heard spreading lies and fomenting protest." Lan laid his hand on the groaning man's head. "This cannot be permitted. Upon which of you shall I render judgment first?" He cupped the woman's chin, and she glared up at him with a mixture of rage and terror. Lan smiled. "You, I think."

The king started to wind his fist back, but a shout rang out to interrupt him. Shock rippled through those gathered on the mage-glass platform, and every eye searched the crowd for who might have dared to interrupt the king's justice. It was not until their gazes fell on him that Garin realized he had been the one who protested. Lan himself stared at him with narrowed, dangerous eyes. So much for subtlety.

Garin stood amongst the kneeling crowd and drew his hood back. Isolated gasps identified a few people who recognized him, but otherwise expectant silence fell.

"Cousin," King Lan said, his face carefully unreadable. "I did not see you there."

Garin was not certain he believed that, but he kept his face carefully neutral. "What...what crimes did you say these folk committed?"

"You question me?" Lan asked, his voice a cold, threatening blade.

"I would never question my rightful lord and master." Garin bowed, growing more comfortable as he made Lan angrier. "I simply wish to relate the story accurately. We should know what terrible misdeeds our fellows have committed, to discourage such treason in others."

The crowd hardly wanted to cross the king, but that suggestion seemed very reasonable. Alcarin looked profoundly anxious, ready at any heartbeat to leap to Garin's defense—to drag him away, swords ringing and casters cracking. They would likely not escape, but it would be a glorious battle. The only safe path he could see was to confront his cousin and not shrink from him, as he had in the palace.

"Very well," Lan said. "They have been heard to spread seditious rumors and lies regarding my royal personage and the glorious city of Tar Vangr."

"*Heard* to spread," Garin said. "They were neither tried nor convicted. Is there no evidence? Let those who accuse them come forth and be recognized."

Anger rippled through Lan at the prince's audacity, but Garin could sense the people supporting him. As long as the Ravalis had been in power in Tar Vangr, they were still guests in the city, and most of the pale faces in the crowd were those of the winterborn. Lan had only been king a short while. If he failed at this, his first public showing before some of the most powerful people in Tar Vangr, it would taint the political capital he needed to gather. And as impulsive as Lan could be, he was enough of a political animal to know this as well.

"That is wisdom, cousin. Let us speak plainly." His armor gleaming, Lan raised his hands to encompass the crowd. "All of you represent the wealthy and influential in this city, and you should know the truth, rather than rely upon rumor and supposition. So here it is."

Lan drew his hands into his chest and laced his fingers in front of him.

"On Ruin's Night, assassins attempted to destroy my Blood," Lan said. "In a bid to seize the throne for themselves, numerous traitors on the Council slew my father Demetrus where he sat, and they attacked me as well. These things you have heard, and I stand before you today to confirm them." He spread his arms and winced in pain. It made him seem vulnerable despite his fantastic suit of red-gold armor. "I still bear the wounds upon my body to remind me of that terrible night."

He let the moment draw out for a few heartbeats, then dropped his hand. "But this attack came not just upon me and my Blood, but upon our city." He pointed toward the rising palace tower on the mountain, where black metal twisted into the sky and smoke wafted amongst the clouds. "Look at the scar their strike left upon Tar Vangr, where all can see."

The king let that pronouncement sink in for a moment, then struck the finishing blow.

"Seventeen Tar Vangryur lost their lives in the assassins' strike," Lan said. "Many of them did not have names, but I know those who did. Eresaar, Fias, and Valla. Three of my personal friends, who left behind Blood and lovers of their own." He hung his head.

Garin knew for certain that the king was…if not openly lying, at least distorting the truth. Regel and Ovelia had slain mostly summerborn warders, while Lan and Demetrus had personally slain several Tar Vangryur councilors and their warders, including the heir of Blood Yaela. Those men and women who had sought the throne, certainly, but not through assassination. Regel's attack later that night had been a much more personal affair, and Lan had only suffered after he had attacked Ovelia personally.

It mattered little. The crowd had begun to turn when Lan had described his wounds, and shaping the story as an assault on the city itself had won them over. They stared with anger now at the two accused traitors, and Garin knew any plea for clemency or truth would go for naught.

"The assassins themselves lie dead, do they not?" Garin asked. "Surely the danger they pose has passed."

"Oh aye." Lan smiled slightly, but only with his eyes. His mouth remained cold. "But the conspirators that attacked me—attacked our city—they were not alone." Lan stepped closer to the two battered Tar Vangryur. "They could not have achieved what they did without their network of accomplices. Thieves, murderers—cowards. Spies and infiltrators are all around us, constantly searching for weaknesses—constantly seeking to undermine those who would protect us. To frighten us. But we are not afraid."

He picked up the big man by the throat, dragging him to his knees. The man gasped, choking.

"Never afraid," Lan said.

The power in the king's gauntlets boiled over and he shattered the man's neck between his fingers. He cast the man over the edge of the mage-glass, and the corpse vanished into the acidic clouds.

"Blood must answer blood, and death must come to those who seek to kill us and our fellow Tar Vangryur," Lan said. "The liars and bloodbreakers who lurk amongst us understand no other tongue."

Lan reached for the woman next, but she mustered up a burst of strength and leaped out of the way of his seeking hand. She made it half a dozen paces before one of the Dustblades put a casterbolt between her shoulder blades and she fell in a heap.

"I am sorry you had to see that," Lan said to the gathered crowd. "Please, fare well on your voyage, and keep your eyes open for suspicious activity and your ears keen for treasonous words." He waved them toward the *Avenger*, then turned to Garin. "A moment, cousin."

As the crowd anxiously filed aboard the ship, Garin waited—trying not to tremble—as Lan approached. They stood, each taking the measure of the other. Around his cousin, Garin could see Alcarin linger at the ramp onto the *Avenger*, looking back, but Ovelia pulled him after her.

"Those people were innocent, weren't they?" Garin asked.

"Perhaps, perhaps not," Lan said. "I instructed my warriors to pull three people at random off the ship." Lan shrugged his shoulders. "An effective demonstration, no?"

Garin forced himself to stand up straight when all he wanted to do was scream and cower. "What would you have of me, Majesty?"

"You are going to Luether," Lan said. "Before you bring me my sword."

"Yes," Garin said. "As you knew I would."

Lan made no argument. "You are leaving a great deal behind to pursue a vain quest."

"And you have a task ahead of you," Garin said. "If you are to find these spies and infiltrators. Particularly one with hair of silver and another named for a sword of ice."

The king leaned close, and Garin could feel his hot breath on his face. "If you knew where they were," he said, "you would tell me, no?"

"Of course, your Majesty." He tried his best not to gaze after his allies.

Lan looked at him so intently he might have been staring through him. "Narfire light your way, cousin," he said. "Go save our city, if you can. I'll be down to burn your bones at Midsummer if not."

Without a word, trying not to shiver, Garin turned and climbed aboard the *Avenger*. He was the last passenger to do so, as the crew started to undo the ties and cast off the chains that bound the skyship in place.

"Oh, and cousin!" Lan cried from the dock.

Garin looked back, only to see the king heft the murdered woman's body and toss it over the side of the skyship dock to plummet the thousand feet to the rocks below. Lan said no more, but merely smiled. Then he turned and walked away, his retinue behind him.

Garin shivered.

"Such wasted effort," came a voice behind him. Garin would recognize that raspy, aged voice anywhere.

Vhaerynn the necromancer stood perhaps two paces from Garin, draped in his black cloak. They were of a height, he and the sorcerer, but that was where the resemblance ended. Garin was built on a robust scale: wiry, strong, vital. Vhaerynn was the opposite: almost skeletally thin, sickly, and so weak in appearance one imagined a stiff wind might break one of his limbs. Underestimating him based on his visage, however, would not do at all. The necromancer wore a simple black robe and his ornate gold dagger strung on a chain around his right wrist. A more powerful relic, Garin did not think he had ever known—except perhaps Draca.

"I—apologies, Lord Necromancer," Garin said, scrambling to get his wits about him. "I must not have understood you."

"Such wasted effort." Vhaerynn cocked his head to the side. "Unless His Majesty's attempt to intimidate you proved successful, Summer Prince?"

"Hardly, Lord Vhaerynn." Garin stiffened his spine and bowed. He would not give his cousin's creature the satisfaction of seeing his unease. "You do honor to this humble peddler of chemics and devices."

"Yes, yes, project your false modesty," the sorcerer said. "But fear not. I've not come to betray your confidence. I come as an ally."

"I'm sure."

Vhaerynn's mouth turned downward in a grimace. "I am also not given to brash theatrics, as is his Majesty."

"My cousin did not order you here?" Garin asked. "To keep me in my place?"

"He did not. I am here of my own will," Vhaerynn said. "To make sure you are…prepared. I admire your determination. It is only your ability I doubt."

He held up a hand, and Garin felt his arm begin to tingle as Vhaerynn's foul magic seized his blood and turned it to his will. Through his blood magic, the sorcerer manipulated Garin's arm as though it were his own. The prince struggled, but he was fighting himself.

A sea of humanity parted around them, filtering into the skyship's lower decks. On the aftcastle, Alcarin stiffened, looking at the old man like he wanted to plant a knife between the aged shoulder blades. Garin wanted to scream at him to stay back, but managed instead only a sharp glance. For her part, Ovelia increased their guise: she feigned a coughing fit and dragged Alcarin over to tend to her. Thankfully, the necromancer seemed oblivious—to him, they were simply nameless faces in a crowd of folk climbing onto the *Avenger*.

"Release me," Garin said through gritted teeth.

"In a moment."

Garin felt his trembling hand brush aside his cloak, revealing the bound hilt of Draca at his belt, counterbalancing his thaumaturgical warpick on his other hip. Vhaerynn nodded in satisfaction. "At least you're not entirely a fool."

Then abruptly the magic was gone, and Garin owned his arm again. He rubbed at his wrist, which still tingled. "You could have just asked."

Vhaerynn smiled. "I thought your cousin's longing to see you submit was childish of him, but now I understand. For all your determination, you are as weak as he is. As any of you are."

71

Garin's face felt hot. Ovelia's hand was on Alcarin's arm now, fingers white at the strain of holding him back. The Fox of Luether felt a swell of adoration for his squire, but to attack Vhaerynn now would undo all he had fought for. He stood up as straight as he could.

"Is that why you've come?" Garin asked. "To insult me and bully me like Lan? I thought such things beneath you, Blood Mage."

Vhaerynn bowed his bald head slightly. Despite the lightly falling snow, his pale scalp seemed dry as bleached bone. "A passing trifle," he said. "Since I do not think we will see each other again for some time, I came to offer you a parting gift."

He reached into his voluminous robes and drew out a small gold ring, set with a ruby in the shape of a drop of blood, which he put in Garin's hand. Small runes decorated its circular length, though he could not read them. Even at a glance, Garin could tell the ring was ensorcelled, but not with any thaumaturgy he knew. Blood magic.

"And what is this?" Garin hefted the heavy thing. "Are we betrothed, now?"

Vhaerynn smiled thinly. "Every member of the Blood Ravalis bears my protection and falls under my aegis," he said.

Truth, finally, Garin wanted to say, but thought better of it. Vhaerynn's protection was weak, whether by accident or malice. King Demetrus had fallen while Vhaerynn ostensibly protected him, and Garin had his suspicions about Paeter's fate as well.

"Usually, I do this task through a simple blood ritual," Vhaerynn said, "but as I suspect you would refuse such a thing—"

"You suspect rightly," Garin said.

"—I have woven the enchantment into this ring instead." Vhaerynn's hands disappeared back into his robe and he shivered against the cold. "If you are wounded—if your blood spills upon the ground—the magic of that ring will call me, and I shall come forthwith to defend you. Wear it or not, as you will."

The old man nodded and turned away. Garin closed his hand around the ring, as though he could crush it in his palm.

"But why would I accept any gift from you?" Garin said. "You are my cousin's creature, and am I not a threat to his rule?"

At that, Vhaerynn smiled thinly over his shoulder. "The Eunuch King will not rule forever, and he will leave no sons to carry his line," he said. "It is a poor sorcerer who does not consider the future."

And with that, he strode away into the swirling mist.

Alcarin was by Garin's side in a heartbeat, steadying him. The prince wondered when his legs had gone weak, but now he was having trouble standing. He felt…not himself. Violated.

"That monster," Alcarin said. "What did he do to you?"

"Nothing. I'm well." Garin opened his tight fist and revealed the gold ring. He'd squeezed so tight he had marks in his skin. "Gave me two gifts—this, and something to ponder."

Ovelia was there as well, staring at the ring in his left hand, and also the ring he already wore on one of the fingers of his right. She didn't have to speak. He knew her thoughts.

Garin looked to the skyship, which had loaded most of its passengers. More folk were setting out for Luether than the ship usually carried, and its hold was stuffed with goods.

"Come," he said. "If we want a berth, we'd best hurry." Then to Alcarin, loud enough for the Ravalis guards to hear him, he said: "Have a care with those valises, boy! Drop one, and I'll sell you and your grandmother for scraps."

Alcarin gave him an adorably defiant look, and Garin knew he'd have to make up for that barb later. He looked forward to it.

He looked off into the gray sky, its color bleeding away as night approached. He thought about flicking the gold ring out of his palm and off into the empty sky. He would watch it fall, turning end over end with a faint hum, and vanish into the clouds. The idealist in him wanted to watch that very badly.

The pragmatist, however, shut his eyes with a sigh and closed his hand around the ring.

ACT 2: DECEIVERS

Before the Fall—The Long Dawn—Luether—959 Sorcerus Annis

SONG AND DANCE RIPPLED along the streets, and the aroma of a thousand flowers wafted into the broiling evening. Every tavern in the city swelled to bursting with people from both tiers of the city, and lifts full of inebriated revelers raced up and down all day. All of Luether rose in celebration of Paeter Ravalis's return: the handsome prince who had swept back home after his first state visit to Tar Vangr, all but fulfilling the alliance between the Ravalis and the Denerre, two great Bloods who had been rivals for centuries. Bound in common purpose and in blood, the two cities could stave off the encroachment of Ruin and lead their people into a new era of cooperative prosperity.

For young Garin Ravalis, the alliance could not come soon enough. In Tar Vangr, his own particular eccentricities would be welcomed rather than despised. Luether remained steadfast in its limited views, but perhaps with increased trade, and shared culture, attitudes in his home city would begin to shift. It had occurred to him more than once, in the darkest hour of the night, that he could flee northward. He could go keep court with Lenalin and Ovelia and all the pale folk of the wintry lands, there to live as he wished, never caring what anyone thought. But he was the crown prince of Luether, and he could not abandon his city and his people, no matter how much they loathed what he was.

The ruling Blood of Luether historically held itself above such revelry—preferring boring, proper balls in their palace in High-City—but under King Cassian, they joined the people in their joy. Garin had followed the Ravalis entourage to six different taverns so far, and Cassian yet had the energy to keep dancing even as night fell. At Garin's subtle prompting, they'd ended up at his favorite, the Long Dawn. The unmarried king had his pick of the most beautiful ladies of Luether, but he danced with anyone and everyone. Rich or poor, it did not matter to him: he mingled with his people rather than standing above them, and that Garin very much respected. And he'd always liked dancing.

At some point in the night, he noted his cousin Alistra watching the revelry from a private booth set aside for the Blood Ravalis. He saw her yellow eyes peering out through the cracked shutter, barely open to allow her to watch largely unseen. Garin gently excused himself, waved for fresh wine, and pushed through the curtain of crystalline beads to join her. The booth featured benches with numerous pillows as well as a round table hung with its own shimmering curtain.

"What say you, Lissa?" he asked as he slid into the booth.

Drawing her attention mournfully away from the dancing, Alistra glanced at him with mild distaste. Her unique eyes—vivid yellow, like those of a wolf in a child's story—flickered with jealousy. They were her best feature: the rest of her was large, unwomanly, and sedentary. Most nights, she hardly moved from one spot, but sat like an overfed hound long since fallen from its master's good graces.

"Oh, I pass quite well up here," she said. "Sitting and watching this thing I can never touch."

"I know exactly what you mean."

"Do you? Truly?" Alistra sighed and gazed out the open window over the revelers with their brightly colored dresses, sweat-lathered skin, and flashing smiles. She politely ignored her cousin.

It saddened Garin that Alistra could take no part in the revelry, but such was Demetrus's decree for his only daughter. All decent men, he insisted, despised girls who disrespected themselves enough to flirt or spent time with men not her own blood or her husband. To him, such promiscuity was the province of gutter women, far below his daughter in dignity, and for her to indulge would be an admission of her own filth. Such expectations might have crushed a lesser girl, but Alistra embraced the expectations put upon her with a righteous fire. Men had never shown much of an interest in her body, so she gladly crafted herself as a non-sexual being. So far as Garin knew, she had never so much as kissed a lad, let alone shared one's bed. But he could see the longing in her—the same that had burned within him, until that last year. And she had carried it for far longer.

"What?" Alistra had caught him staring at her. "Does his highness have some witticism to share?"

"Always," Garin said. "But none particularly appropriate for this festive occasion."

Alistra rolled her eyes and went back to ignoring him. Of all his cousins— and Demetrus had many children—Garin could most appreciate time spent with Alistra. He always claimed he did it to save her from constant boredom, but in truth he did so out of sympathy for her plight. They could not have been more different, but they shared one important facet in common: Luether would not let either be what they should be.

Free.

And so they seized their moments where they could. Alistra admired from afar and Garin did the same, settling in to watch his beautiful cousin Paeter with no small amount of longing. Unlike with his daughter, Demetrus not only allowed but actively encouraged his sons to flirt, dance, and rut with as many women as possible. Paeter was an indifferent dancer at best, but the number of women who flocked around him at all times rendered his skill irrelevant. They fed him morsels of food—oysters, grapes, bits of bread and cheese—and he drank small goblets of watered wine with each of them. As always, Lan followed him doggedly.

"Cousin," Alistra said. "A professional opinion."

Alistra nodded toward two Vultara girls—Vilaer and Utora, if he remembered their names aright, the youngest of their Blood. The twins were of a dangerous age, this being their sixteenth summer, and they drew the attention of almost every man in the tavern at one time or another. And, of course, the Blood Vultara had a reputation of old as the Blood of the Harlot, descending as they did from the city's most ignoble villainess: Lady Vulta, who had almost destroyed Luether in the hour of its birth. No self-respecting Luethaar wanted anything to do with a Vultara, which meant everyone wanted them. Badly. The twins played the game particularly well: dancing rather closer together than sisters should, embracing and kissing. Their strategy succeeded in drawing a horde of admirers, which was probably the only reason they remained in the Long Dawn with the Ravalis. Their respective Bloods were well known to be fierce rivals from old. That, and Garin could tell by Alistra's sneer that she liked them as little as she liked any slim girl.

"Do men truly find such lurid, disgusting behavior attractive?" Alistra asked.

Garin chuckled. "You're asking the wrong Ravalis, cousin," he said. "But their admirers seem to approve. Don't you know having twin lovers is a summerman's greatest fantasy?"

Alistra made a disgusted sound. "Shouldn't you be down there trolling and whoring like my brothers?" she asked. "Not wasting your time with your fat spinster of a cousin?"

"Like that, you mean?"

With some disgust, he nodded to Lan, who lurked on the edge of Paeter's entourage, badgering some poor merchant heiress who was just trying to get closer to Paeter. Her cheeks blushed redder and redder, and she eventually managed to extricate herself, complaining of some sort of stomach malady. Lan watched her go for a moment, then turned back to Paeter's group, sniffing at the edges like a hound searching for a new fox to torment.

"He's like a little puppy," Alistra said.

"Not so *little* anymore." Despite having seen one fewer summer, Lan had always been bigger than Garin, and over the last year that had all turned into chiseled muscle. Garin might have found Lan as lovely as his dashing brother, but after that last summer…Garin spent as little time around Lan as he could manage whilst maintaining a veneer of etiquette.

"Don't you want some tight body to warm your bed this night?" Alistra asked. "My brother may be the hero who united two cities, but you're the prince who will rule Luether. You could take any one of his strumpets."

The word—Demetrus's word—made Garin slightly ill. "Meh," he said. "You're the only woman I can stand, Lissa—you know that. Those others have only their looks to offer."

"That's the point, fool boy." Alistra rolled her eyes. "Is this not your fifteenth summer? Surely you'll grow up and start looking at girls one of these days."

"Ugh. Revulsion!"

The handsome serving lad who'd brought them mulled wine came back around, and he gave them both a deep bow and a wink for Garin. This reminded him of the previous night, in this very tavern, upstairs in that beautiful boy's room…Garin felt his stomach lighten and sweat broke out on his neck. He looked away, nervous and uncertain, until the server had left.

Alistra saw the look that had passed between them and sighed. "Lan says you were there when Paeter's betrothed came to visit last summer. The beautiful Lenalin Denerre, jewel of Tar Vangr."

"What of it?" Garin took a long draught of weak ale, then peered at her shrewdly. "Are you jealous?"

"No." Alistra looked put out. "Well, yes. Father didn't let me out to see her. The first time in my life I could have met another princess, and I'm locked up in the tower the whole time, weaving some stupid tapestry."

"Sounds abominable," Garin said.

"It was." Alistra leaned across the table. "I've heard the stories of her beauty and grace. It is said that she is lovelier than fresh snow—as delicate as ice and refined as cut marble."

"It's all true," Garin said. "But what's your question?"

Alistra caught his hands in hers. "Can you honestly tell me that you looked upon her, and felt nothing?"

Garin looked in Alistra's predatory eyes, considering his reply. They'd had this conversation—or near enough to it—several times before. Of course he had told her the truth, but that did not mean she accepted it—at least not fully. She rationalized it as a strange quirk that he would eventually outgrow, as a boy who surrounded himself with boys would eventually realize that girls were not as disgusting as he had once thought. She never protested it, and had on more than one occasion shared bemused gossip about his endeavors, but there was ever the suggestion of impermanence to their converse. Garin loved Alistra more than anyone in Luether, but she had a wall just as thick and strong as everyone else. He wondered if she would ever truly understand.

At length, Garin shrugged. "She was fair and lovely, if one wishes for such a thing," he said. "But in truth, I found her handmaid far more interesting."

Alistra frowned. "I heard tell of her handmaid—Ovelia Dracaris, yes?" she asked. "Bastard born: half summer, half winter. Not much to look at, so the story goes, but she's heir to an old Blood and true." Her frown turned into a glower. "Lan also told me she's a loose-legged slut."

Darkness rose up inside Garin at those words, and he saw Lan's face contorted in rage. He pushed the image aside as best he could. "No," he said. "She isn't."

"If you say so," Alistra said. "I rather think she would have rutted with Lan if she was. Regardless, I'm sure a smallborn strumpet would welcome the attentions of the Crown Prince of Luether."

"Welcome me into her bed, you mean," Garin said, just to see the scandalized blush on Alistra's cheeks. Embarrassing her made him feel better, and the darkness inside ebbed. He sat up straight. "Mayhap I'll put a babe in her belly and damn the politics!"

"I'm sure you would win her to your heart, your handsome highness." Alistra clasped her hands in mock worship. "Would that not drive my father mad? To see some gutterborn whelp on the throne?"

"Mine would hardly care," Garin said. "Good King Cassian would throw up his hands and welcome new Blood to join with ours. But yours—Demetrus Ravalis." He thrust out his lip and narrowed his eyes in imitation of his uncle. "There is a proper and righteous way to do all the things," he said condescendingly.

Alistra laughed behind her hand. "Stop it!" she said. "It's too true."

The night wore on. Garin realized that at some point, the server had stepped back into the booth and insinuated himself close to him. Had he drunk less wine, he might have noticed earlier, or been able to keep himself from smiling at the lad like a besotted fool. The server took the invitation and sat between them, and before long the three of them were having a fine time around the table, drinking and eating and laughing at one another's impressions and jests. And when the server put his hand on his leg—a hand that quickly slipped between his thighs—the prince thought little of it. He sat back and enjoyed, forgetting for the moment where he was. He felt, in that hour, like Luether's true prince.

At length, Garin became aware of Lan lurking just outside the curtain of beads, much as he had done at the edge of Paeter's circle. Apparently, he'd failed in securing any pleasurable company for himself, which should have been simple considering his standing as cousin to the crown prince and brother to the hero of Luether. Alas, Lan seemed incapable of interacting with anyone—male or female—without offering some manner of offense. And yet, somehow, he was worthier of Demetrus's love and respect than his prim and proper sister.

Belatedly, Garin seized the server's hand and held it still. He flashed the lad a warning look. Alistra perked up and looked at them, her brow furrowed. Then she saw Lan and averted her eyes as though from a slug. "Hail, brother."

"Reveling, as is proper." Lan glared at her. "Certainly not being a snooty fat wench, pretending to be better than everyone."

"Only the ones I'm better than." Alistra seemed unconcerned, but Garin could see her jaw working to keep back a sharper barb.

"Eh?" Lan perked up. "What was that, woman?"

"Leave off, cousin," Garin said. "No one invited you."

He'd tried to be brave, but Lan's angry glare cut Garin off at the knees. His vile cousin flopped onto the bench across the way and seized Alistra's wine goblet for himself. Garin and the server sat rigid in their seats, while Alistra gave her cousin a curious look. At least Lan hardly seemed to notice the tension: he was focused on sloshing the wine around in Alistra's goblet. The server made to leave, but Garin held his leg to keep him in place.

"Shame you couldn't win the winter slut yourself," Lan said to Garin. "Beautiful women like that are hard to find. Especially here in the south." He smirked at his sister, who rolled her eyes.

"Oh no," Garin said, his voice dry. "What a shame. However will I live?"

"No use crying about it, little boy." Lan missed his sarcasm entirely, of course. "Paeter told me he already rutted the princess, and she squealed for more. Good bed-play is the foundation for any strong marriage."

"Don't be crude, little brother." Alistra made a face. "And I doubt you know even *bad* bedplay, let alone good."

Lan replied with an obscene gesture involving his tongue and two fingers. Alistra's face went red, and she lashed back with a sharp word of her own, and quickly the discussion devolved into bickering between the siblings. Garin loathed Lan's presence under any other circumstances, but he had to admit he loved watching Alistra tongue-lash the hapless bully. Perhaps she'd sit on

Lan's head and all their problems would go away.

Lan hadn't just been crude, though. The common rumor on the streets held that Paeter had put a babe in Lenalin's belly already, but rather than being a scandal, this whipped up the revelry to new heights of congratulatory ferocity. Garin realized that it would be quite the opposite, of course, had Paeter been a woman and Lenalin a man. In that case—if Luether's princess had rutted her betrothed before their official binding—there would have been no revel, only private censure and an attempt to keep her shame silent and hidden. He'd thought Luether's attitude quite normal until the previous summer, when Ovelia had shown him a different path. Now it made him more than vaguely sad to see his beloved city so bound up in its own hypocrisy.

Rather than rise to the challenge, Lan looked back to the revelry, and specifically to his brother. Paeter had lost his shirt somewhere and now had half a dozen women hanging on him as he sat in a private booth of his own. Garin would not have been surprised if one or two were under the table as well. The thought made him feel warm, and he realized the server's hand was back, this time inside his breeches. Garin gave the lad a wide-eyed look and received a coy smile in return. He couldn't believe this was happening—not a pace from where Lan sat, oblivious—and he was just drunk enough not to stop it.

A soft cough drew his attention to Alistra, who gave him a concerned, uncertain look. Garin realized she knew what was happening, and he gave a tiny shrug. She returned a faint smile, picked up the wine jug, then shifted over to sit beside Lan. "More wine, brother?"

"Uh?" Lan looked up at her drunkenly. "Yes, fine."

She poured for him. "Have you seen Laegra Vargaen recently?" she asked. "She was asking about you earlier today. I think she dreams of you."

"Really?" Lan looked intrigued. "I didn't know—"

"Oh yes! Why just today, she praised your warm skin, your strong jaw—"

Alistra went on with her story, distracting Lan, while Garin enjoyed the server's attentions. His caressing fingers turned to a tight grip, one that slid up and down, and it was all the prince could do to keep from crying aloud. The tension on the edge of discovery made it all the more exciting, and Garin almost could not breathe. The lad stared at him, green eyes like deep pools in which the prince could sink and drown. This was folly and Garin knew he should have stopped him, but he was so tired of carrying the weight of his secret. So tired and so very *angry*.

Somewhere, in the depths of his building pleasure, Garin realized his cousins had begun arguing, and he didn't quite understand until Alistra failed to stop Lan from turning back to the table. Garin could only imagine what he looked like with the serving lad touching him. At least it had all come to pass hidden under the table. Lan looked unsteadily in his direction, and his eyes narrowed.

"What…who's that?" His voice slurring drunkenly, he pointed toward the serving lad. "What's he doing?"

Garin opened his mouth but could think of nothing to say. Across the way, Alistra looked stricken. The gorgeous lad with the bright green eyes—who was more sober than any of them—gave a slight bow and tried to flee, but Lan lunged out and caught his arm.

"You," Lan said to the server. "You're a whore, aren't you?" He turned his glare on Garin. "You. I warned you about this. Didn't I?"

The prince tried again for words, but his tongue wouldn't work. The room suddenly felt stifling. The server was looking at him with sheer panic on his face, and Garin wanted nothing more than to assure him all would be well. Even when he knew it would not.

"Lan." Garin finally managed to speak. "I didn't—"

"He's mine," Alistra said.

They both stared at her, stunned. "Lissa," Garin said, but Lan silenced him with a sharp look.

"What do you mean?" Lan grasped the server's arm tighter, wrenching a yelp of pain out of him. "And be *specific*, woman. Acts. Lascivities."

A wave of revulsion passed over Alistra's face, but she straightened up tall like the perfect princess. "He's mine," Alistra said. "My lover. We've rutted… half a dozen times, at least. Him atop me, me atop him, his cock in my…" She raised her chin. "I do not regret it."

A faint smile cross Lan's greasy face. "You will."

Then he hustled the server out of the private booth and into the mass of dancers. Alistra sank back down into her seat, seemingly calm despite the gravity of what had come to pass.

"Lissa, by the Fire," Garin said.

"See to yourself," she said. "Your laces are yet open."

Hurriedly, Garin secured his breeches once more. "Do you have any idea what you've done?"

"What I had to." Alistra poured a fresh goblet of wine. "Far better for father to punish me for a transgression than you for a perversion."

"This cannot pass." Garin rose from the table and paced about, too anxious to do nothing, too scattered to do anything. "We need to go. That's it. Flee."

"And where would we go?" Alistra asked. "Steal aboard the next skyship bound for Tar Vangr, perhaps? I'm sure father would never look for us there.

Or perhaps you meant exile in the wilds of Ruin, where we'd not last a day. No." She raised the goblet to her lips with a hand that shook only a little. "I shall wait here, sipping wine, and suffer the consequences of my actions."

"You cannot do this for me," Garin said. "I cannot allow it."

"You cannot *allow* it?" Alistra's yellow eyes blazed in the candlelight. "All my life, men have told me what I can and cannot do. I will not have the only man I do not despise do the same."

Garin felt as though she'd slapped him, and he hung his head. "Thank you," was all he could say.

Alistra went back to watching the revel with the same serene detachment as before.

Footfalls on the steps announced an imminent arrival, and Garin sucked in a sharp breath. None other than Paeter pushed through the bead curtain into the booth. Alistra glanced at him briefly, sighed, and went back to crowd watching. Before Garin could speak, Paeter strode through the pillows around the table, leaned over, and closed the shutters fully. Alistra sighed.

"I don't know what you said to Lan," Paeter said to Garin. "But he left here in a hurry, with a sly-looking lad bundled under his arm."

"Mine," Alistra said.

"Yours." Paeter wore a dubious expression. "Regardless, Lan's on his way to get father."

"And you came in here to what, spare us the public shame?" Garin indicated the windows. "Perhaps the Luethaar should see how their rulers view their progeny."

"And who would it surprise?" Paeter asked. "No. I came to give you privacy and to warn you—"

"Warn me of what?" Alistra asked. "That father will rebuke me? Surely he will. But unlike you and our child brother, I have never crossed Demetrus's wishes. I am older than both of you, and I know him far better than you do."

Paeter shrugged. "I hope you speak truly."

Garin grasped Paeter's arm and whispered in his ear. "Please," he said. "Do something."

"Such as what?" Paeter asked. "Tell my father the truth, perhaps?"

Garin's face felt cold. Paeter *knew*. Somehow, he knew.

More footsteps, and none other than Cassian Ravalis pushed through the curtain of beads. The King of Luether looked weary, sweat glistening on his forehead, but generally in good spirits. A robust man even at his advanced age, he was a man of great jest and a sparkling eye. Never one for politics, he'd never married and put off having children until duty insisted, and he'd stopped with Garin, his bastard son by a mistress, born a few seasons after his fiftieth summer.

Cassian's wide smile shrank slightly when he saw the dour faces of his son and nephew, and the cold passivity of his niece. "By the Fire," he said. "You lot look a mess. Did something pass poorly?"

Garin opened his mouth to reply, but Paeter gave him a warning look. "A bit, Majesty," the older prince said. "My dear sister has been indiscrete with a lover, and I fear a scandal will soon befall."

"Oh." Cassian looked to Alistra, and his expression softened. "I'm so sorry, niece."

Without looking, she nodded solemnly.

They waited a few moments, and the beads made their familiar skittering sound once more. Even before he looked, Garin knew who had come, and he recognized the thick voice that filled the booth.

"Unclean."

All eyes turned to the door, where Demetrus Ravalis stood straight and tall. Where his brother Cassian had two summers over him, with his thick, graying beard and grim manner, he looked much older and far harder. His manner suited his position as Luether's general well, and under his tenure, the Luethaar navy had never stirred as much fear in any era of living memory. Garin found the man terrifying—an older, smarter, and deadlier version of Lan in almost every particular. Behind Demetrus stood Stevron—his equally intimidating, eldest son—and Lan himself, who wore a smug, vicious smile.

As subtle as an axe between the eyes, Demetrus strode into the booth and immediately commanded the attention of all. He stepped past Cassian and thrust open the shutters of the booth so all could see. Dutifully, Alistra stood, smoothing her crimson skirts.

"Father," she said, keeping her eyes appropriately downcast. "I have spoken truly to your son, and will repeat as much to you. I accept whatever punishment—"

Demetrus pounded one fist on the table to cut her off, knocking over goblets and upsetting the wine jug. A shudder passed through Alistra, but she stood firm, hands curled into fists at her sides. She believed firmly that Demetrus would rebuke her with his words, but Garin thought in that moment that he would strike her. He clung tightly to Paeter, who held his hand to reassure him.

When Demetrus reached out toward Alistra suddenly, Garin flinched, but the general merely raised the girl's chin so their eyes met.

"Your indecency shames me," Demetrus said. "It is not your fault. You are only a woman—a little girl pretending to be something she cannot be." He drew his hand away with a creak of leather. "Worthy."

Alistra flinched as though struck and her mouth opened but nothing emerged. In the end, the weight of her father's words stayed her. She looked down at the floor.

"From this day forth," Demetrus said. "I have no daughter." He glanced over his shoulder. "Stevron. Bring this…*thing.*"

Alistra loosed a deep breath as though all the life had left her in that moment.

Demetrus swept from the room with his confident stride. Lan turned up his nose at Alistra and all but skipped gleefully after his father. Garin looked to his own father, and King Cassian wore a sober, pained expression. The king reached out as though to touch Alistra, then drew his hand back at the last moment. He left. Stevron stepped inside the booth, seized Alistra roughly by the arm, and dragged her out. She offered no resistance.

Garin and Paeter sat alone in the back chamber of the Long Dawn once more. The revelry had ended, and though many out in the common room snuck glances into the booth, they hurried about their business. No one wanted to be associated with the spurned girl, declared by the brother of the king to be unclean and unworthy. Casually, Paeter reached over for the toppled jug of wine, swished it once, and poured the remainder of its contents into the last surviving goblet.

"Poor Alistra," Paeter said. "She thought she knew better, but Luether has its rules—men and women their appointed roles."

Rules and roles. Garin realized he'd not seen the green-eyed server with Lan. "Where…what will happen to him?"

"To the serving lad?" Paeter asked. "You don't even know his name, do you?"

Garin shook his head.

"He nipped the bud of Lord Demetrus's only daughter." Paeter shrugged. "If a man ruts an heiress, it's only partly his fault. In my father's mind, she seduced him. Probably a firm beating is all. They'll batter up his pretty face but cut him loose." He sipped his wine. "If they knew the truth, he'd wind up with his throat slit in a ditch, no doubt. Is that what you want?"

"But—" Garin could hardly think. "I—"

"I know." Paeter shifted closer to him on the pillowed bench and pressed the goblet into Garin's hands. "Put it out of your mind. You have more important matters to consider, Prince."

"I'm not—not thirsty." Garin put the goblet down on the table. His hands were shaking. "I can't let this happen. I can't—"

"You must." Paeter leaned in close, his breath warm on Garin's cheek. "And you should be more wary. I could teach you, if you wish."

Garin's heart beat faster. "What do you mean?"

Paeter smiled. "Politics," he said. "Hiding the truth. Doing what you wish—what you need—despite all the eyes upon you. Is that what you want?" Their noses almost touched. "Do you want me...to help you?"

Garin longed to kiss him. He'd spent countless nights tormented by dreams of Paeter—strong, handsome, clever—but he'd never before been so close. So intimate...

He restrained himself. "Yes," Garin said. "Teach me."

Paeter's smile widened. "Good lad."

SIX

OVELIA STOOD AT THE rail of the Avenger as it sailed south through the skies toward Luether, the cold wind stinging her face. She'd left behind her aged disguise, because it made no great difference. Even if a Ravalis agent had followed them onto the Avenger, he could not send word back to Tar Vangr before they arrived in Luether. Hiding in the city was part of the task that lay ahead anyway.

The first time she had been to Luether, it had seemed a far happier occasion, even if her heart had been breaking every moment. Considering it now, Ovelia wondered what she might have done differently. To think that twenty winters later, all would come to pass as it had…Ovelia shook the speculation away. She had learned long ago that regret served no purpose but to torment the living. The dead and lost had no stake in the matter.

Instead, she thought about how, as a girl, she had looked forward to the rare occasions when she and Lenalin would ride the winds together, side-by-side and sometimes hand-in-hand at the rail. Even now, standing here, she could sometimes imagine Lenalin had just slipped away for a moment and would return soon. The princess would attempt to surprise her, and Ovelia would pretend to be surprised just to see Lenalin smile. Those days had passed in happiness, but in time they had both grown to majority, and the larger world had intervened.

Now as Ovelia stood at the railing, the world had grown larger and emptied out. No Lenalin. No Regel. No sight, even. The sky was a vast blackness to her, punctuated with the shadows of Draca. The world smelled rotten around her, and she constantly lusted for the numb euphoria of sweetsoul.

A tiny impulse invited her to push herself over the railing and be free.

It would be so easy. What had she left in this world? Lenalin was long gone. Orbrin lay dead at her hand. Her quest to avenge the Blood of Denerre had failed. And though she had found Semana alive—a dream she hadn't dared imagine— the wayward princess had rejected her. Regel had broken his oath to slay her, or at least he had not let her die. Her eyes were gone and her strength all but rotted away in a drugged haze. Her whole vile life had come to a dead end.

Except for Garin.

The Bloodsword told her of the Ravalis prince's presence before her senses detected him. "Again you try to steal upon me," she said.

"I know, I know." Garin leaned backward on the rail beside her. "I just like watching you. I'm quite good at telling what people are thinking, but you present me with a challenge."

Ovelia put her chin on her arms. "I should not have come here," she said. "I should be following Semana. Protecting her."

Garin put his hand over hers. "We talked about this, my lady. You're in no shape to go after her—and even if you did, what then? She killed you last time you came near her."

Ovelia remembered the agonized look on Semana's face, and the stirring in her heart when she saw it. Semana both loved and hated her, she knew, but how could she explain that to Garin?

"Besides," Garin said further. "The Lord of Tears gave us specific instructions to stay away."

"And you always do what anyone asks of you, I suppose."

"Don't we both." Garin blew out a sigh. "He said—let me remember—he said 'you have taught her all you could. For now, at least.'"

Ovelia gave a wry chuckle: "Aye, that sounds like Regel."

She lapsed into silence and considered the vast emptiness before her. Ovelia's world had become a blurry canvas of bright and dark, of moving shadows that might or might not signify anything. She felt the tiny currents in the air and the fluctuations of heat upon her face. She could smell the salty sea spread out far below, tinged with the varying scents of sodden wood, rotting kelp, and other dying things. The world itself was dying, but it was only now—that she could no longer see it—that she *felt* it. Her own body felt the same: rotted and worn thin.

Again, she had that unsettling urge to jump, all the more powerful for her realization.

"I understand now," Ovelia said.

"Understand what, beautiful?" Garin asked.

She pushed away from the rail and smiled. "There was never anything to see anyway."

Garin turned to her, about to speak, then went still as a stone. She felt the sudden tension in his body—sensed him seize up and go rigid in surprise.

Apparently, there *was* something to see.

A skyship rose before the *Avenger*, surprisingly silent until it hummed nearly atop them. Ovelia perceived it as a massive vision of fire in the sky.

She'd not heard it over the comparatively deafening roar of the *Avenger*'s own mage-engine. The great vibrating rings that swept around the smaller craft came so close to the edge that she could have reached out to touch them. She smelled pitch-sealed wood and corroded metal and tasted the hot fumes of boiling magic. She glanced down at Draca at her belt, where warning shadows overflowed the scabbard. She had allowed her nostalgia to distract her.

"Shard's pirates," Garin said. "But why risk openly attacking?"

"It doesn't matter who they are or why," Ovelia said. "Get behind me."

Far above, armored figures threw themselves off the deck of the pirate ship and floated down through foul-smelling clouds of smoke. The magic was in their cloaks, which expelled force to let them float down unharmed. As they came, they leveled casters or drew blades. All this Ovelia saw in Draca's shadows inking her world.

The first pirate landed a pace from Ovelia, just an instant before the pommel of Draca found his face and sent him staggering back to the rail. She bulled ahead and shoved him screaming off the deck, then turned and drew Draca in a wide arc that parried aside a seeking sword coming from her left.

The pirate behind that sword staggered back, perhaps taken by surprise to face a blindfolded woman who could not only fight, but knew exactly how to react before he attacked. Ovelia pressed him back, sliding the flaming Draca along his sword. Its wavy blade made the handle vibrate painfully in his hand. Then she twisted his blade harmlessly wide, put Draca across his chest, and wrenched violently away, opening his hardened leather all down his body. He fell, screaming in pain.

Ovelia turned back to Garin, who drew a device from his back that she saw vaguely but could not identify. The weapon had a shape like a caster and smelled of oil and woodsmoke, but it lacked the reek of thaumaturgy. He pointed it up at the boarding party and cast, and the weapon cracked like a spent caster. It fired no bolt but a bright beam of magic that streaked through the air and struck one of the pirates, center mass. He twisted in the air, gurgling in sudden pain, and floated limply away.

The shadows curled, making Ovelia's eyes widen behind the crimson cloth. She threw herself forward and flattened Garin beneath her, just before a casterbolt slammed into the deck where he had stood. They rolled over one another and came to a halt against the rail. They held each other an instant before Ovelia sprang up. She crouched over Garin protectively, her legs ready to spring. In the shadows, she saw no attackers for the moment.

"I chose rightly to bring you," Garin said.

"You do well enough." She nodded to the odd weapon clutched in his arms. "What is that?"

"A proper alchemist must have his mysteries," he said.

Battle was joined across the *Avenger* as the crew engaged the boarding pirates with blades, maces, and casters. Streaks of fire fell upon the deck, making the skyship rock under Ovelia's feet. She steadied herself on the rail while Garin held fast to her leg. Thunderous reports tore apart her senses and the air reeked of expended magic. Ovelia consulted Draca's shadows, and she saw casters discharging in their direction. They had to find cover—they could not stay in the open.

"Come." She took Garin's hand and dragged him toward the stairs below decks, watching the flames carefully. The shadows twisted and shifted, forming new threats so fast she could hardly follow them. She headed for the open staircase that would lead below.

A pirate landed in front of her on the open stairs, sword drawn and ready, and Ovelia met her with Draca. This one had more skill than her fellows, and managed to parry and lock their swords up high. Ovelia shoved her back, but the pirate danced down the steps in perfect balance. They reached the lower deck and pressed together against the wall. Ovelia felt the woman's face come in close proximity to her own, but could not make out the woman's expression. It was an unsettling feeling

The shadows and her instincts made Ovelia turn, and the woman punched a dagger just wide of her side. The blade slit open leather and flesh like cream, and immediately Ovelia gritted herself against the rising pain. She fell back, disengaging their weapons. She felt Garin behind her at the top of the stairs, his body taut with tension. Ovelia held up one hand to soothe him and pointed Draca with the other.

Casually, the pirate stood and stretched, blades ready. "I didn't expect someone so skilled."

"Neither did I," Ovelia said. "Yield, and—"

A massive *crack* thundered through the air, deafening in such proximity. The pirate pitched forward, her hands going wide, and a caster bolt burst through her chest. Ovelia flinched, but the dying woman still slammed into her, driven by the force of the blast. They fell in a tangle, the pirate choking and sputtering and bleeding all over Ovelia in a flood. They struggled in a floating, muted world. The woman's fingers ground into Ovelia's arms, and blood and drool flowed from her mouth all over her face. Ovelia thought, for one horrible moment, that the pirate was trying to bite her. Then her body convulsed and froze in shock. She was dead within three shuddering heartbeats.

Ovelia lay beneath the pirate's corpse, breathing and struggling to make sense of a world spinning wildly. Everything hurt, but especially her head.

She could see moving shadows above her, but she didn't know them. She heard a persistent ringing sound, and beneath that two muted voices. Garin, she thought, and Alcarin. They held each other for a moment, then renewed their argument.

"Wait," Ovelia said. "Wait—"

One of them—Garin, she thought—turned to her and knelt beside her. She felt his hot breath on her brow. "Lady Dracaris," he said. "Can…stand?"

She started to get up, failed, and shook her head. The corpse was too heavy a weight, and she felt dizzy as soon as she moved. At least her hearing had started to clear.

"Wait," Garin said. "I'll return. Allie—stay with her!"

He vanished down the stairs, leaving the two of them alone. Alcarin stood over her, a smoking caster in his hands. Ovelia could smell the discharged magic and practically taste the corruption it had left in the room. He simply stared at her, and not for the first time, she wished she could make out expressions. Reading faces would be much more difficult than she had ever learned.

"Alcarin," she said. "Help?"

She had not intended it as a request, but it became one. And for a heartbeat, she thought he hadn't heard her at all, or perhaps that he had and it made him consider. His expended caster was pointed at her chest, and though it seemed a casual oversight, he held the caster with a grip so firm his hand trembled. She did not need Draca's shadows to know his intentions. She understood something about him in the moment—something they had in common.

"Pass well," she said, trying to reassure him. "Do not be afraid."

Alcarin inhaled sharply, and she felt his whole body shiver. "I—I don't—" Then he shook himself and leaned toward her. "Let's just get this mess off—"

Together, they moved the corpse off Ovelia, and she found herself able to move once more. Her blood-soaked clothes clung wetly to her sore body, but at least she could stand. With Alcarin's help, she climbed to her feet and fought to steady her breathing. The battle had almost put her down. By the Fire, she wanted a draught of sweetsoul—for the pain and for the longing.

"Where's your master gone?" she asked.

"He's—" Alcarin rewound his caster with fumbling hands. "Getting something to help."

She heard muffled screams from above, but they had decreased in frequency as she lay stunned. Casters rang out and steel clashed, but less than before. She climbed up the stairs and ducked just below the level of the main deck. Above, the world was a mess of clashing steal, burning magic, and weeping people. Still Draca's shadows lay quiescent, telling her nothing.

"Alcarin, what do you see?" A sudden clatter startled her. "Alcarin?"

The youth knelt on the stairs beside her, his whole body trembling. He was whispering something to himself that she could not quite make out over the sounds of battle. The caster lay on the step below him, and he stared at it as at a serpent. She could smell the terrified vomit building up in his throat.

"Alcarin." She seized his shoulders and put his face to hers. It made no difference to her—she could not see his face regardless—but his attention shot to her instantly. "I need you. Garin needs you."

Whatever his expression, he nodded at length, and she felt his muscles relax.

"I need you to see for me," she said. "All this noise. I can't—"

He nodded again and immediately snaked away from her to look out over the deck. "No one's moving up there. The ship's defenders have barricaded themselves at the access points. The pirates…Silver Fire, three are coming this way!"

"Yes." Ovelia saw the shadows of Draca start to form into three figures, swords and casters ready for battle. They moved with grace and purpose—no mere brigands but a trained cadre accustomed to fighting together—and she did not see any obvious vulnerabilities. She had recovered somewhat from the beating of a moment ago, but she was still weary. Could she defeat three trained warriors? She looked to Alcarin. "Ready your caster. Stay behind me."

Footsteps behind her warned of Garin's approach—she recognized his perfume immediately, and also the sense of purpose that infused his stride. There was something in his hands—a weapon, like the one he had used before. "Three, you say?" he asked.

"Yes, but—" Alcarin said.

Garin strode right past them out onto the deck. Ovelia heard the pirates exclaim in surprise, and then there came a mighty roar, as of the thunderous crash of ocean against rock. Ovelia felt a massive force wash through the air that felt not unlike Mask's unseen hand magic. Alcarin gasped, and Ovelia watched as Draca's warding shadows abruptly boiled away and vanished.

"Come." Garin shouldered his curious weapon and held out his hand for Alcarin. "We have a skyship to rescue."

SEVEN

A s HE BALANCED AWKWARDLY on the empty deck, Garin felt the ripple in the air making every inch of his exposed skin vibrate. The world felt hostile to him, as though the air itself thrashed in protest of what he had just done. The dizziness, he had expected, but not the lingering vibrations.

"Fascinating," he said.

"What is?" At his side, Alcarin looked subdued and thoughtful. Shame. Garin had been hoping to impress him.

"This." Garin held up his nameless weapon. "When triggered, it produces a burst of sound, like a thundercaster. Not lethal, but extremely painful." He nodded to the three stunned pirates who had borne the brunt of the blast. "What I didn't expect was the air being disturbed after and *what are you doing?*"

Ovelia knelt over one of the stunned pirates, Draca reversed in her hands for a killing thrust. He scrambled over and caught her wrists. Her blindfolded face turned to him, her mouth set in a hard line.

"No killing," Garin said. "Not without need."

Ovelia stared at him blankly for a heartbeat, then nodded. "As you say."

Garin nodded and turned to include Alcarin in the discussion. "We need to get to the bridge," he said. "Shard would be going that way."

They left the three senseless pirates and headed across the wind-swept deck of the *Avenger*. Lockdown alarms blared from corroding horns, their magic sending tiny plumes of gray into the sky. Fewer bodies littered the deck than he had expected, and that he credited to King Lan's edict that no pleasure travelers would journey to Luether. The remaining passengers were desperate merchants, warriors, and other generally sober folk, who knew to take shelter when the alarms sounded. The golden rings that encircled and propelled the skyship scythed over them, briefly blotting out the sun. Shard's skyship had disappeared from view, and Garin felt a little uneasy not knowing where it had gone.

Most of the fighting was done, with surviving defenders sealing themselves below-decks while skyship pirates roamed above, testing the trapdoors and generally keeping watch over any would-be attempt to retake the ship. One such group of pirates turned in their direction, raising weapons, but Garin leveled them with another thunderous blast that left them writhing on the deck, clutching at their ruptured ears. Like as not, the alarms had drowned out the sound of Garin's weapon.

Captain Hyldir commanded the *Avenger* from the rear of the skyship, on an elevated aftcastle that offered a clear view not only of the rest of the deck but also of the world around them. Though the burning summers had worn away or seen replaced most of the once-warship's armament, the circular command bridge maintained its rusting iron-clad walls and murder holes. Even the mighty windows that permitted a complete panoramic view of all horizons could be shut with stout iron shutters. A handful of warriors could defend the place against a massive boarding party, which was exactly what Garin found when they arrived. A dozen pirates, all clad in dark leathers and bearing the mark of Shard—six silver triangles on a black field—stood between them and the bridge. They were not attacking, but rather guarding, which suggested that Shard was already inside.

"What are they doing?" Alcarin asked, his voice small and uneasy. "Why not just blast the bridge with the main cannon and have done?"

"And lose the prize? Shard is too canny for that." Garin peeked at the locked-down bridge. "Hyldir is captain of the *Avenger*, and the mage-engine is attuned to her. Should she perish, the *Avenger* falls. Figuratively *and* literally." He flexed his fingers. "They have to take her alive."

His concussion cannon slung against the small of his back, Garin pressed himself against the wall below the bridge platform and motioned to the others to hide as well. Taking cover, they managed to approach undetected until they came, crouched, to the eight steps that would lead up to the aftcastle. While the three approached, the pirates had occupied themselves attacking the armored bridge, but now they stood restless guard. Vaguely, Garin heard the sound of converse within, out of which he recognized Captain Hyldir's gruff voice. Negotiating from a place of weakness, unfortunately.

Behind him, Ovelia wore a composed expression and her body conveyed an impression of calm readiness. She had sheathed Draca once more to hide its crimson shadows. Not for the first time, he counted himself fortunate to have crossed her path. Alcarin, on the other hand, shook with nerves. In his current state, even with the precise caster Garin had built and calibrated specially for him, the man couldn't hit a target within an arm's length. He kept glancing furtively at Ovelia, as though concerned she would see him sweat. However dire the situation had become, Garin couldn't help but appreciate the irony of trying to hide an expression from a blind woman.

"Ay," he said, drawing Alcarin's attention. Garin could see the whites all around Alcarin's eyes. Poor man was terrified. He smiled reassuringly and held out his hand. "Come."

Alcarin looked bewildered. "What? Now?"

"Garin," Ovelia said under her breath.

He ignored her and took Alcarin by the wrist. "Come."

Garin pulled the man to him, caught his neck in one hand, and pressed his lips to his Alcarin's. He felt the tension flood from Alcarin, leaving his body relaxed. Ovelia looked vaguely disapproving.

The kiss broke, and Garin gave Alcarin a little smile. Then he stood and strode up the stairs, leaving behind his companions' startled protests. He approached the pirates, hands wide.

"Hail!" Garin said to the pirates, beaming. "Well are we met!"

Perhaps it was the audacity of his plan, or perhaps it was that he had materialized seemingly out of the air. Either way, the assembled men and women in leather and bits of plate turned toward him with startled expressions rather than weapons. They had various features—northerners, southerners, islanders, and even a few from more exotic locales Garin did not know. Their armament varied as well, from blades to bludgeons to sleek, deadly casters. The pirates did not immediately cast or charge, so he continued forward peaceably.

"I have come to see your master, of course," Garin said. "I would not be wrong in assuming he is within, yes? Conversing with the *Avenger's* captain? Shard has always struck me as a reasonable sort of pirate." An angry murmur ran through the group, and more than a few tensed. Garin kept walking, ignoring their brandished weapons. "My apologies. I meant *free sailor*, obviously. I'd not want to put moral judgments upon you folk."

The woman at the front of the group stepped a pace forward of the others. She wore spiked shoulder plates and bore a double-hooked sword, almost like two falcata joined at the pommels. Garin had never seen such a sword. She pointed the curious weapon in his direction, making him hesitate a step lest he walk right into one of its points. Her deep voice filtered through a mask of black and white patches.

"I am Aeldad, first mate to Shard, captain of the *Reaver*, the ruler of these waters and skies, and you are now my prisoner," she said. "Who are *you*, madman, to make such—?"

He spoke right over her without stopping. "Your hostage, good lady. Garin Ravalis, Prince of Tar Vangr and rightful King of Luether, once those troublesome barbarians are gone." He pushed her blade aside with his leather gauntlet. "And worth a fair cask of gold in ransom, I might add. Even a *king's*."

That gave Aeldad pause, and Garin saw several faces behind her light up. That was good. Several of the pirates, however, were not distracted. When the woman had stopped him, he'd lost control of the moment, allowing them to react normally. They fanned out to encircle him, which was bad. Two headed toward the stairs where he had appeared. Doubly bad.

He had no choice.

Garin reached for his belt, which drew as much attention as if he had screamed at them. All the pirates looked to him, casters drawing a bead on his head and chest.

"Ah, no—stand easy, good friends. It's only aescama lotion." Garin raised one hand to show he had no weapon, with the other he drew a small flask from his belt. "But of course, goodly sailors such as yourselves may know little of alchemy. Aescama is a protective ointment brewed from the sap of a certain tree that grows east of Luether. Nothing dangerous." With nimble fingers, he uncorked it and dipped his fingers against the edge, smearing them in a greenish jelly. This he touched to his cheeks and nose. "The sun is very hot today, is it not? And you'd hardly want your hostage to burn himself unrecognizable, would you?"

Aeldad stepped forward and seized his forearm as he reached for his ear. "You belong to me now, little madman," she said. "Your face will burn as I see fit."

"Certainly." Garin looked at the foul-smelling substance on his fingers, just above her hand. "Just let me finish with this, unless—" He reached toward her sleeve as though to wipe the stuff off.

Aeldad slammed the hilt of her sword into Garin's face, and he sprawled to the deck. The world rocked for a moment, and he inhaled the stink of blood-stained wood and his own spittle. She had split open his lip with that strike. The other pirates roared with laughter, and Aeldad raised her arms as though to welcome their adulation.

Good enough. Garin put the last of the substance in his ears, and the world instantly went silent. At the same time, he twisted a knob on the weapon still lashed to his back. He felt more than heard the low whine of the cannon powering up, then overloading. Aeldad was screaming something, but Garin only heard her dimly through the aescama protecting his ears—its true purpose.

Then the cannon exploded in all directions with a wave of thunder, sending all the pirates flying. Those not knocked senseless in the initial blast slumped to the deck, cradling their heads and moaning.

Garin climbed shakily to his feet. He could hear a dull ringing in his ears, but the aescama lotion seemed to have worked. He looked to the disabled first mate on the deck before him. Aeldad had borne most of the blast and fallen disoriented to one knee, where she struggled to right herself, blinking rapidly. Her mask had fallen askew, revealing her dark, deeply lined face. She was older than Garin would have guessed, and very tough to have taken the full force of a blast that put all her compatriots on their backs.

"What?" she said, her expression confused. Blood trickled from her ears. "What is? What—?"

Garin drew another vial from his belt and passed it under her nose. The pirate's eyes rolled up in their sockets and she fell into a deep slumber. He caught her and lowered her gently to the deck.

"Ancestor's cocks, I'll reek of this stuff for days." Garin scratched at the dried lotion on his skin. "Aescama isn't for the skin, you know."

Alcarin and Ovelia hurried across the deck toward him, the former blithely and the latter carefully with sword drawn. "That was amazing!" Alcarin smile became a frown and he caught Garin about the shoulders. "And incredibly stupid!"

"Shame," Garin said. "I was aiming for *brave*."

"It was certainly that, but you scared me." Alcarin put his arms around Garin. "Your recklessness will be the death of us both, one day." He sniffed at his master and scowled. "Ugh. That's awful."

"Oh stop, flatterer."

As Alcarin held him tightly, Garin looked over his shoulder to Ovelia. She regarded them silently, but he thought he caught the tiniest hint of a smile about her lips. He was glad to see he was not the only one of their band afflicted with the madness of courage.

The sounds from within the bridge had faded to silence, and through the cracks in the iron shutters Garin could see faint shadows moving. Surely Shard was expecting them. The door to the bridge was slightly ajar, but he heard no voices inside.

He looked to Ovelia. "Perhaps you wish to go first this time?"

Without reply, she drew Draca from its scabbard with a whisper, leaking crimson shadows in its wake. She gazed down upon the blade, and Garin wondered what the magic looked like to her. He made a mental point to ask her about it later—if a later came to pass. Finally, she nodded and gestured to the door, then fell into a casual fighting stance, ready to spring forward. Garin pushed the door inward and had barely pulled back before she was past him, moving low and fast, blade above her head.

A caster bolt flashed through the air where her head would have been and shattered into the opposite wall. An instant later, an axe cut across, propelled by a hulking man in Shard's colors. Ovelia ducked before it came at her, and the blade skipped along Draca before it buried itself into the opposite wall. She came up inside the bruiser's guard and smashed the pommel of her sword into the center of his chest, sending the man stumbling back a step. Ovelia stalked toward the pirate who fumbled to recharge her caster for a second shot. Blind as she was, the woman moved on sure feet like stalking death.

"Enough."

The voice was soft but powerful, filling the room with the undeniable tone of command. It emerged from a slight figure that stood near the back of the chamber, draped in black robes and a flowing veil wrought in intricate, jagged lines like shards of broken fabric. She raised one hand to gesture her warriors back, and they obeyed her command without hesitation.

"The infamous Captain Shard is a woman," Garin said under his breath. "Burn me. There goes my brilliant plan to seduce him."

The woman in the veil seemed unmoved. "You have an advantage at this moment, Prince Garin Ravalis," she said. "But so do I." From beneath the folds of her robes, she drew a handcaster and lined it up with Hyldir, who lay coughing on the floor at her feet.

"I wouldn't," Garin said. "If you slay her, we all die."

"Ask your pet Dracaris if you doubt me," Shard said. "What does her sword tell her?"

Ovelia was staring at Shard, her expression startled and her hands trembling on Draca's hilt. Shadows leaked around the sword, and Garin could tell the uneasy calm of the room stood balanced upon a keen edge. One wrong step, and violence would erupt, culminating in their fiery doom thousands of paces below. He wondered how Shard had recognized both Ovelia and himself so easily, but he knew enough not to press the issue.

Abruptly, Ovelia perked up and whirled toward the door, Draca up and burning. Behind him, Garin heard casters crackling and swords rattling against bucklers. Some of Shard's minions had roused themselves and awaited their mistress's command. Alcarin stepped closer to Garin and pointed a shaking caster at Aeldad.

"We have danced this dance before," Shard said, her voice betraying not the slightest concern for her circumstances. "You know my price, but you refuse to pay it. I could kill you, but...you are so amusing to watch dance."

"Then we have reached an impasse," Garin said. "What happens now? How stupid will this be?"

They faced one another for a long moment, and only deep, uncertain breathing broke the silence. Ovelia stood ready, sword dripping with flame. Shard's pirates had recovered and held their weapons in trembling hands. Behind him, Garin could feel Alcarin struggling to control himself, his breathing rapid and his armor rattling. Finally, Shard broke the silence.

"I suggest an...*understanding* between us. I have my fleet, you have your quest—they need not interfere with one another." Shard waved her hand toward the open door onto the deck. "I shall walk out that door and leave this ship, and you shall continue on your way. Should you succeed, I would relish having the good ear of the new king of Luether."

"Fair enough." Garin stepped aside and gestured toward the door.

The pirate queen strode toward the door, her black robes trailing past like waves of silk. As she passed Ovelia, her head shifted slightly, though Garin could not make out her face to know why. When she was about to go, he caught her by the shoulder. She stopped immediately as though stabbed and turned her shrouded face toward him.

"And you will owe me a boon," Garin said.

Shard raised her chin. "I do not like laboring under a debt."

"And I do not like pirates threatening to kill me and my allies," Garin said. "But such is the way of Ruin."

Shard considered. "Very well," she said at length. "I will owe you a boon. Think carefully on what you would have of me. I suggest you make it a worthy request."

Then she was gone, and her warriors followed her. They gave Ovelia a wide berth, but she was not paying them any attention. Instead, she stared after Shard, and Garin could see the confusion on her face. They would speak of this later, Garin thought.

"Well," Alcarin said. "That passed well."

Garin pointed toward Hyldir, who had begun to moan and stir. Alcarin knelt beside her and uncapped a vial under her nose, making the woman flinch to wakefulness. As his squire tended to her, Garin turned to Ovelia, but the woman had already rushed past him out the door. He followed her out into the howling wind.

Shard's pirates had gathered at the *Avenger*'s railing and—one by one—leaped off into the air, letting their cloaks flare out around them. The captain remained until last, both hands on the railing, gazing out over the gray horizon. In the distance, perhaps a dozen leagues away, Garin could see the broken spire of Atropis rising from the sea. And beyond, he saw rising smoke that marked the City of Flame he meant to save.

"Hold!" The wind caught Ovelia's cloak and the ends of her crimson blindfold. At her side, Draca flowed with foreboding shadows. Her stance seemed desperate, and on her face Garin read a challenge.

Shard looked over her shoulder at Ovelia, and though the veil hid her expression, Garin could swear that she was smiling. Then she stepped over the railing and fell from the *Avenger*.

Ovelia rushed to the rail and Garin followed just behind, only to see Shard's own skyship rise up from below. The craft was a beautiful, deadly thing of silver-plated darkwood that bristling with charged ballistae and cannon. It floated upon rings that gleamed like pearls in the sunlight. The name *Reaver* shone along the hull, inlaid in silver lettering. Shard stood on the deck, her robes flowing like water in the wind. Then the ship disengaged and floated in the opposite direction. He watched the dark figure of Shard recede from view until her sleek skyship pulled up into the obscuring clouds.

"What passed there?" Garin asked. "Was she lying to us?"

"I thought—no." Ovelia stood watching the retreating ship, though of course she could not see. "She spoke of an understanding between you. Do you know her?"

"Not personally, until today," Garin said. "But Shard has operated in these skies for over ten years now. We've rarely corresponded, but I know Pervast sends his hunters after hi—*her* frequently, so she is no friend of his. Apologies. I did not know Shard was a woman until today. She's fond of secrets." He scratched his head in thought. "She is neutral as regards my quest, and she has never before suggested any sort of understanding between us, so that's progress. Perhaps she liked you?"

Ovelia looked troubled. She watched sightlessly as Shard's skyship sailed away.

Alcarin appeared at Garin's side. "Hyldir passes well, and the crew suffered only a few injuries, no deaths," he said. "Do you pass well?" He looked fleetingly to Ovelia. "Both of you?"

Ovelia glanced in Alcarin's direction. Even though her blind eyes hid behind a crimson blindfold, he still flinched from her blank scrutiny. She looked to Garin. "And now, Highness?"

Garin looked out at Shard's retreating skyship and nodded. "Onward to Luether," he said. "I suspect she won't save herself."

"One never does," Ovelia said under her breath.

EIGHT

Luether

PLUMES OF THICK BLACK smoke boiled up and diffused into the dawn air, and through it the rising sun painted the southern horizon with an astonishing palette of crimson and hazy russet, violet and vivid ochre. This Ovelia could not see, but she knew it well—could picture it in her mind. She touched her fingers to the porthole, feeling the heat through the mage-glass and imagining how beautiful the sunrise must be. She lay back on her bed in the sumptuous cabin, remembering.

Regel had explained the coronas around mage-cities to her, as they stood undecided at the prow of this very skyship. She'd been able to see it then—the colors and corruption over a different city—and she'd thought it so beautiful. That moment seemed so long ago now. It had fallen away from her to become part of a different life.

That night, Ovelia had dreamed again of fire, silver flames that boiled in front of her, kept at bay behind a shimmering wall that she could perceive only at a touch. She felt the roaring heat on her face—strong but endurable. She could not say why she stood in front of the flames, or what she meant to do. They burned silently and without answers. Abruptly, the fire took shape, starting to form a face…Then the flames roared forth to swallow her whole and she awoke, craving sweetsoul and fighting hard not to ask Garin for it.

The memory of the dream burned away, leaving Ovelia once more in a world where she could not see the fire awaiting her on the horizon.

The last time Ovelia had approached the Burning City, it had representing an end to her—the last step in a journey that would finally bring justice for her crimes. Succeed or fail, she would die in this place, and she had spent five winters making her peace with that. Now, however, she lacked that sense of inevitability and it left her unbalanced. She floated in a new world that she could not see. In Draca's shadows, she perceived danger on the horizon. Even if she could not see Luether, she knew it.

Ovelia could *feel* it, too, and she found no beauty in it now. Even at this distance, the rising stench of fumes filled the *Avenger*'s decks, tickling her nostrils and making her feel oily. It turned her stomach and made her breathing shallow as her lungs clenched. Her fingers felt vaguely numb, and she moved them faster to keep them supple. Sight had blinded her to these more subtle effects of the bad air, but now she could not ignore them. She coughed despite herself, disturbing Garin where he worked on the other side of the room.

The suite of rooms—formerly the captain's chambers—was lavish, much larger than their old guest cabin and copiously stocked with liquor and all manner of higher quality food than the kitchens normally produced. Captain Hyldir had insisted they take her cabin for the remainder of the journey, out of thanks for saving her and her ship. Ovelia suspected it had something to do with the revelation of Garin's identity as the rightful Prince of Luether, and she could not say Hyldir's knowledge of the truth pleased her. By all accounts, however, the captain seemed loyal, and Garin had sent Alcarin to watch for any sign of treachery.

Garin's squire looked up from the table in irritation, and Ovelia didn't need sight to perceive his glower. Since she had laid her hand on Draca's hilt after losing her sight, Alcarin had always seemed so clear to her. Most people wavered on the edge of her awareness, but Alcarin she could always see clearly enough: there was danger in the man, of that she could attest. Just at the moment, Alcarin had grown particularly discontent. She could smell his unwashed flesh and his angry murmuring made it clear he had run out of patience. Like as not, Garin had kept him up all night.

The Fox of Luether lounged on the bed, a book in one hand and the fingers of the other hand tracing through the air. He mumbled to himself under his breath and constantly moved, as though he couldn't wait to dock and get on with it.

"Ah, Lady Dragon, you're awake, I see." She only vaguely perceived his wave. "What about Nalcaer—any reports from him, Allie? Perhaps he's too busy with that beautiful boy of his?"

"Surely not," Alcarin said. "Since our visit to Tar Vangr, word has been sparse."

"Can't wait to get back into it. Can I pour you a drink, Ovelia?" He sloshed a bottle of murky liquid on the table. "Have some nyssa. Our grateful host found some for us. You'll not find a finer drink in all of Luether to break your night's fast."

"My thanks, Prince, but no." Ovelia sat up and crossed her legs, uncertain what to say, particularly when Alcarin was there. "If there is kefa, I will have some of that."

"Of course, of course," Garin said. "Allie, we have a pot steeping on the kettle, yes? Make yourself useful."

His squire looked up irritably, but did as Garin had asked. The kefa, served in a small porcelain bowl no bigger than the palm of her hand, smelled of sweet cardamom and jasmine. Ovelia tasted the hot, milky beverage and immediately regretted it. It reminded her uncomfortably of sweetsoul, and her body ached in sympathy and longing. She set the cup aside.

Garin bounded to his feet and began pacing in front of the bed. His feet made a series of quick *pat-pat-pats* on the floor, and Ovelia realized he was running in place. How he came to possess his boundless reserve of energy and irrepressible enthusiasm, Ovelia couldn't guess, but she did admire that about him. Lenalin had been like that, too—impossible to keep down against her will, but much more subtle about it. She remembered exceptions, of course—days spent in darkened rooms, weeping earnestly into pillow after pillow—but Lenalin had always sprung back to her full grace within a day or so. When it came to Garin, Ovelia had never known him to falter. If any man could fly without magic, Garin would—if only he had the focus.

Alcarin must have noticed it too, for he sighed and his pen went back to scratching out letters.

"It's been too long," Garin said. "We've been away from Luether nearly twenty days now. Anything and everything could have happened in that time. I need news. Answers. Reports." He drummed his fingers on his opposite forearms. "Some word came in Tar Vangr, but not nearly enough. It's been interminable." He paused. "Ovelia, you're watching the sunrise—what of our progress?"

The irony of asking a blind woman such a question made Ovelia smile wanly. She could sense it, however. "Luether draws close," she said. "We'll arrive within two hours, I expect."

"Excellent!" He flounced back down on the bed. "It couldn't have come soon enough."

Alcarin hesitated, and Ovelia realized he was looking at her. Again, she could not read his expression, but she could feel his resonant distrust. "Might we speak alone, Highness?" she asked.

Garin stretched languidly. "I keep no secrets from Alcarin," he said. "You can speak freely in front of him."

Ovelia bit her lip, uncertain how to proceed. She wondered if Garin truly had told his squire all their secrets, and whether she should reveal this one. "I was just thinking of lost friends."

"Ah. Personal business, then." Garin looked over to Alcarin. "Be a good boy and confirm our landing procedure with the good captain. I'll want to debark and get right to it."

Alcarin turned his attention on Garin, and he solidified more clearly into Ovelia's perception. She turned her sightless gaze to Draca's shadows and immediately dropped her hand to the weapon's hilt. Neither of the men seemed to have noticed, but instead focused on each other—communicating without words. Alcarin faded to a shadow at the edge of her perception. He left the room, and it was not until Ovelia heard the door click shut behind him that she relaxed her guard.

"What was that about?" Garin asked when they were alone. "Don't think I didn't notice you ready to draw steel on my squire." His amiable disinterest had turned into sudden intense focus. "A less patient man might have taken that personally."

"Nothing." Ovelia crossed to the desk where Alcarin had sat, felt around for the chair, and finally took a seat. "I...thought I saw something."

"Alcarin? In Draca's flames?" Garin shrugged. "After that duel in Tar Vangr, I'm not surprised the lad has some lingering feelings. Even a fight to finish. You damaged his pride, after all."

"I did not mean to."

Garin lay back and chuckled. "No fear. It won't jeopardize our task."

Ovelia bit her lip, unsure what to say. She had seen nothing in the flames—not really. Rather, her unease about Alcarin fueled her general perception, as though her intuition demanded she pay attention to him. Trying to tell her something, no doubt, but she could not understand the warning. "There is danger in him," she said at length, deciding on something vague rather than trying to explain. "I feel it."

"Danger? In Alcarin?" Garin drummed his fingers on the headboard. "I should certainly hope so. This business of rebellion may seem like a game for civilized men, but I assure you, without savagery we wouldn't last half a day." He stretched. "I've witnessed what those hands of Alcarin's can do—and felt more than my share, if you wish to know. Why, I remember one night, we were celebrating after making Pervast slay one of his own generals and Alcarin came up with a rather fine use for a wine bottle..."

He wanted to make her blush, but the matter was too serious for Ovelia to let him shrug off her concerns with a sordid tale of debauchery and glee. "All knives on the table, Garin," she said over his story. "I don't think Alcarin's aggression is focused on me, but more broadly. He's angry, and it's only a matter of time before he lashes out. Are you certain of him?"

He sat up, and his easy affability cooled considerably. "Yes," he said. "No doubt. The lad is hot-tempered, but he would never do anything to hurt me. He wants the Children out of Luether as much as I do. I'm sure you two won't get on—at least for a while—but I know my own squire and lover."

"You—" Ovelia nodded. "Yes. I trust your judgment." She shook her head. "I'm sorry. This is all new to me. I can't be sure what I saw."

"Has this happened with others?" Garin asked, interested now. "Is that what happened with Shard? What *did* interest you so much about her, anyway?"

A fair question. Ovelia hadn't given herself space to consider. When they had confronted Shard, Ovelia had faced her as an enemy, but something had drawn her to the pirate queen with an inexplicable but irresistible force. She hoped they would encounter Shard again, and also wouldn't deny a little thrill of uneasiness at the prospect.

"Shard was the opposite," Ovelia said. "I could barely see her at all. I could hear her and…smell her. I sensed no danger in her at all. I can't explain it."

"I see." Garin cracked his knuckles. "Does this mean she is a friend?"

"I wish I could say." Ovelia shrugged her shoulders. "I will caution discretion before trust. We cannot know who our friends are—only our enemies, and then, only after they have acted against us."

"So says the spymaster of the Winter City?" Garin asked. "Or so says my friend, Ovelia Dracaris?"

Ovelia paused. She hardly knew Garin, and yet she felt deep in her bones that she could trust him. They had become friends, of a sort. But it would make her a liar to tell him so. "I swore to aid you," she said. "I will advise you as best I can. I cannot force you to listen to my advice, however."

"True enough." That made him smile. "I choose to see friends in the shadows, while you may see them as enemies. One reason I need you."

"Will this serve?" Ovelia asked. "Do you truly think you can recapture Luether in a season?"

"Of course," Garin said. "I have spent twenty summers working on it. Surely I can accelerate my plans to the span of a single season. It's hardly an epic quest, right?" He no doubt meant that as a jest.

Ovelia nodded but said nothing.

The silence between them stretched, and either one might have broken it, but knuckles rattled on the door and Alcarin appeared. How long he had waited without, listening to their converse, Ovelia could not rightly say. "Hyldir says we arrive within the hour," he said. "Time to prepare."

"Good." Garin's affability boiled back over and he sprang to his feet. "Can't sit around here all day! Have to get back to it." He opened the locker at the foot of the captain's bed and drew out a bundle of leather masks. "You'll want one of these, my lady."

Ovelia took the garment, which felt rough to the touch and smelled of old leather oil. She put it on over her face, thankful for the filter to block out the smoke and trying not to think of Mask.

NINE

A HOT WIND SENT smoke billowing around them on the Avenger's approach, and the cracked towers of Luether loomed out of the haze. Garin had never been away from the city for so long, and this homecoming filled him with renewed vigor and also a deep unease.

It was the air, he realized—thick and bitter, like rancid oil in his mouth. Unlike Alcarin and Ovelia, Garin wore no mask: he had never shielded himself in his homeland, even those first terrible days when the Children had loosed the Narfire. Like most Luethaar, he'd developed a persistent cough over the bleak summers, but the cleaner air of Tar Vangr had soothed his breath and he'd hardly coughed since his arrival. The instant he came out on deck, however, the cough returned with a vengeance, and Alcarin looked at him with worried eyes. He thought he'd grown accustomed to Luether's blight, but that moment reminded him how terrible it had become.

Then, when the *Avenger* put into Luether's skyship dock, Garin knew something had gone very wrong. Simply put, he saw too many people.

The Luether of his boyhood had been a beautiful and vibrant place: a city of spires that challenged the skies, of industry that produced wonders the world had not seen in a thousand years, and of passions great and small that made it the loudest mage-city of old Calatan. He'd spent much of his time amongst the marble towers and lush gardens of High-City, navigating through a sea of smiles. Even more had dwelt below, in Low-City, where things became rougher but also more honest. He remembered how packed the city had felt twenty summers gone: dancing with youths in the streets, listening to the boasts of tavern bravos, flirting with coin-lads and lasses in the windows overhead. One could wander the streets of High-City into the darkest hours, drinking and brawling and whoring without the slightest fear.

Since the Children of Ruin had overrun the city, however, all that had changed. They'd confiscated or destroyed food stocks, slain revelers in the streets, burned buildings, and generally shit all over everything that had made Luether great. Not a single tower stood unbroken, the despoiled gardens lay fallow and stank of human waste, and every vandalized statue in High-City lacked a face or limbs. Most had vanished altogether, leaving nothing but rubble. The barbarians had murdered or exiled most of High-City's residents but didn't have it in them to sit in the stolen houses and do nothing, so at the best of times the place felt like a graveyard patrolled by roving bands of disfigured, insane killers looking for brawls with one another. Garin recalled days over the last two decades where he hadn't seen a single person in High-City whose eyes lacked the madness of Ruin.

Today, however, so many folk lined the streets that Garin's little party could scarcely push through. It seemed the whole population of Luether had gathered, and perhaps it had. Thousands of people clustered on the street corners and filled the cracked mage-glass thoroughfare that led from the dock to the palace. Many wore shabby clothes held together with patches and poor stitching, and some wore nothing at all. Garin passed one wispy-haired old man who milled about, mumbling incoherently to himself, as he scratched absently at a festering scar across his lower back. Not far from him, an emaciated woman greedily clutched a scrawny rat that squealed and thrashed in her hands. A pet, or perhaps a meal for later.

If there was ever an encapsulation of the poverty and suffering the Children had brought to Luether, it was that moment, on that day, on that street. It made Garin's heart ache and his stomach crawl.

"Burn and rot the Children," Garin said.

"Where?" Ovelia scanned subtly, shifting her attention in multiple directions. Her hand gripped the hilt of Draca tight. She'd abandoned her elaborate disguise as the old woman and instead opted for a simple hood over her mask. Garin doubted anyone would be looking for her, anyway.

"They'll be at the dais in the center," Garin said.

Ovelia nodded her understanding. "Why have so many gathered?"

"It can only be one of two things," Alcarin said from Garin's other side. "A rally or an execution. Both, probably."

"Come." Garin pushed through the crowded street. Whatever befell, he had to see it.

Not everyone he saw was poor. A few Bloods of wealth and privilege yet remained in Luether, though the distinction meant less in the City of Pyres than in Tar Vangr. The most comfortable folk stood in walled compounds near the center of High-City, watching along with all the others but from a place of relative safety atop high walls and crumbling crenellations or behind fences studded with broken glass and sharpened wire. Blood Gultras, Blood Meleten, and Blood Harska—all were present, and if Garin remembered their numbers rightly, all their members stood to bear witness to the activity at the center of High-City. The warders of Blood Luyra had engaged in some kind of spat with a band of enforcers, and armed men and women shouted at each other and rattled the corroded gate to their compound. The rest of the Blood

Luyra stood watching silently, the wind nipping at exposed skin and clothing.

Garin and his allies drew close to the raised dais at the center of High-City, the focal point of the people's attention. The square was full, except for one section where the mage-glass had fallen free into the city below, leaving a vast hollow where an ill wind sent smoke rising into High-City. Garin remembered that day: he had met Regel and Ovelia in Luether, and had his first glimpse of this path ahead. Many lives had been lost, however, and he wondered how many yet would die before he could see the barbarians pushed out of his home.

Above the platform towered the only statues left largely undamaged in Luether: golden, scale-armored King Raval, the first ruler of Luether and progenitor of the Blood Ravalis, his boot upon the neck of silver-plated Queen Vulta, his rival for the crown of the summerlands. In the center of the great dais at their feet burned a constant silver flame—the spot through which the Narfire had always burned to light High-City day and night, to light the statues always and remind the Luethaar of the source of their power. Raval boasted a heroic stance, as befitted a warrior who had quelled an uprising and set out the bold first law of Luether: that no woman would ever rule over a man—a law Pervast had seen fit to maintain in his new City of Pyres. Garin had always found it odd that his Blood would rally around such an image, which he found in poor taste at best. Since he'd met an incorrigible princess named Lenalin and her headstrong warder Ovelia nearly thirty summers ago, he'd learned quite well the ridiculousness of that tenet.

And yet, it played out today before his eyes, in a way that made his stomach churn. Before the statue stood a hulking Child of Ruin: fully a head taller than the tallest man Garin had ever seen, with bulbous shoulders and arms wider than the average man's torso. He wore spiked plates strapped onto his massive shoulders and arms, and Garin realized that he had another set of arms—smaller and with sharply clawed hands—protruding from his chest. He wielded a thrice-barbed war spear, point up so that he could hold a prostrate form on the ground with its butt. The woman in the tattered white dress before him trembled: he may not have trod upon her neck, but the similarity of her situation to that of Queen Vulta in the statue was clear. Bright blood leaked from her mouth—livid against her dark skin—and Garin realized the barbarian must have struck her to the ground. He tensed.

Alcarin swore quietly, but his mask mangled the words. Garin agreed with his assessment.

"Who is it?" Ovelia asked.

"Utora Vultara," Alcarin said. "Pervast's latest queen. She's—"

"I know what they're doing to her." Ovelia tightened her grip on Garin's hand. "Hold fast."

Garin hardly noticed. He was staring at the dais before her, where the Narfire had once climbed through a tall chimney in an elegant display honoring the first Ravalis, the dais stood torn open into an exposed pit wide enough for two horses and a wagon to fall in. The opening admitted a torrent of silver flames crackling just below the surface. The Narfire burned with no smoke, leaving only the wavering air to mark its ferocious hunger. A dozen barbarians huddled around the pit, two of whom operated a fiendish contraption that looked like a cage with manacles at the four corners. The two hooded Children of Ruin were locking a naked man into place on the rack. He showed signs of having been beaten savagely: his head lolled and blood dribbled from his face.

As Garin watched, the spearman moved the spear, and Utora pushed herself shakily to her knees, then to her feet. The filthy ground and rough treatment had mangled her white gown: torn, smeared with dust and blood, and barely hanging onto her frail body. Her life balanced on a knife's edge: at any moment, a barbarian could easily run her through or shove her into the fire pit. One of the barbarians reached for her, and she flinched, but instead he wrapped a circlet around her neck and clicked it shut. She tried to stand up tall and strong, like the queen she was, but terror made for an implacable foe. The barbarian gestured rudely, and Utora cleared her throat. The choker made her voice loud enough for all in High-City to hear.

"My...my lord and master, the great Pervast the Unseen," Utora said. "He...his will and word are law. And he says that this man..." She paused, visibly shaking. Then the barbarian with the spear her nudged her in the back with the butt of his weapon, and she flinched as though struck. She stood up straight, though her thin shoulders still trembled. "That this man, known as Thestis, has committed lascivious, unnatural acts, has conspired against the throne, and has murdered the king's appointed agents. Thestis is hereby denounced and condemned as a traitor to Luether."

"Thestis," Garin said. "I know that name. He—"

Alcarin's face had gone stark white.

The barbarians secured the prisoner in the metal cage. He only then seemed to come to his senses, for he began to struggle against the bonds. One of the barbarians smashed a fist into the prisoner's groin, and his whole body shuddered in pain. He spat vomit onto the blistered mage-glass. The other operated a panel of levers, and a metal arm whirred and lifted the cage over the pit of fire. The prisoner heaved and tried not to cry out as the cage began to lower.

Across the crowd, a man in a scourged brown cloak shoved through the gathered crowd. A caster was in his hand, and the brutalized folk scattered out of his path. "Summer Lives!" he shouted. "Summer Lives!"

"Nalcaer," Garin whispered. "Burn it all. Thestis is his lad."

In the cage, Thestis screamed as silver fire made his skin start to blister and his hair smoke. The flames put off no smoke of their own to smother him—only the heat to sear his flesh from his bones. The barbarians of Luether cooked him like meat over a grill.

Nalcaer burst through the crowd to the foot of the dais. The nearest barbarians turned toward him, spears at the ready, and he blasted one in the chest with his caster. The struck man—whose face wept with dozens of crudely-stitched cuts—staggered back into Utora, who fought off his hands as he tried to catch her. He toppled into the fire with a brief scream and a burst of sparks as the Narfire devoured him. The battered queen scurried a way and tried to break free, but the big, four-armed barbarian interposed himself, brutal spear lowered at her chest. Utora crouched low, covering her head with her hands.

Garin started to move, but Ovelia held his wrist tightly. "Let me go," he said. "I have to help."

"No," Alcarin said. "There's nothing we can do, except be killed."

Garin struggled but they were right. His stomach sank.

At the foot of the dais, Nalcaer was fighting two barbarians with his falcat. He managed to cut one down, but the other barbarian jabbed him in the back with her spear, leaving it in him. He whirled with a roar and raked his bloodied sword across her face, putting her on the ground. He turned to charge up the dais, but a spear took him in the gut. He staggered back, and then a second spear hit him high in the chest. Nalcaer fell to his knees and his curved sword clattered down the steps of the dais. One of the nine barbarians still standing drew out a hooked dagger and made his way down toward the wounded man.

In the cage, Thestis continued to scream, and the reek of charred flesh assailed Garin's nostrils. His heart thundered in his head, and he wanted to run. This, though, he had to see. Had to bear witness.

Nalcaer's shaking fingers fumbled at something, and Garin realized he was trying to recharge his caster for another shot. The barbarian stalking toward him smiled widely—she was missing most of her teeth. She seemed not to have noticed the threat, or else she did not consider it a serious one. Behind her, Thestis's screams reached an inhuman pitch.

"Come, Nael," Garin said under his breath. "You can make it. You—"

Nalcaer's caster abruptly clicked and whirred to life once more, and he raised it high. The barbarian paused, her expression stupefied, and Nalcaer took that moment to aim. He cast with a sharp crack, and Thestis's blackened head exploded in a shower of blood and skull fragments. The screams mercifully ceased. Nalcaer smiled, and blood trickled down his chin.

The barbarian who had been stalking forward shook herself, glared at her snickering allies, and charged with a roar. She stabbed Nalcaer in the chest with the dagger up to the hilt, and it burst out his back. The caster fell to the steps as she lifted him, his body jerking spasmodically, into the air. Then she hurled him onto the cage, where he struggled and danced for a moment. Then Nalcaer and the condemned Thestis burned together, seared onto the cage.

The horror turned Garin's stomach, but what broke his heart was the reaction among the folk of Luether. The square lay dead silent, like a lonely crypt rather than a mortal place filled with people. Not a single person looked so much as displeased, let alone disgusted: they stared at the execution with cold indifference, as though they had watched thousands like it and saw nothing of any note. Had they sunk so deep in despair that horror meant nothing to them?

Garin thought his fast breathing and pounding heart were the only sounds in the world. Surely they would give him away if he did not leave. "Enough," he tried to say, but pressure swelled in his chest and exploded out his mouth in a coughing fit that shook the world around him. How the barbarians did not hear and descend upon him, he could not say.

Dimly, he heard chanting: a chorus of evocations to "Live!" "Live!" "Live!" The Children of Ruin celebrated death with mockery as they always did, challenging the condemned to live despite the horrors befalling them.

Garin turned away, as much to hide the tempest of anger on his face as his coughing. His heart raced and his hands trembled. He wanted so badly to act—to end all this madness—but anything he did now would only see him and his allies dead, his cause lost. He'd made himself bear witness to his agents' execution, but he did not have it in him to watch the others. He had seen enough death.

"Fox of Luether!" Utora cried, making Garin shiver to his full height. She might have shouted in reaction to him turning away, as though she addressed him directly. The world slowed around him.

Garin turned back to the dais, but he realized Utora hadn't spoken to him. She stood closer to the edge of the mage-glass where the segment had fallen into Low-City. The wind made her white gown flutter madly and angry tears streamed down her face. If she had looked frail before, she looked hardly there now—so close to the edge of destruction. Everyone was staring at her, including the Children of Ruin with their spears leveled at her back.

Utora's gaze shifted over the crowd, taking them all in, and it was her expression that caught at Garin's heart. With so much doom around her, he would have expected her to look beaten down and broken, but instead he saw something he could not have imagined on her face: hope. She was searching for him in the crowd—though they had never met, she looked as though she sought his face anyway. Perhaps she would recognize his spirit rather than his body. It seemed like she might say something, but instead she bowed her head as though in defeat—or perhaps in reverence.

Then she ran, slipping past her barbarian escort, and hurled herself off the edge of the mage-glass. Wind sent her tattered gown streaming behind her as she vanished soundlessly into the smoke below.

The world shook and fell away, and Garin suddenly could not control himself. He felt like a passenger in his own body as he charged forward, screaming without sound. Alcarin and Ovelia restrained him in their strong arms and bundled him away despite his protests. Dimly, Garin saw Ovelia run into someone, who bounced off her and said "away!" He had a vague glimpse of yellow eyes like discs of gold sparkling in the sunlight.

Alcarin was whispering in his ear, but Garin could barely hear him over the rising darkness inside him that drowned out the world.

TEN

WHEN THE QUEEN OF Luether condemned the prisoner to death and the man broke through the crowd, caster and sword drawn, Alistra all but clapped her hands in triumph.

"Ha," Alistra said under her breath. She put a hand over her mouth to restrain her mirth. "Ha ha!"

Davargorn saw nothing amusing, and from his sour expression, neither did Vhaerynn.

After a day and a night of pushing the sleek black ornithopter Lan had granted them, they had landed at the skyship dock perhaps an hour after the *Avenger*, dashing Davargorn's hopes of arriving in the city first. He'd gone immediately to the much larger ship's berth, but the only ones he saw debarking were servants unloading the ship's cargo. To have traveled hundreds of leagues at speed only to miss his quarry by so brief a span filled him with fury. He'd been able to pace only a few moments before he felt Vhaerynn's insistent tug on his blood and he'd had to return to the ornithopter, where Alistra had cursed him for making them rush to no great purpose. She wanted nothing more than to find accommodations in Luether and revel in her newfound—if limited—freedom. Vhaerynn had kept silent on the issue.

A public execution—complete with unexpected heroics—seemed exactly the remedy for Alistra's mood, however. From their position near the back of the gathered throng, the three of them watched as the rebel, transfixed with two spears, fell to his knees. He struggled to rise, even as one of the barbarians came toward him, drawing a blade that was more sickle than dagger. Alistra was watching with wide eyes, hardly able to contain her excitement. Considering her obvious relish, Davargorn suspected that she hadn't seen much in a long time.

Vhaerynn looked entirely indifferent to the drama unfolding at the foot of King Raval's statue and instead busied himself trying to keep his gray robe from picking up too much dust and grime. He never would have suspected such fastidiousness from the sorcerer, whom he had personally seen climb out of a pool of blood. The strange contradiction made his head ache.

For his part, Davargorn was scanning the crowd in Luether's High-City square. Most of the anonymous faces passed his sight without making an impression—dirty, slack, devoid of hope—so he stopped looking at faces but rather at stances. Most of those gathered stood disconsolately, hands thrust into pockets or hanging listlessly at their sides, and those he ignored. What he sought was tension—anger, even: folk standing tall, shoulders back, jaws tight, eyes fixed upon the horror at the foot of the statue. He looked for folk watching with growing rage at the injustice on display.

Once he knew what to look for, it took him only a matter of moments to find the ones he sought.

They stood not too far away, nearer than Davargorn to the dais where they could see more clearly. He did not know their faces, but he would know Ovelia's profile anywhere: tall, proud, and unbroken. The stance was deeply familiar: the way she balanced her left foot just slightly ahead of the other, ready to leap into battle at any instant. She had stood the same way when she claimed triumph over him in the temple of the Summer Goddess, when Mask—Semana—had deserted him for his failure. He'd spent every night since that day dreaming of his vengeance against her, and he would not be denied today.

Hand on the hilt of a hooked dagger, he slipped away through the crowd toward his quarry.

Davargorn half expected Vhaerynn's blood magic to draw him back, but the sorcerer had apparently sufficiently preoccupied himself with concerns about hygiene. He glimpsed Alistra at the edge of his sight, and she cast him a wink when he parted from them. She had noticed, and she approved. Then she too disappeared, leaving Vhaerynn alone, grumbling over his stained hem.

Even with legs weakened from long captivity, Davargorn cut through the crowd, skirting the assembled folk like a wraith in his dark leather armor and light red cloak. He'd thought the color a fool choice when King Lan insisted he wear it, but in Luether—amongst so many bright colors and the constant heat—a darker hue would have made him stand out. As it passed, not a single eye lingered on him longer than a breath, and he was on his quarry before he could credit his own speed. When he had come closer, he saw a hint of red hair peeking out of her hood. She'd barely even bothered to disguise herself. *Insulting.*

He reached for the woman at the same time Vhaerynn's magic flared in his blood, making his movements suddenly sluggish. He meant to pull her head back and cut her throat in one fluid motion, but instead all he could do was punch her awkwardly in the shoulder. He hadn't even drawn his blade yet.

She whirled, and he saw her sun-blackened skin and bright blue eyes—not Ovelia Dracaris. Her face went from surprised to angry and disgusted. "Ware!" she shouted. "Stupid boy!"

Davargorn might have killed her anyway, but for the blood magic restraining him. He mumbled something like an apology and looked back toward Vhaerynn, whose glare he could feel even through a dozen interposed bodies. He felt the call in his blood, pulling him back toward the Necromancer, and he had no choice but to obey.

"Fox of Luether!" someone shouted, and he craned his neck to look.

The woman at the center of the plaza had called out for Garin by his symbol. Her eyes swept the crowd, and Davargorn tried in vain to see where she was looking. He saw only one face he recognized—that of Alistra, about a hundred paces from him, back toward the skyship dock. What was she doing?

Then Utora ran and threw herself through a gap in the mage-glass below their feet.

The gathered crowd had reacted with impassivity and aplomb to the public execution—horrific as it had been—but when their queen leaped to her death, it shook them from their stupor. Confused murmurs passed through the crowd, and more than a few shouted or screamed in protest. The Children of Ruin left standing on the dais brandished their spears to keep the mob at bay. Closer to Davargorn, a bearded man slammed his fist into the belly of his neighbor, and a grappling match erupted between them as a woman nearby screamed. He would have cut them both down, but the blood magic drew him on.

An emaciated man with desperate eyes lunged at Davargorn, grasping at his throat with bony fingers. The blood magic made him sluggish, but Davargorn still had enough control to plant his dagger in the skinny man's ribs. The beggar stared at him with wide eyes, coughed up blood, and slumped to the ground. Shouts of "blood!" and "steel!" rose into the air around him, and Davargorn found himself running back to Vhaerynn under the cool shadow of a rattling awning. The sorcerer waited, his face carefully neutral. Alistra arrived a breath after him, distantly smiling.

"Why would she do that?" Davargorn asked. "She was not under attack. That was pointless."

Alistra gave him a hard look, then rolled her eyes and turned away.

"It does not matter," Vhaerynn said. "This chaos serves our purpose. Did you mark our quarry?"

"You know that already," Davargorn said. "I—"

Vhaerynn ignored him in favor of Alistra, who nodded. "It was as you suspected," she said. "She didn't perceive me as a threat with that sword of hers. Couldn't see me at all, it seemed. And something else about her—she's weak. Addicted to a toxin. I could have killed her just then."

"Fortunately, you did not." Vhaerynn looked out over the plaza, which had fallen into chaos. "Come. We will discuss this later."

"What?" Davargorn asked. "What do you mean—?"

"Later. I'll see to accommodations." The necromancer gestured toward the crowd. "Follow them. Deal with any Children who get too close. It does not serve our purposes for them to die just yet."

"Pity." Alistra turned to Davargorn, her expression pensive.

"What?" he asked, then flinched when she laid her hand on his cheek. "Don't."

Alistra's expression remained unchanged, but her yellow eyes glittered with amusement. "Am I taking the boy or do you have him?"

"I'm not a boy," he said. "You—"

"You take him," Vhaerynn said. "I can follow. Spill blood, Lady Ravalis."

Alistra glared at him. "Don't call me that."

Vhaerynn hesitated, then headed toward the nearest lift.

She stood looking after him for quite some time, her fingers clenching and unfurling at her sides. After Vhaerynn had so casually commanded and dismissed her, Davargorn expected to see a visage of defiance or at least annoyance on her face, but instead she looked thoughtful. *Tactical.* But was she a general planning her next move on the battlefield, or a child scheming at a game? He did not know her and could not say for certain—an uncomfortable but familiar feeling.

"Come along, boy," Alistra said at length. "Can't let them get too far ahead of us, now."

Through exertion of will, Davargorn forced himself to release his hold on the hilt of his falcat. He followed her silently, though inside he burned to act. *Not yet,* he told himself. *Not yet.*

Soon.

ELEVEN

Luether

GETTING GARIN AWAY FROM the square and into Low-City proved simple enough, but doing so without attracting the attention of the roving Children of Ruin took no small effort. Half-leading, half-carrying a man through the streets as he sobbed and cursed uncontrollably made for poor stealth. Ovelia lost count of the times she and Alcarin had to backtrack or take a shortcut through an alley. It never came to blows, but twice she put her hand to Draca's hilt in expectation of an ambush. No assault came, however: every time, the roving barbarians found something else to occupy their attention, allowing Ovelia and Alcarin to slip away with their uncooperative bundle.

Garin's protestations grew weaker the farther they got from the site of the horror, and by the time they made their way along the Way of the Confessoras in Low-City, he had grown feeble indeed. No more did he try to impede their progress but instead stared at nothing, mumbling but quiescent. It almost seemed as though his mind grew weaker with every step they took. Ovelia had never seen Garin like this, but it fulfilled the expectation she had formed on the *Avenger*, when she had observed his similarity to Lenalin.

The more Garin weakened, the more uneasy Alcarin grew, stressing the need for haste. This, Ovelia granted happily. She also noted that he offered a series of hand gestures to numerous folk in the street, no doubt signaling their safety in approaching. Had she not been able to see Alcarin burning clearly, Ovelia would have missed the signs entirely. Or, jittery and distracted from her racing heart, she might have walked right past the tavern and never noticed.

They came to a tavern called the Long Dawn, its arms marked by a half-risen sun over a set of dark mountains. Ovelia scrutinized the sign, uncertain why Draca's fires chose to show her that while the rest of the tavern was a mass of black and shadow. The mountains resembled the Broken Fangs in the northern range, visible from Tar Vangr's High-City on a clear day. A good omen. She suspected most people in Luether had not seen those mountains and probably never would, so the resemblance would be lost upon them.

They carried Garin through the front doors of the tavern, and Ovelia felt as though they had entered a battlefield. The folk within made no pretext

116

of calm or casualness, as the Circle of Tears in the Burned Man always did. Instead, they hurried about, shouting angrily at one another and occasionally launching blows. Without her sight, the cacophonous common room became a storm of shadows and outbursts, making Ovelia immediately dizzy. She knew immediately what kind of organization Garin ran: sloppy, disorganized, doomed. And now, they only had until Midsummer…

"This is your revolution?" she asked. How these people were not dead already, she had no idea.

"I'll talk," Alcarin said in her ear. "You get Garin into the back. Do you need help?"

Ovelia shook her head. "I can find my way."

Alcarin immediately headed into the mass of people, issuing instructions and attracting their focus. Ovelia looked to Garin, who whimpered something in a language she did not know and slumped heavily against her. "Almost there," she said, even as she noticed Draca smoking. "Just wait—"

Ovelia sensed the big man in front of them—a hulking shadow that stank of sweat and fish—before he spoke, and she reached up to catch his hand when he tried to grasp her shoulder. To his credit, the man didn't waste time with words but instead immediately grabbed for her. Ovelia managed to sidestep and twist his arm out of the way, but Garin encumbered her other arm and she could not abandon him. She put her back to her attacker—she had no need to face him—and he tore the back of her shirt open in his attempt to grasp her. When he predictably tried to wrap his arms around her throat, she ducked low and hurled him over her shoulder. By the Fire, he was heavy, but his momentum worked for Ovelia. He ended up slumping down along the wall, startled and confused.

Casters sizzled to life and steel scrapped free of scabbards. Ovelia had not meant to draw attention, and she'd thrown her attacker by reflex. Now, she could not say how many foes stood against her in the cloud of angry shadows swirling before her, but she knew that to draw Draca would be to invite doom. Instead, she held up her hands in surrender.

"Hold, hold!" Alcarin stepped between Ovelia and the rest of the room. "Aegis! Stand down, Jeggs." He pointed at the big man who had attacked Ovelia, who had climbed to his feet and was shaking his head to clear it. "This woman is under my aegis."

A woman pushed out of the group and confronted Alcarin. Though most of her features hid in shadow, her mouth caught Ovelia's attention—big and full and loud. She was missing a few teeth, making her voice oddly wet. "What are you thinking, Alcarin?"

Garin murmured something untoward.

Alcarin glowered. "I was hoping everyone wouldn't see him like this," he said. "I need to mollify everyone. Try not to get in any trouble." He vanished into the shadowy flurry.

"I'm Biaza, second sword of Summer Lives," she said. "Garin may have the vision of a returned summer, but we're the ones who see to it that it does not die." The woman took Ovelia's hand. "Come with me quickly. And bring *him*."

They headed into the back, following Biaza's lead. The woman walked with a shuffle—one long stride, then a shorter one—and carried herself with great confidence. They deposited Garin in a small chamber hidden behind a tapestry. The room smelled of potions, unguents, and all manner of alchemical supplies, and Ovelia recognized it as one of the laboratories Garin had spoken of during their time together. He kept half a dozen such rooms hidden throughout Luether, where he could lock himself and work for hours or even days at a time.

"There." Biaza locked the door behind him and turned to Ovelia. She spoke in the thick, full-throated accent of Low-City Luether, and a slight slur to her words made her voice echo almost imperceptibly. She sucked her teeth while not talking. "He's in one of his voids, but the chemics will pull him out, you wait." A pause. "Alcarin said you're with him, no?"

Ovelia realized Biaza was holding out an arm to shake, and she returned the gesture, hoping the hesitation not too long. "I am Lea," she said, hesitating to give her full name. Her ignominious reputation as the Bloodbreaker would not help matters. "I've come to help Garin."

"With that?" Biaza clucked her tongue in mild disapproval, likely at Draca. "I don't mean to alarm you, lass, but you're wearing a blindfold. Makes your fight a bit tricky, no?"

"No more than your limp impedes your walk," Ovelia said. "Or your missing teeth your speech."

Biaza sucked her teeth in thought—those traits hardly seemed obvious to one who was blind—then smiled big in Ovelia's hazy vision. "You've a few surprises, girl. Not the least is your mouth."

"I've been told that before." Ovelia found she genuinely liked this woman. She listened at the concealed door and heard the clashing of glass on stout wood, as well as a few garbled curses she did not care to understand. "Will he...?"

"He passes well, no doubt," Biaza said. "What did he see?"

"A public execution," Ovelia said, as coolly as she could under the circumstances. "Two of his men, I—I don't remember both of their names. Nael, something? It was awful."

Biaza drew up short and breathed in sharply as though Ovelia had punched her. Of course—Biaza likely knew both men, if she was a member of Garin's movement. Ovelia winced at her oversight. The day grew long, and she felt increasingly weary.

"I should go," Biaza said. "No doubt Alcarin's in need of friendly steel by now."

She walked away, leaving Ovelia near Garin's room, just as someone else approached. Ovelia recognized his strong musk and the weight of his steps as those of the man who had attacked her. The shadowy corona that told her of his movements warned her of imminent danger once more.

"You! Woman!" he said. "I am Red Jeggs, and we have unfinished business."

"Lea," she said. "And I suppose we do."

The man held out his arm, which Ovelia cautiously took—ready this time. Red Jeggs immediately pulled her toward him, going for a hold, but she ducked under his arm and twisted it up behind him. Now that they were touching, her sight disadvantage became moot: she could feel his every movement. Pitting her strength against his, she slowly forced him back toward a lock, but he slammed them both against the wall. Her grip faltered and he wrenched his arm free, putting them once more on level ground.

"Ha ha," Red Jeggs said. "Good."

She acknowledged his assessment with a brief nod.

After that, the bout became friendlier. They wrestled back and forth, comparing strength and technique. Ovelia could tell from the dying chatter in the room that more than a few had turned to watch their grapple. Red Jeggs was her better, but Ovelia fought like an animal. Finally, Jeggs caught Ovelia in an arm lock she could not escape, and she tapped him twice on the arm to signify her submission.

Red Jeggs released her. "Burned and broken," he said. "You're not a true grappler, Dragon Daughter, but you're a scrapper, no? Are you really blind?"

Ovelia nodded. "Why do you call me Dragon Daughter?"

"Rumors travel quickly," he said. "You tell me your name is Lea, but I think Dragon Daughter fits you better. For the ink on your back."

That, Ovelia could accept. "You are one of Garin's men?"

"Armsmaster," he said. "Swords to casters to any of the tricky alchemics he brews up, I teach it and wield it all. Best warrior in Summer Lives, but if you're half as good with that sword as you are with your hands, I suspect that's *second*-best now. Is it true you're the Bloodbreaker of Tar Vangr?"

Ovelia nodded. "I have spent much of the last year trying to redeem myself of that distinction."

"Apologies," he said. "Didn't mean to stir hard thoughts. You seem honorable. I have this sense about folk. Especially beautiful women."

He was flattering her, and Ovelia could feel his ardor even when his crotch wasn't pressed against her. "Do you always flirt this shamelessly with fresh recruits?"

Red Jeggs at first look confused, then rose to the challenge. "Only hardened veterans—the pretty ones," he said. "It's been a while since we had any of those. I may be out of practice."

"No, it passes well." Ovelia shook her head. She could hardly think about that now. "I worry for Garin. Losing his men cut him deeply."

"Aye to that," Red Jeggs said. "He's in one of his voids—who knows how long that will last? The others take it well, but it wears on them to see him in distress."

His *voids*. Ovelia would remember that. "Biaza passes well enough," she said.

"That's because Biaza has slain six Children of Ruin, two of whom used to be hers," Red Jeggs said. "The woman is made of well-tempered iron. Shame about her third son."

"What?" Ovelia's heart skipped.

"Thestis, who died today," Red Jeggs said as he stepped away. "Shame."

Ovelia barely heard him. She felt Biaza's eyes on her, and though she could not see the woman's expression as she spoke in hushed tones with Alcarin, Ovelia could sense well enough the darkness there. Thus far as a rebel in service of Summer Lives, Ovelia had nearly broken the arm of their best warrior, made a horrible mistake with their second in command (one that stood only to grow worse when the truth was revealed), and stood guard outside their leader's room while he raved about a darkness few could understand. She sank to the floor and blew out a long sigh.

This road would prove long indeed.

The trek from High-City to Low-City had been long and bloody, but Davargorn relished it all the same. Nothing eased his weary heart quite like stabbing a man through the groin and leaving him to bleed out in the gutter. And Alistra—Narfire bless her unburnt body—had provided more than one such opportunity.

"Come along, boy," she said as he drew his blood-smeared dagger out of a choking barbarian. The man collapsed, weeping and snarling by turns, onto the shit-stained cobblestones, and Davargorn kicked him in the stomach to silence him. "We'll lose them if we don't hurry."

Davargorn gave her a derisive sniff, wiped his blade on the dying man's vest, and hurried after.

Following Garin's little band, picking off would-be ambushers, redirecting patrols, and silencing likely informants had proved a diverting challenge over the last hour. After his long imprisonment and the uncomfortable ornithopter, Davargorn relished the chance to stretch his muscles and return to what he did best: killing. The blade felt good in his hand, as though it had always belonged there. And though he lacked his cutting cloak or handcaster, Davargorn felt more like himself than he had in a long time.

Surprisingly, they'd only slain three of the ten or so would-be assailants, while the others they'd eluded or sent off in the wrong direction. Davargorn had to confess that being constantly restrained had begun to wear on him. Alistra seemed so casual—almost haphazard—while he itched to move forward and waylay their quarry.

"You're weaker than I expected," Davargorn said as he joined Alistra under an awning near a corner of a cafe. Garin had made it most of the way down the street around the corner, with the help of his little slut and Ovelia. "Has bondage taken your taste for blood?"

"And you're just as stupid as *I* expected," Alistra replied. "Kill too many, and we draw attention to ourselves. Kill only a few, and it could be a series of unfortunate accidents. You're too eager for sense. Honestly, I'm to believe you survived more than a few days on the street as a slayer?"

Davargorn bristled, but Alistra held up a hand to stop him before he could speak. She gestured with her chin, and he looked out after their quarry. Ovelia and the others had stopped below a sign depicting mountains, and went inside without further hesitation.

"Good," Davargorn said. "Allow them to fortify themselves before we kill them. Brilliant."

Alistra gave him a dubious look. "Were you listening at all to my brother's directive?"

"Listening, yes," Davargorn said. "Caring, not at all. I'm here to kill the Dracaris woman, your cousin, and anyone who gets in my way. Then I disappear."

"And go where, boy?" Alistra asked. "You truly believe his bloated Majesty will forgive your betrayal and won't send agents to hound your every step? You *are* a fool." She indicated the tavern their quarry had entered. "We—"

Davargorn stepped into her, forcing her back against the building before she could react. Her hand went too late to the hilt of the axe at her right hip, but his curved blade was already at her throat. Her bright yellow eyes burned into his.

"Yes?" she asked.

"I'm not a boy," Davargorn said. "I'm not a child, I'm not your pet, and you don't command me." He pressed the honed steel against her throat. "Say you understand."

"I understand." Her eyes never blinked or left his. "I am not your enemy."

"No?" he asked. "Your Blood all but destroyed me: killed my family, killed my master, imprisoned me, ra—*violated* me." He shivered. "Why would I not kill you right now and have done with it? I have sworn to destroy your blood."

Alistra gazed at him levelly, betraying not a shred of fear. "My Blood," she said. "Not *me*."

"I fail to see the difference."

"My Blood," she said again. "Which has done all the same things to me."

Davargorn could not say why, but he would let her speak. He lowered the dagger and pressed it instead against her ribcage. A simple thrust would drive it into her heart, and from the look in her yellow eyes, she knew it as well.

Someone passed by in the street and glanced in their direction. A warding glare from Davargorn, however, sent the woman on her way. He turned back to Alistra, who waited patiently. There was no fear on her face—no urgent tension in her body, ready to spring at the first chance to escape. He both loathed and respected that. She was like no other woman he had ever met and no man either: utterly fearless, whether through courage or madness.

"Your Blood hurt you and locked you away," he said, "and yet you do their bidding. You are a convenient tool to them."

"As you were to your previous master?"

"No." He pricked her through a gap in her hauberk so that she felt the blade. "You do not talk about Mask."

"Such pain. I thought as much." Alistra still seemed entirely unafraid. "You have no subtlety, Tithian Davargorn—no nuance. You are a cudgel in the street, where I am a stiletto in the dark. The things I could teach you about being a slayer." She shook her head. "No, ugly boy: I only *seem* to serve my brother's purposes, but in truth I serve my own. I follow his course and use the weapons he has given me until our paths diverge."

"What do you mean?"

Alistra smiled. "Follow me, and find out."

Davargorn tensed his grip on the dagger. "And if I decide to kill you instead?"

"Then you continue to walk a path laid before you," Alistra said. "Rather than learning to choose your own."

They stood a long moment, clasped against the wall like lovers and like mortal foes. Davargorn wouldn't deny a tingling thrill that ran through him to hold Alistra under his power, but part of him knew matters passed not strictly how they seemed. She had just as much power as he did, and he found the line intriguing to walk. He lowered his blade.

"Not so stupid after all." Alistra touched his face—the very gesture that had made him flinch before—and he stood firm. "Still so ugly, though."

Davargorn gave her a grotesque smile.

TWELVE

THE SUN RARELY SHONE brightly in smoky fallen Luether at the best of times, but it had long since set when a knock came on Garin's door. The rest of the day had been a blur: the march to the Long Dawn, securing him in his laboratory with as much wine as he could manage, and ignoring the cries and curses of his friends outside the door. He thought near midnight the worst of it had passed, and he must have slept since then.

He came to his senses and noted his surroundings in an analytical way. His body: slumped against the wall. At his side: a mostly empty cask of wine and a half-full bottle of nyssa, cork missing. His clothes: torn and stained. His knuckles: bloody, which matched a place on the stone wall he vaguely remembered punching at least fifty times. The nearby table: overturned. Glass beakers and sample dishes: shattered. The rest of the room: a mess.

He didn't remember the intervening night, but he could guess what had happened. He awoke coughing, as though his lungs sought to crawl up his throat and out his mouth.

The knock sounded again, making his head begin to pound with the same thudding rhythm. He uttered a guttural reply, then—with effort—formed a word. "Come."

The door shuddered, but Garin could see at a distance the latch kept it shut. He muttered and pulled himself up along the upended table. His feet seemed barely attached to his body and didn't want to obey his instructions. He had to force each leg ahead of him and hold it in place with one or both hands, but eventually he made it across the room and got his hand on the latch.

"Come," he said, and the word sounded more coherent this time. His head felt muddy.

Alcarin stood in the doorway, his expression a quiet storm. His eyes were hollow and glazed, he wore the same smoke-reeking clothes he'd had on since the *Avenger*, and his hair had become a rumpled mess. He looked terrible.

"You look terrible," Garin said.

Alcarin's neutral grimace deepened into an open scowl. "So do you," he said. "And you stink."

As he closed the door behind Alcarin, Garin sniffed experimentally at his shoulder. Indeed, he stank of stale wine, nyssa, and not a little vomit. And if even *he* could smell it, well...

123

"You've made quite the mess in here." His squire looked around the room with the same sour expression. With his boot, he brushed aside the broken shards of a beaker, then righted an overturned jar on the nearest table. He crossed his arms and glared at Garin. "You made a mess out *there*, as well. Nalcaer…he left a void, and you weren't there to fill it. Everyone's panicking—half of them want to abandon the cause, half of them are demanding to talk to you."

"I'm surprised half of them don't want to kill me," Garin said.

"More than half, I think." Alcarin looked not at all amused. "We've talked about this so many times. Everyone loves the brave Garin Ravalis who can't be weighed down, but when you fall, you fall hard, and if everyone sees…" He shook his head. "You can't do that. You can't simply vanish when we all need you here. When we need you to be strong. To be fearless."

Garin felt anything but fearless. The concept of simply speaking filled him with terror, but he did it anyway. "You need me," he said, pulling the words together through sheer force of will.

Alcarin gave him an odd look. "Yes," he said. "You are our leader."

A big smile on his face, Garin stepped toward Alcarin. He put his hands on his squire's biceps. "You *need* me," he said. "*You.*"

His squire looked discomfited. "Yes, but—"

Garin leaned in and kissed Alcarin despite his protests. His squire went taut at first, then relaxed in his embrace. Their kiss lingered as Garin pushed them back against a table, his hands tracing the contours of Alcarin's muscles. It made Alcarin soften, his body inviting Garin to explore further. In his drunken lust, Garin could think of nothing better than to oblige.

"Garin," Alcarin said. "You taste of wine. Don't—"

"Don't stop. *Right.*" Garin slipped one hand down Alcarin's breeches to wrap his fingers around the man's blade. Hard as steel. "You need me. You need this."

As gracefully as he could, Garin crouched before his squire and went about his business. Alcarin arched back over the table and loosed a loud groan. He entangled his fingers in Garin's hair and shuddered with pleasure. Garin squeezed his squire's firm backside the way he knew he liked.

"No. *No.*" Alcarin gave Garin a shove, and he landed on his backside amongst the broken glass. Garin stared up, dumbfounded, as his squire pulled up his breeches.

"Just a small poke," Garin said. "Not even a thrust. Come—"

"I won't do this again," Alcarin said, his face furious. "I won't be your burned *crutch*. I—"

He trailed off, and Garin did not at first understand why. Then he saw Ovelia at the door, watching them sightlessly. With her eyes hidden behind that strip of crimson cloth, she seemed more like a sculpture than a woman—a thing, rather than a person. Garin hoped it was the wine that had made him think so.

"You talk to him," Alcarin said, his tone dry and dismissive. He wiped his lips with the back of his hand. "He isn't listening to me."

"Allie—" Garin said, but his squire pushed out the door and let it bang shut behind him. Garin sighed and let his face fall into his hands. "Burn *me*."

They remained that way for a long moment—Ovelia standing silently, Garin huddled on the floor, tasting Alcarin and mourning himself. Then, slowly, she approached and sat on the wine-stained floor beside him. She did so gingerly, feeling out the location before she sat, and then she faced him without meeting his eye. Sometimes, Garin forgot about her blindness until she did something of the sort.

She held out her hand, and he put the half-empty bottle of nyssa in it. She drank deeply, scowled, then wiped her lips. "What are you thinking about?" she asked.

"Today," he said. "Naelcar. His lover, Thestis. Utora Vultara. All of it. It's just—just so much."

He expected her to rage at him as Alcarin had, or perhaps express undeserved sympathy for his plight. What he did not expect was her silence. She sat and gazed blankly at him, waiting.

And Garin found himself speaking. He told her about his boyhood, and the summers during which Luether had seemed so bright and shining—the beautiful city on the mountain, overlooking a tranquil sea. He boasted of the flowers and the people and the singing and dancing. He spoke of Luethaar bravado, of bitter rivals who dueled in the streets, then settled their differences by who could drink the most nyssa. He captured, in his half-drunken poetry, a life and world that he'd lost long ago, and spent the intervening decades striving to rediscover. And by the end of the story, his eyes felt wet and full.

"Am I a fool to want that back?" he asked. "To think I can have it?"

"Of course you can have it back," Ovelia said.

Garin shook his head, unconvinced. "We've fought for twenty summers," he said. "Since I was a boy, I've watched my friends fight and die trying to make my people rise up and throw off Pervast and his horde. Everything we try has failed. Every attack, every sabotage, every theft—none of it lasts. And now we have what, a season? Most of a spring and half a summer to do what we have spent twenty summers failing to do? It is too much. There is not enough left of Luether to save."

"I do not believe that," Ovelia said. "And neither do you."

"You saw what has become of my people," Garin said. "They witnessed abject horror yestereve, and yet not a one of them so much as flinched. Let alone stepped up to stop it."

"Nalcaer did," Ovelia said.

"Because his lover was the one being burned alive," Garin said. "Silver Fire, we should have done something for him." He coughed fiercely and she extended the bottle. He took the nyssa back and drank deep. The biting fire knotted his stomach.

"Alcarin was right," Ovelia said. "There was nothing we could have done. You are but one man, too important to risk. Alcarin is a firebrand, but hardly fit to face a dozen Children of Ruin. And me—" She shook her head. "In my prime, with Draca in my hand, I could have slain them all and won the day, but I am blind, Garin. I'm still learning to fight this way, and I would have died yesterday. Died and revealed you, and then you would have died as well."

"Yes, I know all that," Garin said. "Utora…she saw what I did, and she chose escape rather than face another day of this empty horror."

Ovelia shook her head slightly, but she was smiling.

"Something is funny?" he asked.

"I want a draught," Ovelia said.

He shook the bottle—a little left—and held it out to her, but she shook her head. "You mean sweetsoul," he said.

Ovelia nodded. "I feel so selfish," she said. "Here you are, telling me your story, and all I can think about is forgetting my own." She looked down at the floor. "My world was taken from me, too, and she was all I had left of it. The last legacy of the man I once served—the last reminder of the woman I… the woman I loved." She shook her head. "Now I've lost her, and against that, nothing matters to me. My sight. My health. This city. None of it." She held out her hand for the bottle. "You've lost so much—seen so much doom—and all I can see is my own darkness. Selfish."

"Not selfish," Garin said. "Honest." He handed her the bottle. "I'm the one who's been selfish. I still have my life—my sight—my lover." He gestured vaguely toward the door. "You've lost as much as I, and more. There is no more fight to get back what you have lost. I am mourning myself when I have not died. Selfish."

Ovelia shook her head. "I know enough of despair to know it is real." She reached up and pulled off her crimson blindfold. "It drives us to drink or harsher venoms. It slows us in battle and steals our spirit to push on. And though we may fight it, we cannot defeat it alone." She looked directly at him and held out her hand.

Garin stared at her hand for a long moment, then looked up at her dry hazel eyes, mottled and glazed from Mask's ravaging magic. A warm pressure rose within him, not unlike when he had stood in the square and watched the horror the previous day. This time, instead of threatening to send him screaming into that dark corner of himself, the warmth that stole his breath instead pushed him toward the light. Tears welled in his eyes, and he could not stop them as they fell. He took her hand, and she drew him into her embrace—not like a mother holding a child or a lover clinging desperately to a lover, but a friend. Exactly the friend he needed.

"I think," he said. "I think I have an idea. Something new."

"New?" Ovelia asked.

"Mad, actually," Garin said. "But in a city fallen to madness, what choice do we have?"

He pressed himself into her embrace. Ovelia held him as he wept for a time, and it was not until his tears had dried that he realized he was holding her as well.

~

Light burned at the edges of the boarded-over window, and Garin realized morning had come. Perhaps he had slept, or perhaps he had only drowsed beside Ovelia, leaning his head against her shoulder. Whatever had passed, he awoke feeling refreshed and ready to go. He rose, and helped Ovelia to her feet.

"Time to go rekindle a revolution," Garin said.

Ovelia nodded.

The common room had slowed somewhat since their arrival, but the tension yet remained. Alcarin looked particularly harried, his clothing and hair askew and his eyes ringed with red circles. Garin suspected his squire had slept not a single moment, and his heart ached for that. He felt selfish, letting Alcarin bear the brunt of the chaos of his return while he lay in stupor in his chamber. Alcarin flashed him a small, angry look, and Garin nodded slightly in response. He would make it up to his squire, somehow.

But first, he had an announcement to make. These were his core agents—warriors sworn to the cause and proven over and over again, each of whom exerted influence over a cell of rebels in the city, all unconnected socially or politically but united by the common goal of driving the barbarians from Luether. Garin had not elevated all of them personally, but he trusted implicitly the judgment of those who had. They deserved to hear the news first, dire as it might be.

"Twenty summers ago, Luether was a city of laws and justice," Garin said. "A city where we could live and celebrate life, free from fear and violence. Then Pervast came, and destroyed our world—our way of life. For two decades, we have struggled and died under his tyranny." He shook his head. "This summer, his reign ends."

Stunned silence greeted his pronouncement, and the common room descended into still attention. All eyes fell upon him, and Garin took a deep breath to steady himself. Slowly, he stepped to the wide circular table in the center of the common room, drawing out the movement to lend weight to his words. Ceremoniously, he drew the warpick from his belt and laid it gently on the table, as was the custom for commanders addressing their men. Disarming himself in this way but showing the weapon to the hall ensured he had their undivided attention. Then he leaned heavily on the table.

"I have kept a secret from you this night," he said. "You've heard the rumors that Demetrus, my uncle and true king of Luether, is dead. Also, that my cousin Lan has ascended in his place. This is true."

Murmurs rustled around the common room, and Garin held up a hand for silence.

"What is also true," he said. "Is that my cousin plans to march south with the armies of Tar Vangr to reclaim Luether by force at Midsummer." He drew himself up to his full height and crossed his hands behind the small of his back.

No murmurs this time. Mostly, the gathered agents stared at him with shock on their faces. Garin sensed Ovelia looking at him, and turned to note the expression of disapproval on her face. He nodded.

"Many of us call Tar Vangr the Winter City, but it was named the City of Steel first, and Lan has reclaimed that name for it. The forges beneath the city and within the mountain have worked to produce war machines and weapons for this effort, and when Lan marches south, it will be with an army the likes of which the World of Ruin has not seen since the last Ruin Fall, two hundred summers gone."

He could hear the excited whispers, and even a few muted cheers broke out at his speech. For the first time in years, his people saw light ahead on their dark path.

"Lan sails south at Midsummer," he said. "We have until that time to set out his path."

The murmurs fell silent, as the full weight of their dilemma sank in. The task that lay before them seemed overwhelming enough to Garin—he could only imagine how his agents felt.

"This is not impossible," he said. "We have worked for twenty summers toward this moment. I have brought with me Lea, a fine warrior, but we two cannot do this alone. Our plans must accelerate, but they will succeed if you all do your part and follow me." He looked around at his gathered rebels. "I have not always been the best leader for you. I am impatient, arrogant at times, and very, very stubborn. But I have a plan for our success, and I ask you to trust me one last time." He took a deep breath. "Will you do this?"

The room fell silent as a tomb. No one spoke or even stirred, and Garin could hear his own heart thudding in his chest. The darkness rose from where it had fallen asleep inside, and he could feel it clawing at his stomach and lungs. Had he made a mistake? Would this all come to nothing?

Then a heavy tankard clunked down on the bar, and Red Jeggs stood up. A huge, barrel-chested man with a veritable crimson forest of a beard, he had long proved one of Garin's best warriors and most loyal supporters. The man loved a good challenge, and the prince had hoped this would do.

Red Jeggs stepped out of the crowded rebels toward Garin, over whom he towered. He sent a brief, speculative look toward Ovelia, and she raised her chin in answer.

Red Jeggs smiled widely and clapped a hand on Garin's shoulder. "I will fight beside you, my liege," he said. "You offer a man's challenge, and this man will answer it."

Then, as if the assent had broken some barrier, all in the common room began to name their approval, raising hands and clapping plates and tankards. Red Jeggs inspired them to speak out. Matronly Biaza, whose thick jowls and graying hair hid a devious tactical mind, raised her hand and pledged her support. From the back of the room, Corvus—a scarred veteran from Luether's fall and his most trusted warder—gave a grudgingly optimistic nod. He'd never accepted Garin's personal proclivities—particularly where Alcarin was involved—but he had always respected the prince as a leader. His approval meant a great deal just at the moment, when Garin most needed it.

A chorus of rebels came to Garin to offer congratulations and renew their pledge of fealty and support. More than one joke passed around the common room about this particular summer's life being a shortened one, and Garin laughed along with them. They could do this. They *would* do this.

Garin felt hope bloom once more inside him, where it had spent so long withering. When his uncle had summoned him to Tar Vangr that winter, he'd been near to surrendering to the inevitability of failure. But seeing Ovelia's determination, watching Regel use his magic, and seeing Princess Semana miraculously return from the dead—all these things had planted it once more in him. And now Ovelia would nurture the fledgling growth until it would become a deep-rooted, immovable object.

He smiled at her, even if she could not see it. Like as not, Ovelia had no idea how important she had become to Garin's plan.

At the back, leaning against the far wall, Alcarin glared reproachfully at Garin from across the room. He'd muddled that particular bit of diplomacy quite a bit, but Garin had an idea of how to make right with his squire.

When it was all over, Ovelia padded quietly to his side and whispered in his ear. "Was that wise?" she asked. "Telling them Lan's plan? They are as like to panic as rise to the occasion."

"All respect, Lady Dracaris, but you do not know my people," Garin said. "Perhaps you should get to. I see Red Jeggs eyeing you in particular."

It was true. The big man had barely taken his eyes off Ovelia since they had emerged from the back room, and even a child could tell what that meant. Of course, the unsubtlety would be lost on Ovelia, since she could not see Red Jeggs's fervent gazes.

"I hadn't noticed," she said. "You're walking a dangerous path here, Garin. Can you trust these people to follow you?"

He nodded without hesitation. "I trust every one of them with my life."

The moment stretched until finally, Ovelia nodded. She stepped to his side, and together they watched the gathered rebels move about, talking excitedly, planning and boasting. His speech had reinvigorated them for the task at hand, and they would need every bit of courage and energy. He felt a warm lightness in his chest and could breathe easy for the first time since the previous day.

Ovelia seemed far away, lost in her own thoughts, and Garin knew why.

"You need not fear for yon princess," he said. "She is more than capable, and even then, the Lord of Tears walks by her side. Surely you do not think he will allow harm to befall her. As I trust my people, you can trust yours."

Ovelia returned an unconvinced smile. "I hope you are right."

ACT THREE: DREAMERS

Before the Fall—Palace of Tar Vangr—Spring, 960 Sorcerus Annis

THIS WAS WRONG—ENTIRELY, INCREDIBLY wrong.

Ovelia knew that, but couldn't say it.

The colors arrayed below turned the great hall of the palace into a garden such as Tar Vangr had never seen in her lifetime. Vibrant purples joined with passionate reds, and rich yellows whirled and entwined to enact a scintillating dance of such beauty and wonder that watching it made his head hurt. Rich perfumes rose like the aroma of cut flowers the day after a heavy rain. It put Ovelia in mind of Lenalin's garden—the modest but beautiful patch of land on one of the lower terraces of the palace that Orbrin had set aside for his queen and their daughter.

It was clearly a Luethaar revel as much as a Vangruyr one. The bright colors adorned the men as well as the women, and they danced entirely too closely and vigorously for the palace. 'Twould be a scandal, had not Lenalin laughed and delighted so. They danced amongst tables piled high with food and drink while attendants scurried at the edges of the crowd, catering to their every need. Meanwhile, the musicians pushed themselves harder and harder to pipe out notes at a dangerous pace Ovelia would have thought impossible before her visit to the summerlands.

For all the obvious joy in this room, Ovelia felt only sorrow as she watched from the balcony. She gripped the stone so hard her fingers turned white.

"Do you hate this as much as I?" she asked aloud, seemingly of no one.

Regel the Frostburn appeared at her side—dark, rugged of feature and cold of eye. Ovelia had not known for certain that he was there, but it made sense. Of course he would be watching, just as she was. She regarded him for a moment, then went back to watching the revelry from afar.

"These Ravalis and their summerborn entourage bring strange customs." Regel said as he stood beside her, arms crossed. "I cannot approve of Denes Hall becoming a rainbow of color and passion."

"I cannot imagine why they'd not ask *your* opinion."

Ovelia felt waspish, but the barb hardly seemed to sting Regel. Without a word, he produced a crude wooden figurine—a dove, she thought—and went to work on it with a small carving knife. She'd never been entirely comfortable around him. He was older, for one—a man grown when they had yet been girls—but it was more than that. If pressed, she would claim that it was the stench of death that lingered about his entirely too appealing features. In truth, though, it was because she knew they both wanted the same thing, and that made them rivals.

"Almost finished?" she asked in part about the carving, but only in part.

His knife went *skritch-skritch*. "Why are you wearing a dress?" he asked.

Ovelia made a face. "It's a *gown*—far richer and finer, apparently. This frippery cost several hundred silvers, if you can believe it." She held out the edges for him to scrutinize the thing.

"It looks…well? On you?"

"Ugh." Ovelia plucked at the folds of the cumbersome monstrosity of crimson silk. It was cold and bulky and hadn't even the thinnest protective padding. "My father insisted, as a gesture of good will. The Ravalis demand their women wear these stupid things."

"And you are a Ravalis woman, now?"

They stood in anxious, companionable silence.

Lenalin's wedding day might have proved insufferable, had Ovelia not had Lenalin to watch. As always, the princess had made herself the focus and spirit of the revelry, taking dance after dance with partner after partner. Lenalin moved with grace and vigor, embracing the frenzied dance of the Luethaar as though born to it. The music woke something inside her, and she reveled in the freedom the dance inspired.

As she had for so many winters, Ovelia imagined herself in place of Lenalin's partners. The crazed dancing of Luether complicated the familiar fantasy, but her mind could cut through that. The musicians would take a pause and play something slower—deeper and more powerful. She would lock eyes with Lenalin and no words would be needed. Their hands would touch and they would melt together as they had when they were girls. They would dance together, before everyone but also completely alone, and just for a moment, the world would be perfect.

But of course, Ovelia could not touch Lenalin—especially not on the day of her bonding to Paeter Ravalis. It would never be the same between them. Not after today.

She noticed Lenalin's husband—still a strange word to her—standing at the edge of the floor, watching Lenalin with the same sort of focus Ovelia paid her. Something other than admiration tinged his expression, however: he wore a slight, self-satisfied smile. That, coupled with his confident stance, put Ovelia in mind of a conqueror looking out over a battlefield. The look made her uncomfortable.

"What do you think of him?" she asked.

Regel looked surprised that she even remember he was there, much less spoke to him. "Paeter Ravalis?" He scraped a ream off his carving. "He is a talented warrior and field commander."

"That's not what I mean," Ovelia said. "You see how he gloats over Lena, as if she were his spoils. Is that the sort of man he is?"

Regel looked at her levelly for a moment, then went back to his carving.

Ovelia suppressed a growl of frustration and leaned heavily on the banister.

Lan Ravalis was there as well—a boy more than a man, of perhaps six and ten winters. Laegera Vargaen, the eldest daughter of the Blood, was talking with Lan, though she kept making eyes at Paeter. Her hair had come undone and her dress showed a good stretch of her endowments, but Ovelia could tell that her apparent drunkenness was an act. Seeking to seduce her way into an alliance, perhaps?

Regardless, she saw no threats to Lenalin or potential disruptions of the gathering. She had all the time in Ruin to gaze down and dream of what might have been, if only…

Regel tensed, and Ovelia realized they were no longer alone. She turned just as a man spoke in a slurred voice. "Fancy that. I didn't think anyone was up here."

Garin Ravalis stood at the mouth of the disused servants' stair, his frilly noble shirt unbuttoned to his waist, the image of a Fox emblazoned on his chest glimmering in the ambient light. He was raging drunk, judging from his slurred speech and uneven gait, and the half-empty bottle in his hand. Ovelia wasn't sure he even saw Regel, lurking there in the shadows in his gray cloak. The King's Shadow put a hand to Frostburn's hilt in readiness, but Ovelia touched him on the arm to stay him.

"Your highness." She bowed.

"Ha!" Garin took another drink of his bottle. "You even bow like a man. Marvelous."

"Prince Garin." Regel bowed.

"Ho! Hail, guardsman. I hardly saw you there." The prince swayed up to Regel, caught him by the arm, and leaned on him as he spoke to Ovelia. "I quite seem to have lost my way, Lady Dracaris. Is this the way to the rut-rooms?"

Ovelia flinched at the distasteful term and saw Regel grimacing in the gloom. Revels at the palace incorporated a number of rooms where attendants—male and female and anywhere between—cared for the highborn Blood heirs and their guests in need of a rest from the more formal revel, or whose interests fell on a more intimate encounter. Sex was one diversion such rooms offered, but leave it to the summerborn to think of the tradition in such terms.

"No, your highness," she said. "This is the balcony. We warders watch from above, for your safety and that of the other guests."

"Oh." Garin frowned. "In that case, would you ward me a moment? I need a moment away from the glittering horde." He leaned heavily on the stone banister with a thick sigh. "I find I like this cold city. You appear stiff and proper, but you're much more...open as regards society. We Luethaar might dance faster and shout louder, but we have more hesitations."

"Guardsman, if you might leave us?" Ovelia said.

"Nay—nay!" Garin pawed at Regel's arm. "Stay a while, my goodsyr. I find your face appealing, in a dark and terrifying way." He eyed Ovelia pointedly. "He shall ward me, while you take a moment."

"As..." Regel paused. "As you wish, your highness."

He looked to Ovelia for a cue, and despite the odious day, she had to smile at the sheer terror on his face. She did not often see Regel the Frostburn— he whose sword could rend lightning, 'twas said—made so uncomfortable. She guessed Garin would not make a fool of himself and try anything with Regel, but even so the King's Shadow would keep it private. Secrets were his specialty, after all.

And the message Garin was sending Ovelia—drunk as he was—seemed clear enough. He understood her need to be alone, and perhaps steal a moment with Lenalin if she could.

"I shall take my leave of you, then." Ovelia pushed off the banister and headed for the stairs.

"Wonderful, yes—yes." Garin smiled woozily. As she walked away, Ovelia heard him engage Regel with a riddle of some sort. "But first, tell me this: what's missing from this revel?"

"My lord?"

"Don't be coy, goodsyr. Give it a try. Think of the *colors*."

Their voices faded as Ovelia made her way down the stairs, toward the main hall where the dancing consumed most of the available space. It felt warm and cramped down here, the atmosphere stifling for one who had not imbibed as much as the other revelers.

Colors... She found herself wondering as to the second part of Garin's riddle.

All the expected colors were here—warm reds, deep purples, shining yellows, majestic blues—all but one: green. Many of the present Bloods should have worn green but did not. This confused her for a moment, but she remembered her heraldry and it began to make sense. As a girl, she'd gone over the writs of the Bloods in great detail, memorizing the markings and sigils of the powerful in Tar Vangr. Her father Norlest might have given her studies a wide berth, but King Orbrin had demanded nothing less than perfection in his only daughter's companion. She knew all the Blood colors, crests, and words by heart. And here at the revel, several Bloods wore the improper heraldry, trying specifically to avoid green.

The most glaring lack of green came from Blood Vargaen. "Blood and Strength" were their words, and the colors red and green represented them respectively. As first heir, Laegera wore a red gown, and she had an amber pin in her hair—whenever she'd seen her before, Ovelia had noticed that she favored emeralds. A purposeful lack of green. Now that she thought on it, she'd observed a disturbance earlier in the evening at the gates that fit her emerging theory. The scholarly Blood Forthuse had sent its eldest and brightest, and she'd watched as the guards made some sort of objection to their white and green attire. Finally, the Forthuse heirs had left the gathering in a huff. Again, the revel did not tolerate green. The only exception seemed to be Blood Dracaris itself, for which red and green were ancestral colors. Norlest, standing beside Orbrin on the dais, wore a red surcoat and a green sash. Ovelia's gown was crimson, but she wore a green sash as well to connect with her ancestry. Perhaps that was why she'd gathered some odd looks, particularly from the Ravalis retinue. Lan especially had glared at her, which at the time she'd attributed to his unreasoning hatred of all things female. The Ravalis hated green. When she and Lenalin had visited Luether, Ovelia realized that she'd not seen a single scrap of green other than what they had brought.

Only then did she understand. Green was the color of the Ravalis's rival Vultara, the Blood that had betrayed Luether centuries ago and almost destroyed the mage-city before it even arose. They were the reason that no woman would ever rule over a man in Luether. And green must be a reminder of that.

Was that what Garin had meant, with his riddle? That they should look to the missing, even if it is uncomfortable?

And with that thought, Ovelia realized Paeter was gone.

Lenalin's husband had vanished from his own bonding revel, and that made her skin begin to itch all over. Lan had disappeared as well, along with Laegra Vargaen.

She shoved her way awkwardly through the hall, wishing she had Regel's grasp of subtlety. The guards at the front door seemed lax, as though they had not moved in some time—the prince had not passed them by, or they would have jerked to attention. King Cassian had not interrupted his story, so Paeter's departure must not have caused a disturbance. Paeter must have slipped away deeper into the palace—through the doors toward what Garin had called the "rut-rooms." Even as she thought so, the doors opened and a pair of beautiful lads came striding out, looking rather shaken. An encounter with Prince Paeter would do that, Ovelia suspected—he had that sort of effect upon men and women both.

She headed that way, but a hush abruptly fell on the crowd. She saw Regel near the edge of the dance floor, obviously angling for the same corridor she moved toward. Lenalin had stopped him with a hand on his wrist, and Ovelia watched Regel shake her off before recognizing her. They stood, staring at one another, for a moment that seemed to stretch. Ovelia could feel the shocked silence in the room like an oppressive weight. Ovelia started toward them, slipping between revelers, her heart racing.

"Always so tense!" Lenalin cradled her own wrist, then laughed loudly.

"Princess?" Regel looked confused and frightened. "What—?"

"Learn to relax, Regel." She held out a hand and smiled at him with the earnestness that comes from too much drink. "Come. Dance with me, my lord."

What was she thinking? She had approached him before everyone. The other nobles were staring at them, and a cold shock of fear swept through Ovelia. Not here—not on her bonding day—not before a hundred witnesses. She could hear whispers and quiet speculation as she slipped through the crowd. She was almost there—almost in time to save them from disaster.

"Your highness." Averting his eyes, Regel bowed but pointedly did not take her hand. "I think her highness has confused this simple soldier for another. Please, pass me by." Then, in a whisper so that only she would hear, he mouthed the word: "*Please.*"

Ovelia could see the shuddering tension in Lenalin's stance, and sudden anger radiated from her at his dismissal. Could she have drunk away her inhibitions such that she risked so much by approaching him openly, before so many people? Even the royal table had begun to watch: Cassian in confusion, Demetrus with analytical curiosity, and Orbrin with grave focus. All eyes fell on the princess, waiting on her decision. Lenalin drew in a breath to speak.

Then Ovelia was there, stepping between them with her hand on the hilt of her sword. She coiled herself into a fighting stance. "Is this man troubling you, highness?"

Outwardly, Regel shrank away as though cowed, but Ovelia could see his relief.

"Ah ha!" The break in the moment returned Lenalin's natural charm. She smiled broadly. "Methinks summerwine is truly wonderful. Another bowl!"

The princess's joviality diffused the tension in the chamber, and most of the listening nobles laughed behind their hands. Lenalin hurried back toward the floor and took a new partner, and most of the attention followed her. A few nobles kept eyeing Regel suspiciously—already planning their rumors, no doubt—but Ovelia glared them down, one and all. All the while, she kept one hand on Regel's strong forearm, guiding him subtly away from the dance floor.

Finally, when they were mostly alone, Ovelia turned her full attention upon him. The two of them had never passed well in each other's company, but they had learned long ago that they could at least tolerate each other. They both wanted the same thing, after all, and that was to protect Lenalin. Just at the moment, though, he had to find a way to get away from her, and he thought he saw an opportunity.

"What are you doing?" Ovelia asked, her words accusatory. "It's her *bonding* day!"

Regel stepped toward the wall, and she turned to track him. "She approached me," he said.

"You think that matters to the Ravalis?" Ovelia's temper flared. "You cannot touch her. You cannot have her. You cannot even *look* at her. You know this! And now—now you're endangering her!"

Regel took a sudden step toward Ovelia, and her training kicked in, making her step back into a fighting stance. He did not attack with any weapon, however—only words. "As though you are not."

Ovelia glared at him. "I'm not—"

At just that moment, a server opened the door to the hall and ran full into Ovelia. If Regel hadn't made her turn, she would have seen him, and if he hadn't provoked her to step back at the right instant, he would have avoided her. As it passed, the attendant's tray full of emptied platters and half-full tankards fell all over Ovelia and the servant both, and they staggered in a tangle of limbs and curses. The surrounding nobles turned to the commotion and burst into laughter.

Face going beet red, Ovelia flicked away wine from her sopping dress and pawed at the sticky cream in her hair. She rounded angrily on Regel, but he was gone. Of course.

The server, mortified, attempted to brush the worst of it from Ovelia. "My lady, I'm so sorry—"

"Nevermind that," she said. "Did you see the prince? Where did he go? Which room?"

"Chandlis," he said. "But the prince said he wasn't to be disturb—"

Ovelia pushed past him and out of the hall, leaving the jeers of the nobility behind.

The wide hallway led to a number of rooms of various functions, each named after a particular famous ruler of Tar Vangr, much like the great hall took its name from Queen Denes, first of the Denerre line and the founder of the city. She passed Daritin, a sitting room full of thick white pillows and lacy frippery to honor the man of leisure whose name it bore, as well as the laconically-named kitchens of Duldurin, a king known more for his famous appetites than any conquests or victories. She came upon the chambers of Aritana, the most recent chamber named, which took inspiration from King Orbrin's royal mother—Lenalin's greatmother. Despite her distaste toward men, Aritana had borne children to perpetuate the line—ironically, two healthy children who turned out to be boys—but in her later winters, she only kept the company of women. As such, it was a chamber that did not allow men inside for any reason. That chamber featured prominently in Ovelia's dreams, but she had never been inside.

Finally she came to Chandlis, named for a king of Tar Vangr known for his indulgences in both male and female company. It was one of the few chambers in the palace that was reserved exclusively for sex, patronized by the king and many of his favored courtiers. Paeter's purpose in leaving the hall and coming here made Ovelia feel warm and angry all over. She understood little of the institution Luethaar called "marriage," but she had listened to enough of the vows exchanged to know that it expected the participants to hold lover's fidelity to one another.

The door was closed and locked, and he could not get in without causing a commotion. Instead, he headed straight for the nearest entrance to the secret tunnels, in the hall of Denerre's Tree. The antechamber was amongst the oldest parts of the palace, endowed with the sacredness that comes from long history and shared experience. Hidden behind a tapestry that muffled sound and blocked all sight, it offered a place for heirs of Denerre to sit in contemplation in the presence of their ancestors. Upon the wall spread a silvery tree connecting the scripted names of the Blood of Winter, from Denes to Lenalin—empty space to the right of her name would host her children, and their children thereafter.

Ovelia nodded to the tree and its magic flickered in reply, drawn to her body's warmth. She touched one of the names—Chandlis—and a small passage opened below the tree, leading into the space between the walls of the prince's borrowed chamber. Different names could be pressed to lead to different rooms, but that was the one he required just then. She crawled through and slipped between the walls to a pair of spyholes cut at waist height into the Chandlis chamber. The palace boasted countless such observation mechanisms, dating from the reign of the notoriously paranoid King Durus Denerre. Ovelia peered through, and gritted her teeth at what she beheld.

Paeter Ravalis stood in the center of the room, shirtless with his breeches pulled to his knees and a look of supreme pride on his face. The jackal inked on his bare chest sparkled and seemed to laugh in the candlelight. Laegra Vargaen knelt before him, her gown pulled open to the waist, her head buried in his crotch. With the fingers of one big hand woven through her golden curls, Paeter guided her at her work, looking quite pleased with himself. Moans and smacking sounds emerged from the heiress, and her hands grasped his backside for leverage.

"You see?" Paeter asked—not to Laegra, but to someone Ovelia couldn't see. "It's simple. What you want, make her provide. What other purpose does a woman serve, but to please a man?"

He grasped Laegra's head hard and pulled her in sharply. She made a sharp sound of surprise, gagging on him, but then Paeter pulled out of her mouth and let her breathe. He stroked himself idly, while she panted for breath and looked up at him dazedly. She smiled. "You are pleased, my lord of Summer?"

He ignored her. "Well, brother?" Paeter asked. "Strike."

Ovelia watched with growing anger as Lan appeared, stripped to the waist like his older brother, his hands hesitant on the laces of his breeches. He had only an incomplete tattoo on his own chest—a bear, it would be, when the Ravalis inkers completed it on his day of majority. The Bear of Luether was yet a cub. The tattoo reminded her unsettlingly of the dragon inked on her back, but that mark she'd got for love, not out of devotion to a backward city and its disgusting ways.

"Brother—" Lan trailed off. Based on his uncertain expression and the nervous tension in his body, Ovelia thought he might never have been with a woman before. Good. "I am not…"

Paeter looked to the half-naked woman on the floor. He said nothing, but the command he gave her was clear.

"Let me be your bride for the eve, my lord," Laegra said, the words barely her own. She rose up on her knees, pushed out her chest, and spread her arms wide to Lan. "Give me the honor of your love."

Lan looked at first confused, then his face shifted into a look of smug superiority much like his brother's, albeit tempered with a touch of impatience. "My love? My cock, you mean."

He strode toward her and cupped her chin with his hand. The suddenness of his movement shocked her, and she sat up straight and taut as though he held a knife to her face. Thoughtfully, Lan ran his thumb over her lips while his other hand worked at his laces. His breeches were straining now, as though the look of her fear excited him more than her body. Laegra composed herself with an effort, though Ovelia could see the tension linger in her back and her trembling hands. It disgusted her and yet.

And *yet*.

Then Lan freed himself and shoved into Laegra's mouth with enough force to make her gag. Reflexively, she pulled away, but he grasped her head in both hands and held her fast. She strained, slapping at him as though he held her underwater.

"Not so much, brother," Paeter said. "Slowly. Don't spend yourself so—"

Lan pulled back, then shoved again just as hard. Over and over he did so, wrenching choking sounds from Laegra as he did. Her hands curled into fists, then splayed out into trembling fans. She could not breathe. Ovelia found she could not breathe either. She felt warm and wet and itchy.

What was this in her that responded to such barbarism?

"Enough!" Paeter snapped. "Lan!"

Finally Lan drew himself out, letting Laegra slump panting back onto the soft rug. He stood over her, one hand on his engorged blade, a look of anger on his face. He looked over at Paeter, who was watching quietly, his expression unreadable. Something passed between the brothers, and both nodded.

"My lords." Laegra wiped her mouth and crossed her arms over her bare chest. She looked, in that moment, much smaller and more vulnerable than she ever had. "I am honored, but I—"

Paeter crossed to her and ran his fingers along her cheek, far gentler than his brother had. "I am sorry, beautiful one," he said. "My brother is coarse and untrained. Do not take it amiss."

He knelt beside her, one knee bending over her as in an embrace, and kissed her soundly. Laegra softened under his touch, reassured and drawn to him, and wrapped her arms around him as well. His hands dipped down her body to the inside of her thighs.

Finally she broke the kiss and looked at him uncertainly. "My lord, the lover's kiss is one thing, but that—" she said. "You are my lady's husband. I cannot—"

"I am your prince, and one day your king." Paeter's embrace grew tighter. He hiked up the skirts of her dress. "Will you bow before your king?"

Trembling, Laegra nodded. She gasped as Paeter thrust into her, and they worked in concert. Lan stepped around behind her, stroking himself to a purpose.

Ovelia drew away. She had seen more than enough.

The crawlspace closed behind Ovelia as she climbed back into the ancestral antechamber. Whether she was making her way back to Denes's Hall to denounce the Ravalis brothers before the assembly or into the Chandlis chamber to cut both their throats, she couldn't quite say. She felt like a passenger in her own body, born along on the winds of rage and injustice.

She felt numb and disgusted, and deep inside her, a fire brewed—a longing that had gone unsatisfied. She'd been with men before, but never quite like *that*. She'd not even thought such a thing possible. Ovelia found herself sitting back against the wall beneath the glimmering tree of names, sweating and trying to slow her raging heart. She wanted…By the Fire, what was happening to her?

Only when the darkness moved did he realize she was not alone in the alcove. In the soft silver light of the runes, she could make out a dark shape that she'd not seen before. "Shadow?" she asked.

"Yes, Tall Sister." The leaves of the tree of Denerre brightened, illumining Regel's face beneath his cowl. His body hid under the folds of his cloak, seemingly made of the night. "I know what you saw."

"You—" She swallowed. Her throat felt so parched. Her body ached. "You do?"

"I can guess."

He knelt down before her, and she could see her sweaty face reflected in his dark eyes. The spreading radiance made Ovelia's fiery hair a ruddy flame and her hazel eyes became golden coals.

"This won't part them," she said. "Regel. You'll only make it worse if you speak of it."

Without a word, he stepped away from her toward the corridor. She scrambled to her feet and caught his arm, but he fought her. What would he do? What madness?

She took hold of his shoulders and thrust her face into his. "She already knows!"

Ovelia's assertion stopped Regel cold. He turned back to her, his face confused. She looked past him and behind, then took his hand and drew him deeper into the lineage alcove. The wintry tree of the Blood of Denerre gleamed faintly on the wall, its luminescence fading without being touched. They stood alone in the dark, breathing shallowly and in time. She leaned against him, shoulders heaving.

It was ridiculous. The server had made a mess of her gown, her face, and her hair. She looked afright but she felt beautiful. Powerful. This was wrong but *right*.

"Lena knows about Paeter," Ovelia said into his chest. "This isn't the first time. He's rutted a dozen women since they were betrothed—at least, that we know about. Not one of them has made a bit of difference." Her face darkened. "Infidelity is hardly a match for politics."

He felt wiry and strong, his muscles flexed and hard as stone. Ovelia had rarely touched the king's shadow, let alone been this close to him. In truth, she'd never wanted to be, but now—after what she had seen…His darkness called out to the darkness she had only just discovered inside herself.

"But…" Regel shook with obvious rage.

She pulled away, holding him against the wall so he couldn't leave. "Regel, you need to stop," Ovelia said. "Lena is married to Paeter. It's over. Let her go."

She clenched her finger into the muscles of his shoulders. So hard. Pitiless.

"You told her," Regel said. "About the others."

"Yes." Ovelia narrowed her eyes. "The first. The second. All of them. She ignored me." Her fingers clenched so tightly she might have drawn blood if not for his thick leathers. "It's over. She's not coming back. She's not—" A sob rose from the depths of her guts, choking off her words. She pressed herself against him, and he raised his arms awkwardly around her.

Ovelia realized that she wasn't trying to convince *him*.

At that moment a pair of laughing nobles passed in the corridor. Regel and Ovelia both averted their eyes, though the tapestry hid them quite well. Ovelia looked up at Regel's angular face and read in his features the same impotent feeling that gripped her. They were both of them trapped—both of them screaming for escape. His love for Lenalin had been obvious to Ovelia from the moment they three had met, and it burned just as brightly this night, if not hotter. She wondered if he could hear her heart breaking, just as his did. For the first time, she saw beneath the intimidating armor he never took off, and found within a damaged soul not unlike her own. Her body moved against his, and she did not stop it. Did not even try. He did not seem to mind.

"You still love her," he said.

"So—" Ovelia shivered as she rubbed against him. "So do you."

He closed his eyes. "Yes," he said, whether in reply to her words or her actions, she did not know.

Her fingers found their way to the buckles of his hauberk, and he did nothing to stop her. He should have. Pushed her away—left it all alone. His icy dark eyes remained shut, his mouth a tight line. She drew open his breastplate and pressed her smeared face against his chest, kissing the soft hairs slick against his skin. He had so many scars, and she wanted to touch them all. She slipped her hand into his trousers, and his blade pressed hard against her hand. "Yes?" she asked, wrapping her fingers around it.

"Yes," he said. "*Yes.*"

A deep, animal sound rose through Ovelia's throat, starting as a rumble but becoming a cry. All her love-sick frustration bubbled up inside her and burst forth in a rush of angry desire. She caught Regel's face, one hand on either side of his head, and kissed his lips. Hard. It was not an amazing kiss. Neither of them had much practice with such things, but they made up for it with ardor.

He tensed, and for a heartbeat, she thought that might stop him. That he would awaken from whatever stupor she'd put him in, push her away, and flee, leaving them both alone and miserable.

Then he put his hands around her head and held her to him, crushing them both against the wall. The lights of the Denerre lineage spread outward from Regel's hands and Ovelia's head, naming ancestors who had walked these halls for hundreds of winters.

Ovelia swept Regel's leg out from under him and used her superior strength to push him down to the floor, where she straddled him. She tore open his clothes and hiked up her dress around her waist—at least this frippery was good for something. She kissed him again, cupping his blade with her left hand as she did. His mouth was cold but inviting, his cock burning between her fingers as she stroked it. He was no longer the shadow of the Winter King—no longer death that drew breath—but a *man*. A man in pain and needing heat and passion and *sex*. Just as she needed it.

Then it happened. He glanced up at the wall and saw the name there. It slipped from his lips.

"Lenalin," Regel said.

Ovelia considered him carefully, poised over him like a hunting animal. He throbbed painfully in her hand. Uncertainty boiled up inside her too, and something told her to run. That this was not her. That he did not want to rut *her*. That doing this would kill her. Perhaps not today—but someday.

"We should not do this," Regel said. "Ovelia, I—I love Lenalin. So do you."

She knew how to assuage the darkness and to find some solace in a world falling to Ruin.

"No." She stopped his lips with a kiss. "Not her." She kissed him again. "*Her*."

He furrowed his brow. "I don't—"

"Do not love *me*." She put her fingers to his lips. "Love *her*."

Finally, she saw understanding on his face. He closed his eyes. "Lenalin," he whispered.

She guided him in line, then slid onto him with a shiver and a sigh. She began to move, slowly but with power. Uncertainty and hesitation fled. She squeezed him and whispered of need and desire, and even to her own ears she did not sound like herself. There in the dark, with their hearts racing, she became another to him and to herself. She closed her eyes and pictured not herself, but Lenalin.

"Regel," she said, increasing her crescendo. "My shadow."

"Lenalin," he said, the world thundering around him. "My light."

There was pain and there was pleasure and there was fire.

When it had ended, they embraced and wept together in that darkened chamber, while the impassive heirs of Denerre watched from the shadows.

THIRTEEN

Luether

Flames.

In her dream, she stands before a thin wall she cannot see that separates her from roaring flames she cannot feel. She is aware of their heat but it does not touch her. She can see them, but they seem impossibly far away. And yet they become no less dangerous for their distance.

She is about to turn and go when she hears the voice. Somewhere in the depths of the world of fire, behind the invisible barrier, a scream emerges. She looks back and sees a feminine shape thrashing among the flames. The woman in the fire moans and cries out in agony, unable to escape her awful fate.

In her dream, she knows the woman in the fire, but she cannot remember her name.

She does not think—she only acts. She lunges against the wall, hands outstretched to break it.

The barrier she cannot see dissolves under her touch, and the flames wash over her. Her flesh scalds and flakes away, but she pushes through, desperately reaching for the woman she saw in the fire. Pain such as she has never imagined rips through her, but she must...

There is no one. She is alone. She has failed.

And then she is the one screaming.

~

OVELIA AWOKE IN THE dim light of dawn, with the city's smoky light streaming through the crack in the boarded-over window. Where the rays touched her skin, she saw faint steam rising into the air, which she at first took for a lingering remnant of her dream. After all, she could see so little in her shadowy world, and in her dreams all became vivid and clear. The fire had come to her again, pulsing and raging just beyond her touch, only to burst free and devour her. Only when her skin began to prickle in the heat did she realize it was genuine, and she shifted into the shade to escape the burning ray.

Marked by his familiar musk, Red Jeggs shifted where he lay curled beside her, his massive body trapping her against the wall. When Ovelia moved, he murmured and curled his muscular arms tighter around her. For all his bravado, he grew extremely vulnerable when he slept, not unlike a child finally given permission to stop pretending to be a man grown. He rutted a bit like a boy as well, strong and enthusiastic but only middling in terms of skill. Perhaps he expected Ovelia to teach him better technique, just as he taught her grappling, or perhaps he simply expected her to love the sex regardless. Either way, he offered a fine diversion, and she'd all but forgotten the cravings for sweetsoul thus far.

She blew out a sigh and lay back against Red Jeggs's arm. After ten days in Luether, she felt restless, and she could not quite leave behind the feeling that they were all doomed.

Summer Lives was not in a bad place. Considering their scant numbers and general lack of discipline, the rebels had achieved a great deal. Garin had worked hard for twenty summers to forge alliances, gather key information about Pervast's operations, chart the routes of supply caravans and the schedules of ships, and generally oppose the usurpers at every turn. And they had done so, remarkably, through little enough violence, though Ovelia had seen personally that they were suitably equipped for combat. Bringing Garin out of his void that first day had made a significant difference: he had emerged from his ruined laboratory with renewed energy, practically leaping with each step, and immediately seized full, competent control of his people.

As she'd feared, however, the old ways proved insufficient. She heard the murmured discontent growing: the rebels' increasing unease with the announcement of Tar Vangr's impending invasion, the disagreements that boiled over into arguments too easily, the calls to more decisive action. As she had predicted, Garin should not have revealed the truth of their situation so quickly. He should have worked them up to it, achieved a few victories before he told them. The task had changed, and Garin needed to prove himself anew. She had told him that more than once, but he always replied with that none-too-serious laugh of his to dismiss her concerns. "Have no fear," he would say. "I've a plan."

Truth, perhaps, but his plan could not keep the rebels content. Even as they lay the groundwork for their coup, the rebels ached to launch an offensive—to secure a victory they could measure in blood. At first, Garin had been content to brush off their complaints and urgings to strike, but she could see it wear on him. His high-minded ideals of seizing the city without bloodshed had ceased to placate them. They demanded violent action, and Ovelia knew Garin would have to grant it to them.

"Dragon Daughter," Red Jeggs rumbled.

About the only advice Garin had followed was to hide her true identity, and even that had raised questions over the last days. Who was this blind woman who fought so well, whose counsel Garin trusted? More than once Ovelia had caught Neblen—Summer Lives's best thief—riffling through her things, ostensibly looking for valuables. A time was coming when she could no longer conceal herself, and how would the rebels react to the infamous Bloodbreaker revealed amongst them? And how would her presence match Garin's stated goal of peace?

She rose and fought off Red Jeggs's hands when he tried to haul her back into the bed. The big man mumbled his way into wakefulness as she shook out her breeches.

"The Dragon is up early," Jeggs said, his voice low and suggestive. "And so is mine."

"Good for you." Ovelia had grown adept at dressing herself without sight, so long as she had a chance to place her clothes somewhere near to hand. Red Jeggs's tendency to hurl garments around the chamber in his haste to get to bed often disrupted such plans, however. One of a handful of reasons she'd taken him to her bed only twice. Thrice, now, counting last night.

"Good for you, too." He came up behind her and hugged her with his big arms, and she felt his ardor prodding warmly against her lower back. "If you're not ready for a proper rut, you could work that magic you did last night with your mouth? Summer wenches can't do half what you can." He shivered at the memory.

His bashfulness despite his ostensible confidence was another reason. He probably thought it charming, but she mostly found it tiresome. *If you want me to suck your cock,* she thought. *Just say so.*

"Perhaps later." Ovelia broke his grip using a slip he had taught her and reclaimed her shirt where she'd hung it on the chair. "The sun's already up. Garin should be starting his briefing soon."

"Oh, how *exciting.*" Ovelia heard the bed creak and knew Red Jeggs had sprawled across it. "Not half as exciting as what's happening over *here,* though. Come, Dragon Daughter, so I can show you."

She saw no reason to respond, so she focused instead on buttoning her shirt.

Red Jeggs made a petulant little noise, halfway between clearing his throat and a sigh. "I can watch at least," he said. "For a woman of forty summers, you have a burning body. And that dragon…"

He'd meant it as a compliment, but it hardly sounded like one. More of an attempt to get her back into bed, like a petulant squire offering false praise to a master for a pat on the head.

Why had Ovelia let this go on as long as she had? Perhaps because she had so few friends here, and Garin had sought her counsel less and less. And at least training with Red Jeggs and rutting him by night gave her something to take her mind off Garin's struggles.

"Are you coming?" Then, when Jeggs chuckled, Ovelia amended: "To Garin's morning brief."

He made some sort of gesture, which of course she couldn't see, then yawned loudly. "I can sleep just as well here," he said. "Even better, if I had company—"

Ovelia suppressed the urge to snap at him. "Stay, then," she said. "I'll return afterward, unless Garin has some new task for me."

"What is about him that inspires you so?" Red Jeggs asked. "You're not from Luether—I know that much. And it isn't his body that draws you, or you're in for a rotten disappointment. So what is it?"

She looked back at him over her shoulder. "Not everything is rutting and blood, Red Jeggs," she said. "One day perhaps you'll understand."

"Doubt that," the man said under his breath. Likely, he hoped Ovelia wouldn't hear.

She dressed, affixed her swordbelt with Draca's soothing weight, then paused. A familiar scent wafted up to her nostrils, and she looked back toward Red Jeggs. The big man stooped naked next to a table, where he'd set out tankards of fresh goat's milk and was busy stirring some sort of powder into one of them.

"What," she said. "What is that?"

"Sweetsoul," he said. "Drink a little every morning. Care for a taste?"

Ovelia clenched her fists to keep from shouting at him, or perhaps pleading, or perhaps lunging across the room to seize the powder and devour it. Instead, without a word, she took her leave of that sweaty room. Red Jeggs didn't know it, but Ovelia privately hoped this would be the last time. Until she'd smelled the sweetsoul, she'd been sure it would be. But her body longed for it. Would do anything to have it.

When Ovelia reached the common room, she immediately felt something was amiss. The Long Dawn seemed slower than usual, with only half a dozen patrons, none of whom she recognized. She saw no sign of Garin or Alcarin. Ovelia felt her temper rise.

She found Biaza near the bar, where the woman was cleaning tankards. "Where's Garin?"

Biaza fairly radiated dislike, the contempt clear in her clipped sigh and curt words. "Gone," she said. "Hours gone. Thought they'd wake you, but perhaps—" She nodded down the hall toward Red Jeggs's room. "Perhaps you was a bit distracted."

"What?" Ovelia ignored the condescension about Red Jeggs. "What do you mean, *gone?*"

~

"I can't believe you didn't bring that woman," Alcarin said.

"I know," Garin said. "It's so stupidly dangerous, but that's why you love me, right?"

Alcarin gave him a sour look, then shook his head and smiled impishly. "I do appreciate having a chance to talk to you myself," he said. "It seems like she's been attached to you ever since Tar Vangr, like a…third arm. Like you'd grown a woman of a sudden."

"Amusing as that image is," Garin said, "is that a hint of jealousy I hear, Squire?"

"Not at all, Master." Alcarin snuggled closer to him and their noses touched. "Only appreciation."

Garin smiled widely.

This day, the mechanical carriage carried them to the Mines of Tuerine, where Garin would make his next appeal to the hearts of the Luethaar. The people had known nothing but oppression so long that a show of compassion would flare brightly into what Garin hoped would become a raging blaze. After he liberated the Mines, of course.

"You've never been to Tuerine, have you?" Garin asked.

Alcarin shook his head. "Anything I should know?"

Garin shrugged. "Tuerine was one of the first mines constructed after the Return—its wealth made Luether strong in those early centuries," he said. "Luether sent its criminals to work alongside heroic excavators and the strongest of the strong. Ten thousand free men working alongside as many slaves, who could earn their freedom through their own sweat." He sighed. "You should have seen it, Allie—cart after cart floating up, all of them sparkling with harvested minerals. Like we discovered treasure just lying on the ground and just took it."

"The mine remained open for a thousand summers?" Alcarin asked. "It never ran dry?"

Garin shook his head. "They kept finding new veins of minerals," he said. "It became a…*tradition*, as much Luether as the mage-city itself. Those who acquitted themselves best found positions of honor in the city. One of the great Bloods—the Duldur—rose to power in just that fashion. My uncle never approved, but some of my earliest friends carried that blood—good men and handsome."

"It sounds wonderful." Alcarin scrunched up his nose. "Not now, though."

Garin nodded grimly. "After Ruin fell upon Luether, everything changed," he said. "Pervast proved a canny ruler, which no one expected. The long siege had complicated the city's mining operations, but once Pervast controlled Luether, he opened the Mine back up with his people. He understood immediately that to control Luether, he needed to wrest the economic reins from the great Bloods of the city, and he got right to it."

"But how?" Alcarin asked. "You spoke of thousands of workers. They did not rise up and fight?"

"They resisted at first, but Pervast was crafty," Garin said. "Most of the foremen had died in the initial assault, and he replaced the rest with Children. The workers he gave immediate freedom, regardless of how many summers they had yet to work, and he treated them better than the other people of Luether. Not a single execution. At first, they received it as a blessing, but over the summers he ground down their wages and rights, provoking them to rash actions against the establishment. Pervast's minions punished any transgression with harsher measures, making sure the workers knew the responsibility for such crackdowns lay upon their foolish fellows who had overreached what they had earned. In time, even the most concerted opposition efforts had ended, and the miners shuffled along in helpless obedience."

Alcarin nodded. "I always wondered why Pervast remained in power so long."

Garin blew out a sigh. "I've heard nothing from the Mines since I left for Tar Vangr," he said. "None of the agents we sent have returned."

"So you don't know what we'll find." Alcarin reached into his coat. "Good thing I brought this."

The orb in his hand pulsed gently with inner thaumaturgy, a slowly churning soup of gemstones and shards of metal bound within a thin crystalline lattice. The cunning craftsmanship took hours of work and no small amount of skill, particularly considering the dangers of such a device. Fox's Maelstrom, Alcarin had named it, and Garin wished he had never invented the devilish thing.

"No." Garin immediately put his hand over the grenade in Alcarin's hand. He'd done so suddenly, tense, but then he relaxed. "No," he said more gently. "We haven't come to fight. I would settle this with words before weapons."

"Diplomacy." With a contemptuous roll of his eyes, Alcarin put the grenade back in his coat. "As though these barbarians even understand such things."

"And your alternative is to kill everyone in the room, dead as you can?" Garin asked. "How did you even come by that monstrous thing? I thought I had sealed them all up."

"The Maelstrom?" Alcarin patted his coat pocket. "You keep secrets from me, master, but not as well as you think." He drew his caster. "One of these days, your optimism will see you in mortal peril."

"We'll see," Garin said. "I hope you're wrong."

"So do I." Alcarin checked his caster, making it hum quietly at full charge. "But I'll plan for *you* being wrong."

"Stirring." Garin gave him a soft round of mocking applause. "Truly. I felt my heart lurch."

Alcarin returned a disapproving grimace. "It's still another hour until we arrive," he said, fingering the caster. "Plenty of time for all manner of accidents to befall."

Garin reached out, took the weapon, and set it aside. His and Alcarin's eyes met and Garin moved into his squire's arms. "Let's make it a pleasant accident, shall we?"

Alcarin smiled for the first time since they had returned to Luether. "There's my master."

Their lips met.

FOURTEEN

THE CARRIAGE LET THEM off outside a ramshackle dig site studded with half a dozen broken-down lean-tos and a few hunks of corroded machinery. The winds that blew sediment into the air ranged from gentle breezes to gusts that could strip the flesh from human bones. A deep, funnel-shaped pit tore down into the ground, ringed with a narrow, steep path like a spiral staircase. The sun had mostly set, but a hot wind swept through and scoured dust from the bald earth. Not a single person was in sight, giving the place a profound sense of abandonment. This had ceased to be a place where men could live and work.

Girded and masked against the dust, Garin leaped out first, and Alcarin followed with his caster ready. What he saw made his smile evaporate as surely as a pool of Ruin's bile under the rays of the rising sun.

"Silver Fire," Garin said as he climbed down from the carriage. "I knew it was bad, but…"

He kicked a rock skittering through the barren land. He peered up at the crumbling stone hulks at the edge of the bowl that held the primary mineshaft, baking in the sun, and remembered the bright pennants flying over towers to mark the progress of that day's work.

Garin closed his fists tight. "This ends today," he said.

"If all goes well, you mean," Alcarin said.

Garin had to smile a little at that. Summer Lives had spent decades planting allies within the Mines, but with Lan gathering his forces, they had no more time to wait for their seeds to grow. It was time to reap what they had sown, and hope the yield would be enough. He had confidence, even if his advisors did not. Alcarin's doubts kept him grounded, even if he meant to disprove them this day.

They stepped amongst the stones and dust, searching in vain for the contact who was to have waited for them. The place seemed deserted, and Garin did not like the odor that wafted up from the pit along with the black smoke. The smell was acrid, like sulfur and other mining chemicals, but it also carried the stench of blood with it. From his disgusted expression, Alcarin smelled it too.

"We should make haste," Garin said.

Alcarin nodded grimly. "Assuming anyone remains to be saved."

Garin became aware of someone watching, and he had only just begun to reach for his belt pouch when a gangly form shook itself free of dust and

152

trash to rise before them. Alcarin got his caster up, and the creature hissed in warning and slithered back. Its bloodshot yellow eyes resembled those of a frightened dog. "Who?" it demanded, in a voice like that of a serpent.

"Hold." Garin pushed Alcarin's caster down with his arm and addressed the dust-covered urchin. "My squire is unfamiliar with the ways of Tuerine. Forgive his rashness." He pulled open his shirt to show the animal emblazoned on his chest.

"The mark!" The creature narrowed its eyes at his tattoo, then gasped. "The Fox! The Fox."

"That he is." Alcarin's voice and body language were wary. "And what are you?"

"Dust. Shadow." The creature shook itself, and enough dust fell free to give Garin a sense of her identity. She was a small woman, painfully thin from malnutrition, dressed in filthy rags, and all but hairless. Her legs and arms bent oddly, and she was missing at least two fingers and three toes. Her eyes were yellow, and Garin suspected sickness was the cause. "Dustling."

Garin reached out, and the woman flinched away. "Pass well," he said. "What is your name?"

The dustling looked confused, as though no one had asked her such a thing in living memory. She seemed to think about it for a moment. "Lis," she said uncertainly. Then, with more confidence: "Lis."

"Lis, then—a good name." Garin touched her hand, and the woman smiled, delighted. "I have come to fulfill a pact made long ago," he said. "Take me to the taskmaster."

"Down below?" The dustling looked away, refusing to meet his eye. "That way lies pain. Evil. Are you afraid?"

"I am," Garin said. "But this thing must be done."

"As the Fox wishes." The woman nodded grimly. "Follow."

She hurried off, loping unevenly on all fours down into the yawning entrance to the mine. She moved with a strange gambol, more like an insect reduced to four poorly-matched limbs than a woman with arms and legs.

"What was *that?*" Alcarin asked as they walked.

"The dustlings are key workers at the mine," Garin said. "Fitting in cracks the stronger workers can't, running messages back and forth, and keeping watch." He brushed dust off his hand, and it danced in the burning sunlight. "The name wasn't as literal when I was a boy."

Carefully, they made their way down the spiraling path down into the mine. The shaft offered some relief from the sunlight, but it also plunged into pitch blackness not a dozen paces down. Alcarin pulled out an alchemical torch and bathed them both in pale green light, which failed to illumine the hot gloom of the shaft. As he couldn't see the bottom, Garin had the unsettling sensation of looking down an infinite maw into the darkness at the heart of the world. His own darkness stirred in response, but he choked it down.

"This way, Fox," Lis said ahead of them, the echo of her voice racing around the stone walls. "Ware the steps."

Garin made the mistake of touching the corroded railing fifty paces down, and it gave a groan and leaned precariously out into the darkness. Alcarin gave him a warning look, and Garin smiled sheepishly. They hugged the wall for safety, particularly in spots that had no rail remaining at all or where the steps had begun to crumble. It grew warmer the lower they went as well, until Garin found himself sweating more than he had in the sunlight. They shed their cloaks and opened up their tunics to breathe. Smoke rose through the shaft, but they could breathe as long as they kept away from the edge.

As they descended, they heard the sounds of work being done. Tools chipped away at stone, machines hummed and smoked as they ground away at dense patches, and every so often a shout of alarm or warning rang out. Primarily, though, Garin heard something he remembered well from his youthful visits to Tuerine: a deep, resonant hum of low voices raised in harmony.

The miners sang as they worked, a ballad from the ancient days of Luether's rise. The words were those of old Luether, even before the advent of the Calatite Empire, when the mage-city had been but a dream among the first of those to Return. His father had brought him often to hear the song of Tuerine—a ballad that spoke of dust and stone and buried gold, hidden beneath the burning world above. It told of valor that lay buried beneath the ruins of an ancient world, and of a people that might rise again. That last, he thought, was the most powerful symbol of all.

"I've never heard anything like it," Alcarin said.

"It is the song of a shackled people," Garin said, "but not a people who have abandoned hope."

"And yet Pervast allows them to sing it?" Alcarin said. "He allows the spark to linger?"

Garin nodded. "Perhaps he has no mind for metaphor," he said. "Or perhaps hope is how he torments the people. I told you before how he broke their spirit—perhaps this is how he maintains it."

In the shadows of the green torch, Alcarin's face looked stormy.

The bottom of the mine shaft loomed suddenly below them, and Garin waved Alcarin to a halt. He felt a great sense of space spiraling around them and lifted the torch to see. Indeed, the path continued down like a staircase but much of the nearby walls had been hollowed out to form a vast cavern of sorts deep under the ground. Thousands of candle flames made the mine sparkle like the night sky, but Garin could hardly breathe for the thick smoke they produced. The vast open cavern did not match Garin's memory of this place: he recalled tight quarters and a dozen passages snaking off in all directions, with thousands of support structures in place to secure the mines as a safe place for all. Safety, after all, had always held first priority in the Mines of Tuerine.

Pervast, however, did not hold the same concerns as Garin's father had. Instead, in the name of expediency, the miners had hollowed out and destroyed much of the earth down here, like ants eating away at the walls of their tunnels until a bubble of air remained where all those supports had been. Columns of stone still held up the ceiling, but they looked thin and weak. Garin could see several parts that had collapsed already, and he shuddered to think of the lives lost through such carelessness. It would take at least a decade to secure the mine once again, if such a thing could even be done.

Lis waited for them at the bottom of the steps along with half a dozen sweaty, blank-faced miners who squinted in the bright green light. At first only mildly curious, they looked up at Garin with rheumy eyes that widened in growing recognition. Soon, whispers began to spread through the cavern, and Garin and Alcarin had not gone more than a dozen paces through the growing crowd of miners before the word "fox" had begun to echo around them. Most just stared at them, unbelieving.

"Too late to go back now," Alcarin said.

Garin nodded. He slipped a vial from his belt and downed it surreptitiously.

Lis shuffled close to Garin. "You take me with you?" she asked. "When you leave?"

"*If* I leave," Garin said. "I promise."

As the crowd continued to form around them, they followed Lis toward a well-lit compound a few hundred paces from the stone steps. Hovering platforms that blurred the air beneath them floated past, bound for the surface or a deeper tunnel, but they glided to rest as their guides paused to look at the newcomers. By the time they reached the radiance of the command post, Garin and Alcarin had accumulated hundreds of onlookers who followed them in silence.

Stalagmites strung with razor-wire closed off the area of the command post: a small, fortified hut from which the foreman supervised the work in the Mines of Tuerine. As a boy, Garin had once visited the facilities on a tour of Luether's holdings, and he remembered a cordial welcome in a cozy cavern tucked off the main corridor. Now, with so much of the stone carved away, the place felt barren and entirely too exposed.

Also, the six Children of Ruin standing guard with casters and blades did little to assuage his unease. They focused on the crowd of miners, sweeping their casters across to track targets. Four of them looked like any Luethaar one might encounter on the street, albeit scarred from thousands of battles and carrying better equipment. One barbarian had studded his left arm with so many blades and nails it resembled a club wrapped in razor wire. From the way he swung it through the air with an ugly *thwup-thwup* sound, his arm seemed to be the only weapon he needed. The other barbarian was a woman, Garin thought, though her body was encased in such thick hides and tarnished plates bristling with spikes, making it difficult to say. How she breathed in the oppressive heat of Luether and particularly Tuerine, Garin couldn't guess, but her mad eyes were visible even at a distance and full of raving fury. He had a sudden image of her leaping on a foe and grinding him to death under her horrific armor.

Lis looked back at Garin, her face terrified in the darkness, and he knew he had to go alone from here. He waved her back and stepped to the razor wire gate. "I would speak with your master."

Two of the guards turned their casters on Garin while the others kept their weapons trained on the crowd. One said something in their guttural tongue that Garin didn't understand, and grumbles spread among them. He felt a doubt, but had to stand strong.

"*Vash tat.*" A woman pushed through the hanging leather strips over the command post door and stepped into the fenced area. The chamber behind her became briefly visible as she stepped out, hung with blood-stained implements such as one might find in a butcher's shop. Garin saw movement in the darkness: someone she had just come from torturing, it seemed.

The barbarian woman gestured and the two guards closest to the fence pulled it open. She pointed to Garin. "You. Come." She glared at Alcarin. "Alone."

Alcarin sucked in a sharp breath. Garin touched his hand and gave him a reassuring look. He hoped he came across more confident than he felt.

Garin stepped into the fenced area and came face to face with the woman, who had easily a head over him and half again the weight. A series of metal studs traced surprisingly delicate patterns up her neck and across the left side of her face. For a Child of Ruin, she looked well groomed and even pampered, suggesting a high rank. She stared at him, her mottled gray eyes seeming oddly wide until he realized she had no eye lashes.

"I am the Fox of Luether," Garin said.

"I know your face." The taskmaster had a deep voice like water flowing over sharp stones. "And yet you come with only one warder? I did not know you a fool."

"I've been called worse," Garin said. "I've come to inform you, Lady—?"

"Ortur." She laid one gloved hand on a four-tailed whip, studded with shards of metal and glass, that hung coiled from her belt: a makeshift scourge. "No lady."

"My mistake," Garin said. "I've come to inform you, Ortur, that your time here is done. Luether no longer belongs to Pervast, but once more to its people. You have one day to leave this place."

Silence greeted his pronouncement. Ortur stared at him, absolutely thunderstruck, and the other barbarians—whether they understood the words or not—looked equally surprised. The hundreds of miners who had now amassed around the fenced compound seemed shocked to silence. Garin fancied that the sound of picks and hammers had ceased in the deep so that the entire mine could hear him. Good. Behind him, he could feel Alcarin's eyes burning into the back of his head, and he resolved not to look.

"What?" Garin asked. "Have I something on my face?"

Ortur's mouth opened and a rumbling laugh burst from her throat, wrenching her entire body into a fit. A barbarian with a sense of humor—wonderful.

"I appreciate the flattery, my lady," Garin said. "But I speak in earnest."

The laughter ended, and Ortur glared at him, her expression become vengeful and violent. "No lady." She uncoiled her scourge.

It struck before Garin could even see her move, much less react. It raked down his shoulder and across his chest, and one of the barbs split open his chin. A tingling, scratching sensation surged through his torso and face, and he fell to his knees on the stone. He cradled himself, exposing his back to her.

"Fool," Ortur said. "You have no power here. I feed you to Narfire."

Garin looked up at her. "Strike me as you like," he said. "I'll not fight you."

The scourge whistled and Ortur hit him again, this time tearing his tunic and laying his back open. Blood welled, and Garin could feel its flow tickle his shredded skin. He grunted.

Around them, the gathered crowd watched in terrified silence. Alcarin was breathing so loud and so quickly Garin thought he might collapse. His hand was in his coat, reaching for the Maelstrom, but Garin shook his head sharply to forbid it. If he drew that weapon, they would all die.

"Think you are brave?" Ortur asked. "You are mad."

"There has been enough blood shed between our peoples," Garin said. "Leave this place—go in peace. There is no power in your swords."

Ortur roared in frustration and struck him again, and this time blood flew through the air. His body shuddered and his hands clawed furrows in the stone. Garin thought that if he hadn't drunk the potion to block out pain before confronting her, he would be screaming himself senseless right now.

The beating went on and on, and Garin lost count of how many times Ortur struck him. Every time, blood bloomed, but it congealed instantly and did not fall. More than one voice would speak thereafter of the unbreakable Fox of Luether.

Finally, it paused, not because he had succumbed but because Ortur grew weary. She breathed heavily, her massive chest heaving as she raised the whip once more in the air with a trembling arm.

Garin raised his head. "Your time is over," he said. "Leave—"

A boot caught him in the face, knocking him onto his back. Garin's head struck the stone, making the world blur. Blood streamed from his nose and split lip. Ortur stood over him, scourge in one hand, a hooked knife in the other. It looked like a blade intended only for torture.

"Enough," Ortur said. "Luether belongs to Ruin, not fool whose words mean nothing." She grasped his collar and spat in his face. "On your feet, and I kill you like man. Mercy."

He looked up at her and spoke through bubbling blood. "I will not fight you," he said.

Rage crossed Ortur's face, making her eyes almost bug out of her head. "Have it as you wish." She raised the blade for a killing blow.

A sound stayed her hand: the clatter of metal on stone. It sounded not unlike the chipping sound Garin had heard earlier, but much closer. Just outside the fence, one of the workers was pounding her heavy pickaxe against the stone at her feet. One of the barbarian guards pointed his caster at her and shouted orders, but the sound started coming from other directions around the compound. The confrontation had attracted an audience that swelled beyond the score of miners who'd attended them at first to a sea of faces beyond count. Each and every gathered miner banged a hammer, pick, or shovel against the stone. Alcarin stood among them, looking at first terrified and then righteously furious. He joined in, pounding his fist in the air. Even the skinny dustling Lis took up the cry. From the depths of the cavern arose a deafening racket that swelled like rising thunder as if to shake the fundaments of Luether and make all the Summerlands tremble.

The barbarians looked to one another, fear clearly writ on their faces. They were terrified animals, incapable of understanding. Ortur signaled, and they lowered their weapons.

Garin raised his chin to Ortur and smiled through blood-smeared teeth. "Your time is over."

For a moment, he felt certain she would kill him. The hate in Ortur's eyes was palpable, and her body shook like that of a feral cat with its back against an alley wall. Had he miscalculated? Was he a fool for making this attempt? The darkness rose, filling Garin with doubts. A ten-count, and he would lose his spirit, and with it, his revolution. Even as Luether rose up around him, he felt himself falling into a deep, dark pit, and there was no Ovelia Dracaris to pull him back out. Alcarin stood on the other side of the fence, too far away to help. Garin faced the growing despair alone.

Then a voice sang out from the barbarian's hut. "Go," it said.

A disheveled woman staggered out of the hut, obviously wounded and bleeding from half a dozen cuts on her arms and torso. Her white dress had been torn and cut away in places, leaving her deep brown flesh exposed to the torchlight. Fresh wounds stood out livid against her skin, and her appearance spoke of recent, brutal torture. She raised her face so that all could see, and her bright eyes burned with righteous anger. She was the exact twin of another woman Garin had seen not so long ago, who had thrown herself from High-City. But where Utora had evinced only despair, this woman showed something else entirely: anger.

"Vilaer Vultara," Garin said, hardly able to comprehend.

"Go now." Vilaer stretched as best she could to her full height. She was a diminutive woman, but her stance spoke volumes. She sucked in a sharp breath. "You heard him, Ortur. Your time…is done."

Ortur hesitated a painfully long moment, then nodded. She barked an order in the barbarian tongue to her fellows, who put up their weapons.

"Safe passage out of the mines." Garin rose shakily. "The Fox of Luether is a merciful one."

She looked down at him with disgust. "A stupid one," she said. "This is not over."

"No." Garin locked eyes with Vilaer, who nodded to him. "It is not."

The barbarians marched out of the compound, the workers parting to form a path to the ramp. Garin watched them go, at least until they were out of sight, then collapsed to his knees. Vilaer suffered a similar fate: like a puppet suddenly deprived of strings, she slumped down and lay unmoving.

Alcarin burst into the compound, hands cupping Garin's face. "You idiot!" he said as Garin pushed himself up into a sitting position. "You mad *idiot!*"

Garin chuckled raggedly, then nodded to Vilaer. "See to her," he said. "She is as essential to this cause as I." When Alcarin hesitated, Garin kissed his hand to reassure him. "Go."

Garin looked out over the sea of miners gathered around the compound. Hundreds, he thought—even thousands. All of them standing with him. One of them clapped her hand on her chest, fingers spread, and the salute spread to her neighbors. Soon, the entire cavern offered Garin the same gesture of fealty.

Perhaps, he thought. Perhaps this just might serve.

FIFTEEN

A SANDSTORM RAGED OVER the entrance to the Mines of Tuerine, ripping at any creatures of flesh and blood who dared face it. The mechanical carriage had barely coasted to a stop before Ovelia was leaping out of it, Draca drawn and smoking in the swirling dust. The storm battered at her masked face and body and distorted her senses, filling the world with an impossible haze. Fighting for focus, she crouched below the worst of the cloud and tried to detect what she could.

The place was dead or nearly so. She smelled dust, old bone, and smoke. The air choked her lungs, and she took to breathing shallowly through her nose only. Ovelia reached out to feel for combatants near the yawning mine opening, keeping the blade up to defend against any sudden attack. There was another carriage—the one that Garin and Alcarin had taken, no doubt—but she sensed no one inside. She shivered with hunger, but not for food, and the seemingly abandoned mineshaft matched her hollow feeling.

Red Jeggs stumbled out behind Ovelia. She hadn't particularly wanted him to come along, particularly not with the half-full skin of sweetsoul-infused milk he'd brought after she'd interrupted his morning meal. She'd so far been able to resist the urge to seize it and guzzle it down. Also, by the half-hearted way he protested, he didn't entirely seem to have *wanted* to come along, either.

"We shouldn't be here," he cried. "Garin has a plan. We should respect—"

Ovelia raised a hand to cut him off. She *did* sense someone present near the mine, but barely. Draca's shadows gave no clues, but Ovelia scented a faint, familiar perfume on the rushing air. The winds began to abate, and she pointed the sword in the direction she could best guess, trying not to let it tremble and reveal her weakness.

"I know you are there," Ovelia said, having to shout to hear herself over the wind. "Show yourself, Shard."

At first, there was only the howling wind, but after a moment, the pirate queen's voice rose from the dusty ruin of the mine entrance. The storm passed as she appeared, as though it answered to her will. "Impressive," she said, the wind almost entirely gone. "I see blindness hardly stays you, dear one."

The way Red Jeggs stiffened told Ovelia that Shard had concealed herself from normal sight as well. The woman seemed damned capable of avoiding notice when she wished. Ovelia still could not see her, but her ears could point her in the right direction.

Red Jeggs strode in front of her, raising his twin axes to ward off an attacker. Ovelia might have found his desire to protect her sweet, had it not also felt so patronizing. She had already defeated Red Jeggs once—if anyone should be the warder, it should be her, even blind.

"Shard, as in Shard the Pirate?" Red Jeggs inclined a slight bow toward their foe. "An honor. I did not know you were a woman."

"Yes." Shard sounded bored. "I don't know you, but if you stand with her, I suppose you'll pass." She turned her attention to Ovelia. "Did you bring this slab of a man for a shield or for fodder?"

"Why are you here?" Ovelia pushed past Red Jeggs and took a menacing step toward Shard's voice. She could faintly see her now, a slightly lighter spot against a forest of shadows. She wore her black robe as usual, despite the oppressive heat. "Are you part of this trap for my Lord Ravalis?"

"*Your* Lord Ravalis," Shard said. "What singular phrasing. I almost didn't know whom you meant." When Ovelia did not rise to the bait, the pirate queen scoffed. "As to your question, dear one, no—and as far as I can see, this is no trap. I have come merely to bear witness."

That gave Ovelia pause. "Witness what?"

"There." Shard raised her arm to point. "I'd stay my blade, were I you."

Ovelia did not need to see her gesture to understand. Draca went mad with warning, and she could sense the rage stomping up the path from the mines. Half a dozen Children of Ruin appeared, cursing and hissing insults in their guttural language. Their leader—a tall woman with a scourge coiled at her hip—seemed particularly angry. She practically burned in Ovelia's eyes. The barbarians paused when they saw the three folk standing at the opening of the mine, and hands went to weapons.

"I wouldn't." Shard raised her hand, and abruptly a hundred dust-covered pirates rose from the ruined area, training casters on the barbarians. Needlessly, Draca's flames spoke of a rain of casterbolts that would leave the barbarians little more than pulp on the cracked earth.

The woman who led the mine barbarians stepped to the fore. "Fox of Luether speak of peace," she said to Shard. "You enforce with war."

"I see you understand," the pirate queen said. "Better a live hypocrite than a dead idealist."

The barbarians lowered their hands from their weapons and slowly, tense at every step for a coming attack, marched out of the dusty bowl. When they had gone, Shard gave a circling gesture and her pirates filed away with surprising organization into what Ovelia expected were skyships waiting to bear them hence. Shard gave Red Jeggs and Ovelia a nod, then turned to walk away.

"I don't get it," Red Jeggs said. "You're leaving? Before we see what passed?"

"You would have me steal your master's moment of glory?" Shard asked over her shoulder. "We are not formally allies, and so it would not do to deprive him." She paused. "Unless you can give me a reason to stay, dear one."

Ovelia raised her chin. "No," she said. "And I am not your *dear one*."

"As you say." Shard hitched up her dress, climbed the slope of skittering rock, and was gone.

"What was that?" Red Jeggs asked. "Do you know her?"

Ovelia shook her head. She doubted she'd seen the last of Lady Shard, however.

They had only moments to wait before a troop of half a hundred people came up the ramp, including Garin, Alcarin, and a scrawny woman Ovelia did not know. The Fox of Luether had taken a bad beating, which Ovelia could see in his halting step and hear in his labored breath. The woman seemed wounded as well, barely able to walk even with Alcarin's aid.

Garin saw them immediately, and a bright smile lit his face. "Many apologies," he said as they drew near. "I should have taken you along, it seems."

"Yes." Ovelia touched at his face and shoulders, and he winced with pain. "You're hurt."

"I'll live." Garin indicated the woman leaning on Alcarin's shoulder. "This is Vilaer, eldest heiress of the Blood Vultara and Pervast's latest consort. The Ruin King had set his best torturer to breaking her."

Red Jeggs made a strangled little sound. "The Ruin King's whore?" he managed. "Highness, you can't possibly want her for an ally! By the Fire, the Vultara opened the gates to the barbarians! Luether hates her Blood almost as much as it does Pervast."

Shocked silence hung among them for a moment. Garin stared, too stunned to speak, and Alcarin looked as though he actually agreed. The harsh words struck Vilaer like another lash of a whip, and Ovelia could see her lose just a little more of her strength.

"Apologize to her," Ovelia said.

"What?" Now it was Red Jeggs's turn to look stunned. "Woman, you do not command me—"

"Whatever she is, I am far worse." Ovelia put her hand to Draca's hilt. "Apologize."

All eyes fell upon them, and Ovelia could feel the scrutiny like a palpable thing. Particularly Vilaer was watching Ovelia closely now, holding her breath in anticipation. She could not see the Vultara princess's expression, but she grew warmer and brighter moment by moment.

"You would fight me?" Red Jeggs asked. "Here? In front of so many?"

"Yes," Ovelia said. Then she spoke softer, so that only he and those nearest her could hear. "I'll not kill you, but leave you battered and wounded. *Defeated.* Can your pride stand the humiliation?"

Red Jeggs boomed with laughter, but there was an edge beneath his mirth. It was a shadow of warning against such provocation. Should Ovelia continue on this path, she would threaten his need for dominance, and that would mark open hostilities between them. Ovelia could handle the consequences, but losing Ovelia would not serve Garin or his quest.

"I am not my Blood, syr, and I hate Pervast as much as you do." Vilaer's eyes flashed, and she spoke up with greater passion than Ovelia could have imagined from the small, nigh-broken woman. "You think I can look at what he did to my sister—to my Blood—to my *city*, and not want him gone?" She raised her chin. "And even if I did not, I have power and influence you cannot even imagine. Summer Lives *needs* me."

Red Jeggs considered for a moment, then chuckled once more—this time, without artifice. "Well said, 'princess.' Prove yourself a friend to Luether, and I shall follow you." He walked away.

Vilaer nodded, betraying no sign of weakness. Ovelia could sense her relief.

"Lady Vultara." Ovelia bowed her head. "Please accept my sorrow for your lost sister."

"Thank you," Vilaer said. "And for what you did for me. I shall not forget it." The woman nodded to Ovelia and looked back to Garin, who had been trading whispers with Alcarin. "Can we leave this place now? I'm so tired, and in a great deal of pain."

"Of course, princess," he said. "Of course. And again, well said."

Garin pushed away from Alcarin, able to stand on his own, if shakily. He turned back to the crowd that had gathered behind him, even down the ramp into the mine. Ovelia could feel the anticipation in the air, and when Garin raised his hand, it built to a near-boiling fever. "Friends and countrymen," he said. "You have heard my words and know what you must do. Go forth, and be brave! Dawn is coming!"

Then he clapped his open hand on his chest—the traditional salute of the Ravalis—and the miners erupted in cheers and cries of support. Garin beamed in the wave of adoration.

"What have you done?" Ovelia asked.

"Declared victory, and it worked." Garin grunted. "I'll tell you all, back at the Long Dawn."

Ovelia moved to take his arm, but Alcarin interposed himself between them. "Take her," he said, offering Vilaer. "I'll help him."

The curt dismissal took Ovelia aback, but she stooped to help Vilaer instead. She was slim, her body soft and not at all wiry or muscular. She bled from a dozen shallow wounds—the marks of obvious torture. Ovelia could not see, but the way Vilaer stiffened when Garin hobbled away and the sigh she uttered at his absence told clearly how she felt about the man who had—apparently—rescued her.

"Wait," Vilaer said. "Your Highness! My Lord Ravalis—"

"Heh." Red Jeggs chuckled. Even he had picked up on the woman's growing ardor. "Our Lord Fox is a hero, aye, but I fancy you'll be disappointed there. His tastes don't run to lady—"

Ovelia turned her head toward Red Jeggs, sharp as a slap, and he shut his mouth. It would not do to offer idle words, when the truth was close to the jest.

Vilaer seemed at first confused, then she nodded in comprehension. She relaxed against Ovelia's arm and loosed a deep sigh. "It seems it has begun," she said. Then she slumped down, all her energy spent. Ovelia caught her, and fortunately she weighed so very little. Ovelia expected Red Jeggs to insist on carrying her, but for a relief, he said nothing. She hitched up Vilaer into her arms.

"What?" Red Jeggs asked as he took a draught from his sweetsoul infused milkskin. "What did she mean? What has begun?"

Ovelia tried to ignore the sucking hunger in her gut. "Dawn for Luether," she said. "It's good that you didn't fight me. Garin did this all on his own, and I feel very ignored."

"You are a bold one, Dragon Daughter." Red Jeggs cast his milkskin aside—empty, thankfully—and slapped his hand on his chest. "I look forward to rutting that spirit out of you when we get back."

"Do you."

Ovelia met his flirtation only half-heartedly. Instead, she found her thoughts drifting toward the woman drowsing against her shoulder, breath warm on her neck. They were almost of an age—Vilaer lacking a few summers on her—but something in the Vultara princess kindled something inside Ovelia she'd thought lost so long ago. Vilaer reminded Ovelia of another fiery princess, the last of her Blood, whose birthright lay just out of reach.

This princess, Ovelia would not fail.

SIXTEEN

The Long Dawn—Luether

SPRING HAD ALMOST REACHED its zenith in the form of Hopedawn—the longest day of the season, a few days hence—and the Summer Lives revolution pressed forward with growing speed.

Summer Lives had taken over the Long Dawn, securing it against barbarian patrols or stragglers alike. Window shutters were closed despite the heat, the door latched shut with two burly rebels on watch. From outside, the tavern appeared not to have opened yet for the day, which could be for any number of reasons, from an innocuous supply shortage to violent intervention from the ruling Children. Passersby would think better of trying to enter the Long Dawn and instead amble on to more welcoming establishments. It granted the conspirators a great deal of privacy and quiet at need.

"My friends," Garin said to the gathered agents. "You've all heard tales of what has transpired. I have come before you today to lay them to rest, and to speak of our new path going forward."

He hoped earnestly that this would pass well.

They had all come, following his summons to join in the largest assembly of Summer Lives in recent memory. Biaza, Corvus, Neblen, and Red Jeggs were there, of course—the leads of the various cells of the operation—but so too were their squires and many of their agents. They had packed the Long Dawn almost to bursting, all of them eager to see this madman Luether was calling the "Merciful Fox." After the incident at Tuerine, word had spread of the man who sought to end the oppression of Pervast and his minions without bloodshed. It seemed that Luether could talk of little else, now that the workers had gone on strike and all but crippled the mage-city's economy.

Vilaer Vultara sat gracefully near Alcarin, trying to be unassuming and failing badly. Ovelia had so far managed to avoid making her identity widely known, but Vilaer shared a face with Utora Vultara, who for many summers had been the public face of Pervast's rule. Nor would any Luethaar forget that the Vultara had opened wide the gates to the barbarians in the Fall. Everyone in Summer Lives knew Vilaer; most distrusted her at best or hated her at worst, and her presence in the Long Dawn had caused no small amount of unrest. He'd had to clear up more than one argument that threatened to turn violent. Fortunately, Vilaer seemed quite content to suffer such barbs in demure silence, working diligently to prove herself despite their mistrust. And Garin could honestly assert that she had proved crucial thus far, having played a major role in his victory at the mine, even to her great peril.

That victory, he reminded himself, had cost *him* as well. The bruises and scars of that incident had mostly healed, but he still felt sore and weak. The discomfort was well worth the gain, however: they were making real progress, and it filled him with courage and hope. Perhaps this new course would not prove mad after all. The difficulty, of course, was selling compassion to the rest of the rebels. Looking around at the impatient faces of his compatriots, Garin began to doubt, but he had to try.

Garin's words had inspired quiet, and all eyes fell upon him. He could hear not only his own breath but that of Alcarin two paces away. He could feel his squire's support, and resolved not to make a fool of himself as he had that first day back. He could also sense Ovelia lurking just a pace to his left, hand on the hilt of Draca. After he had tricked her out of accompanying him to the Mines of Tuerine, he had found it impossible to get her to leave his side. He admittedly deserved the scrutiny, and it did not bother him. Rather, he found it comforting, as he would need all the support he could muster.

"No doubt you've heard many things about what transpired at the Mines." Garin saw the hooded figure of Lis at the back of the room, cleansed of dust but recognizable by her hunched posture. She offered him a slight nod, keeping her eyes averted as she had at the Mines. "But what is more important than the details is the purpose: giving the people something to follow other than bloodshed and death."

Uncertain silence greeted his pronouncement. Not unexpected. What he had to say next, however, would evoke a far more violent reaction. He took a deep breath. Lead them into it. Coax them.

"For twenty summers, we have struggled against Pervast the Unseen and his horde of killers and monsters," Garin said. "Those who dare speak against Pervast's rule suffer beatings, torture, murder—whatever humiliates and ruins them, the barbarians will do. And we have been Luether's only protectors, answering blood for blood, destroying their goods and crippling their trade where we can. Summer Lives has proven a constant, unclosing wound to Pervast—a reminder that he cannot simply do what he wants without consequence."

He paused to let the gathered agents absorb his words. They generally nodded in ascent and pride, their unease soothed by the reminder of their efforts. Every one of them hated Pervast with a deep, consuming passion, and they looked back over their achievements with grim satisfaction for the barbarian blood they had shed in Luether's streets. Behind his smile, Garin braced himself for the impending fight.

"But consider, my friends," Garin said. "Where has this strategy brought us?" He spread his hands. "We kill one of their warriors, they kill ten of our people. We destroy a shipment of arms, they burn down a communal home, displacing hundreds. I ask you now, when does it end?"

"When all the barbarians are dead," Red Jeggs said, his voice a grumble and his eyes livid.

The answer brought rumbles of assent and even some cheers from the crowd. Garin had not coached Red Jeggs on what to say before this council, and for good reason: the man followed his own path. But he had been at Tuerine and seen the defeated barbarians, and so he would likely prove a support in any case. Garin held up his hand, and the room fell silent once more.

"Yes," he said, when they had quieted down. "Yes, if Pervast and all his barbarians were to die, the killing would end, but at what cost? Look around you." He gestured around the common room. "There are how many of us, thirty? Perhaps twice as many additional agents in the city? Pervast has thousands of barbarians roaming the streets at all hours of the day and night. Even if we could slay all of them, what cost to the city? And how long would it take?" He shook his head. "We don't have time."

"Then we strike smart," said another of the agents, a woman Garin did not know. She had a series of red gouges across her face and was missing one of her eyes. "We know the names of Pervast's ministers. We throw them down—leave him crippled on the rocks when your cousin comes with the hammer. A *massive* hammer."

She pounded her fist on the table, making more than a few nearby rebels flinch. In particular, Neblen—a twitchy street thief known for her expressive, credulous face, who was the best information gatherer in Summer Lives—yelped and put one hand on her neighbor to steady herself, the other to the grip of a handcaster at her belt. The gathered rebels cheered even louder, and many banged their fists on tables as the scarred woman had done.

This was not going well. Garin had to make them understand somehow, but they turned his words against him so easily. What he was proposing would seem like madness.

"I'm sorry," he said to the scarred woman. "You are?"

The woman scowled at him. "I am called Svista, Fox Prince," she said. "I've had the honor to fight and bleed for you for two summers. This"—she indicated her missing eye—"I sacrificed for you."

Her tone made that sound like a mild rebuke, but Garin let it pass.

"Yes, Svista," he said. "Tar Vangr marching to our aid is a wonderful thing, and yes, it represents a chance to throw down the usurper." Garin gestured around the room to encompass his agents. "But consider—if my cousin arrives with his army, what will Pervast do? He will round up the people and throw them in front of the soldiers and their casters. He will conscript all of Luether to fight this enemy before he risks even a single one of his own people. And those who will not fight? He will hurl them from High-City to take the hearts from the invaders. You know this. You have seen his men do this."

Again he paused, and this time a series of murmurs broke the silence. This news diminished their enthusiasm, and now they watched Garin again with rapt attention. Their expressions conveyed their displeasure, however, and Garin knew that he would have to tread carefully lest they blame him for such dire circumstances. In particular, Biaza was glaring hard at him, and Garin felt a sharp pang about her son, lost his first day back in Luether. No more blood would be shed.

"If we do nothing, the armies of Tar Vangr will lay waste to Luether, and our losses will be far greater than any we have seen these past twenty summers," Garin said. "That is why we have been unable to triumph—because they hold the knife over us in the form of our people. But what Pervast does not realize is that Luether is a double-edged blade—the very doom he holds over us will prove his own."

That perked their interest—some flicker of hope in their dark hour. Garin clung to it fiercely. Behind him, Alcarin drew in a sharp breath, while Ovelia looked on edge. She had not wanted him to do this—advised against it with all of her logic. Perhaps he should have listened to her.

Vilaer watched him with bright eyes, thoroughly believing every word he said. He felt her support, and it gave him strength to push on.

"We will inspire the people to rise," he said. "Pervast has ground them into the dust under his boot. But we have seen what power they hold. It is time to awaken them from their sleep and break their chains. With their aid, we can conquer Pervast's empire without drawing steel." He looked around the room, meeting all of their eyes. "Through mercy."

Absolute silence. Garin saw the confusion on their faces, as he had expected.

"Mercy," Svista said. "You mean, for our people?"

"For our people, and for our enemy," Garin said. "Our city is a damsel in chains, forced against her will into a cycle of torture and pain. Do we free her by strengthening those chains with more of the same or by breaking them with something new?" He spread his hands. "Think of it. How much of their blood have we spilled, and they have returned every act of aggression ten, twenty, a hundred fold. The people have known nothing but violence for an entire generation—"

"*Stop?*" Svista got to her feet. "You want us to cease our fighting. Stop killing barbarians."

"Yes," Garin said. "Defend yourselves as you must, but fight with words and deeds, not with steel." He rose up to his full height. "Show our people an alternative—that strength is not power."

"I have watched Pervast's public executions," Svista said. "And they seem plenty powerful to me. Maybe we should execute some of his rabble—show our own strength." She pointed at Vilaer, who flinched away as though struck. "We can start with Pervast's own whore. Is her Blood not as guilty of murdering our people as Pervast?"

Rumbles spread through the common room. Vilaer's face went white, and Ovelia stepped protectively between her and Svista. The Vultara heiress looked up at her with gratitude and—Garin thought—something like adoration. Too bad Ovelia could not see it, he thought: that look would certainly have propped up his spirits, had Vilaer aimed it at him.

"If we cling to our hatred," Garin said, "the violence will never end."

"And why should it?" Svista asked. "Pervast had my husband killed. My two sons. The youngest had just seen his fourth season. They threw him from the battlements because I wouldn't give you up. *You*, prince." Svista pointed at Garin. "I am the last of my Blood for your sake. And now you ask me not to seek revenge? Now, when the means is within our grasp?"

"I know it is hard," Garin said. "We have all lost someone to this war—"

"Oh?" she said. "Your fancy squire stands beside you. Not a scar mars your pretty face. You've even got one of the enemy following you around like a doting little puppy. And your foreigner is there to back up whatever you say. You've not suffered as we have. Who have *you* lost?"

Alcarin took a step forward. "How dare you—?" he started, but Garin stayed him with a gesture.

"My father." Garin looked down at his hands. "My mother." He looked up again. "My city."

Svista's face slipped into an expression of surprise, but she grimaced in disapproval. She sat once more, placated for the moment.

"This." Biaza spoke in her soft but commanding voice from the back of the room. "This path of mercy." She stepped forward, drawing the attention of all. "This is what you advocate, even as an assassin stands beside you?"

At first, Garin thought she meant to heap more slurs upon Vilaer, but when Ovelia rose up to her full height, the truth dawned on him. This, he thought, would help not at all.

In the shocked silence, Biaza pointed toward Ovelia but spoke to the gathered agents.

"Oh yes, Lady Dracaris—I know you." Biaza kept her gaze on Ovelia but addressed the common room. "She may hide her true identity, but she is Ovelia the Bloodbreaker, she who betrayed and slew the Winter King five summers gone. A fitting champion of this new path, yes?"

The common room erupted in angry shouts and clamorous argument. Ovelia stepped forward, but Garin put a hand on her wrist to stay her. He shook his head, and even if she could not see him, she seemed to understand. Alcarin glared with burning eyes, and well he did. He had spoken against keeping Ovelia's identity a secret, after all, and now his dire words had come to pass. At least they had not begun to shout for Ovelia's blood as a traitor and regicide. Small comfort as the darkness rose inside him.

"Hypocrite!" Svista made the word a sharp dagger. "You would stand there and judge *us*? You, who make alliances with vipers and butchers of kings?"

Garin realized he had stood and said nothing for too long. Alcarin was shouting in his ear, trying to stir him, but all he could do was look around in confusion. Summer Lives was disintegrating before his eyes, and he felt powerless to stop it. Corvus had broken away from the wall and held the hilt of his short sword at the ready, moving toward Garin protectively. Red Jeggs held two arguing agents from each other's throats. Neblen had vanished— hiding, no doubt, until the fighting ended. The common room would erupt into a brawl in seconds if Garin did not act. But the darkness consumed him and he could not move against it. He felt like a child watching the sand castle he'd erected crumble in the surf.

And in that darkness, another word rose unbidden to his mind—a terrible secret he could not bring himself to name.

Hekatomb.

Surely it had not grown so bad. Not *yet*, surely.

But what if he was wrong? What if the only path that lay before him was one of death?

Then a hand touched his, and he looked up at Ovelia's blindfolded eyes. Her expression was patient and kind, and suddenly the darkness inside him did not seem so overwhelming. It lifted, and he could think for himself once more.

"Stop," he said.

170

The sounds of the arguing agents rushed back in, and he witnessed the pandemonium in the common room. Summer Lives had almost boiled over into utter madness, and he could see more than a few drawn blades.

"Stop!" he shouted.

Silence fell as voices trailed off and blades lowered, and all turned to him.

"This is not an easy thing I ask of anyone," Garin said. "But from this moment forth, no agent of Summer Lives will spill the blood of anyone—barbarian or Luethaar—without absolute need. If you cannot follow this edict, you should go now, and take my best wishes."

The tense silence that followed was the longest of Garin's life. He watched his agents consider his words—his offer and ultimatum—and he could see the hope rise and fall on their faces. Finally, one of the chairs grated against the floor, and Svista rose, glaring, and slowly walked from the room. Half a dozen more agents followed her, casting contemptuous looks back. They would sway their own cells as well, and Garin expected Summer Lives would diminish significantly this day, but it could not be helped.

At least his chief advisors remained. Corvus stood near the back, loyal to a fault even in his disapproval. Garin had half expected Red Jeggs to go, but the way the man looked at Ovelia reassured him. Of all of them Biaza had lost the most blood to Pervast but she remained a constant fixture at the bar as ever. Of all of them, he felt most grateful for her.

"For those who stand with me, thank you." Garin let out a sigh, and the tension relaxed in the room. "Now then. A brief respite—all of you take several days, and we'll meet again on Hopedawn to assign tasks. Sleep well, and prepare yourselves. This will not be an easy path."

Garin pushed his way through the crowd, delirious and dizzy after his speech. The agents of Summer Lives spoke excitedly and uncertainly among themselves. Lis appeared, eyes bright, and she whispered some sort of encouragement he could not hear over the din. Passing her by, Garin retreated into the back room for relief. His hands were shaking, he realized, and he felt the darkness threatening to overpower him at any moment. Alone, he could let it wash over him freely.

The door opened behind Garin, and he turned to find Alcarin—eyes bright and excited—standing before him. They embraced, more for mutual support than affection. "That went better than it might have," Alcarin said. His expression turned wry. "All of that could have been avoided, you know, if we just told them about *Hekatomb*."

He'd meant it as a jest, Garin realized, but the word stung like a needle in his belly. He seized Alcarin's wrist and looked him straight in the eye. "No," he said. "Don't even say that. *Ever*."

Alcarin's expression slipped into confusion. "But," he said. "I thought—we talked about this."

"If I am to rule these people, it will not be as the monster Pervast is," Garin said. "I have to believe we can do this peacefully."

"As though these butchers understand peace," Alcarin said. "You need to punish Biaza. She confronted you before all, and cost you dearly."

"No," Garin said. "There will be no punishment. Biaza spoke true, and she did me a favor."

Alcarin tensed. "You need to get Svista back," he said through gritted teeth. "Follow after her. Plead with her to return."

"No." Garin shrugged ironically. "Who is she? I'd never heard of her before today."

"Well *I* had," Alcarin said. "You're the charismatic figurehead, but I'm the one who keeps track of our commanders—who takes note of their dealings and past indiscretions. Svista was a loyal friend, and now that she's on her own, she is dangerous."

"She'll not move against us," Garin said. "She wants Luether liberated."

"But by you?" Alcarin asked. "You've thrown your lot in with her enemies. You turn your back on her and her allies and elevate her foes. How is that any better than what the Ruin King offers?"

Silence cut between them like a sword. Garin stared. Alcarin blanched.

"In…in her eyes, I mean," Alcarin said.

"I know what you mean." Garin felt beyond tired. "What are we arguing about? It's not about Biaza or that Svista woman. What is the matter?"

Alcarin's eyes glittered at him. "I've fought beside you. Bled beside you and for you."

"And I thank you for it. You've been a constant support. The best friend I could have."

Alcarin's brow drew tight. "And as your friend, I must rebuke you," he said. "You choose a whole new path without consulting me—one that can only lead to failure."

Garin shook his head. "We've spoken of this before."

"And we'll speak of it again." Alcarin's face grew darker in his growing anger. "Why change strategy now? We have only days before your cousin comes in force. Why waste the time we have left on a course doomed to failure?"

"I am not convinced it is doomed to failure. You've some convincing rhetoric for me?"

"You've always known there was a chance," Alcarin said. "You built our answer. Biaza and Corvus both know we need it. Silver Fire, even *Red Jeggs* can see we need it. It is almost ready and now, when the time has come to use it, you hesitate?"

"You're burning *right* I hesitate." Garin clutched Alcarin's wrist tightly, and their eyes met. "I will not use *Hekatomb* unless there is no other option."

"There *is* no other option!" Alcarin checked his voice, glancing again at Ovelia, who had stirred. When he spoke again, he did so in a whisper. "If so many lives must be lost, let them be theirs, rather than our own. No victory without sacrifice."

"The sacrifices you would have me make," Garin shook his head. "They are too many."

"Is the cost higher than at the mines?" Alcarin said. "You tried your way, and the taskmaster nearly killed you. She was *one woman*. Now you would throw yourself on the mercy of Pervast, who has murdered thousands of us? No." He shook his head. "I cannot lose you. Not when there is another way."

"*Hekatomb* is not that other way," Garin said. "That—" He sighed. "I said no."

Alcarin glared. "You think you are being selfless, because you will sacrifice yourself before you slaughter animals," he said. "But in truth, you are too much a coward to do what must be done."

"Allie—" he said, but his squire was already stomping from the room.

Wiping the sweat from his brow, Garin found himself suddenly shivering in the humid room. It felt cold and so terribly lonely.

"What's *Hekatomb*?"

In the excitement of the gathering, the heat of the argument, and the precipitous crash thereafter, Garin had almost forgotten about Ovelia, who was leaning against the doorframe. Without her eyes to watch, the woman became almost a fixture of the room when she kept silent, which was often these days. She must have followed Alcarin, or perhaps she'd been waiting to confront Garin alone. Either way, she'd heard enough. Vilaer stood beside her in the doorway, her eyes wide.

"Is it a weapon?" Ovelia asked. "One of your devices?"

Garin took Ovelia's hand and looked at Vilaer . "I cannot tell you," he said. "I have to show you."

SEVENTEEN

THE PATH THEY TOOK led Ovelia through parts of Luether she had never known. She could see only in fits and starts, so she had to imagine her surroundings through her other senses.

They descended below the sizzling street to escape the oppressive sun, replacing the smell of burned wood and corroded metal with the stench of mildew and human waste. The air hung thick and humid in the sewers, making their clothes stick to their flesh mere moments in. Here, the people of the city sought refuge from the burning sunlight in the rough-hewn tunnels and catacombs of an earlier age.

The three kept their hoods low despite the heat, hiding their features from the filth-covered refugees. Ovelia could smell the people well and sense them well enough. They cowered in their alcoves and peered out at them from the shadows of crude tents and lean-tos, curious and anxious. Some had violent intent, but simple fear defined most of them. Ovelia could see the shadows leaking from Draca, but she made a point not to touch its hilt, lest they interpret her caution as a threat or a sign of fear.

Vilaer exhibited enough unease for the three of them, breathing heavily as they passed through the tunnels, jumping at every shadow. She clung to Ovelia's hand like a talisman, which felt warm and comforting. Ovelia knew Vilaer was not timid by nature from the way the princess had risen to Red Jeggs's insults at the Mines of Tuerine. Perhaps such long captivity under Pervast had broken her spirit, and Ovelia felt great sorrow for it. How majestic would she be, rid of the monster who had ruled her?

"I've never been this deep," Vilaer said, her voice soft. "How many people live here?"

"Thousands," Garin said. "More than dwell above."

"Why?" Ovelia's exposed skin tingled, and her clothes felt like the exterior of an oven, trapping all her body's heat inside. "It's so much hotter down here." She sniffed and made a face. "And fouler."

"Safer, too," Garin said. "The barbarians don't patrol down here. Easier to deal with sweltering stench than with coughing up blood after a beating."

Ovelia frowned. "How evocative and specific."

"I've seen enough for a hundred such stories," Garin said.

"That's—that's terrible," Vilaer said.

174

No one disagreed with her.

They turned a corner into an alcove like any other, but Ovelia sensed something odd about one of the walls. Sure enough, Garin removed a false stone and she could faintly make out three circular shapes like dials. Garin spun the last dial, and Ovelia heard a click. Steam puffed around a rectangular section the wall before them, and she could dimly see a shadowy outline emerge in the stone. A door slid open in the stone, and Garin led them down into the depths as it ground shut behind them. Here, the stench of the sewer vanished into a mélange of dust, lamp oil, and various alchemical substances, only some of which she could identify. The heat diminished slightly, its edge blunted, but Ovelia still sweated in the lonely darkness. Vilaer breathed softly and faintly, holding Ovelia's hand tightly.

"These are my secret laboratories," Garin said. "I reclaimed them from a particularly ruthless, amoral practitioner of thaumaturgy in the early days of Summer Lives. Since, I've put them to good use."

Ovelia barely heard him. She marveled at what she could see in these new tunnels. Before, the darkness had seemed all but complete, punctuated with shadows of strong feelings and furtive movement. Now, Ovelia could see the faint traces of the steps they descended, illumined by a dull, silvery light from below. It melted up through the hard black floor like rising water. Along the way, they found door after door that vibrated slightly with red magic. It was the only source of color in her shadowy world.

"None of these doors will open for anyone other than me," Garin said. "I calibrated their magic to respond to my touch and mine alone."

They reached one particularly large door, illumined in such bright white that it made her dizzy. Whatever lay behind it glowed with such power that she could make out every detail of the doors.

Garin must have heard her faint gasp, for her made a small, approving sound. "I think, my lady, that your blindness is not complete," he said as they descended. "You've spoken before of shadowy forms and auras around some people. But these things are not consistent—they come and go by the hour, and you cannot summon them when you have the need." He touched the wall, which lit up with guiding magic, not unlike the tunnels beneath Tar Vangr. "There is, however, one thing you always seem to see. The shadows of your sword, the hum of skyships, the whine of a charged caster."

"Magic." Ovelia traced her fingers along the glowing runes, which she could almost read.

"Indeed."

Garin guided her down to a platform, and they paused before a stout door that burned at its edges. There they paused as he put his hand to the latch. Ovelia watched in wonder as crimson radiance flowed from his body into the door. The magic that was Garin reached out and unlocked it.

"So if you always see magic, my lady," Garin said. "Then you'll want to brace yourself."

With that, he flung open the door, and Ovelia had to catch herself against the opposite wall at the sudden revelation. They stood on a narrow, long platform that stretched around deep chasm of darkness that fell away into a pit of pure, silver Narfire that churned and bubbled. All around her she could see worktables and desks stacked high with scrolls and tattered parchments, the materials of a skilled, prolific thaumaturgist. Somehow, Ovelia could sense the long hours and stretching days of work that had transpired in this place, copious effort expended to a single great purpose.

And floating in the pit before them—secured by massive chains that held it fast to the opposite walls, burning with potential power and ensorcelled thaumaturgy—was a skyship.

Ovelia had seen many aerial vessels in her time: huge transports that carried hundreds of soldiers, sleek ornithopters that could carry a small cadre or a single iron-clad war machine, or floating barges that could transport many tons of heavy goods from place to place. The skyship before her dwarfed them all in size and sheer power. It bristled with weaponry: softly humming heavy casters mounted in turrets, no fewer than four thaumaturgical cannon she could see, and the silver rings that hung suspended around it bristled with serrated edges for ramming other ships. It boasted thicker armor than Ovelia had seen on the *Avenger*, and all of shining new iron smelted on the anvils of Luether. It bore as its masthead an angelic figure she could not perceive well, but she could easily picture its drawn sword calling for blood.

It was a floating engine of doom, and gazing upon it made Ovelia feel small and terrified.

"This is *Hekatomb*," Garin said. "The warship that is my life's work."

"It's—it's beautiful," Vilaer said.

"It's new." Ovelia marveled at it. "I have never seen such a thing that was *new*."

"It only shines so brightly on the outside," Garin said. "You should see the inside—a mess of cobbled parts and replaced components that would shame even a journeyman magewright. But it is powerful—no lie. It has enough power to destroy Luether, Tar Vangr, and anything else that stands in its way." He crossed his arms. "It has never flown, and it never will."

Ovelia looked to him, confused. "What?" she asked. "Why?"

Garin looked to Vilaer. "Would you give us a moment, your highness?"

The princess drew in an anxious breath, then blew it out. "Of—of course, your highness. I'll just—" She let go of Ovelia's hand and meandered along the ledge, examining the ship in more detail.

Garin blew out a great sigh. "I was not the first to work on this great undertaking," he said to Ovelia. "My greatfather commissioned *Hekatomb* before I was even born, and I only rediscovered it just before the fall of Luether. This weapon against any enemy, to be turned against our oppressors."

He reached out his hand and ran his fingers across the sharp iron of one of the skyship's rings.

"At first, I thought this ship was the answer to my rage against Pervast and his barbarians," Garin said. "I was young and foolish, and all I wanted was revenge. And *Hekatomb*—it could deliver that." He curled his hands into fists. "I spent most of those early summers working on the ship day and night, stealing shipments of iron, bribing smiths, enlisting the aid of fellow thaumaturgists, developing concoctions in my laboratory to harden the iron or strengthen the weapons. Few knew—only Alcarin and a few agents I trusted, as well as a few magewrights who kept their secrets for coin." He closed his eyes and shook his head helplessly. "I spent two decades of my life to craft a perfect weapon that could destroy my enemies, and I have succeeded beyond all speculation or doubt."

"But," Ovelia said.

Garin crossed his arms and looked down. "Twenty summers I worked on *Hekatomb*, until Dark Solstice last year—just before I went to Tar Vangr," he said. "The night of the revel—Ruin's Night—I was to tell my cousin Lan about the existence of the skyship: to make it the anvil while his army would be the hammer. Crewed by fewer than a dozen people, *Hekatomb* alone could destroy Luether to keep it out of the hands of the barbarians who've brutalized and tortured our people and defiled our birthright."

"But you changed your mind," Ovelia said. "Why?"

"You." He looked up at her. "Well, not *just* you. My cousin, too—seeing the animal he was. But watching your devotion to your princess after what Lan did to you. It all seemed so insane, so impossible; that only a madwoman would do as you had done. The World of Ruin was too dark and cruel for such love—it could not but crush it."

He shook his head, and Ovelia thought he was smiling ruefully.

"Then I watched Regel snatch you back from death's dark gateway, against everything I thought possible, and I…I stopped," he said. "I could no longer hate Pervast or the barbarians. They were as much mortal men and women as you or I, twisted and horrible as they are. I could stop and look at the path I was walking, and look ahead to see where it would end."

"Not where you want," Ovelia said.

"Yes." Garin swept a hand out toward *Hekatomb*. "It ends with the destruction of my city, the needless deaths of thousands, and a triumph for Ruin," he said. "I would have won, but what would I leave behind? A city of ashes and corpses? A legacy of death? No." He set his jaw. "I will not be remembered as the man who killed my city to save it. The price my people will pay is too great, and the price I will pay is greater still. I will find another way."

He glanced over in Vilaer's direction, and the woman smiled back. Hope radiated from her.

"And if that other way cannot be found?" Ovelia asked. "If your cause of hope and mercy bears no fruit?" She looked out over the skyship, and the answer dawned on her. "*Hekatomb* is your second plan, should your primary plan fail."

"I have to try." Garin nodded solemnly. "The idealist in me would sever the chains that bind *Hekatomb* and let it sink into the Narfire, but the pragmatist will not allow it." He hung his head. "What if I am wrong, and the skyship is needed after all? What if you and the Lord of Tears have driven me mad? Am I not worse than Pervast to dash the last hope in pursuit of a folly that will not serve?"

Ovelia nodded. "I will not tell you to destroy it or to use it," she said. "That is a decision only you can make. Or not make, as you will."

"I've spent many summers not making this decision," Garin said. "It can wait a bit longer."

Ovelia turned once again to the mighty ship. She had to confess it was beautiful, and not just because it was the first thing she had seen clearly since Ruin's Night. Its lines were marvelous, more like those of a bird in flight than a ship. She could sense its potential to wreak devastation, not just on its appointed targets but also upon an unwary pilot. *Hekatomb* reminded her of a finely honed blade: beyond deadly in the hands of a master and just as dangerous to a novice wielder.

"Is it not a risk to leave it here?" Ovelia asked. "You said the doors could only be opened at your touch, but surely a powerful sorcerer could force them. Turn your own weapon against you?"

Garin chuckled behind her. "That, at least, I need not fear."

Draca's flames stirred, and she looked around to see Garin with a drawn blade behind her. Her body reacted defensively, half-drawing her sword, but he paid her no mind. Instead, he pressed the dagger to the palm of his opposite hand, and blood welled. He cast it on the floor at their feet.

Ovelia sensed something then, a growing pressure in her head. Draca became a hot iron in her hand, putting off so much smoke it might have been quenched in a bath of blood. She'd felt this warning once before, far to the north and on the last night she had been able to see, but it had not been nearly so intense. The blood on the floor twitched as though alive.

Vilaer hurried back over, drawn by the sudden commotion. She saw the blood and gasped.

"Back away," Ovelia said. "Highness! Princess!"

The blood parted and a man pulled himself out of it as out of a pit cut into the stone. Vilaer screamed, her voice echoing in the Narfire-lit cavern. Gore evaporated from the man like sweat and in a heartbeat Vhaerynn stood before them, his hairless skin glistening as with a fine dew. He looked older than a withered tree, and he wheezed like a leaky sieve trying to breathe. He gazed at Garin, then turned to Ovelia with a distasteful frown. His form lit up like a burning sun, glowing with the magic of thousands of trapped lives.

"Stand away!" Ovelia pointed the magic-drinking Draca at Vhaerynn. "We are under attack."

"No," Garin said. "I have invited him."

Ovelia stared at him, aghast. Her limbs shook to strike. "But—"

"He is, after all, court vizier to my family," Garin said. "Do you think he owes my cousin any more loyalty than he owes to me?"

"Just so, Highness." Vhaerynn sniffed in Ovelia's direction. "Apologies for my reaction to your call. I expected to find you alone." Then he glanced at Vilaer, who hid behind Ovelia. "And a Vultara as well. You keep such interesting company, my prince."

"Apology accepted, odd compliment unnecessary." Garin waved. "You came very quickly to my summons. Suspiciously, one might say. Are you here to keep watch over me?"

"The blood pact has no distance," Vhaerynn said. "But yes. I am in Luether. Your cousin the king commanded me to follow you. To ensure your success."

"How kind." Garin chuckled. "So long as he knows nothing of *Hekatomb*."

"It is our secret, my prince," Vhaerynn said. "Until you free me of our pact, of course, by your word or by your death."

"Of course."

Now that the initial shock had passed, Ovelia found herself staring at Vhaerynn, quite unable to comprehend what she saw. Since losing her sight, she had never gazed upon a sorcerer—one who wielded magic from within, rather than in the form of artifacts. Almost like an over-full sheep's bladder, his skin held a coursing morass of glowing spirits all tied together in an impossible grapple. Some glowed brighter than others, and she watched

179

spirits fade and vanish before her eyes: digested inside Vhaerynn. A pair of spectral hands caught hold off his chest and heaved as though to pull a body to freedom. She saw a horrified face, its eyes stretched impossibly wide, and caught her breath.

Vhaerynn caught her staring and glowered. He crossed his arms, holding in the spirit that tried to escape. "Highness, I have fulfilled my vow and come to your summons. What would you have of me?"

Garin shifted uncertainly, but he let it pass. "Necromancer, tell Ovelia of the pact we have made," he said. "Tell her of the magic you wove into this beautiful monstrosity at my urging."

Vhaerynn eyed Vilaer, who was trying unsuccessfully to fall beneath his notice. "You wish me to speak plainly?" he asked.

Garin nodded.

Vhaerynn made a distasteful clucking sound with his tongue. "Fear not, Daughter of Dragons," he said. "*Hekatomb* slumbers, and it will awaken only by Ravalis blood. Garin holds the key to its flight and its fate. And unless he has summoned me here to complete the ritual—?"

"I have not," Garin said.

"As I thought." Vhaerynn arranged his robes artfully around him. "Then I shall take my leave."

And with that, he vanished once more into the puddle of Garin's blood, which immediately dried up and turned to a black, congealed mess. His sudden appearance and leavetaking stole words from the chamber, and the three of them stood silent for a long series of moments.

"That," Vilaer said, breaking the tension. "That was horrific."

When Ovelia spoke, her voice was somber. "You spoke of the greater price you will pay."

Garin nodded. "Alcarin wants me to use *Hekatomb*, but he does not know what it will require of me," he said. "One more reason I can never allow the ship to fly, unless there is no choice." He looked at her, and she guessed an expression of fierce determination hung on his face. "Do not mistake me. There is no sacrifice I will not make for my people, but I would much prefer not to have to make this one."

Vilaer looked hurriedly back and forth between them, then focused on her feet.

Ovelia nodded. "Then we should see to it your mad path leads to victory." She wished she felt more confident.

Garin was staring at her. "I know what you're thinking," he said.

"Do you?"

He moved to a nearby desk scattered with parchments: notes, schematics, and maps. There, he began stacking the various writings and sketches. "You're wondering if my cousin could activate *Hekatomb* as easily as I could. Ravalis blood, as Vhaerynn said."

Ovelia nodded solemnly. "Could he?"

"Certainly." Garin set down the stack of papers and began to pile more things atop it: shards of metal, small gemstones, empty vials, and the like. "As long as I live and can control *Hekatomb*, it is safe. But if my cousin comes in force and wrests the knowledge from Vhaerynn or myself, he will certainly awaken *Hekatomb* and use it to conquer Calatan's last heirs and grind the World of Ruin under his boot. Thousands will die, and none will have the power to stop him." He hefted his burden in his arms. "Precisely what I cannot allow to come to pass."

He crossed to the cliff edge, where he hurled the papers and gewgaws out into the voids. They alternately floated and whizzed down into the darkness, catching fire and burning even before they had reached the pit of flame. Ovelia looked back to see Garin shove an entire table off the edge, and it cracked in half as it bounced off the cavern wall in its fall.

"What are you doing?" Vilaer asked, her voice rising.

Ovelia understood. "Exactly what he needs to," she said.

Ovelia went to his aid, and together they shoved the contents of his laboratory into the fire. Vilaer at first only watched, shocked, but eventually she joined in. In moments, they stood before the floating *Hekatomb*, which now seemed like a great, forbidding mystery without anything to even hint at its identity or construction. Ovelia watched Garin as he breathed heavily in the sweaty darkness.

"I still don't understand," Vilaer said. "Why destroy so much work? Decades spent crafting this weapon that could save your city?"

"Because I cannot risk another finding it and using it," Garin said.

"But you may yet need it," Ovelia said.

He nodded grimly. "Does that make me a coward?" he asked. "Am I sacrificing needless lives and losing my city because of my own fears, that I will not be able to overthrow Pervast? That I cannot protect them from Lan and his own manner of barbarism?"

At length, Ovelia shook her head. "It makes you a pragmatist," she said. "Svista and the other agents who left you cannot see that. They see only an idealist, and idealists make poor leaders. You, though—you are willing to do what must be done."

Garin nodded. "Let us hope it does not come to that."

Gazing at *Hekatomb*, Vilaer blew out a long sigh. "Let us hope."

EIGHTEEN

Ruktha's Redoubt—Luether

THE FADING SUNLIGHT THAT fell upon the soaring balcony made the water sparkle on the woman's burnished skin like diamonds strewn across a golden cask. She ducked her head under the water and rose afresh, letting it cascade over her sinuous body, scouring the dust and grime away. Water traced the tight curves of her small breasts, flowed along her raised ribs, and disappeared into the dark chasm between her thighs. Her eyes opened— yellow, predatory eyes—and she gazed out at the purples and oranges of the setting sun. She laid her head back against the discolored bronze tub and let out a long, contented sigh.

Only after a moment did Alistra look into the chamber and address the growing darkness with a faint smile. "Are you there, boy?"

Davargorn drew in a steady breath but did not move. He hadn't meant to watch her at all, let alone for this long. When he'd entered the High-City villa to deliver his report, he'd found Alistra scouring herself beside the tub on the balcony. He'd thought to speak, but then the light glimmered off her naked flesh and instead he'd found the shadow of a massive wardrobe from which to watch. Alistra climbed into the bath only after her skin was all but clean.

This odd dance proved more irksome every day. Thus far, since Vhaerynn had forbidden him to hunt rebels, Davargorn had spent his days in Luether killing every Child of Ruin he could find. It hardly presented exercise, much less a challenge. The winters he and Mask had spent in the city ducking patrols and learning how the barbarians operated had prepared Davargorn well for this task, and he went about it with grudging efficiency. His need to do it without being seen added spice to the entertainment, but it was too easy. Every day, he went forth to stalk and murder lone barbarians, then returned, covered in blood and lusting for battle, to find whatever fresh game Alistra meant to play with him that evening.

After a time, Alistra's caution waned, and she relaxed again. She loosed a soft hiss and her face took on a look of concentration. Davargorn could not see her hands from this angle, but the growing pleasure on her face told him enough. His pants felt tighter. When she moaned and clasped her left breast in her hand, his blade strained uncomfortably against his belt. She knelt in the bath, fingers working fast and diligently between her thighs, and cried out in a quickening series of utterances.

He didn't understand. Alistra had the face of a scrapper—bold features, oft-broken nose, thick jaw, scars on her lips, cheeks, and eyebrow—and her roughly treated body carried the same legacy. Her captors had cut off fingers and toes, scarred her all over with whips and branding irons, and subjected her to torments Davargorn could hardly imagine. Alistra's manner, too, was horrible: vicious, crude, and insulting. There was nothing of beauty about the wretched woman—so far did Alistra stand from the radiance of Semana Denerre nô Ravalis as if to seem a mere caricature.

And yet, Davargorn could not deny how firmly he stood, or the dull ache that seeped into his loins the longer Alistra worked and the longer he watched and listened.

Finally, with one last moan, Alistra was done. She slit her eyes open to scan the room one last time, a rueful smile on her face, then collapsed back into the bath with a great sigh. Water warmed from the day's sun sloshed over the sides to sizzle on the stones.

"Too bad," she said with a sigh. "I could have used a good rut."

Davargorn felt an overweening urge to stride out and confront her, but he held back. The familiar tingle in his veins told him Vhaerynn drew near. He stole from the room even before he heard the creaking door below that announced the necromancer's return. The water sloshed in the tub behind him, meaning Alistra had heard and would be more alert, but Davargorn had already reached the comparative safety of the stairs. He'd never thought he would find Vhaerynn's company safer than that of Alistra.

He left the room just before an anxious steward swept past him with a platter of bread, cheese, and steaming meat for the evening meal. Ruktha's Redoubt had once belonged to the Blood Tolutar, vassals of the Ravalis from before the fall of Luether. The barbarians had long since slain or chased out the heirs to the blood, but the surviving servants had been all too happy to serve Vhaerynn, emissary of Lan Ravalis, the King in Exile. Davargorn hoped they also feared the necromancer enough not to sell them out to Pervast, and so far they had not. He suspected that if they knew Alistra's identity as an heir of the Ravalis, they might have thought the potential gain worth the cost, but surely she could deal with such an eventuality in her own unique way.

The steward did not see Davargorn of course, who headed to the top of the stairs to listen for Vhaerynn. The necromancer puttered about in the hall for a moment, then began the long climb up the spiral stairs. Davargorn heard him punctuate each step with a sharp breath, and thought better of hiding. With his distinctive blood, the sorcerer would simply sniff him out wherever he lurked. Thus, Davargorn turned right back around and pounded his fist on the wall beside the half-open door of Alistra's room.

"Come," she said. Her tone—both sweet and suggestive—made Davargorn shiver.

He thrust the door open and stepped inside boldly, like a knight asserting his dominance over the chamber. Not at all like a cowardly thief who might have crept in to spy upon bathing ladies. To his great relief and disappointment, Alistra had donned a gauzy white robe, though she left it undone at the waist and it revealed a long line of her brown body beneath. He tried to keep his eyes on her face.

"Ah, the ugly boy," she said with a dismissive wave. The steward all but fled from the room. "Had a productive day, did you?"

Davargorn watched her closely, and realized she was hiding a smile. Now he understood. She'd known he was there, watching her bathe, and she'd put on a show for him. And now she would pretend otherwise. He did not understand this game, nor did he like it.

"Good enough," Davargorn said. "Killing barbarians never loses its savor."

"That must be sweaty work." Alistra gestured to the tub she had recently vacated. "Care to purify yourself? I'll not watch, unless you wish it."

When Davargorn gave her only a glower in reply, the woman chuckled and crossed to the table. She picked up a half loaf of black sweetbread and inclined it toward Davargorn. He shook his head, and she shrugged.

"Be as coy as you like, but I've seen you looking at me," she said. "I remind you of your princess, perhaps? She must have starved herself quite often, to fit into those horrid leathers of hers."

"You don't starve yourself." Davargorn pointed toward the feast set out for her. "You've done nothing but eat since we arrived. Eat and sleep and insult me."

"Only because you deserve it." Alistra broke off a hunk of bread and slathered it with hot pepper sauce. "I was quite the beauty with some heft on me. Maybe you'll live long enough to see."

A ragged cough at the door interrupted them. "Much as I would *loathe* to watch you children play your little rut-game," Vhaerynn said. "We have more important business to attend."

The necromancer's presence made the blood pound in his head, but Davargorn had accustomed himself over the last days to blocking out the pain. The old man smelled like blood as always, but beneath squatted a befouled foundation of rot and vomit. His skin looked thin as crackling parchment, the lines on his face had deepened to chasms, and his long teeth projected just over his lip. He walked with a slight limp, dragging along his steps. All these clues told Davargorn that he'd not fed his dagger recently, making him apt to prove foul tempered.

"Hmm." Alistra's expression showed she had noted the cues as well. She swayed to a dusty, bowl-shaped seat, slumped down, and threw one leg over its gilded arm. Davargorn averted his eyes. "And what important business is that?"

If Vhaerynn even noticed her forwardness, he made no sign. "As you may but probably do not know," he said. "The so-called merchants of Luether have consolidated their holdings since the workers at the Mines of Tuerine declared open revolt against Pervast two days ago. An act for which we have your cousin to thank." He glanced at Alistra. "My agents only now have the details: by all accounts, the Fox of Luether walked in and challenged the taskmaster without preamble or strategy. He should have perished, but instead he…*inspired* the miners."

"Bold," Davargorn said.

The others looked at him with surprise that he had spoken. Davargorn usually listened mutely to dialogues between Vhaerynn and Alistra, with nothing of any import to add. But the sheer nerve of Garin's action had sparked a tiny flame of admiration, which Davargorn immediately doused. He looked away, as though he hadn't said anything.

"It *is* bold." Alistra thumped her feet up on the table and stretched languorously in her seat. "Which was the point. My cousin does love his drama."

Davargorn's skin prickled. What was she doing?

"Mayhap," Vhaerynn said. "His scheme proved successful, and now Luether's economy stands on the brink of collapse." He coughed to clear his throat. "This is…unexpected."

"Perhaps by you." Alistra flicked a hunk of bread off the table with her toes, loosing a bemused snort as it bounced along the floor. "I, on the other hand, have never underestimated my cousin or his resolve. How does it feel to be surprised?"

The Necromancer glowered at her. Davargorn could feel his growing anger in the rush of blood pounding in his head.

"But this is old news you bring, necromancer." Alistra swept one hand across dismissively. "I knew of Garin's stand in the Mines even as it passed. Would you like the details? How many times the barbarian scourged him? Or how his body refused to bleed? Even you would have found it inspiring, I think, had you any poetry in your heart."

Vhaerynn frowned. "Your cousin is making his move to draw Luether out from under Pervast's feet, and we must move with him," he said. "We—"

"Let me guess," Alistra said. "Queer little cousin Garin refuses to wield his greatest weapon, and we must secure it from under him. Yes?"

"His greatest weapon?" Davargorn asked. "An alchemical device?"

The necromancer shot Alistra a disapproving glower. "It need not concern you, boy. Lady Ravalis, I require—"

Alistra interrupted the command with a loud belch that made them both look over at her in surprise. She held a greasy drumstick in one hand, her face smeared with its juices, and smirked at Vhaerynn. "No no, by all means," she said. "Tell Tithian about *Hekatomb*."

The necromancer looked surprised, if not stricken. It only lasted a flash, but Davargorn saw it. "You do not command me," he said. "I command *you*."

"That's adorable." Alistra tore off another hunk of meat and chewed loudly. "That you still think that's true."

Davargorn drew back, hands at the hilts of his falcata. He felt the tension rise between Vhaerynn and Alistra, even though neither moved to threaten the other. This was a duel between them, one in which he did not relish participating. Neither seemed to notice him.

The necromancer drew himself up to his full, imposing height. "You watch your tongue, whore."

"Oh yes," she said. "There it is. That word you hide behind as though it will shield you." She cast down the drumstick and wiped her face with a piece of bread. "It is so sad that you do not know the depth of your defeat already."

"Indeed." Vhaerynn's voice was calm, but Davargorn could hear its exasperated edge. "Enlighten me, scorned daughter of a dying blood. How have you defeated me?"

"That's just it." Alistra took her feet from the table and stood. She wiped her fingers on her silk robe, heedless of the stains, then plucked up her wine goblet. "I haven't defeated you. I was never your enemy. The *world* has defeated you." She gestured out to Luether beyond the balcony. "My brother rules Tar Vangr through fear—well enough. My cousin sees how to inspire—how to lead. Mercy! Imagine that." She looked back to Vhaerynn, her expression mildly disgusted. "By contrast, you can only muck around in the mud and blood with the pigs. You've already lost, and you can't see it."

"I'll tell you what I *do* see." Casually, Vhaerynn touched the golden dagger that hung from his neck. Pain rose in Davargorn's head, and he could feel the blood itching in his veins. "I see a whore who needs to learn a lesson about angering her master."

"That's the second time this eve." Alistra voice darkened. She drained the last of her wine and tossed the goblet aside to shatter on the floor. "Call me that thrice, and I will make you regret it."

"Will you?" Vhaerynn held up the dagger, making its edge glitter in the light of the setting sun. "Do you think your curse will protect you from the power of a god?"

"Who can say?" Alistra scoffed. "Men and their daggers. Is that the only weapon you can draw?"

"Hardly."

As Vhaerynn grew angry, Davargorn's body stiffened as the blood magic built in him. Now was his last chance, but he hesitated, uncertain how to move. Which of them should he strike down?

"You may have been born free of magic, but you are still just a woman," the necromancer said. "I told Lan this was a mistake, to bring his willful, insane sister, and you prove it with your every breath. Do you truly think you can speak to me thusly and not face the consequences?"

"We shall see." She looked to Davargorn. "Now. Kill him."

Her command surprised both of them by equal measures, but Vhaerynn acted first. He shot a glare at Davargorn, who stood ready to draw steel, and capillaries rose in the whites of his jaundiced eyes like blood-red cracks in tainted snow. Before the slayer could speak, his limbs went rigid as the blood magic seized him. Vhaerynn had been taking hold of him since he arrived—he'd never had a chance.

"No," the necromancer said. "I think he will kill *you*."

Alistra looked to Davargorn, her expression cold. "Will he, indeed?"

Davargorn struggled to speak against the choking magic, but his body was not his own. His falcata hummed forth into steady hands he could not control. He stepped and slid his twisted foot.

"You waste your last breaths appealing to him," the necromancer said. "He is *my* weapon."

Davargorn stepped toward her, his arms raised through Vhaerynn's will. He stared at Alistra, willing her to flee or at least defend herself. They gazed at one another, locked in a battle unseen.

Finally, Alistra's calm expression fell into a sneer, and rage rose back up. "Come then!" She slammed her fists on the table, making the dishes of food bounce. She swept all the food aside, hooked her hands under the edge, and threw the table aside with a snap of her muscular arms and back. "*Come!*"

That gave them both pause, and Davargorn was able to stop moving, and he succeeded in loosening his grip on his blades. Vhaerynn quickly reasserted control, however, and he took another step. He shuffled into the space vacated by the table, within arm's reach of Alistra. The swords shook in his hands and grew still once more. It all felt like a cruel game.

"Kill me!" Alistra tore open her robe, exposing her unprotected breast to Davargorn's blade. "If you cannot control yourself—if you will always be under another's boot—then kill me now." She raised her head, baring her throat. "Be stronger than you think you are, or I'll have none of you."

Davargorn laid his crossed blades on either side of Alistra's neck. The blood inside him burned as brightly as Alistra's wolf-yellow eyes. She gazed at him with righteous anger and staggering contempt.

The moment stretched, and Davargorn could tell time passed only because the crimson sun dipped lower, lengthening the shadows in the chamber. His blood thundered in his head, but somehow he could see and think. Had he slept all this time, standing like a statue with his swords at Alistra's throat? She heaved before him, matching his own cycle of breathing. He thought he could hear her heart beating as well, in time with his.

Every impulse in his body wanted to shove the steel through Alistra's body—part her head from her neck—but he would be his own man. He no longer even had to fight, he realized.

Vhaerynn loosed a frustrated growl behind him, like something not human. Davargorn managed a glance, and what he saw made him shiver. Any vestige of vitality had fled him: his extended arm had become the gnarled branch of a dead tree, his body shook like withered leaves in the wind, and his face shrank into a hollow skull. Blood trickled from his nose and mouth, and he choked for breath. Such a pathetic creature presumed to command *him*?

With purposeful smoothness, Davargorn turned halfway toward the necromancer—the most he could manage—and dropped the swords from his shaking hands. They rang loudly on the warm stone beneath his feet. Distantly, his hands reached toward them, but he held himself firm.

Alistra nodded.

Then she stepped across the mess of food, shattered crockery, and keen swords toward Vhaerynn.

"Back!" the necromancer said. "I abjure you, whore!"

He slashed the deadly golden dagger at her, and it opened up a gash in her left hand. Alistra staggered back a step, grasping her hand to her breast.

Davargorn caught his breath, remembering the awful destructive power of that blade.

A moment passed and nothing else. No ancient magic smote Alistra into a dusty corpse. Blood dripped from her hand, and she raised it to her lips experimentally. When she drew her cut hand away, it left a bloody print across her lips and cheek.

"Thrice." Alistra took the golden dagger out of Vhaerynn's trembling hand. "I promised you."

Vhaerynn whimpered. "Wait—"

Alistra slammed her elbow into the necromancer's sweating face. The old man stumbled back, and she hit him with a flying knee to the chest. He tumbled down and crunched into the floor. Alistra leaped on his chest and punched away, pounding his face and head and neck. Blood spattered everywhere: Alistra's robe and naked flesh, the walls and the floor, and even spots on the ceiling. She laughed uproariously and madly, and only the meaty slap of fist on flesh punctuated the reverberating glee. The smell of blood mingled with the reek of fresh shit filling the old man's robes.

The sun set fully. Davargorn watched the beating from a distance, his body shivering as the last vestiges of the blood magic waned. Then it was gone entirely, and he could no longer feel his blood beating in his head. He became his own man once more as night fell.

Vhaerynn's gurgling cry caught Davargorn's attention, and he saw Alistra driving her thumbs into the necromancer's eye sockets. The old man struggled, but he could not escape her powerful legs and hands. For such an ancient, withered creature, Vhaerynn erupted with blood like a burst waterskin. Blood soaked Alistra's arms to the elbows and made a ruin of the silken rag she wore.

There came a loud, wet *snap*, and abruptly Vhaerynn stopped thrashing.

"Hnn." Alistra climbed dizzily off Vhaerynn, a gore-covered mess drizzling blood onto the floor. She looked down at herself and smiled through the ruin. "And I just had my bath."

Davargorn shivered, as much with admiration as revulsion. In that moment, he knew he would follow Alistra anywhere.

He put out an arm to steady her, but Alistra brushed past him. She plucked up a chipped jug of wine, sloshed it around, and raised it to her lips. She drank as though it were water and she dying of thirst.

"Did you know the dagger wouldn't hurt you?" Davargorn asked at length.

Alistra interrupted her drinking to glance at him sidelong. "No."

"And that I could resist the blood magic?" he asked. "Did you know I wouldn't kill you?"

Alistra finished the jug and tossed it aside to bounce and roll toward the door. Davargorn noted the steward and one fearful maid lurking there, drawn—no doubt—to all the shouting and crashing. He gave them a slight nod and they hurried away, breathing hard and heavy. If they had feared their guests before, they knew abject terror now.

"No," she said. "Victory requires risk, or didn't your princess teach you that?"

Davargorn nodded. "Only too well."

She reached down and took the golden dagger from the floor. Vhaerynn's fingers twitched feebly for the handle of the blade, but Alistra stomped on them with her heel, producing a vicious cracking sound. The necromancer

189

gurgled in protest, and Alistra kicked him savagely in the face. He rolled onto his side and drooled a mess of blood and shattered bone onto the floor.

"Hey." Alistra knelt over the broken man and gave him a chiding slap to put him on his back, staring up through a ruined face. "Hey—listen. Look at me." She pulled his face up to hers, and blood bubbled up in his throat. Her eyes narrowed and she spoke in a sharp, guttural voice Davargorn had not imagined she could muster. "*Look at me.*"

Vhaerynn groaned and choked in agony. His one eye that could still see fixed on her face, and Davargorn could see the hate and fear written in his expression. Sickly black blood trickled from his nose.

"Blood sorcerer, necromancer of the last mage-city of Calatan. You came at me—*me*—not at your peak, and now, what have you to show for it?" Alistra hefted the golden dagger. "Without this, what are you? Just an old sack of bones and shit that doesn't understand death."

Davargorn grimaced in disgust. "Kill him and be done with it," he said.

Alistra held up the golden dagger, poised over Vhaerynn's eye. He stared up at it like a drunkard at a bottle—a drowning man at the surface of the sea above. Davargorn had witnessed the dagger's magic at work, and he wondered what the broken wretch saw in its golden surface. Perhaps he imagined the souls trapped within, screaming for vengeance.

"It's what he wants, and I'll not give him that." Alistra drew the golden knife away. "Let him expire here, pitiful and weak. I wonder if the age he's eluded for decades or the bleeding kills him first." She prodded Vhaerynn in the ribs with her toe. "Enjoy it, old man."

She left Vhaerynn in a spreading puddle on the floor.

"Come, boy," she said. "We're done with this place anyway. We have a rebellion to aid." When Davargorn gave her a perplexed look, she continued. "Garin stands more chance of overthrowing Pervast than anything that wretch could devise. We do this my way now. Agreed?"

At length, Davargorn nodded. He collected his swords from the floor and joined her on the balcony. She leaned against the bannister, overlooking a mechanical carriage being readied below.

"You've a plan?" he asked. "An inside agent?"

"Better." Alistra stood naked but for blood in the warm evening air and took a deep breath. She gave him a crooked smile. "A fresh bath. Then, I've a pirate to see about a boat. But first."

"First?" Davargorn caught her hungry look.

"I need something to offer."

She drove the golden dagger to its hilt in Davargorn's ribs.

ACT FOUR: OPPORTUNISTS

Twenty-one years previous—Ruin's Night—The Palace
of Vultara—Luether, 961 Sorcerus Annis

THE SUN HAD ONLY just begun to sink from its zenith through the crimson curtains, and Garin was already well on his way to a drunken oblivion. A mess of discarded clothing and empty phials of hard drink, his silk-festooned boudoir stank of wine and perfume and sex. Idly, he traced the lines of the fox inked onto his smooth chest, leaving dregs of nyssa over his skin. It felt like nothing but it amused him.

He loved his life of idleness and hated it.

The Crown Prince of Luether had built an impressive reputation for debauchery as he came of age. He'd imbibed quite a bit over the last few seasons, to dull the ache that was every Ruin-blighted day. When he wasn't drinking, he lost himself in flirtatious nonsense with a stream of giggly would-be princesses and their achingly handsome brothers or attendants. In his less lucid moments he'd even had sex with a few of them, though try as he might, he never enjoyed it.

One of the Vultara twins—Utora, he thought—even now had her face buried in his crotch, and he had just now realized it. She was skilled, certainly, but she lacked what he himself most wanted in a lover—through no fault of her own, but only an accident of birth. Fortunately, he could gaze through the gauzy skeins of silk that fell from the ceiling of his room at the thickly handsome Edric of Blood Duldur as he sat with the equally beautiful Radicci on the opposite couch by the window. The two lads spoke animatedly and drunkenly about philosophy or the weather or whatever—he hardly cared.

"Remis Thalavanter evoked the fundamental dignity of both men *and* women," Edric was saying. He was wise despite his Blood's humble origins as workers in the mines, and that only made Garin swoon harder. That and his shoulders. And his backside. And his frontside. *Mmm.* "That despite tradition, each should have as much right as the other to—"

"Thalavanter was a heretic and a fool." Radicci flipped his dark hair out

191

of his eyes. His was a feminine beauty—the stuff of bawdy tales of boys who served in gutter brothels until they rose up to become the dashing hero of a swashbuckling tale. "His arguments relied upon a false equivalence: that men and women are born equal. Obviously that isn't the case. See how much stronger we are, and faster, and just *smarter*."

Edric sighed. "I'm not sure that's what that means."

Garin pictured Edric's strong hands on his body, his thick lips wrapped around—

With a groan, Garin spent himself, keeping his eyes carefully shut while Utora swallowed his seed and cleaned him with her tongue. He didn't want to spoil the illusion, even if he knew he could never have it. Drained, he lay back on his divan while she went to fetch herself wine to cleanse her palate. No doubt, from the coy gaze she cast him, she thought this meant something between them—that in a season or two, she might be his queen of Luether and do this for him every night.

And perhaps she would. They would wed, he would ascend the throne, and they would have disappointing sex every night. In a few summers, she'd churn out squalling heirs, gradually grow to resent him in a few more, and finally kill herself as his own mother had done when he was a boy. It made little difference to Garin. In truth, he had befriended the girls mostly because their Blood name angered his noble father and because his other attendees wanted the loose sex. He took another draught of wine and listened to the obviously exaggerated gasps of Vilaer as one of Garin's other hangers-on rutted her silly on the other side of the room.

He hated it. All of it. The lies, the pretending, the boring sex…himself, most of all.

The rules of polite, gruff Luethaar society no longer applied once one entered his boudoir, and he took pride in indulging his entourage in their every desired taboo. While Garin celebrated wanton behavior here, outside these halls the Vultara girls would be roundly condemned as sluts and harlots, and the lads publically chastened but privately praised. That was, unless they knew about the time Garin had convinced the curious Radicci to bed down with him behind several of the curtains. They'd agreed never to speak about that night, of course, but Garin ached for such a touch once more—even if Radicci had proved such a pompous, self-loathing ass about it. It would not do for Garin to retract his favor, however, so he'd let Radicci stay on, with the promise of occasionally rutting one of the Vultara sisters or one of the other young women they retained for their sordid endeavors.

As long as Garin could stave off the world, he would.

He knew it could not last forever, though. Outside his sweaty, humid chambers, an anxious pall suffused Luether this Ruin's Night. A force of Children of Ruin had camped outside the city since the previous Ruin's Night, but the armies massed outside the gates had grown truly massive in the few days since Dark Solstice. Luether's superior mobility and force—skyships, war machines, thaumaturgical marvels—had so far proved more than enough to repel any invasion and to keep a steady flow of supplies coming into the city. The City of Flames would survive to see another summer, at least.

Even so, the extended siege had begun to take its toll on the Luethaar, both economically and psychologically. Bringing in so much food by skyship meant clamoring hordes of people in High-City all the time, and rising prices from the Bloods that controlled the supply. Mobs brought more Dustblades out in force, and King Cassian had even set Ironclads against his own people on more than one occasion. Many street philosophers shouted shrilly about the coming doom, claiming that it would fall upon the city any given night. For their part, the barbarians seemed content to wait. And wait. And wait.

Even blurred with drink, Garin was no fool. He knew Luether could not stand forever. Eventually, some spark would ignite the growing tinder and the resulting blaze would bring the mage-city toppling down. He only wondered if he cared what happened to him during the fallout.

Utora was building to a crescendo, and Garin went through the motions of pleasure. He'd established long ago that he would not necessarily spend himself when stimulated, and Utora either believed him or was decent enough not to argue the point. After a few not unpleasant moments, she stopped and rose up before him, her voluptuous body barely wrapped in a thin robe of green silk woven with tiny cut sapphires like raindrops, and snuggled up to Garin's side.

Had he been the sort of man who prized women—the normal sort of man—he might have found her touch arousing, but instead it did nothing for him. He had learned long ago to feign appreciation, though, so he did so now, idly tracing the contours of her breasts with his fingers and trying not to sigh in his lingering distaste. She giggled.

"Did my prince enjoy his pleasure?" she asked in a whisper. "I found it delicious."

"Huzzah the day," Garin replied, trying not to yawn. He'd become an adept liar. In truth, he envied her sister Vilaer, who was getting soundly plowed by a very handsome lad only a few paces away.

"Perhaps you wish to taste me as well?" Utora's violet eyes glimmered at him. "Or perhaps—?" She shifted one leg over his chest so that she straddled him.

"Well," Garin said, his voice slurred. "'Twould hardly be noble to decline such a generous offer."

193

A discreet knock on the door stirred Garin from his lethargy but failed to disrupt the babble of voices in the chamber. Longing for a distraction, he rose half-way, shoving Utora lightly aside. She took the gesture playfully, hugging him around the middle and pressing her cheek into his bare back. Endearing but annoying.

"Come!" he shouted.

Gutner, his long-suffering steward, pushed the door open and poked his head into the room. He wore a barely patient expression on his face. "Your Highness," he said, taking great pains not to look at Utora pressing her naked bits against his back beseechingly. "The king, your father, again bids you attend him at the council."

Oh yes. There was Narfire-burned *hope*.

The palace of Ravalis buzzed this day with all manner of news and excitement. Twice King Cassian had violated a centuries-old feud with the Ravalis' bitter rivals from the north, Denerre the Blood of Winter: once in arranging the marriage of his nephew Paeter to Semana, and now again in requesting northern aid against the Children of Ruin. King Orbrin Denerre had responded by bringing his whole Blood to Luether, including a very-great-with-child Lenalin. Garin's father was even now in council with the other great Bloods of Luether as well as King and Queen Denerre to determine if Luether would put aside her stubborn pride to accept their swords and war machines. There was hope, but not a great one.

This wasn't the first nor even the second time today that Gutner had interrupted him. This morn, the poor servant had awakened Garin and his guests from a late night, and they'd chased the hapless man out with thrown pillows and insults. When the man returned an hour later with delicacies to eat and—particularly—more nyssa, they'd welcomed him into the salon with good cheer, then driven him off the instant he mentioned the council. As of this third attempt, Garin could see Edric and Radicci tensing, pillows in hand, and even Vilaer had gone silently from the back alcove. Bracing for a battle.

"Well you can tell the king, my father"—Garin swatted Utora playfully on the rump, making her laugh—"that I am otherwise occupied." Utora crawled around to take him in her mouth again, and he listlessly twined his fingers through her hair.

"As you wish." Gutner hesitated on the threshold and leaned back in. "Your Highness, I was also given a message for you from Lady Dracaris."

Garin looked at his servant directly for the first time, suddenly interested. "Ovelia sent for me?"

"Not as such, Your Highness." Gutner straightened where he stood. "Lady Dracaris sends her apologies she cannot attend you today. Her Highness, the Princess of Winter—"

"Is otherwise occupied. Of course."

Garin sighed and waved his steward away. No doubt, Ovelia waited upon Lenalin's every whim and need. While she remained beautiful and elegant as ever, marriage to Paeter and carrying his child seemed to have made the Winter Princess harsh and bitter. Garin had seen Lenalin only once during this visit, and the pleasantries they had exchanged upon her arrival had been anything but. He did not envy Ovelia her duty to ward Lenalin during the end of her term, but such was love. What he wouldn't give to have a lover he could dote upon as completely as Ovelia did her Princess of Winter.

In the wake of Gutner's visit, the intrusion of reality into Garin's careless den of perversity left a lingering unease. Edric and Radicci fell to pointless bickering, then silence. Vilaer finished up quickly, then shoved her way free of whatever hapless slave she'd picked to satisfy her that day. And as for Utora— she put in an effort, but Garin couldn't fake it anymore. After a few moments, she gave up and flopped naked by his side to entertain herself with one of the bound romances she always carried with her.

"What was that all about?" Vilaer appeared from the back, tying the belt of her azure robe dotted with emeralds—the inverse of that of her sister. She had green eyes too, where Utora had blue, but otherwise they looked much the same. She cast her sister a sneer. "Should we be jealous?"

"Oh no, Ovelia—" Garin smiled and shrugged it off. "The lady I spoke of rather fancies women."

"Truly?" Vilaer looked scandalized. She sat by Utora's smooth legs and pinched the sole of one foot, prompting her sister to hiss in surprise and pain. "A woman with a woman. How deliciously vile."

"Yes." Garin felt his stomach churn. "Indeed it is."

"Those barbarians of the north," Utora said with disgust, bending her knees back to put her feet out of Vilaer's reach. "Thinking anything is acceptable." Idly, she teased the toes of one foot inside Garin's thigh, but he swatted her ankle in what he hoped would be a playful way.

"As it should be," Garin said under his breath, unable to keep from muttering.

"What?" Vilaer narrowed her eyes at him. "I didn't hear, your Highness."

Even through the haze of drink, Garin realized everyone was watching him: Vilaer and Utora, Edric who he wanted and Radicci who irked him. Others whose names he did not know—lesser scions and pathetic spendthrifts who hadn't worked a day in their lives. Idle youths like himself, but at least they could be honest in their frowned-upon lecheries.

"I suppose we are hardly ones to judge." Garin lifted his mostly-empty goblet of nyssa from the table at his elbow. "As mortal foes grow numerous and bold at the gates of Luether, so do we drink and make merry. We, the disappointments of our Blood—the wastrels of youth. There is no future for us, and hardly a past worth speaking of. Only the now. The terrible, awful, succulent *now*."

No one seemed pleased by that, though they raised their glasses dutifully anyway. He was the Prince of Luether, after all, and these people needed him. What else would they do, these castoffs that better members of the Blood wanted gone? It was all false, and he wanted to spit in every one of their faces. Or perhaps not Edric—him, Garin wanted to kiss so very badly. But since he could not, he resolved to hate the man instead.

Garin relaxed back into his divan, resolved to experiencing yet another wasted day in his wasted life, when he became aware of a distracting din from below in the courtyard. The sound made him perk up and look around. His lank companions seemed not to notice, going back to their favored activities with a murmuring hum of mindless converse and flirtation. A riot, no doubt, and he settled into drinking certain that the Ravalis warders would soon crush it.

He settled in and listened to his companions babble. Radicci was off making wooing sounds somewhere back in the room. Edric had returned to the window and sat by himself, gazing off into the warm sunlight. The Vultara sisters were arguing, per usual.

"We should call for more nyssa," Utora was saying. "Should we get more nyssa? We should get more nyssa."

"Only because you drank all of it," Vilaer said, her voice droll. "You always get the best things, sister. The best drink, the best lad, the best dress…though that one's stained, isn't it?"

Vilaer went red with indignation. "It is not," she said. "Yours is torn!"

At the window, Edric's expression became a perplexed one. Garin might have found it funny, but the lad seemed upset by something. Thus, Garin climbed off his divan, pulled up and secured his silk trousers with the drawstring, and wandered dizzily toward the source of sunlight. The wine and nyssa left his footing uncertain, but he made it well enough, leaning heavily on one elbow beside the thick, manly body he so often dreamed of. "What is it, Edric?" he asked. "You seem—"

Without looking at him, Edric pointed down into the courtyard. "That."

Five stories below, Garin expected to see a horde of upset citizens trampling the well-sculpted courtyard of the Ravalis palace, with its delicate fountains and exotic flowers. He would smirk down at them and offer some sort of witticism about making work for the groundskeepers come that evening. Then they would go back to drinking and wasting another day.

What he did see, however, made Garin's stomach clench hard as a fist. There were people gathered in the courtyard below the palace, but not peaceful protestors or even an unruly mob. What he saw was a vicious, bloody melee between gray-cloaked Ravalis warders in blue and red surcoats against a horde of screaming, thrashing attackers in mottled skins and bits of armor, wielding axes, picks, and hooked swords. They roared in rage, more like animals than like mortal men and women.

"By the Fire," Edric said. "What does it mean?"

At first, Garin couldn't quite credit what he was seeing, and wondered if he'd lost his senses after days of numbing his mind through drink and flesh. Then it dawned on him, with a terrible power that made him absolutely sure of what had come to pass.

The barbarians had breached Luether, and with them came Ruin.

A fist knocked on the door to the boudoir, prompting a startled gasp from Radicci. Garin spun on his heel and almost fell, but Edric put out a hand to steady him. The prince cursed inwardly that he'd drunk so much that he couldn't even walk straight. He started toward the door, under which he could see shadows moving.

Utora caught his arm, and when he looked down at her, she shook her head rapidly. "Wait!"

The disturbance rose and Garin realized with a sinking certainty that turned his legs to sludge that the sounds had come not just from outside in the courtyard but from *inside* the palace.

"We don't know who's out there," Vilaer said. "It could be slayers."

Utora's eyes flashed with panic. "Bar the door!" she said. "Maybe they'll pass us by."

The heavy fist pounded on the door again, more insistent this time, and they all breathed in sharply or exclaimed small curses to the Narfire. Radicci, half-hidden behind a folding curtain, had gone so white Garin could no longer see the Free Islander in his face. The rank smell of fresh piss arose, but no one made a sound. Garin certainly did not begrudge anyone their fear—his bladder felt on the verge of release itself. His heart thundered in his chest, and he heard it in his throat and head.

"Go away," he said softly to the door, willing their would be guest to pass by. "Go *away*."

197

Another knock—fainter. Then came a voice—one which made Garin's heart clench tight.

"Son," it said. "Son—"

Garin tripped over himself in his haste to get to the door, and he wrenched it open. "Father?"

Cassian Ravalis, King of Luether and master of the Summerlands, lay slumped against the door jamb, his royal robes sodden with blood. He oozed from dozens of wounds and a long-spent caster trailed from his hand. His handsome, thickly bearded face had drawn long and haggard, and his body trembled as he moved. Garin couldn't understand how weak and frail he had become, when he had always seemed immovable. A man nearly in his seventieth winter should not have to endure such treatment.

"Father," he said, taking the king in his arms. "What has—?"

Blood bubbled up to coat his fingers, and Garin trailed off in rising horror. He held on firmly, as though he could hold all the blood inside the king. Cassian felt like a bundle of sticks strung loosely together by twine that was even now coming unraveled.

"My son…" Cassian said, his face racked with pain. "You…you must—" He coughed, spitting blood in Garin's face. "S-sorry…"

"No." Garin shook his head, his eyes welling. "It's well. All passes well."

Behind him, the prince could feel his friends watching. Utora was wheezing, on the verge of swooning dead away, while Vilaer steepled her fingers against her nose and watched. Edric ran his hand back through his hair over and over. Radicci had not emerged from hiding. Half a dozen other faces he did not know watched him stupidly, not comprehending. How could they? How could they even *exist*?

"Garin," Cassian said. "My son…you must…"

"Wait, Father," he said. "Don't—don't try to talk."

The hall was littered with corpses, Garin saw, and he could hear the sounds of violence down the stairs. Many Ravalis warders must have spent their lives so that the king might make it to Garin's door. Shadows played up the stairs, and Garin heard heavy footfalls ascending toward them. He pulled, but Cassian felt like so much dead weight.

"Help me!" Garin cried.

Edric was just standing there looking at him stupidly, and he tried to repeat his command to get the brute's attention. It was only when Vilaer stepped forward and took hold of the king's arm that Edric finally stooped to help haul Cassian inside and onto the bed. Utora shut the door behind them and shoved a chair under the latch. The king coughed and wretched up blood, murmuring nonsense words Garin desperately wanted to understand. His face was wracked with pain.

"Radi," Garin said, then turned to hiss at the cowering lad. The Islander looked dazed. "Radicci! Bring me the sweetsoul. I know you have some."

"But—" Radicci looked ready to bolt—where, no one could say.

"*Now.*"

Snapping to attention with the sharp command, Radicci did as Garin bid. For the first time, Garin saw Radicci's love-slave of the day—a woman whose name he did not know. He kept looking for the man he thought he had heard rutting Vilaer, but there was no one else. Drunkenly, he wondered if the headstrong Vultara sister had indulged herself in a lover of the feminine persuasion. Immediately he hated himself for the thought. He felt sick—like a child caught in a child's games when men bled around him.

Radicci arrived with the sweetsoul powder, which Garin dissolved in his half-empty goblet of nyssa. Gingerly, he eased it between Cassian's lips, hoping it might help with the pain. The king's eyes fluttered and he gazed up at Garin dreamily. Seeing his father focus through the agony but also the glossiness in his eyes was enough to make him swear never to take sweetsoul again.

"Garin," Cassian said. "They're coming…betrayed…you have to go."

"Go?" Utora said, her voice trembling. "Go where?"

"Shut up!" Garin shouted at her, far harsher than he meant. "Father, not without you. Rest a moment, and you'll come with us."

Cassian shook his head weakly. "It's…too late for me."

He gestured down at the welling mess of blood in his middle and Garin realized for the first time that sticking…by the Fire, sticking out of the king's *belly* was a warpick. Garin had no idea how he hadn't seen it before, but now he did. It was a brute, ugly thing—a piece of a machine torn from its proper moorings and perversely lodged instead in flesh. His fingers touched it, and it sent a shock of terror through him.

"Garin," Cassian said, his voice barely a whisper. "Luether…needs you."

"I—I'm sorry, Father," he said. "I'm barely a son to you. I'm weak. I'm like a child. I'm sorry I couldn't be Paeter or burning *Lan*—"

"No apologies. All that…I never…doubted you. You…"

The king descended into a coughing fit, and Garin held his hand tightly throughout it. He opened his mouth but couldn't summon the words. A deep darkness rose inside him, stealing words and thoughts and threatening to take his breath. He tried to focus through all the drink and the wasted days.

"Now…now is the time," Cassian said. "To set…set it aside. To be…who you must be."

Boots stamped by in the corridor and a man shouted something, his words muffled through the wall. Fists pounded on the door. Utora started blubbering, and Vilaer took her by the shoulders and shook her. By the look on his face, Radicci would have wet his breeches if he hadn't already, and perhaps he even now held his bowels clasped tight to keep from voiding himself. Edric looked confused, gazing up at the door when the knock sounded like a frightened animal that hears the hunter drawing near.

"Who you must be," Cassian said, voice crackling. "To save…our city."

Garin felt cold to the world outside his dying father. His heart beat slower, in time with that of the king. Cassian seemed to be summoning up his own focus, mustering the last of his strength to convey something of dire import to him. He would not miss it, though barbarians came to take his life.

"Beneath…" Cassian's voice meandered in and out of coherence. "Long Dawn…"

Garin shook his head. "I don't understand," he said. "Father, what do I do? Father—?"

The king gave a great shudder and a long gasp rattled out of his throat. For a long moment, as fists pounded on the door and his companions tried to talk to him, Garin couldn't breathe. He waited and waited for Cassian's next inhalation, but nothing came to pass. Perhaps he'd simply fallen asleep.

"Father," Garin said, trying to rouse the king. "Father."

The door caved in around the lock, sending the chair skittering across the floor a few paces. Two men burst into the room, haggard and spattered with blood and dust. Utora shrieked and would have collapsed had not Vilaer caught her in her arms. Edric held out a heavy tankard like a shield, but it trembled in his hands. Garin himself looked up lazily and noted the stained blue and red surcoats they wore, marking them for Ravalis warders. Had they been Children of Ruin, he'd have looked at them in the same way.

"Majesty!" one said, then pulled up short with a stricken expression. His eyes widened and dampened, and the skin pulled tight away from a mouth wide open in shock. The other man huddled away, cursing in some foul dialect Garin did not immediately recognize. It was their faces—full of pain and shame and the agony of defeat—that finally convinced Garin the king, his father, was dead.

"Stand," Garin said, his voice a broken whisper. He cleared his throat. "Stand and speak. What are your names?"

"Corvus," said the second guard, who still wouldn't look at the king. He nudged his companion, who did not react in the slightest. "That there is Jorak."

"Corvus and Jorak." Garin smoothed Cassian's hair idly, as one might that of a doll. His middle and arms were covered in his father's blood. "What has passed?"

"Betrayed, your Highness," said Corvus, his voice dripping with poisonous anger. "Someone has opened the gates and brought the horde into the city. At the same moment—"

Jorak shook himself. "They struck in the council chambers, as though they knew exactly where and when to strike," he said. "So many great Bloods broken. The king…we got him out, wounded, but we got separated. He must have…"

The man trailed off, unable to speak the obvious. Cassian had known he was dying, and come to see Garin one last time. After a lifetime of misunderstandings and inadequacy, Garin wished they'd had more time.

"My uncle?" Garin asked. "My cousins? Lan? P—" He swallowed the name. "Paeter?"

"Escaped, your Highness," Corvus said. "With the Blood Denerre."

"Denerre!" Vilaer scowled. "Those blood-traitors from the north must have done this. Betrayed us to those vermin!"

"No, my lady," said Corvus, his tone gruffly dismissive. "The barbarians struck at them just as easy. Demetrus's First Shield saved King Cassian's life— at the cost of the Winter Queen."

"By the Fire." Garin thought instantly of Ovelia and Lenalin. "The Winter Princess. Has she been secured?"

Corvus shrugged, but Jorak nodded vigorously. "That man—Syr Norlest, the warder for the Winter King! He went up to find them. We came down, following the king."

Garin nodded. He'd only met the man once, but if the legendary Syr Norlest Dracaris had gone to rescue Ovelia and Lenalin, they would escape. He heard the fighting dying away out in the courtyard but growing louder in the palace itself. Time was running out. "Pass well," he said. "There is an ornithopter standing by?" He nodded around at his companions. "To take us all out of here?"

Corvus looked dubious, but Jorak smiled widely. "If we all get cozy, yes," he said. "We need to move, before they cut off the corridor—"

"What of our mother?" Utora asked, interrupting him.

The warders seemed to notice the Vultara girls for the first time, then, and though they might not have known them personally, their twin faces and the blue and green dresses identified their blood plainly. Jorak's almost manic smile turned quickly to disdain—even contempt. "We've no time to waste for the Blood of the Harlot," Corvus said.

There it was.

Utora paled and shrank back a step. "What did you say?" Vilaer asked, eyes narrow.

"Shut up, slut," Jorak said, chiming in. "You are guests of the prince, and so we will not turn you out like dogs. But speak out of turn again, and I—"

"You'll *what?*" Garin rose and addressed Jorak directly. "Who are you to rebuke my companions?"

The warder paled. "I—I only meant—"

"Your Highness, we've no time for this," Corvus said. "The King was clear in his orders. We are to take you immediately to the 'thopters—"

"Is the king dead?" Garin asked, resting one hand on the warpick that had killed Cassian.

The warders looked confused. "Yes—" Corvus said.

"Then *I* am your king." Garin ripped the warpick from his father's body as he shouted, and his voice filled the space like thunder. He hadn't realized he had grown so angry, but he would not stop himself. "I am your king," he said again, softer this time. "And you will obey me."

The warders looked to one another and nodded.

"Is Lady Vultara alive?" Garin asked.

Corvus shrugged, but Jorak narrowed his eyes in thought. "I believe so," he said. "She left the council chambers shortly before the assassins struck. If she took shelter in her guest chambers, she might have survived."

Garin nodded. All the High Bloods of Luether had chambers in the palace set aside, decorated in their style and kept neat for use on short notice. Even Denerre had chambers, though they'd not used them in centuries and most generations of Ravalis had let them gather dust or treated them like rut-chambers. Garin might have commanded Corvus and Jorak take them there, but that would be higher in the palace and thus farther from escape. The chambers of Vultara were below and would be on their way.

"I cannot advise this, Highn—your Majesty," Corvus said. "Even if Vultara survived, we may have to fight our way through burning dozens of Children of Ruin. Syr. Do not do this."

Garin raised his hand to silence the man. "Then it is settled," he said. "We will save Lady Vultara and anyone we can."

The warders crossed their arms over their chests and moved to obey. Jorak went to the door and cast wary glances in both directions. Corvus looked at Garin with something like paternal pride.

"Gather yourselves," Corvus said. "Quickly."

~

They moved as smoothly through the halls as a disheveled group of two warriors and six entirely untrained youths could.

Corvus and Jorak moved with the disciplined grace and cold efficiency of rigorously drilled warders. They stalked from alcove to shadow to stairwell, constantly taking cover as they peered around corners and waving forward their wards only when they saw no threat. Aside from their battered armor and a single shield, they had between them a caster whining with half a charge, their swords, and a single javelin. Garin recognized the thaumaturgical charge in it—a curling magic that would produce a forest of grasping tendrils upon a strike. That could prove the difference between escape and being overwhelmed.

A quick assessment of his companions, on the other hand, promised far less. He had the warpick he'd taken from his father's belly, but he had more rage than actual training in how to swing it. Edric and Vilaer were the only ones who seemed remotely capable, and Garin attributed that primarily to his great strength and her resolve. He'd broken off a chair leg to use as a club, while she'd produced a wicked knife from somewhere. The others fared worse. Utora trembled and shook, constantly on the verge of bolting, and for all his bravado Radicci shrank with fear. If Garin hadn't already regretted having sex with him, the lad's cowardice would have put him off for life. Assuming any of them lived out the day.

The sixth of their number—the slave-girl whose name Garin still did not know—lingered at the fringe, keeping very quiet. She glanced frequently at Vilaer and trembled slightly, then went back to looking at her feet. If Garin had to guess, he'd have put her age at fifteen or so. Perhaps younger. He dearly wanted to speak with her, if only because she looked as alone as he felt.

Corvus raised a closed fist to stop them at the landing of a stairwell just above the Vultara's guest chambers. "Wait," he said, sniffing at the air. "Something smells foul. I'll go ahead and see if it is clear."

"No." Jorak laid a hand on his arm. "I'll go. You stay with them."

Corvus looked at him doubtfully, then nodded. "Take the caster," he said. "I'll keep the javelin."

As Jorak stalked down the stairs, the remaining warder took up guard. Garin sat on his haunches against a wall, leaning on the butt of his warpick. The six youths sat, thankful for the chance to rest. Utora had held it together thus far, mostly with Vilaer's constant encouragement and coaxing. Radicci huddled so close to Edric that Garin was given to wonder if he had protested a bit much after their tryst. Seemingly unable to get comfortable, the nameless girl stood and shifted, stood and shifted ever closer to Vilaer. Finally, when she mustered her courage, she touched the brave Vultara sister on the shoulder, her expression on the verge of weeping. "My lady," she said.

"Away!" Vilaer slapped her hand away like a hateful insect. "I've no use for you, slave. Do not badger me."

The girl shrank away and cowered in a nearby alcove, refusing to meet anyone's eye. Garin's heart wept for her, but he could not think of the first word to say. After this was over, perhaps, he would find the words. He would do for her what Alistra had done for him, those summers ago. And perhaps it would even help her. For Garin, what his cousin had done that night was the only reason he had lived—for spite. Now…now he had a different purpose. And perhaps this girl could as well.

Abruptly, Corvus perked up and drew his sword, disrupting Garin's musing. Shortly thereafter, Jorak appeared up through the stairs, beaming. "Clear," he said. "I heard fighting farther on, though."

"Lady Vultara is in there?" Corvus asked.

He nodded. "Someone is," he said. "Door's locked from the inside, and someone knocked back. Had they been Children, they would have attacked. Barbarians aren't smart enough to set an ambush."

Corvus seemed uncertain. He looked to Garin, who nodded. "Take us."

Cautiously, they made their way down the stairs toward the chambers reserved for the Blood of Vultara. Dying light trickled through the windows that ringed the round common area, with blue and green curtains swirling easily in the breeze. It seemed oddly peaceful. Here on the third floor of the palace, the Vultara chambers were far removed from most of the main thoroughfares, intended to inconvenience Vultara courtiers when they stayed here for councils. It had always been this way, since the ignobility of Queen Vulta's betrayal centuries ago. The facilities were spare but functional, their arching mosaics and tapestries gaudy and the least artistic in the palace. Garin had never personally felt the same level of hatred toward the Blood Vultara that his own Blood was supposed to, but he understood tradition. Best of all, he saw no barbarians lying in wait.

"Stay alert," Corvus said, as though in answer to Garin's thoughts. The young ones raised their make-shift weapons, trembling in the semi-darkness.

"Just through here." Jorak went to the double-doors to the main chambers and gave a very specific knock. A moment later, a lock clicked, and the door swung slightly ajar. Jorak gestured them inside. "Quickly, quickly."

Corvus went first, and Edric and Vilaer after him. Garin entered fourth, and was immediately struck by the heat of the chamber. It felt stuffy and close, even if he could see only a single person waiting in the center of the room. The warders sheathed their swords and bowed deferentially.

Lady Vortan Vultara had seen perhaps fifty winters or so. She had ruled her

Blood from a young age, and many ascribed to her the same iron determination and will that marked many of the great women of her Blood. Too bad for her that King Raval had decreed that no woman would ever rule over a man in Luether. She certainly looked every bit the queen, and her mind for ruthless politics would have served the Summer City well. Today, she looked at him as though she couldn't quite believe what she saw.

"Lady Vultara," Garin said. "We've come to escort you to safety. Have you attendants? Servants?" He looked around at the empty chamber. "Bags, perhaps?"

Vortan's expression went from one of incredulity to sorrow. She looked past him at Vilaer and Utora. "Oh my daughters," she said. "I am so sorry. I tried."

A man stepped from the shadows—a shambling hulk, nearly thicker than he was tall. His thick, upturned nose and tiny eyes seemed porcine, completing the image of him as a hog. His flesh—which he hadn't bothered to cover other than with a loin cloth—rippled with crude black and red tattoos depicting animals, trees, and mountains. His stench almost made Garin swoon.

"Child of—" Corvus reached for the javelin, but Jorak pointed the caster at his face.

"Apologies, Cor," Jorak said. "Vortan may be a slut and a traitor, but she paid me too well."

"Traitor," Corvus said, his hand trembling on the hilt of his sword. "I will kill you for this."

"No, you won't," said the barbarian, his voice ugly and high-pitched. "I am Pervast, King of Ruin." He looked to Garin and pointed one stubby finger at the tattoo on his bare chest. "You must be the Fox of Luether. The crown prince, if I understand it."

"King," Garin said. "I am the last Ravalis left in Luether, if that is what you mean." His companions trembled at his side.

"King?" The barbarian shook with laughter. "I am the king of Luether now. I, Pervast the Powerful. Pervast the Devious. Pervast the—"

"Corpulent?" Garin raised the pick. "You may be king today, but not forever. Not while I live."

"Well." Pervast's wide grin was disgusting. "As you will have it, then, *Prince.*" He threw back his head and bellowed. "Live!" The word echoed through the room and out in the common hall. "*Live!*"

Doors erupted open all around the common hall and barbarians boiled out on their every side.

The battle moved so fast, Garin could hardly keep track of it. A yowling woman with a face full of teeth and twin axes in her hands rushed at him, eager for the glory of his death. Edric stepped forward to block her path, shouting a warning and pulling his club back. The woman hacked the weapon aside along with Edric's right hand, then buried her other axe in his neck. He fell, gurgling and dying, and she pounced on his body to drive it to the ground, then sank her teeth into his fountaining throat.

Garin stumbled away, temporarily forgotten, and Corvus grasped his arm to pull him into a protective circle.

"Stay close to me!" Corvus hacked his sword through a half-armored man's skull. "Steel high!"

Garin nodded and held his pick up. They stood, back to back, lashing out at barbarians who swarmed around them. They managed to get to the wall, where they could defend themselves without being flanked. Jorak stood a ways away, aiming his caster, but he couldn't get a clean cast.

"We need to get out!" Garin shouted.

"We can't get to the 'thopters," Corvus said.

Radicci gave a shriek and tried to flee, but a spear burst through the small of his back and nailed him to the wall. A barbarian raked his jagged gauntlet across the slave-girl's face, sending blood and one of her eyes flying. She collapsed, shrieking and gurgling against the wall. Garin regretted that he had never talked to her.

A caster thundered and the world exploded next to Garin's head. Jorak had cast at them, and narrowly missed. Corvus seized the opportunity to pull him toward the window.

"No," Garin said. "The others! We have to—"

"They're dead!" Corvus snapped. He shoved a barbarian back and pushed Garin toward the window. He leaned his sword against the sill and grasped the javelin from his back. "Keep fighting! I need a three-count!"

Garin swung his warpick, warding off a hairy barbarian. The horde fell back slightly, as if deferring to this one to take the prince. The man hissed at him like an animal, then bent low to pounce. Garin's hands trembled, but he had no choice. Elsewhere, Garin heard Utora scream and looked over to see Vilaer defending her sister with threats and her dagger. She slashed at the barbarians with the tiny blade, but Garin thought they were just toying with her before they struck.

"Not my daughters!" Vortan cried. "You promised, Pervast!"

The roar of battle drowned out her protests.

Garin only realized he'd been distracted when the barbarian lunged for him. He screamed despite himself and swung the warpick wildly, hoping against hope that—

The pick caught the barbarian's temple and its point burst through his opposite eye. His body slumped, killed instantly, taking the pick with it. Even had he wanted to, Garin had no idea how to dislodge the weapon. The barbarians looked at him with respect and rage.

Corvus grunted in approval, then hurled the javelin down at the ground, where it burst with a thunderous sucking sound into a squirming mass of purple-gray muck. It looked, Garin thought, like a mass of slick intestines. Then he grabbed Garin and shoved him onto the sill. The prince looked back.

At the center of the room, Pervast laughed and walked toward the girls. A barbarian with bone beads hanging from his flesh grasped the matriarch of Vultara and drove her before him. Finally, when they drew near Vilaer and Utora, Pervast held up a hand to stop them. Another barbarian handed him a dagger, and he seized Vortan by the hair.

"Please," she said. "We had a pact."

"There are no pacts between wolves and lambs," Pervast said.

He kissed her hard on the lips, then slashed the blade across Vortan's throat, spraying blood over her daughters. Utora was screaming and screaming, and now Vilaer joined her.

"Go!" Corvus cried, and shoved Garin out the window.

His body felt light—momentarily weightless—as he fell. Tears streamed upward from his eyes.

The relentless sun beat down upon Luether, even as explosions ripped through the air high above. Garin looked up as the massive crenellations at the peak of the palace broke apart, torn asunder by ferocious magic. Stones showered down around them like falling stars from the sky.

Luether came undone.

NINETEEN

Hopedawn—The Long Dawn—Luether

She dreamed once again of fire.

She stood in a dark cavern, separated from the roiling inferno by an invisible wall delicate as the skin of a soap bubble. She could have broken the barrier open with a touch, but instead she waited, watching the fires. They were dancing and moving, forming shapes that she had never seen before.

Eventually, the flames resolved themselves into a vaguely humanoid form whose face hid in the cacophony of silver fire, but she recognized it nonetheless: Lenalin.

In the way of dreams, Ovelia screamed silently, and the figure did not notice her. She reached forward and placed her hands on the invisible wall, which felt oddly cool to the touch. Always before in the dream, the wall had ruptured at the slightest pressure, but this time it resisted her like thick glass. Ovelia shoved on it, to no effect, then hammered her palms on the wall, breaking her skin and smearing blood through the air. The barrier would not give, and finally she sank down, heaving, and rested her head against the wall.

"Sister."

She looked up, and there was Lenalin gazing back, her face a rictus of scars and burns. She hardly resembled a vestige of herself, and yet Ovelia would know her face despite a thousand disfigurements and deaths. She wept tears of joy to see Lenalin again, and bitterness at her fate.

"I failed you," Ovelia said. "I—"

Then Lenalin reached through the wall and laid her hands on Ovelia's cheeks. Their eyes met, and Ovelia felt a burning in her head as though Lenalin's gaze had become fire. The princess opened her mouth to speak, but all that came out was flame.

Then, as the world slowed, the wall shattered all around them and a thousand shards of dark glass cut into her, rending her flesh from her bones. Then the wave of heat struck, and she felt her body burning away even as Lenalin's grasp grew tighter.

She could not even scream.

~

ARIN ROSE EARLY THAT day to await the gathering of his agents, unable to
Gstay in bed after waking. Since the announcement a few days before, he'd
nursed the lingering dread that many would not return, and when he woke
that morning it came to him in full force. After a few moments of tossing and
turning, sweaty and worried, he got up, dressed, and headed downstairs. He
found Biaza's squire Antilin in the kitchen, and the girl happily gave him the
first eggs and meat of the day, along with the first brewed kefa. It tasted thin
and not quite ready, but focusing on the vapors distracted him from his worries.

At least things had gone better with Alcarin since the announcement. His
squire had seen Garin's pain and soothed it as best he could, for which Garin
was immeasurably grateful. He fully acknowledged how awful he'd been since
Tar Vangr, and matters would grow worse before this was done, but Alcarin
provided a necessary support. As did Ovelia, for that matter: Garin had seen
the increasingly possessive way Red Jeggs looked at her, and it had begun to
distract the big man from his duties. Much as he hated to interfere in the affairs
of others, perhaps Garin would have to discuss the matter with them both.

Biaza appeared at dawn, returned from a clandestine meeting with her
own agents, and gave him a meaningful glance. Garin raised his half-empty
tankard to her, and she nodded in return.

"I'm glad you remain," he said when she came over to him at the bar. "And
not just because you are an excellent hostess."

"At least your pet Vultara isn't here this time," Biaza said.

"That's a relief." Garin nodded. Vilaer had insisted on staying apart from
the commanders of Summer Lives, lest her presence cause further fissures
in the organization. And by mutual agreement, she would take no further
part in these gatherings. He kept her under guard, of course: taking her had
provoked Pervast's forces to crack down harder on the taverns and slums of
Low-City, and just the previous evening they'd had to hide from a search.

"Do you think you can trust her?" Biaza asked.

"Who can say?" Garin shrugged. "I know what she wants, and I trust her
to act to acquire it. What more is needed?"

Biaza nodded, then furrowed her brow. "What I said the other day—at
the gathering."

"Think nothing of it," Garin said. "It is forgotten."

"It should not be." Biaza grasped his wrist. "What I said was harsh and
damaging, but you would have lost Svista and those other agents in time anyway.
You may have fought among us for twenty summers, but you still follow your

great Blood. You take the folk around you for granted, and rarely do you take their views into account. You assume they will agree and follow you blindly."

"Because I am right," Garin said. "You know my path is the right one."

"Perhaps," Biaza said.

The door to the Long Dawn creaked open and Corvus stepped through, with Neblen following close at his heels. The little thief waved excitedly, and Garin nodded back to her. Relief flooded him.

"Perhaps," Biaza said again. "Perhaps not. However righteous your cause, however sensible your precautions, you risk alienating those you would call allies. See that you do not drive away those in a position to do you the most harm."

Garin smiled. "My thanks for your wisdom," he said. "Though I must ask, do you truly support my cause, or are you one of those allies you would warn me against?"

"If you don't know that," Biaza said with a smile, "then you are beyond help."

Garin chuckled.

Ovelia appeared out of the back corridor, looking quite well put together, and Red Jeggs, dressed haphazardly, followed just a moment later, scowling. Garin thought again that he should do something about that.

He made to drink the last of his kefa, but Biaza put her hand over the mug. She leaned in close. "Do not forget," she said, then left him at the bar.

His lieutenants gathered before the sun had risen high in the sky, and Garin took up his customary place in the common room to address them. Fewer arrived than had come to the last gathering, but he reminded himself that this day's briefing was for his lieutenants only. It made Summer Lives feel smaller but its purpose all the greater.

"Welcome, friends and warriors," Garin said. "Here, learn your tasks of the day."

Garin drew a long scroll from his cloak on the chair beside him and rolled it out on the table. The heavy parchment had yellowed at the edges and looked worn, but not a single letter or line stood upon it—it was entirely blank. Neblen frowned in confusion, but he heard a few knowing chuckles. Corvus rolled his eyes and Biaza gave him a dour smile from where she leaned against the bar near the front of the common hall. Both knew his passion for drama, but neither understood how badly he needed to show off to put all that unpleasantness behind him.

"Behold!" Garin drew a vial of yellowish liquid and flicked its contents onto the scroll. Where they hit, moisture spread and dark lines started to appear. The liquid spread across the scroll like creeping waves of flame, and soon enough an astonishingly detailed map of Luether revealed itself on the scroll before the rebels. He took pride in the sounds of awe they made. More personally, Alcarin subtly put an appreciative hand on his hindquarters, which Garin very much appreciated.

"For a first." He pointed to a warehouse in Low-City. "Neblen has informed us of a stockpile of arms moving into Child hands. We don't have enough soldiers to mount an assault, but Neblen has found a back entrance. Corvus, take Red Jeggs and two other warriors of your choice. Secure the steel for Summer Lives, or destroy it. Neblen will advise you on how to make it look like a burglary."

The soldier nodded. "I'll take Tevis and—" His eyes flicked over to Ovelia. "The Bloodbreaker."

All eyes turned toward Ovelia, who stood at the corner of the common hall. At the sound of her name, she gave Corvus a long, unimpressed look. Garin could see her temper brewing and knew it would boil over at any moment. His agents seemed to have forgotten her or at least treated her with indifference thus far, but she stood upon a narrow perch.

"I have plans for her, actually," Garin said. "Acting on information furnished us by the graces of Biaza—" He swept a small bow in the direction of the Long Dawn's matron, and the woman raised her chin in return. "We've secured a meet with a potential ally who will act to disrupt the specified shipping routes. It requires a sea voyage to a neutral island, about half a day's travel. As this is an official offer of alliance, perhaps I should go—" The room erupted in protest, startling Garin out of his speech. "What?"

No one seemed apt to speak up, until Corvus clarified in his voice like the rumble of thunder on the distant horizon. "Your Highness," he said.

"*Garin*," he said. "I've no title or throne among my friends, who I've fought and bled beside. As I've told you before."

Corvus shrugged. "Yes, your Highness, so you've said."

Raised to respect and defer to the Ravalis from birth, the old soldier—who had served on Garin's personal guard as long as the prince could remember—would likely never let his propriety slip. It was a game Garin and Corvus had played for all the summers they had known one another, and he counted the man one of his closest, most trusted allies.

"You see, Highness," Corvus said. "You're far too important to risk like you say."

"I'm taking Lea—*Lady Dracaris* with me," Garin said. "She'll ward me perfectly well."

"She's blind," Corvus said. "On a cadre, she might be useful. On her own, she's not enough."

"Enough for you," Ovelia said, her face burning with temper. She stood with arms crossed, but one hand rested on Draca's hilt. Shadows boiled up around her hand.

Corvus reached for his hammer. "Try it, you half-breed wench."

The common hall had gone absolutely silent, all eyes on the growing tension between Corvus and Ovelia. Both seemed calm, but Garin knew both well enough to see through the illusion. Either could launch into battle at any instant, and he could not say which would prevail. If Corvus defeated Garin's foreign advisor, it would shake the rebels' confidence in the current leadership, and if Ovelia threw down the old veteran, would that not make everyone hate her more than they already did? And if either of them took a wound in the duel, would not all of Summer Lives suffer for it?

"I'll go." Alcarin stepped to Garin's side and laid his belt dagger on the table beside the warpick. "Corvus is right, Master. You are too valuable to risk, at least without dire purpose. I'm your second. I'll speak for you."

At length, Garin nodded. "Very well, Squire," he said. He put his hands on Alcarin's shoulders. "I invest in you my words and purpose. You will speak on my behalf, and for all of Summer Lives." Then he leaned in close and pressed his lips to his squire's ear. "I'm glad of your timing, this time."

"You say that like I haven't saved you from near-mutiny a dozen times before."

Ostensibly chastely, Alcarin kissed Garin gently on the cheek, then pulled away. He reclaimed his dagger and moved toward the door. He and Ovelia exchanged a nod.

"These are the tasks that must be done, as I have instructed," Garin said. "Any objections? Suggestions? Speak up now."

"Ay." Red Jeggs pushed his way through the common room. The big man wore a cream-colored shirt open to the chest, whose color complemented his dark flesh nicely. It seemed to be an accident that he'd picked well, however. His dress was generally unkempt, and his long, dark hair resembled a nest of ravens atop his well-formed head. He must have prepared hurriedly for this audience. "Did I hear you aright, that you're sending Ovelia and Alcarin alone?"

"That I am," Garin said. "You have a problem with this?"

"Only that you're sending a barely-grown page boy and a blind woman on this important task," he said. "Let me go as well. More arms can wait. You know no Child can match my blade."

Ovelia drew in a sharp breath, and Garin felt her eyeless gaze on him. Warning.

"No," Garin said. "I need you where I assigned you. This isn't a discussion."

For a moment, Red Jeggs looked as though he would argue. A glance around the common room, and Garin could see more than a few dubious expressions. Not everyone agreed with his approach, but his announcement of haste seemed to have soothed some impatient tempers. Red Jeggs apparently thought better of challenging Garin, and so he nodded and stepped back.

"Good," Garin said. "You all have your tasks. I shall expect your reports this eve."

The gathered throng broke apart, descending into various smaller conversations and a flurry of activity to prepare. Ovelia glanced in Garin's direction and he gave her a broad smile she could not see. She shook her head in disapproval and started toward the door.

"That—" Alcarin took Garin's hands. "That went better than I expected."

"You always doubt me." He drew his squire a little closer to himself than they usually allowed themselves in front of the others. Alcarin's eyes said he noticed, but he offered no objection.

"I notice, though," Alcarin said with a wry look, "that you're sending me off with your blind pet dragon immediately after, so we can't celebrate."

"You know I love it when you pout," Garin said. "But this is important. If Biaza's source tells it true, winning this ally could be critical. I can't trust anyone else with a task this delicate."

"Oh I know." Alcarin released him and walked backward away toward the door. "Just remember you owe me this favor."

"I look forward to repaying it," Garin said.

Alcarin stepped past Ovelia and Red Jeggs, who stood arguing in sharp undertones by the door. He knew about their dalliance, of course: Ovelia had told him that first time, and they'd agreed that it would not compromise their purpose in the city. Garin saw trouble, though, in the way their bodies interacted—circling warily like opposing warriors.

"What passed there?" Ovelia demanded.

"Just protecting my woman," Red Jeggs said.

"I am *not* your woman." Ovelia said, loud enough for the whole tavern to hear. Without her sight, Garin realized, she couldn't know how many people were watching her. Or else, she did not care.

"But—" he said.

"No," Ovelia said. "We are not wed, nor are we even promised." She touched his chest, then hers. "This? Between us? It is sex. Nothing more. You should learn that."

Red Jeggs stammered a reply, and his face went the color of his name. He made a mewling noise as though she had kneed him full force between the legs. As Ovelia walked away to join Alcarin, the big man gazed after her like a hurt puppy.

"Jeggs." Garin made his way over. "Share a nyssa with me. I'll tell you about northern girls."

Red Jeggs hardly seemed to hear. Instead, he stared out into the street, and his clasped fists shook with rising anger.

"Jeggs?" Garin laid his hand on the big man's arm. "Pass w—"

Violently, Red Jeggs shook off his hand. "Away from me, sword-swallower!" He rounded on Garin. "You're her little gelded dog, anyway. What's she done to steal your balls? Can't be rutting you—you wouldn't know where to stick it in if a whore knelt for you and opened wide." He stormed off.

Garin stood by the door, shocked. Red Jeggs had his temper, for a surety, but never had Garin felt its sting quite like that. And with the number of eyes watching him—Biaza, Neblen, Corvus, and half a dozen others…

The darkness started to swell within, but he choked it down. Now was not the time.

He had his own appointment to keep, after all—a secret one that would require all his wits and will. He'd never intended to go to Biaza's meeting, but used it instead as a test of his allies in Summer Lives. But for Red Jeggs's outburst, all seemed well enough.

He hoped his meeting would yield better results than this one, though somehow, he doubted it.

TWENTY

WHEN OVELIA STEPPED OUT into the bright Luether morning, her world grew lighter. She felt the heat on her skin, but it did not sizzle as it had at dawn. Some clouds, or perhaps a subtle mist? She envied folk who could tell the weather at an easy glance upward.

"Sun's not too bad today," Alcarin said from where he leaned against the wall under the awning. "All that smoke is good for something, at least."

Ovelia nodded and adjusted her hood over her face. Physically, she felt better today than she had in a long time: rested and strong. She'd managed to reject Red Jeggs's constant attempts to give her sweetsoul, politely but firmly, and now the craving had become significantly less. She should have told him to stop offering, but she hated to expose that weakness. She hardly felt it, much less shivered with need. Perhaps the withdrawal was nearly over. In her mind, however, she was troubled.

Corvus's huge, brooding mass loomed into her shadowy world, exuding menace to keep would-be harassers at bay. She could see he posed her no threat—not at the moment, anyway.

"You understand, my lady," Corvus said in his deep, rumbling voice. "What I said and did in there was not personal, and I intended no disrespect. I am simply protecting my liege."

"Yes," she said. "You have every reason to distrust me, and I every reason to earn your trust." She bit her lip. "These are…difficult times."

Corvus responded to her thoughts, rather than her words. For a smallborn soldier, he could be incisive. "You don't agree with Garin's course either. This…*mercy* idea of his?"

Ovelia frowned, uncertain how to respond. After his apparent victory at Tuerine, Garin had conceived an enthusiasm for victory that could not be restrained. He was now convinced, for better or worse, that passive resistance would serve better than blades and peaceful overthrow would be possible. He seemed to be the only one who held such a view: she could tell many of his agents saw his strategy as folly at best, madness at worst. He should have given more time for rumors to spread before he made his announcement, but Garin valued his showmanship above his sense.

"I advised him against doing that," Ovelia said finally. "He lost people, and now our diminished ranks will only prompt more anxiety and foolish mistakes. We don't have time to waste."

"You underestimate us, my lady," Corvus said. "Summer Lives does its best work at the longest, hottest hour." He made a clicking sound with his teeth.

"Right when tempers flare hottest," Alcarin put in, "and our would-be allies are most like to kill us rather than listen."

"You disapprove of Garin's methods," Ovelia said. Not a question.

"You approve of them?" Alcarin burned particularly bright in her shadowy vision. "He's grown reckless, if you ask me."

He had a point. Ovelia had not forgiven Garin for leaving her behind when he went to liberate Tuerine. In his enthusiasm, Garin could make foolish errors, and Ovelia resolved to watch him with more care in the future. She never should have left the Long Dawn this day, but her fury at the man demanded time apart. At least if he stayed in the tavern, he would be relatively safe until she returned from this task, but she'd not put it past him to embark on some half-planned mischief of his own.

"Regardless," she said finally. "I have sworn an oath to follow him, and I'll not break it."

That proved good enough for Corvus, who gave her a curt nod and walked away. Alcarin, on the other hand, still glowed just as brightly as he had before. As Ovelia had observed to Garin back on the *Avenger*, the lad was angry, and while the trek to the Mine had soothed him somewhat, that rage remained and grew by the day.

"So you defer to his judgment," Alcarin said, "but you still question him, no?"

"I will advise him of what I see as folly in his course, but ultimately, it is his decision."

Alcarin nodded gruffly. "That's something, at least," he said. "The last thing Garin needs is one more weak-willed advisor who won't stand up to his ego."

Ovelia frowned again. "He is your master," she said. "Why do you speak of him so?"

Alcarin scoffed. "If you ask that, you must never have had a master whose bed you shared."

The words took Ovelia by surprise, and she could not quite school her reaction to them. Her cheeks felt warm, and she turned away from Alcarin so he would not see. Focused on sharpening his blades, the lad either did not notice or did not care.

Unexpectedly, someone took Ovelia's hands, and she recognized the gutter reek and astringent scent of Neblen the thief. They'd met before, of course, and the girl had immediately taken a liking to her. For her part, Ovelia returned the affection with a disapproving caveat: the girl seemed entirely too young to be risking her life on Luether's mean streets. She could prove rather scattered, as well, as though her mouth spewed every thought her chaotic mind mustered at any moment. Undeniably, however, "Neblen the Nasty" had proved the rebels' most effective rumor-monger, and her information had never failed.

"My Lady!" the sneak said. "We must talk!"

"What is it?" Ovelia asked, instantly alert. Her reception in the Long Dawn had not been stellar.

"You're Tar Vangran, my Lady," Neblen said.

"Tar *Vangryur*," Ovelia said.

Neblen would not be tripped up. "I want to know all about the Winter City. Its customs, its people—their wealth, specifically. And the dresses! If we're to have guests next season, I would know how to treat them."

"Rob them, you mean," Alcarin said under his voice.

Neblen shrugged off Alcarin's barb. "You're so beautiful," she said to Ovelia. "Are all Tar Vangrans as beautiful as you? Did you really kill the Winter King?"

Before Ovelia could reply, a thicker voice shouted over her. "You—girl," Corvus called. "Come away from there. We move."

Neblen giggled. Her optimism had a rich aroma that made Ovelia feel heady. As the thief hurried away, however, the sense of hope withered and fell apart, like a flat, metallic taste on Ovelia's tongue.

"We should go as well," Alcarin said.

She nodded, unnerved.

~

After an hour under the stinking sackcloth, Garin was ready to vomit into the hood regardless of the consequences. He understood the necessity of it all, but resented the application. He'd come as a peaceful envoy, and if all went well, it would not matter if he knew the route to this place. And if it did not, well, that would not matter either. If his would-be ally did not appreciate the purpose with which he'd placed himself into her custody, he would be quite surprised. Probably he would be dead as well, but every day in the World of Ruin offered such a chance.

So far, his plan had worked. He'd ducked his escorts near Niegrim's Rise, then stolen aboard the lift to Luether's High-City. From there, it had proven an easy feat to get himself captured. Fortunately, they'd not slain him out of hand, but instead left him, hooded and bound, in this room where water dripped and wind roared outside some manner of open window. He could feel the cold breeze biting at his cheeks and had the sensation of being very high off the ground.

On occasion, he thought he heard a slight rustle or cleared throat that suggested a less-than-solitary confinement, but he could not identify his captors. At times like this, he envied Ovelia's ability to see without her eyes. Instead, he tried talking. He said nothing of any import, but entertained and annoyed his supposed companions with observations about the weather, or the minutiae of brewing curatives from herbs found in the prairies around Luether. Garin had never struggled to find words, and so he gladly rambled on into the interminable stink of his hood and the uncertainty of his circumstances.

After half an hour, he heard a voice at last. "That's enough babble," a woman said. "Remove it."

Rough hands seized his neck and wrenched the hood away. The scarred enforcer Aeldad stood over him, and from the cold expression on her scarred face, Garin supposed she had neither forgotten nor forgiven her humiliation at his hands on the *Avenger*. He tried smiling at her, and her displeased grimace became open contempt. Her eyes hungered to inflict some violence upon Garin.

"Hail and well met, tall lady!" Garin said to Aeldad. "I apologize that our other encounter was so brief, but things to do, you know?"

She sniffed at him, then nodded behind him. There, Garin saw not a window—as he had guessed before—but a missing section of wall and some of the floor. The chair in which he sat creaked on the edge of a precipitous drop to crashing rocks a thousand paces below. He looked down at a diamond shaped mountain: the sheer black wall sloping down and out far below, then dropping away into nothingness. Even as he watched, one of the loose stones of the floor gave way and went hurtling down toward the sea. It fell a hundred paces, then skipped off the slope, skidded down, and vanished over the edge. If he followed it, he would leave a messy bloodstain on the stone, he thought.

He knew now where the pirates had brought him: to her fortress atop the ruins of Atropis. There, they held him in a truly ancient chamber, one that crumbled in the wind day by day. How hospitable.

Aeldad looked quite ready to hurl him to his doom before the cell decayed, but her keeper spoke up to stop her. "Squire," said the woman that Garin had heard before. "Enough."

As Aeldad backed away, Garin saw his captor seated across from him on a heap of pillows that seemed out of place in his dingy, crumbling cell. Shrouded in black silks, Shard sat at her ease, watching him curiously.

"My Lady Shard," Garin said. "Always a pleasure."

"I trust the hood was an understandable discomfort?" Shard asked.

"Certainly," Garin said. "I wondered at first why you'd blind me if you planned to show me where we were anyway, but then I remembered you have hidden sentries and defenses from which no skyship has ever returned intact."

"A true legend I wish to maintain." Shard's tone shifted from even an attempt at etiquette to something harsher and more efficient. "You may be a fool, but you are not stupid. Why are you here?"

"Right to it then," Garin said. "Very well. I wish to forge a formal alliance with you."

Shard looked to Aeldad, who stood menacingly over the prince. "Leave us," she said.

The woman looked as though she would argue, but finally she merely nodded curtly and strode toward the door. Shard touched Aeldad's hand, making her pause so they could exchange nods. Aeldad gave over her caster to Shard, and then the tall woman was gone. The door ground shut behind her.

Shard checked the caster's charge and tapped the weapon against her knee. "You know my price, Fox of Luether," she said without looking at him.

Garin shivered. "*Hekatomb*," he said in a whisper.

"You know what I want." Shard checked the sights on the caster. "And yet you have never been willing to give it to me. Has that changed now?"

"No," Garin said.

"I see." She rose and pointed the caster at Garin's left leg. "Tell me where it is."

"Or you'll torture me?" Garin asked. "I've never had a taste for it. The answers it yields are imprecise and ultimately useless. Far better to use one's mind than one's savagery."

"I could coerce you through other means," Shard said.

"Oh?"

Shard pointed the caster over his shoulder toward Luether. "I will kill your friends. Starting with that smooth bed-boy you keep at your side. Alcarin, isn't it? Yes."

"Well, that would certainly cast a pall on our alliance, eh?" Garin asked.

They stared at one another—Shard standing, Garin sitting—for a long time, before she finally lowered the caster. "You are a fool, but not stupid," she said. "You would not have come to me if you did not have something more to offer."

"That's true," Garin said.

"But not what I want," Shard asked. "It must be something truly wondrous to make you bear even the slightest hope that I will make common cause with you. It matters little to me who sits the throne of the City of Pyres. My trade flourishes regardless." She peered along the caster's sights. "So what?"

"Ovelia Dracaris," Garin said.

Shard paused in checking the caster. It was slight and brief, but it was there. "What of her?"

"I could ask you the same thing," Garin said. "I saw the way you looked at her, and she definitely felt your interest as well."

"She…intrigues me," Shard said. "I had heard that she was dead some winters ago, and yet, she reappears, wielding that fantastic sword of hers. There is a story there, one that I wish to hear." She looked at Garin directly for the first time. "Do you understand what you have, in her?"

"I'm starting to," Garin said. "Why? What do you know of her that I do not?"

Smoothly, Shard set the caster on the stone pallet that held her pillows and clasped her hands together in front of her. "She is worth every single soldier you can muster to your cause," she said. "That sword of hers alone could slay all of your foes, and in the hands of a true heir of her line…Ovelia Dracaris could topple mountains in her fury. And yet, you keep her carefully leashed, as you do the *Hekatomb*." She raised her chin. "Why?"

"Perhaps I am cautious," Garin said.

"Timid, I think," Shard replied. "Or is it by artifice? I have heard of this 'Merciful Fox' you would have folk call you. You truly believe you can overthrow Pervast the Unseen, what—by words and good deeds? Rather than by the sword?"

"And watch thousands of my people die by that same sword?" Garin asked. "If I can avoid bloodshed, it is worth trying. And I need all the help I can find."

Shard considered. The veil hid her expression, but Garin hoped it was at least a thoughtful one.

A fist slammed on the door, and Aeldad stepped through. She stepped quickly to her captain's side and whispered in her ear.

"What is it?" Garin asked. "What's happened?"

Shard gazed at him through her impenetrable veil. "You've lost your bargaining power, Prince."

TWENTY-ONE

The trek to the docks was a quick one, as Alcarin led Ovelia through a series of shortcuts and narrow alleyways to cut the time she had expected for the journey in half. Fortunately, her curious affinity for seeing him—his inner violence made him the clearest shadow in a world of darkness—made following him easy enough. They passed in silence.

The city seemed like an extension of Alcarin's own body, so well did he know its ways and secrets. Ovelia would have found herself lost and sick within an hour: she found the constantly shifting layout of Luether impossible to track, even without the blindness. The world became a blurry forest of moving shadows and looming shapes, where the smoky reek of burned out buildings and the too-sweet tang of corpses left to ferment in the street assailed her nostrils. Without a guide, she shuddered to think of the nightmare negotiating these streets would have proved.

They also ducked two roving patrols of Children and one of the horrendous street threshers she had encountered on her previous visit to the city. They watched from cover as the mighty machine lumbered along the streets it had once cleaned, raking all in its path with spinning blades and trampling the refuse beneath spiked wheels. If she never faced one again, she would die well pleased.

Ovelia smelled the docks before they arrived: the salty stench of fish, the pitch used to seal the boats, and the dusky mold that grew over almost everything. Sweaty men labored over odd-loaded goods that had arrived that day, and Ovelia heard the whir of a steel crane transporting crates from the groaning ships. The world became an open blur over the water, and she could just make out the hazy shapes of the towering cliffs that formed the exterior of the archipelago. At least the water seemed mercifully free of the foreboding shadows she had glimpsed from the deck of the *Avenger*. She gazed out over the sea as Alcarin negotiated their passage out to the appointed meeting place. He and the boatman exchanged words, and Ovelia could tell he was one of Summer Lives's agents.

"You grew up in this city, did you not?" she asked Alcarin when they were underway, the water lapping at the tarred sides of their small barge.

At first, Ovelia thought Alcarin might not answer her. They'd spoken little in their time together, and she had received the message clearly that he did not particularly like or trust her. She had hoped this would prove an opportunity to reconcile, but he seemed indifferent. Ovelia understood completely why he might feel antipathy toward her, though she wanted to hear him say the words before she took it amiss.

"I was born in the gutter," Alcarin said. "My first memory is of my mother coughing—she took sick and died trying to bear my little brother. I scraped together every coin I could and burned them both, for the price of just her. My brother was still half inside her. I had just seen my sixth summer."

Ovelia felt a rising pressure inside her chest. "I am sorry, I had not thought—"

"Spare me your pity," Alcarin said. "After that day, I had to be a man grown. No father, no one else. Only me. The city became my family. She cared for me, and I learned to please her." He adjusted how he sat in the little boat and drew out a small blade to fiddle with. "And for a time, I lived well enough. Even thrived. But as I learned, the good in life would not last."

"Then Luether fell," Ovelia said, "and the Children lay claim to the streets."

"After my eighth summer," he said. "Little enough has changed in Low-City, believe it or not. Fewer guards to duck, though the patrols became more brutal. I knew the best hiding places by then." He allowed himself a chuckle. "If anything, the barbarians let me survive. In those first chaotic summers, the skills of a thief—a child who'd not be noticed—were always in demand, and I made enough coin to keep from selling myself. That—" He looked away across the vast expanse of murky water. "That came later."

As his reminiscences spiraled down, Alcarin burned more brightly in her vision. She could literally see the darkness rising inside him, and it unsettled her. She almost apologized again, but she remembered the scorn with which he received sympathy. Instead, she tried a warmer topic: "How did you meet Garin?"

"By pure chance," he said. "In a pub where I worked sometimes. During my sixteenth summer, I think it was. I saw him watching me, as men often did around that time. He was not the most beautiful man I had seen—certainly not, but I liked his look well enough for an easy mark. I meant either to seduce him or cut his purse—both, perhaps. As it passed, though, he had come there for a different purpose."

He touched the caster at his belt, remembering.

"I almost spoiled his game, but he played it off so well," he said. "I think it aided him at first, to explain his presence in the pub while his mark—Hrust, a powerful general in service of Pervast—ate and drank to excess by the fire. The Ravalis had laws against men loving men, but the barbarians did not care—to them, lust is lust. So we could flirt and kiss without drawing the general's ire. It let Alcarin line up his cast perfectly." Alcarin permitted himself a chuckle. "The killing was simple, the escape harder. We aided and hindered one another by turns, and eventually he gave in to my requests to follow him."

"He didn't want you at first?" Ovelia asked. "Why not?"

For a long time, Alcarin did not answer, considering his words with care. "Tragedy fills his life, even then—especially then. He wanted to protect me. But I convinced him he needed me to protect *him*."

"I can see that he does," Ovelia said. "From himself and everyone else."

Alcarin smiled distantly. "It used to be just us, you know," he said at length. "Garin and me against Luether, as if we two could save the city. A mad quest with an end we knew we would never see. But we had each other, and that was enough to sustain us."

He reached out and touched the water, and Ovelia could see the ripples emerge out of nowhere. It was beautiful and peaceful to watch.

"It was his drive that drew me, but it was his heart that kept me," Alcarin said. "He had the same anger in his breast that pulsed in mine—a thirst for vengeance against a world that had wronged us, but his had a nobler goal. I needed that so badly. I ran beside him at his highs and held him at his lows. I saw the terrible weight upon his shoulders, and I tried to ease that, however I could." He shook his head. "I'm not sure I can explain it."

"No need," Ovelia said, thinking of Lenalin—and of Orbrin. "I believe I understand."

He looked back at her, and while she could not see his expression, the angry light that made up his body dimmed somewhat. He still posed an ever-present danger, but perhaps it had grown less now.

And behind him, she saw something that made her body tighten in surprise and sudden terror: a burning shadow in the water, almost identical to the one she had seen from the *Avenger* high in the clouds. The blackness slipped toward them beneath the surface, tendrils reaching for where Alcarin trailed his fingers beside the skiff. Ovelia seized Alcarin's hand to pull it out of the water.

"What?" Alcarin sat up, drawing his hand back inside the boat.

The dark shape passed them by and vanished into the mists.

"Nothing." Ovelia blew out a relieved breath. "Thank you."

"For what?" Alcarin sounded bitter.

"For your story," Ovelia said. "You do not know me well, and you did not need to open yourself to me as you did. I am grateful."

The youth shrugged as if it did not matter, but they both knew better.

"Alcarin." Ovelia laid her hand over his. "I have no designs on your master. I'll not take him from you, and if it comes to it, I would give my life before I let any harm befall him. You have my vow."

He did not reply at first, but merely gazed at her long and hard. Ovelia felt the youth softening toward her, as though her words had touched his heart.

He faded, his bright burning violence diminishing and allowing him to melt into the shadows all around her. Then he looked away and became a bit more substantial once more. "So you say," he said. "We shall see."

It would have to be enough.

The boatman clicked his tongue, alerting them to their approach. Ovelia looked out across the water and saw two blurry masses she took to be ships anchored a ways away. In her murky vision, she could make out a small group of folk on a long, rocky island at which the hungry waves lapped. The boatman piloted their skiff into the shallows. Everything seemed in order, but something inside her whispered a warning. She'd allowed Alcarin's story to lull her, and she'd missed the first signs.

"That's strange," Alcarin said. "Biaza spoke of a single captain: Datur, she named him—a respected merchant whose enmity with the Children is well known. Why then is there a second ship?"

Uneasiness rose and turned to dread in Ovelia's chest. "Quickly," she said. "Describe that ship to me. I cannot see it myself."

"White and red sails, some sort of bird in silver paint—" he started.

"The *White Dart*." Ovelia reached out for the pilot, even as the shadows bloomed around her hand on Draca's hilt. "Turn us about. It's an ambush—"

A loud *crack* resounded across the water, and the boatman staggered back, out of Ovelia's reach. A casterbolt bloomed in his chest, still leaking crackling energy from its discharge. The standing corpse teetered and fell into the water, almost capsizing the skiff. Ovelia crouched low to cling to her balance as the boat rocked madly from side to side. Had they still been on the open water, they would all be meat for the creatures of the Dusk Sea by now.

"I don't understand," Alcarin said. "Biaza set this meeting. She—"

Warriors came at them from both sides, spears and swords in hand, and Ovelia heard the whine of casters pointed in their direction. At her back, Alcarin tensed, and she kept one hand on Draca's hilt, the other on his wrist. If he made a move, it would slay them both.

"Hold, all. They'll prove no use to us permanently damaged."

Ovelia recognized that voice, with its thick accent and bombastic grace, which hid beneath it cold steel. The man appeared amidst the other pirates and brigands, a shadowy outline that her other senses painted with the florid brush of memory: rings that clinked like chimes, bone-white hair that boiled away into the burning sunlight, and deep skin the color of fresh earth. Though she was blind, she could almost see his smile like a silver crescent moon, promising a passionate night that would flow into a violent dawn.

"My dear Bloodbreaker!" Captain Fersi said. "Alas, I shall not leave you in peace this time."

224

TWENTY-TWO

The Luethaar Archipelago

TIME STRETCHED AND FELL apart. Ovelia could remember only fragments of their journey, as if from a dream that defied recollection.

The sackcloth their captors had shoved over her head had dulled the world around her. They swatted her head whenever she struggled, tried to speak, or simply didn't move the way they wanted, calling her "whore" and "betrayer" and "bloodbreaker." Her captors seemed intent on breaking her, and she could feel the bubbling rage behind their punches and slurs. Ovelia, who had been a prisoner often enough in her life, knew enough to resist as little as necessary and never respond to any of the insults.

She could not have said the same for Alcarin, however.

It was a true tragedy, listening to them wrench apart her companion, psychologically and physically. In those first brutal quarter hour on the little skiff heading toward their captivity, Alcarin tried again and again to reason with them, but they pounded him fiercely every time he spoke. Thereafter, he sat as silently as possible beside her, weeping quietly while his bony knees rattled together. Ovelia remembered putting a hand on his thigh to comfort him, and he jerked taut, thinking it another torment. When he finally relaxed and reached over to touch her hand, his chains clinked, drawing the attention and ire of their captors. At least they punished *her* this time, with a slap to the cheek that put her on the floor of the skiff and several brutal hobnailed kicks to the midsection that left her ribs creaking.

Ovelia found herself thinking, in those moments, of Vilaer Vultara. If the princess had endured far greater torture and could still pass for a sane, sensible woman, then she possessed reservoirs of strength Ovelia had only just glimpsed. That wasn't all, though: in her darkest moments, Ovelia thought of seeing her again, and it gave her the strength to endure.

She thought of Biaza, too, but not in such a complimentary way. The woman had sent them into a trap, clearly, but had she done so intentionally or by accident? Had she turned on Summer Lives? Was Garin in danger as well?

Ovelia remembered flashes of sensation—hard floorboards, dirt under her nails, spikes of pain. Someone spat on her. More strikes, but she'd mostly gone numb by then. She knelt, naked, while someone roughly inspected her under the ostensible guise of healing any wounds. He—she could only assume from the heavy breathing, deep chuckle, and her knowledge of Luethaar men—gave her heavily bruised ribs a cursory inspection and pronounced her in good order, though every breath brought fresh agony. He then got onto his true interest, which was to squeeze her breasts painfully hard, caress her buttocks, and prod at her recesses with what she hoped was just his finger. She paid little attention to the indignity itself, but rather committed to memory all the clues she could as to the chiurgeon's identity: his particular musky smell, the peculiar nasal slurp he made every so often as he breathed, the length of his nails as he prodded her. She tried to remember.

She would find a way out.

~

When next she woke, it was to someone pulling the hood off her head. She half-knelt, half-sat, naked and chained at the wrists with iron manacles. They'd even taken her blindfold, which made her face feel oddly light and exposed. It made no difference to what she could perceive.

The cramped, stuffy chamber suggested a prison cell or the like. Dimly, she heard moaning from somewhere, as well as the muted sounds of men shouting somewhere above her. Beneath her, the floor rolled gently, though whether that meant she was on a boat or too many hits had rattled her brains. Her blindness painted the world around her in shades of gray and black, and without Draca, she had no flames to scrutinize. Even so, she knew immediately that one big man stood over her. She smelled old blood and sweat and could hear him grinding his teeth—a warrior or a torturer. Both. She detected a second man in the room, one with a distinctive, heavily perfumed stench. She could feel his oily skin even from two paces distant.

"Fersi," she said.

The big man smashed a fist across her face, and Ovelia's face would have hit the floor had not the chains jerked taut and held her up. Her mouth pulsed in pain and she tasted blood.

"Hold, hold." Captain Fersi sat on a stool across from her, relaxing with a cup of what smelled like nyssa. "Lady Dracaris. I'm so pleased to see you again, albeit under very different circumstances."

She inclined her head toward her captor, who said something guttural and pulled back his fist for another strike. She did not recognize the voice, but the way he slurred his words, she could tell his mouth was full of metal. A Child of Ruin, she thought.

"I said *hold*." Fersi's tone shifted from his accustomed affability to something very cold and sharp. "Leave us."

"Lurdh—" the barbarian said, slurring the word.

Ovelia heard the distinctive click and whir of a charging caster. "*Leave*," Fersi said again.

Grumbling, the barbarian left the room, the floorboards creaking under his feet. Ovelia put the distinctive sound together with the smell of tar and the rolling feeling. They were still on a ship—in the hold below decks—which gave her some hope. She even recognized the ship they were on—the *White Dart*, with its smoking mage-engine and low, pervasive hiss as it cut through the waves. She noted as well a vaguely familiar sweet odor, but she couldn't place it. The barbarian left Fersi terrified in his wake, shivering almost as badly as Ovelia herself in her pain. She could smell Fersi's anxious sweat and hear the unevenness of his breath. She wondered if this was what Regel meant when he spoke of smelling fear.

"Oh Fersi," Ovelia said. "What has happened to you?"

The captain shrugged. "Are you in pain?" he asked. "So you must be. I will mix you a tincture of sweetsoul for it."

Ovelia's mouth went dry. "No," she said, her voice a croak. She cleared her throat. "Thank you, but no. Just...talk to me. Perhaps I can help you. Tell me what you have done."

The captain made a disgusted sound in his throat. "What I have done," he said, musing. "What I have *had* to do. To survive."

Ovelia's heart sank. "I took you for a man of dignity, at least—a merchant prince who dealt fairly, if harshly," she said. "How have you fallen in with such monsters?"

"How long has it been? A season? Hardly so long." The stool creaked as he stood. "When last we met, I stood high in Luethaar society—a merchant of respect and means. But you ripped that from me—you and your lover, the Frostburn." He spun something in his hand, which made a sound that was half whistle, half ring. A weapon. "Because of you, now I take what allies I must, however coarse and cruel. I am the monster now—a pirate, not a merchant. As you have made me. Am I not entitled to recompense?"

Indignation arose in Ovelia, and she wanted to correct him that his fate was of his own doing, but to do so would only anger him. She would reason with him—at least she would try. Speaking was an effort, and the more words she used, the dizzier and sicker she felt. The air in here made her want to vomit. She tried to focus through it.

"Is that what this is?" Ovelia asked. "Revenge?"

That made him chuckle. "I'd not taken you for a narcissist, Ovelia Dracaris," he said. "You are but a tool. You are my key to returning to the city and reclaiming my former place. You tell me how to find Garin Ravalis, and my bloodsoaked allies take him. Then we ransom him to Pervast." He sighed. "Not something a civilized man might do, but my choices are limited."

"There is another way," Ovelia said, trying again to appeal to his better nature. "Rather than turn against Garin, join him. I will speak to him on your behalf."

"You suggest I prostrate myself before that man?" He laughed. "You watched as the Fox of Luether attacked me—killed my men. Exiled me by poison. No." Fersi took a drink, and she smelled the nyssa on his breath as he sighed in her face. "But if it is any comfort, know that you will likely survive. I do rather like your face. Perhaps I'll keep you for myself." He brushed his fingers along her cheek.

Well, she had tried.

Ovelia made a sound under her voice to draw him closer. When he leaned in, Ovelia lunged at him, but the chains stopped her just short of his face. To his credit, he hardly even flinched.

"Are you truly blind, my lady?" Fersi asked. "Your little companion makes that claim, and I did not believe him. But now I see the truth." He touched the scars around her eyes. "At least you still have those lips." His fingers traced her mouth. "I look forward to seeing them wrapped around—"

She gnashed her teeth at him, but he pulled his hand out of her reach.

"That fire." Fersi drew in an excited breath. "How I've missed you." Ovelia felt the cold weight of a steel rod under her chin, lifting her up. "What we shared on the ship was real. It can be again."

"No," Ovelia said.

"Yes yes," Fersi said. "You need pretend no longer. There is no Frostburn here—no crew. Just you. Me." He slid the steel bar down her throat to her collarbone. "I know your darkest urge." He traced the line of her sternum between her breasts and lower. "You know I can meet it."

It had been some time since Ovelia had listened to the darkness inside, but now it boiled up to meet Fersi's offer. Red Jeggs had proved an unsatisfying lover because, for all his vigor and all his skill, he did not understand what Ovelia was or what she wanted. Fersi did, even as she hated him with a fury.

"*No,*" she said, though she wanted to say yes.

Fersi took his rod away from Ovelia and leaned back. "Of course, my lady," he said. "You do not ask for my love, but I will give it you anyway. It will take time to break your will—to quench your fire. But first." He pressed the rod once more against her throat. "You tell me where to find Garin Ravalis."

"Or you will torture me?" Ovelia asked.

"No." Fersi chuckled. "I shall torture your friend instead. You cannot watch, so you listen."

As if in answer to the words, the moans resonated through the wall from the other chamber.

Alcarin. Ovelia's heart clenched hard. "Why would I care?"

"I know not," Fersi said. "But you defended him when my friends took you, and you soothed him when he feared. I know not why his pain is your pain, but so it is. Hmm." He considered. "Is he your lover, perhaps? I assumed you shared Garin's bed—the Fox of Luether at least seems worthy of you."

Ovelia realized something important: Fersi did not know Garin's secret, nor did he realize who Alcarin was. With Garin's squire, Fersi hardly needed Ovelia. He could simply dangle Alcarin as a prize, and the Fox of Luether would… What would he do? Negotiate peacefully and surrender in exchange for Alcarin? Descend with the fires of the heavens to rescue him? Ovelia did not know.

She also did not know if telling Fersi the truth would protect Alcarin or condemn him to death. Luether was not like Tar Vangr, which embraced love in all its forms—instead, it condemned the very concept of a man loving a man, as though Ruin had only so much love to offer the world, and only between a man and a woman. She had heard rumors on the streets in Luether, but none outside Summer Lives seemed to credit them as truth. What Fersi thought, Ovelia did not know, but she was not about to risk Alcarin's life needlessly.

An urge rose in her, one she did not at first understand: an urge to say nothing. Ovelia knew, somehow, that doom would come, and that silence now was the best of all her options. And Ovelia knew to trust her instincts. She stared at Fersi with her cloudy eyes, willing him to feel every bit of the pain he had caused her. From his sharp intake of breath, it may have worked.

"You have a hard body, Ovelia Dracaris, but your heart is soft," Fersi said. "I think it will not take long before the sounds of your friend's agony bring the word spilling from your beautiful lips."

Ovelia shook her head. "This is not you, Fersi," she said. "Do not do this."

"Ah." Fersi stood. "But it is, my lady. The man I am now."

"Wait—" Ovelia said, but the captain was already leaving.

The door creaked open, and she heard the moans grow louder, then rise into frantic cries for mercy. Alcarin's voice. Then the door shut again, muting the sounds, which became screams. Ovelia strained at her chains, which clanked but held: the manacles were too strong. The exertion made her head all but explode, and finally she sank to the floor, trembling.

TWENTY-THREE

EVENTUALLY, THE SCREAMS SUBSIDED and Ovelia heard gruff voices whose words she could not make out. At least they'd left Alcarin for the moment, but she knew they would return. She sank back against the grimy bulkhead. Tears of frustration and pain welled in her eyes, and she let them fall.

She might have slept for a time—she couldn't say exactly. The world rocked back and forth, and she hardly felt in control of her body. Finally a new sound rippled through the chamber, rising over the rocking sea to make the walls reverberate. Laughter—low and mocking and without mirth.

She recognized now the source of the sweet smell, and remembered where she had encountered it before. The temple of the Summer Goddess on Dark Solstice, when she had humiliated a man beyond measure. She had not known he still lived, but nor did it surprise her, considering.

"Tithian Davargorn," she said.

"You remember me," the man said. "Truly, Ruin has blessed us this day."

Fersi had chained Davargorn high on the wall, forcing him to stand, and his arms trembled from the effort of staying aloft. His one big, white eye gleamed clear in her vision—some manner of magic burned there. Ovelia could smell the blood on him—some of it fresh, some of it old—and knew that whatever tortures they had inflicted on Alcarin, Davargorn had endured far worse at their hands. The lad was tough, but she knew he could feel pain—she'd learned that much when she'd crushed his bone mask into his face at their first meeting. His body was a slightly darker patch of the shadows of the hold. Deep within him, faint blue light flickered along his skeleton, like sparks cast from a flint. And in his chest was a dagger, burning bright with magic—it hung out of him like a nail between two of his ribs, and she wondered how he could still draw breath.

"Why are you here?" Ovelia asked.

"Same as you, I suspect," he said. "Betrayed. Brutalized. Ransomed to someone more important—my leathery master, perhaps. Many a vile man would give much to hold a hostage over the great Mask." He spat on the floor. "Such a shame your Captain Fersi doesn't know the truth as we do."

"What truth do you mean, Tithian?" Ovelia thought of Semana stripping off the horrible leather mask—remembered the way seeing her sweet face after so many winters, now framed in darkness, had made her shake.

"That my master would sooner give her right hand than have me back," he said. "It makes me a poor bargaining chip." His chains rattled as he strained to no avail. "But you. You are in Garin Ravalis's inner circle, are you not? He will want you back very much. And his young lover besides."

Ovelia caught her breath.

"Heh," Davargorn said. "I noted Fersi's mistake just as you did. How much would that information be worth to him, I wonder? The freedom of a valueless hostage, perhaps?"

"You'll say nothing of this," Ovelia said. "Or—"

"Or *what*?" Davargorn said. "We're both of us prisoners. And you're blind. I beg you to try." He flexed, making the chains rattle. "The only woman I hate more than you is beyond either of our reach."

"Do you crave vengeance so badly?" Ovelia asked. "Semana—"

Davargorn wrenched hard against the shackles, roaring like a beast. "*Don't you say her name.*"

Ovelia shivered at his outburst, then raised her chin. "Your master did what she had to do," she said. "If she'd told us the truth from the start—I do not know if Regel would have agreed to help her. He might have slain her as an imposter, and me as well."

"Perhaps that would have been better." Davargorn coughed. "Spared us all the trouble."

The words were bitter as Thaldrin venom, but they had no conviction behind them. That eased Ovelia's mind. "That, you do not believe," she said.

"You think not?" he asked. "If I were free of these chains—"

Before he could speak the next word, a terrific explosion shook the *White Dart* and threw Ovelia to the floor. Her ears rang and she coughed, trying to pull in air. When the ringing subsided and she could hear again, she became aware of men shouting and the sounds of boots stamping up on the deck above them. The *White Dart* had fallen under attack.

"The fires of the heavens it is," Ovelia said to herself.

"What?" Davargorn was still reeling from the blast.

Ovelia ignored him. The manacles provided just enough give for her to put her hands together. She grasped her left thumb in her right hand.

"What are you doing?" Davargorn asked.

"I'm going to break my thumb and slip free," she said. "Then I'll find a hammer and break your chains too." She set her jaw and took a deep breath. The pain in her head was blinding, but this would hurt worse.

"I'll do it," Davargorn said. "I'll pass well."

Ovelia paused. "I'm blind, Tithian," she said. "You need to be able to wield a weapon if we're to fight our way out of here."

"And what will you do if a guard hears your cry of pain and comes in?" Davargorn asked, just as another explosion rocked the ship. "We don't have time to argue. Tell me how to do it."

Ovelia didn't want to cripple the better fighter of the two of them, but her instincts told her to listen. Perhaps a one-handed fighter was better than a blind one. "It's simple," she said. "Grasp your thumb with your fingers and pull hard, or slam it against the other manacle."

He answered with silence, and she could almost *hear* his angry glare. Then she heard a sharp popping sound and a grunt, then again. Davargorn slumped heavily to the floor and murmured a curse.

"You weren't meant to break both of them," Ovelia said. "How will you wield a weapon now?"

"Worry about yourself, woman." Bone crackled as Davargorn reset one thumb, then the other.

"Quickly," Ovelia said. "Find an axe or a hammer. We're in the hold, it shouldn't be"—she felt the cold steel of a hammer's head at her temple—"Hard."

"My thanks for the aid." Davargorn sounded beyond furious. "If you can think of a reason I should spare you, speak now."

Ovelia looked up at where she imagined his face to be. The ship's movement and the darkness of the hold made it difficult to tell. "I am your only escape," she said, then waited. When death did not come after a three-count, she continued. "We are at sea, under attack, presumably by my allies. Kill me, and they will surely find and kill you. Rescue me—"

"I see." Davargorn lifted Ovelia to her knees with the hammer. "I will have your word, then. I aid you, and you will see to it your man-loving master does not harm me."

"I will." Awkwardly, Ovelia reached forward and laid her hands upon Davargorn's calves. "My word is my shield and my body. No harm will come to you if I can prevent it." She waited in darkness.

Davargorn's fingers clasped her left hand, and she immediately imagined him holding it down as he broke her fingers one by one. Ovelia's teeth ground together. At length, the hammer whistled through the air and shattered into the floor just aside of her right hand. Three strikes made the chain splinter, and she immediately felt the slack in both hands. It was all one chain through a single loop on the wall.

Davargorn took hold of her right hand, presumably to do the same thing, but Ovelia demurred. She pulled the length of chain free of the wall and deftly wrapped it around her left arm. Not a shield, exactly, but it would serve. She took her bearings on the rolling hold floor, one hand steadying herself against the wall. She'd not liked sea voyages when she had sight, and they became even worse when she could make out only vague shadows, or when a deadly slayer lurked nearby, barely seen.

"Now." Davargorn touched the dagger in his chest, but he didn't have the strength to pull it free. "Take this out."

"That's unwise," Ovelia said. "How you survived that strike, I do not know, but the blade could be holding your heart together. If I take it out—"

"Do it," Davargorn said. "I'll live."

Ovelia had a doubt—she needed Davargorn to escape, and if she took that blade out it could kill him—but her instinct told her to do as he wished. She laid her left hand on his chest and seized the hilt of the blade in her right hand. It tingled under her grasp. "Ready yourself."

He grunted.

She wrenched the blade free in one firm, smooth pull. She expected blood, but instead the dagger came out sparkling clean and dry. With a grunt, Davargorn collapsed to the floor like a toppled stack of kindling. With a gasp, Ovelia fell to one knee beside him, pawing at his chest. "Tithian?" Desperately, she groped for the wound to press upon, but could find no blood. He felt very dead. "Tithian!"

The dagger burned in her hand, and she looked down at the white mist swirling around her wrist. She'd seen this magic before…Then she realized what she held: Vhaerynn's dagger. The mist that twisted around her flesh shaped itself into a desperate hand, and she felt a deep, terrible loneliness tinged with hot fear. She dropped the deadly knife to clatter on the floorboards.

A ragged gasp rose from the floor, drawing Ovelia's attention. Davargorn was alive, somehow.

"Told…you," he said. "Give me a moment."

She opened her mouth to ask how this was possible, but she could *see* it. Blue magic extended out from Davargorn's heart—where the dagger had rested in his ribs—spreading like blood through his veins. Soon enough, it mapped out an entire person stirring on the floor. She'd never seen the like.

"Healing magic." She touched his wound, which was only smooth skin. It reminded her of Regel, but she held her tongue.

"Mind yourself, and I'll mind mine." Davargorn swatted her hand away.

"Fair enough."

They both looked at the glowing dagger on the floor, neither wanting to touch it.

"Did you find other weapons?" Ovelia asked.

He made some manner of gesture, then grunted and hefted the hammer. "This will have to do," he said. "I liked those swords. A great deal."

"Point me in the direction of the door," Ovelia said.

When Alcarin's screams renewed from the other chamber, however, Ovelia knew she had no time to take it slow. She plowed in that direction, doing her best not to stumble on the uneven footing.

"Heh," Davargorn said. "And to think, you defeated me once."

She got to the door and seized the frayed rope handle, meaning to fling it open instantly. She thought better of it, though, and nodded to Davargorn. He murmured his readiness, and she forced herself to take a centering breath before she thrust the door open. Startled voices rose within, Davargorn hurtled past like a rush of wind, and the questions became screams of battle and pain.

Ovelia stepped inside, focusing hard to hear despite the clamor of voices and the ringing dance of steel. To her right, Davargorn was fighting at least two men, and she could do little to help him. She did not know his style and would do more harm than good. Instead, Ovelia searched for Alcarin, intent on protecting him from further harm.

His terror proved a boon, as his continued mewling led Ovelia right to him, far from the fighting. Alcarin screamed when she drew near, and she felt a sackcloth bag over his head. She pulled the rough thing off, and his strangled intake of breath for another scream cut off in a sound of disbelief.

"Blood—Bloodbreaker?" he asked.

"Not today," she said, reaching for his manacles. Sturdy iron, not unlike hers.

Then Alcarin went rigid, and she felt an attack coming from behind before his sharp gasp. She couldn't see the blade, but instinct told her it would be a clumsy downward thrust. The man behind her was heavy, she knew, and did not carry himself like a warrior—such men used their strength, not skill. She swung back, interposing her chain-wrapped arm.

When steel rang off her makeshift shield, she knew she'd guessed rightly.

With a hiss, the fat man tried to pull back for another strike, but once she controlled one arm, Ovelia had him. With her right hand, she caught his wrist and locked his arm behind him with a sharp twist. The man cried out in pain, and the knife fell from his numb fingers.

"Move, and I break your arm," Ovelia said. "Say you understand."

The fat man whimpered in Ovelia's hold as she forced him to stare at Davargorn slaying his companions. One was dead or unconscious, while the other pleaded for mercy in a Free Island accent. Davargorn's hammer whistled as he spun it through the air. His blubbering became a cry of fear, then Ovelia heard the dull thud of steel on flesh and the crunch of blood, and the man moaned. A second blow, and the man could only gurgle. Ovelia knew Davargorn had dealt the man a mortal wound, but she heard half a dozen more thuds for good measure.

"I might keep this," Davargorn said. "It makes such satisfying sounds."

Ovelia's captive moaned and she felt and smelled him void himself.

"Key," she hissed in his left ear. She extended her free left hand over his other shoulder.

Trembling, the fat man put a ring of keys in her hand. "P-Please." He half-swallowed, half-slurped snot back into his nose. "If you please—"

"Oh, we do not," Davargorn said. "Shall I kill him?"

Ovelia relaxed her grip, spinning him around, then had a vague memory. She clutched the man's hand again and felt at his nails. Long and poorly groomed.

"What passes?" he asked. "What—?"

Leaning in close, she sniffed at his neck, which gave off the musk of a man often alone, too often self-pleasuring. The ship's chiurgeon.

Ovelia bent low, cording her body into one single movement. Then she slammed her chain-wrapped arm up and into the chiurgeon's groin. She felt a reassuring crack and the squelch of the man's waste thrust back up into him. He dropped to the floor wheezing and weeping.

Davargorn whistled. Alcarin whimpered.

"Harsh," said a woman, "and well deserved."

Startled fear gripped Ovelia, and she cast about for the speaker. She'd not sensed anyone else in the room, nor could she see any other shadows than those of Davargorn and Alcarin. "Who is that?"

"She—she's standing right there," Alcarin said. "Thin. Bald. Summerblood. So...quiet."

"Apologies," the woman said. "I did not mean to frighten you, dear lady. I did not know of your condition." A hand touched Ovelia's own. "It's me, Lis. From the Mine, yes? Do you remember?"

"I do not know you." Ovelia pulled her hand away and raised her chain-wrapped arm that she might ward the woman off, but then she felt Alcarin relax.

"Yes," he said. "The—the dustling. I hardly recognized you."

"I clean up," she said. "You pass well, friend to his Highness?"

Alcarin pawed at Ovelia's arm. "She helped us at the Mine," he said. "We can trust her."

Ovelia nodded, still trying to perceive the woman, of whom she had no memory. She would have recalled a creature such as Alcarin described. Lis made faint noises—breathing, the creak of leather—but otherwise she might as well not have been there. It was unsettlingly like trying to perceive Lady Shard, but with this Lis woman, there were no hints at all. Had she been there at the Mine when Ovelia had gone to find Garin? Likely she had, and been just as undetectable then. And that was a disturbing thought.

As Ovelia focused, she sensed Davargorn at her side burning with greater intensity even than before. He looked like Alcarin in his rage. "Tithian?"

The slayer was fuming and glaring as though he meant to strangle Lis. At length, he calmed. "She cut down one of the pirates," Davargorn said. "She's good with a blade. On our side."

It had not escaped Ovelia that the lad trusted women easily and quickly. "Well," she said to the woman she could not see. "You came to rescue us?"

Lis laughed lightly. "I am one of Summer's Lives, of course—I work for Biaza, after the Mines," she said. "Time passes and we must go. Come!"

Ovelia hesitated, but just at the moment, she could not very well refuse a sincere offer of help. "I accept," she said, turning to Alcarin's manacles. "'Ware my companion. He is vicious."

"Yes," Lis said, her voice sweet and intrigued. Flirtatious. Not reassuring.

"Watch her," Ovelia said to Alcarin. "If we survive this, we'll see what Biaza says."

"She wouldn't know her," the youth said. "Sep—" He shivered. "Separation. Between agents."

Ovelia's heart ached to hear Alcarin sound so far away. They two did not always see the world the same way, but from the first day they had met, Alcarin had ever struck her as a good, upbeat young man—a light in a dark world. To hear the devastation in his voice…She heard Regel say "such is the way of Ruin" over and over in her head, and she wanted to scream in protest. She comforted herself that she had freed Alcarin, and that at least made him breathe easier.

"We must find our weapons," Ovelia said. "Have you seen a flamed blade, its steel red—"

"As though quenched in blood?" Leather creaked as the woman took something from her belt. "Better than seen it. I *steal* it."

Heat suddenly erupted: a boiling mass of flames and smoke in the shape of a sword. It took up her world, burning away the shadows of Davargorn and the torture chamber. It seemed to be floating in the air, as she could not see Lis holding it. At first, the blade pointed toward Ovelia, then reversed itself, handle toward her hands. "It looked valuable," Lis said. "Yours?"

Ovelia reclaimed the sword, and suddenly the room grew clearer. She could perceive the inky blot of brooding shadow that was Davargorn, the dimmed but still burning rage inside Alcarin, and even the crippled chiurgeon twitching at her feet. She still could not see Lis—not even the slightest shadow where she should have stood. Even with Lady Shard, Ovelia had seen hints to her presence. But this…It did not make Ovelia trust her, for certain.

"While you were pilfering the armory," Davargorn asked. "Did you happen to steal a falcat—?"

"Come," Lis said, ignoring the question. "We should join—"

At that moment, a heavy fist pounded on the door leading up to the sterncastle of the *White Dart*. Alcarin flinched and moaned, and Ovelia had to turn aside to protect her battered ear. Davargorn hefted his hammer. If Lis reacted, Ovelia did not perceive it. She was all but exhausted.

The door creaked open, and some sort of device tumbled through. At first, Ovelia didn't know what to make of it, but she remembered the last time she'd seen Fersi—remembered what Garin had done. She turned and shielded Alcarin's eyes just as a bright flash of light ripped through the cabin. Davargorn and Lis staggered but Ovelia blinked, unaffected, as soldiers with casters and swords stormed into the chamber. She marked it an unforeseen advantage of her blindness.

Red Jeggs appeared, his distinctive bulk barely able to fit into the cramped torture room, and she had never felt quite as pleased to see him. He strode to her and wrapped her in a fierce embrace that made her bruised ribs creak. "Dragon's Daughter!" he said. "I knew you'd find your way out of this."

"Of course." Ovelia tried to straighten and winced. She let herself lean on him for support, finding comfort in his strong arms.

"Silver Fire, you're trembling like the leaves of an aspen." Red Jeggs pressed the spout of a skin to her lips. "Drink."

Ovelia had swallowed two mouthfuls before she thought to push the skin away. The milk tasted warm and rich and lent new strength to her body, but no matter how much she craved it, something nagged her not to indulge. A distant voice, one she ignored in the moment. "Does this mean we've won?"

Red Jeggs chuckled. "If you saw who came to our aid, you wouldn't have to ask." He eyed Davargorn and Lis, and his amiability fell away into something dangerous. "Other prisoners?"

"The man was one," Ovelia said. "The woman claims to be one of us. Biaza's agent."

"She's new, but I've seen her before. Lis is her name, yes? Ho!" Red Jeggs suddenly shouted. "Alcarin! I didn't see you there, lad. Pass well? Come with me." He nodded to the other Summer Lives warriors. "Take them into custody. Garin will decide."

Davargorn hissed in warning. "You promised, Bloodbreaker," he said. "Remember your word."

"I remember," Ovelia said as the agents led Davargorn and Lis away. She couldn't say why, but she was sure the woman was watching her speculatively. Wonderful. She drank more sweet milk.

"Thank you, Jeggs," Ovelia said. "I'm sorry about earlier."

"Bah," he said. "Do not think of it. I like a little fire. We both know how much you want me."

Silently, Ovelia wondered if that was still true. "What's happened? Do we control the ship?"

"Better to show you."

Ovelia remembered something important. "Give me your kerchief," she said, pawing at him.

Red Jeggs started to say something suitably blustering, but she found the edge of his embroidered kerchief and flicked it out of his coat pocket. She hurried back into the brig, stumbling a bit where she stepped, and glimpsed the golden dagger glowing brightly on the floor. The rest of the world existed as mere shadows, but such a relic of magic burned as hot as the sun to her. Gingerly, she laid the kerchief over the weapon and picked it up with great care. Through the cloth, she could not feel the magic, and that reassured her.

"My lady?" Red Jeggs touched her hand.

Ovelia grasped his wrist. "Lead on."

TWENTY-FOUR

RED JEGGS LED THE way onto the deck, and Ovelia found the relative coolness and sudden gust of wind both refreshing and unbalancing. She clung hard to his arm for support and felt him relax. Likely, he thought that meant something it did not, but she had no time to clarify. Instead, she took in the scene wrought in Draca's shadows before her.

A vast skyship hovered over them, one whose mage-engines she recognized from the journey down to Luether: Lady Shard's *Reaver*. Many of the caster-wielding soldiers on the deck of the *White Dart*, covering a platoon of kneeling pirates, wore the same distinctive black leather garments of Shard's pirates. The battle must have been quick and decisive, as Ovelia saw few bodies, or perhaps Fersi's crew had surrendered with little bloodshed. The corpses she perceived were those of barbarians: gnarled and twisted things, barely still recognizable as men and women.

The captain himself stood upon the sterncastle with Garin, holding up a caster in what Ovelia took to be a threatening gesture, even though Fersi trembled as Alcarin had under torture. He looked upon the Fox of Luether with mingled fear and loathing. He kept whipping the caster around to aim at various of Garin's allies, holding them all at bay.

"It is over, Captain Fersi," Garin said. "Our pointless conflict is at an end. We have a common enemy in the form of Pervast. You know his ways—you have seen his brutal measures firsthand." He extended his hand. "We should be friends again."

"And *that* is my alternative, Fox of Luether?" Fersi spat. "Offer my sword to a puffed fool? A boy who has waged war against the tyrant most of his life without a victory to show for it?"

"Er," Garin said. "Yes?"

"What happens when Pervast kills you and hangs your body in the fire for all to see it burn?" Fersi asked. "What then?"

"Why, then I shall be dead. I confess I've no plan for failure at the moment." Garin smiled widely. "Perhaps we can work together toward that end—"

"I shall *tell* you what happens!" Fersi was shouting now. "My exile continues, and I drown in debt to my creditors, if the barbarians do not kill me. You are a coward and a fool."

"But the gain, Fersi," Garin said. "You have heard the stories. You can feel

239

the winds. You know I am right."

The pirate captain bared his teeth. "The people of this city will never follow a man-rutting pervert like you," he said.

Ovelia flinched, and she could feel Garin's unease as well. Perhaps Fersi had reasoned out Alcarin's true value to him. Or perhaps he was spouting gossip or perhaps making a wild accusation. Either way, she could feel anxiety sweep through the assembled pirates and Summer Lives agents.

Like the sea beast he had become, Fersi scented blood and his frenzy blossomed. "I knew it." He waved the caster wildly. "Where is your wife? Your heirs? You offer nothing but a useless, dead en—"

A mighty crack split the air, swallowing his next words, and blood bloomed bright into the air. The discharged casterbolt smashed through the rail of the ship, and Garin staggered after in its wake, clutching at his left hand. Fersi, looking at the prince over the smoking haft of his spent caster, exuded terror and confusion. He'd not intended to fire, Ovelia realized.

A cry went up, and the rebels of Summer Lives pushed forward, weapons at the ready, but Garin held up his good hand. The other he held firm against his chest. "Stop!" he cried. "Stop this. I will—"

A caster cracked, and a bolt took Fersi right in the chest. He staggered backward, pitched against the rail, and started to topple over. Garin let out a cry and ran to catch him, but it was too late. The merchant captain turned pirate fell into the dark waters of the Dusk Sea, which frothed around him. He batted at the water vaguely, his strength failing.

"Burn it all!" Garin rounded on the deck. Sweat poured down his face, and Ovelia could feel his agony from a dozen paces away. He was holding his left hand together. "Who was that? Who cast that?"

"I did." Her black robe trailing, Lady Shard swept across from behind Ovelia on the sterncastle, casually tossing her spent caster to Red Jeggs, who bobbled it awkwardly. "The man insulted you. He betrayed you. He tried to kill you. He was no friend to you and never would be."

"Unacceptable!" Garin shouted. "You follow my path, or you are my enemy."

Shard met his vehemence with cold fury. "As you wish."

Shadows boiled from Draca, warning of imminent peril. The assembled pirates braced, swords half-drawn and casters raised, and the operatives of Summer Lives drew their own weapons. Garin and Shard looked on the verge of lashing out at one another. Ovelia stepped between them, holding up her arms with the last of her strength.

"Stop," she said. "Enough of this."

In the silence, Ovelia felt all eyes on her, a weight she could barely hold up.

She raised her head.

"Focus instead on our enemy," she said. "We rise against Pervast. We work together, or we fall apart. Do not do the usurper's work for him."

Quiet murmurs flowed around the ship, and she saw the danger slowly fading in Draca's shadows. Ovelia dared to breathe.

Garin glared at Shard. "I do not kill my own people," he said. "Nor do my allies."

"As you say." The pirate captain shrugged. She reached out and touched Ovelia on the chin. "Hold onto this one, Fox of Luether. She has quite the tongue."

A great shriek rose from over the railing, drowning out whatever Garin might have said in reply, and a shout of alarm went up on the deck. Ovelia knew without looking what had come to pass: that dark shape under the water, the burning well of power she had glimpsed on the *Avenger* and again on the small skiff, had come upon Fersi. She listened to it rip him apart, and it made her sick at heart and in her stomach. She pressed her face into Red Jeggs's chest, and was aware Lady Shard gazing at her sidelong. When Ovelia turned her head, the pirate captain had vanished once more from her view.

The world seemed to stretch, the sounds of the creature mangling Fersi's body dimming beneath a numb haze. Ovelia looked down at her hand against Red Jeggs's chest, and even though she couldn't see it, exactly, she felt as though there were half a dozen hands there.

"What," she said. "What's happening?"

He looked down at her. "Rest, Dragon Daughter," he said. "You're safe. The sweetsoul milk will soothe you."

Ovelia felt heat rise on the back of her neck and inside her skull, even as her stomach grew cold and her body numb. "How…how much was in that milk you gave me?" she asked.

"Sweetsoul?" He stretched. "Just a pinch—to take the edge off. Why?"

Ovelia felt sick. Her mind wanted to void her stomach while her body ached to tear away Red Jeggs's milkskin and drink it down. She shoved at him, her arms like limp things without strength.

"What's wrong?" Red Jeggs asked quietly. "Have I offended?"

"Away," Ovelia said. "Just…leave me."

He did as she asked, resonating with concern. She could tell his pride was offended, but beneath his insecurity she could sense real worry for her. His empathy made it worse.

Ovelia closed her fingers around the rail of the ship and focused on the slurping sounds of the creature feasting below. She tried not to think about what was happening in her own body.

～

When it was over, and the agents of Summer Lives were climbing back into their skiffs and Shard's pirates had returned to their skyship, Ovelia stood at the rail of the *White Dart*, gazing out over the Dusk Sea. Despite his wound, Garin had accomplished great things this day, allying with Shard and defeating a rival in the form of Fersi chief among them. Ovelia heard the sailors talking of his mercy—that he had offered his hand to one of his worst enemies—and that seemed to fit with his bloodless philosophy. Davargorn was safely imprisoned, trading one captor for another, and that strange Lis woman had vanished into the ranks. Red Jeggs hadn't tried to return to her, but Ovelia could feel him watching her from a distance. It might have been well, but for the sweetsoul coursing through her.

Her senses blurred, and the world seemed to persist under a gray, insensate veil. She hungered, but distantly—she hurt from significant wounds, but they seemed so far away. Even a small amount of sweetsoul triggered this reaction in her after her long deprivation, and she could scarcely manage to keep her thoughts in line. All she wanted was more, but she knew she needed to never touch it again.

When Alcarin approached, Ovelia realized that somehow, she had expected him—dreaded him, in fact, though in her addled state she could not have said why. He approached, thin and beaten and wrapped in a blanket despite the heat. She wished she could not see him as well as she could, and she almost cast Draca into the sea to spare herself the sight. Between his thin face, sunken eyes, and the gaunt hand that clutched his blanket about him like a shield, he looked far older than his twenty-odd winters would suggest.

"They told me," Alcarin said.

Through her muddy lack of focus, Ovelia did not understand. "Alcarin—"

"They told me they were hurting me because you refused to answer their questions," Alcarin said. "Is that true?"

"It is." Ovelia wanted to weep but couldn't. She thought that if she did, she would never stop. "They wanted to capture Garin and sell him to Pervast. I could not—"

"I know," Alcarin said. "I know you could not. But…perhaps you could stay away from me? And from Garin? Just for a while." He left her to rejoin his master.

She bowed her head. The request made her heart ache, but she would grant it. She owed Alcarin that much. She could sense Garin looking at her from the main deck—feel his pain and sympathy both—and turned away.

"Ovelia!" Vilaer appeared, breaking through the dispersing crowd. Unexpectedly, she threw her arms around Ovelia and held her tightly.

"Your Highness." Ovelia should have extricated herself, she knew, but she was slow to do so. The princess was warm and inviting, and the sweetsoul made her sluggish—and hungry for touch. "How—why are you here?"

"Garin summoned me, to help him negotiate with Captain Fersi," Vilaer said. "By the time my ship arrived, it was too late. But I'm glad you pass well. *So* glad."

Then, heedless of their many onlookers—including Red Jeggs, who straightened in shock—the last princess of Luether kissed Ovelia firmly on the lips. It was awkward, ardent, and perplexing. They had flirted subtly and touched a few times, but Ovelia had not expected anything like this, particularly not so quickly. Vilaer's forwardness surprised Ovelia. It should have driven her away, but in her sweetsoul-rich stupor, not kissing her felt nigh impossible.

Finally, Ovelia broke the kiss and faced Vilaer. "Your Highness," she said, wanting nothing more than to kiss her again. To do more. "Is—was that a Luethaar custom I do not know?"

"No, I—" Suddenly vulnerable, Vilaer immediately withdrew, casting her gaze back and forth at the pirates and rebels giving them sidelong looks. In particular, Red Jeggs was staring at them as though they'd each sprouted an extra head. "I've...I've never kissed a woman before. Not for true. And I—"

"Obviously," Ovelia said.

"Don't tease me." Vilaer blushed and started to back away. "I shouldn't have. Just forget—"

"No."

Ovelia held her hand, staying her. Just under the skin, the princess's heartbeat quickened. Vilaer looked up at her, poised like a hesitant bird about to take flight. Firmly, Ovelia closed her hand tighter on Vilaer's, and their hearts beat together.

"Come with me, Highness," she said. "I'll teach you."

TWENTY-FIVE

Luether

As the agents of Summer Lives secured him to the wall of a filthy cellar beneath some half-collapsed building in Low-City Luether, Davargorn reflected that he had spent entirely too much of the last year in chains. And he had grown very, very weary of it. The air in the cellar hung thick and rank, unable to escape the confines of the sallow earth below. In addition to the manacles on his wrists, which they attached to the wall over his head, they chained him with the fetter already around his neck. So much for slipping his shackles: he couldn't very well break his head and wriggle free. Or could he?

His escorts left the room, excepting the brute who had carried him most of the way here. That one gave his cheek a heavy slap to attract his attention, and Davargorn glared up at him. Rarely had he seen a bigger man, with muscles rippling beneath his sun-blackened flesh and hands.

"I am called Red Jeggs, ugly boy," he said. "Ovelia says you aided her. That earns you your life."

"Good," Davargorn said. "Does it earn me yours as well? I'll take it soon enough."

"A prisoner with spirit!" Red Jeggs's face lit up with glee. "My favorite."

He punched Davargorn so hard in the chin his neck crackled. That punch might have killed a weaker man. Bloody spit frothed from Davargorn's mouth. He grinned, teeth choked in blood.

"Hit me again, big man," Davargorn said. "Perhaps I'll enjoy the second even more."

Red Jeggs wound back his fist for another strike, but a voice from the door stayed him. A hooded woman leaned casually against the doorframe, her neck cocked back suggestively. She held a candle—the room's only source of light—tilted so that it dribbled wax onto the floor every so often. Her flirtatious posture worked quite well on Red Jeggs, who straightened up and puffed out his chest.

"Hold," she said. "Garin will want to question the lad, and he'll need his mouth for that."

"Lis." The big man smiled. "You proved yourself today, girl, but don't overstep. Lest some big man like me be forced to punish you."

"Mmm," she said, sliding one hand down her hip. "Promises."

Red Jeggs strode from the room, looking as heroic as possible, and sneaked more than one glance at her body as he did. She pretended not to notice. When he was gone, she shut the door behind him and leaned back against it, smiling.

"What now, Alistra?" Davargorn asked. "Come to gloat? You betrayer."

"Whom have I betrayed?" Alistra asked. "My brother? Possibly, though the season is young. Vhaerynn? Doubtless. Luether? Surely by siding with Garin I am her greatest patriot."

"You betrayed *me*." Davargorn wrenched at his chains, which held fast. "You stabbed me with Vhaerynn's dagger. I assumed it was your plan to have me rescue that horrible woman, to make them trust us. That if I proved myself useful to them—"

"I did, and they will," Alistra said. "But you misunderstood my plan. I meant for them to trust *me*. I used you to become their ally. Really." She laid her hand on his chest, her nails scratching at his spare hair. "You are such an easy tool for any woman to use." She pressed her cheek to his chest, right over his heart, and made a purring sound. "So easy." She reached one hand down over his belly and slipped her hand down the front of his breeches. "I've decided your foolishness should be punished, but your patience should be rewarded."

Davargorn stretched taut against the chains. "What do you—?"

Alistra put her finger to his lips, silencing him. "If it helps, imagine your princess," she said. In one smooth motion, she knelt on the floor and pulled down his breeches.

He thought he had never experienced anything as blissfully wonderful as the sensation her mouth produced upon him, and when her tongue went to work, tickling and teasing...It felt like fire crackling up through his body. He strained against his bonds, fingers contorting to cling on for some sort of support. The sounds that she made, humming and purring, pleased his ears and made his body tremble. He'd dreamed of such a thing, and seen plenty of men pleased thusly, but never...He wanted to take hold of her, even if it required breaking his thumbs again. Hold her and never let her go.

Alistra drew off him with a pop and murmured. "You can stop me any time," she said, her yellow eyes flashing in the candlelight. "You know that, yes?"

"Yes." Davargorn could hardly think. "Please...*More*."

"As you command, my lord." She drew him in deep and he shuddered.

Then he made the mistake of looking down at Alistra's smooth brown face between his legs, and found himself gazing into her yellow wolf's eyes raised to his. She was his killer and his lover, a dangerous predator that controlled every aspect of his world. That pushed him beyond all self-control and he flailed against the chains, trying to pull free before the inevitable. But Alistra clung on, like a lion with its claws and fangs in its prey, until he spent himself in her mouth. In that moment, as he trembled on the edge of breaking, he had never felt so vulnerable ever in his life, his entire body at her mercy. He could do nothing but shiver as she sucked on his slackening member.

Alistra pulled away at last, leaving him shaking and weak. She sat on her ankles and licked her lips. "That was—interesting," she said. "You had so much to spend, and yet you did it so quickly. A lass would almost think..." She looked at him slyly. "You've never had a woman before, have you?"

Numbly, Davargorn shook his head.

"Just when I start to think of you as a man, you remind me you are yet a lad." Alistra stood and draped her arms around his neck. He could smell himself on her breath. "Truly? In all those summers with your mad little tyrant you loved so much, she never once did for you what I, little more than a stranger, have just done?"

Another day, Davargorn might have snapped at her for impugning Semana thusly, but at the moment, he couldn't speak. His body still shook inside, and his mind roiled with guilt and anger and desire for more. When she kissed him, her tongue salty and warm, he could only kiss her back—awkwardly and without any skill to speak of, but with ardor that surprised them both.

"Mmm." She pressed her nose against his cheek. "Not that I can blame her. You added little to the experience." She drew away and caught his sensitive blade in her hand, making him stiffen in shock. "Here I am, having little to do but practice pleasing the guards for better food and drink, and sometimes kill them if I have a chance. I'm a master of the sensual by comparison, and you—you are but a poor novice at best. Your princess did you a great disservice, ugly boy."

That word—*ugly*—sparked Davargorn's temper, and he felt a hot flame rise up and burn away his hesitation. He glared at her. "What are you saying?"

Alistra reclaimed the candle from where she'd set it on the floor at Davargorn's feet. He saw hot liquid dancing in the hollow at the top like oily water. Slowly, she dipped it over his chest until the wax scalded across his skin. Sharp, stabbing pain resonated from the places it touched, and he winced against the chains. The agony lasted only a moment, and then it became almost cold, the wax freezing into a scab not his own.

"You never resented her?" Alistra asked. "Wondered why she didn't love you back?"

"No," Davargorn said. "She was my master, I her squire. I could place no demands upon her."

Alistra's eyes flashed. "Good," she said. "What my Blood has never understood is that a woman's only obligation is to herself, not to any man." She stepped close to him once more as though to embrace him. "I pleased you because I wished to." She put her face up to his. "My choice."

Davargorn chose that moment to seize her by the neck with the hand he'd slipped free of the manacles while she pleased him. Alistra coughed as his fingers closed around her throat.

"How," he asked, "was that any better than what the Ravalis did to you in the dungeon?"

"Because it was my choice." Alistra rasped as he closed his fingers tighter.

"And this is mine," he said. "I did not ask for your touch or your…whatever you call that."

"I call it sex," Alistra said. "And you did not ask for it, but nor did you reject it. You could have stopped me at any time. I told you as much."

"Why?" he demanded.

"You are a man, are you not? Do you not live for the chance to shove yourself into a woman? Or another man, as my perverse cousin does? A man—" Her words cut off as he squeezed her throat too tightly for speech.

"I hold sway over my own desires," Davargorn said, anger boiling up. "And they include more than your mouth or the rift between your legs."

"Do…they…?"

Alistra squeezed out the two words, smiling madly. Sense left her eyes as he cut off the blood to her brain. Her body thrashed and ground into him, possessed of an insane urge to embrace the man killing it. His broken thumb was still healing, and it wouldn't give him enough strength to snap her neck. Instead, Davargorn held on, furious and unnerved, determined to watch as she died slowly.

A loud, angry voice ripped through the door, muted but loud enough to startle Davargorn. The stairs to the cellar creaked under the weight of footsteps. His grip eased, and Alistra gasped in a sharp breath as her windpipe opened up. His prize lost to him, Davargorn dropped her on the floor and snaked his hand back up and into the manacle that had held it. At his feet, Alistra coughed, then looked up at him with delirious joy. That, more than anything else, had pleased her. Awkwardly, she pulled his breeches back up and tied the laces shut, though he could feel the hesitation in her fingers.

The door swung open to admit three people. A stout man with a soldier's gait entered first, hand on the hilt of his sword. Behind him came a man who hid his face beneath a green cowl, though his eyes glittered. Behind them all came Red Jeggs, grumbling and trying to convince Garin of something. As soon as he saw Davargorn, his speech fell away and he glared fit to murder. He bore the look of a man overruled and none too pleased about it.

"Garin Ravalis," Davargorn said.

"Tithian Davargorn." The prince reached up, revealing in the process his heavily bandaged left hand. He winced when his bad hand touched the fabric of his hood, and he drew back his hood with his one good hand. He looked pale and drawn in the candlelight. He looked to Alistra, who had backed away and stood watching from the shadows. He paused for a second, and Davargorn hoped he would recognize her, but it seemed her guise was too well established. "Lis, right? It's good to see you again."

"Highness." Alistra averted her distinctive yellow eyes. She never looked him straight in the face. Davargorn wondered if that was why he hadn't recognized her.

"We do not stand upon royal etiquette in Summer Lives." The prince held out his good hand. "Garin. Please."

"Yes." Alistra took his hand and held it gently. "I leave you to your work—"

"No no," Garin said. "Stay if you like. This will only take a moment."

He turned to Davargorn. "Apparently, Ovelia gave her word that she would speak of you to me, and so she did," he said. "She said you might be of value to us, and I should speak with you first."

"And I," Red Jeggs said, "told his Highness speaking with you would waste the day."

Garin ignored his less than supportive escort. "Ovelia told me you were a prisoner aboard Fersi's ship, and that you fought beside her to escape."

"This is true," Davargorn said.

"Oh, I *know* it is true." Garin rustled around in his belt pouch. "Ovelia has no reason to lie to me. You do, however, and thus—" He produced a small vial of a purplish liquid. "This is *meethus*, a chemic of my own design, made from extract of the midnight lotus, sweetsoul, and a few other things you probably haven't heard of. I could tell you all about its composure, but only an apothecary or an alchemist would probably enjoy such a lecture. Suffice it to say, once I administer this poison to you, you will fall into a suggestive state with inhibitions so low I could ask you to stab yourself, and you'd do it gladly."

"Is that your plan?" Davargorn asked. "Drug me and murder me by own hand?"

"That was just an example," Garin said. "In truth, all I seek is the truth. And once this is in your blood, you'll be glad to tell it to me." He drew out a small dagger and slicked the blade with the poison.

Alarmed, Davargorn looked sharply to Alistra, who reassured him with the slightest of nods. She eyed the dagger in Garin's hand, gleaming with venom, then locked her eyes on Davargorn and frowned.

Davargorn understood. "Wait," he said. "I'll not resist. No need to injure me."

"Not a thrust—just a small poke." Garin paused, and chuckled over some private jest. He pressed the blade to the hollow of Davargorn's elbow where it pierced the bulging vein. "You're a fantastic specimen, you know. Extremely well developed musculature, hardly a scar or scratch after hard summers, and that eye." He looked up at Davargorn's milk white eye. "Fascinating."

"Ugh. Perhaps I *prefer* to be drugged." Davargorn sneered at him. "Get on with it."

In truth, however, he could already feel the poison working its way up his arm. It felt at first like a gentle, creeping cold, and the world dipped out of focus. His body relaxed and his mind felt...muddy. Davargorn felt detached from his body, the poison eroding the last ties of spirit and flesh. It might have terrified him, but he had left fear far behind. Anger flowed away, as did all other emotions.

"Tithian?" Garin asked. "Can you hear me?"

"Yes." The reply came automatically and from a distance, startling Davargorn. Not his own word.

"Remember all that flattery from before?" Garin wiped the dagger on a small cloth and sheathed it. "That's part of the process. Opening your mind, so that you see me as a friend. Did it work?"

"Yes..." Davargorn felt his body smile. "We are...friends."

"Good. I'm so glad."

They were certainly *not* friends. It felt like Vhaerynn suborning his body through blood magic, but at least then his will had been his own. Davargorn could not resist, and that made it truly horrific.

Garin gestured to his escorts, who unclasped Davargorn's wrists, including the one he had thrust back into its manacle. He couldn't tell if it made them suspicious and didn't care. He was floating. They drew over a stool, and Davargorn's body sat down on it. He was going to kill this man some day.

"Now." Garin leaned in close. He had started to glow. "Ovelia tells me you leaped in front of a caster to protect your master, who had betrayed you and left you for dead. Is this true?"

Davargorn nodded. He saw no reason to lie. "I gave myself...for her."

Behind them, Alistra laughed loud, and they all looked back at her with a range of perplexity on their faces. "Men," she said, the word seeming to blur in Davargorn's perception.

The two faceless warders looked at each other with derisive expressions, and Red Jeggs scoffed. "Women," he said.

"Charming." Garin focused on Davargorn. "What brings you to this place, friend?"

"You—you do." Davargorn pointed shakily up at Red Jeggs. "That one. And—" He pointed over at Alistra. "And that one. I *like* her."

Alistra chuckled. In Davargorn's perception, her face blurred and twisted in on itself. It became angular and shifty, like that of a cat. He couldn't tell if it was really happening or just his imagination.

Garin smiled tightly. "I should be more specific," he said. "Why are you in Luether? Is it to kill someone?"

"I—" Davargorn felt the poison itching under his skin. He wanted to scratch himself, but Red Jeggs grasped his wrist and held it away from his arm. He looked up, and the man resembled nothing less than a monster made of molten stone and fire. Davargorn flinched at the suddenness of the vision and looked at the other man, who looked like a constantly sprouting mass of razor-sharp fur. No matter what Garin had said, this sight did not soothe Davargorn—quite the opposite.

A fire was burning inside him, which he recognized as his magic fighting the poison.

"Focus." Garin laid his hands to either side of Davargorn's face, drawing his attention. His glow had become as bright as the sun now, blinding the whole room. "Did you come here to kill someone?"

The whole room had fallen apart now, dancing and swirling in shades of darkness and terror. Davargorn's interrogators had become monsters flowing with fire, blood, and doom. Alistra stood behind them, a tall, black, hairless cat with glinting sharp nails. Did she have a knife? But through it all, he felt his healing magic—his single constant companion from his many winters—and that gave him confidence. And, he realized, he once more had control of his own tongue. He stared the shining Garin-creature in the face and grinned, baring his teeth.

"Yes," Davargorn said. "Yes, I *did* come to kill someone."

Alistra, behind them, looked suddenly concerned, but he smiled wider to see her discomfort.

"Whom?" Garin asked. "Was it Ovelia?" He set his mouth. "Was it me?"

"No." Davargorn managed to shake his head slightly. He could control his own speech, and he could lie. The poison faltered before his magic. "Pervast. The Usurper."

"Why?" Garin asked. "Why him?"

Davargorn considered, his thoughts still blurry from the half-burned poison. "Semana," he said. "For...my princess..."

Garin looked dubious for a moment, then a smile spread across his face. "Then we walk the same path, friend," he said. "Will you aid me in my quest?"

Davargorn nodded. "My master once called me a blade forged from a man," he said. "Point me at your foe, and I will see his blood stain the ground."

Garin rose and scratched his stubbled chin in thought. "I see Ovelia's confidence was not misplaced, and I am glad I spoke with you. Tonight, my people will clean and feed you, and on the morrow you will walk the next length of Luether's path at my side."

Red Jeggs flushed a deep, ruddy shade of outrage. "Highness, you cannot mean—"

Garin put up his hand. "That is quite enough from you," he said. "You were wrong once—do not compound the error by playing the fool."

For a slip of a moment, Davargorn thought Red Jeggs would protest. His hand raised halfway, as though to strike Garin. He noted the way Alistra was watching, noting that little bit of defiance. Garin and his men left, though this time the door remained open. For a time, Davargorn and Alistra stared at one another wordlessly, and the growing smile on her face disturbed and allured him. When the footsteps on the stairs had receded, finally he broke the silence.

"My magic fought off the poison," Davargorn said. "How did you know that would happen?"

"A guess." Alistra shrugged. "Did you see when that big hunk of flesh nearly boxed my cousin about the ear?"

Davargorn nodded. "Garin does not control his agents as well as he supposes."

"A weakness for us to exploit." Alistra sat down on the stool and rested her chin on her palms. "I've changed my mind about you."

"How?" Davargorn asked.

"Before, I thought you a fool boy, easily led around by your cock," she said. "Now I see greater depth to you." She put her hand over her mouth in mock surprise. "You gave your life for the master who had rejected and left you? If that is not love, I do not know what it is."

Davargorn scowled at her. "I've had enough of mockery for five lifetimes worth."

"Oh, poor little boy." Alistra spread her legs wide and beckoned to him.

His mind screamed at him to stop, but his body moved toward her. He stepped into her embrace, reaching for her, and she deftly twisted around him to put him on the ground while she straddled him and kissed him soundly.

251

"I nearly killed you," he said.

Alistra murmured noncommittally in his mouth. "You've impressed me." She pressed her hips against him. "I know you want me—why not take me? I am your spoils."

"You are not," Davargorn said. "I have not won you. I could not win you."

"True." Alistra's eyes glittered at him. "This one time, it will be by your choice. Kill me or rut me, as you choose."

Davargorn gazed upon her. Rage mixed with desire in his belly, and his body felt warm all over. Slowly, he pushed her off, rose, and wiped his hands together. "No," he said.

"I did my job too well, then," Alistra said. "You've not the strength to spend yourself again?"

"Perhaps." Davargorn shrugged. "Perhaps I simply do not owe you my body or my heart."

Alistra's cheeks rose slightly in something like a smile. "Good lad."

TWENTY-SIX

The darkness was there to greet Garin when he left the cellar beneath the Summer Lives safehouse, and it followed him up all the way back to the Long Dawn. The common room was filled with celebration, but in his void, he felt no thirst for drink or for joy.

He looked immediately for Alcarin, but the lad had retired immediately upon his return, wanting to speak with no one. Garin had managed to convince him to accept a soothing draught to help him sleep and poultices for his wounds, but more substantial treatment would have to wait. Perhaps that was for the best. Garin's own hand was wrapped heavily in thick bandages, and the last time Alcarin had looked at it, he'd fumed and heaved until he practically fainted.

The battle with Fersi had proved a mixed victory at best. His newfound alliance with Lady Shard had held strong—even now, the woman was taking control of Fersi's substantial section of Luether's black market. Between her efforts and the revolt at Tuerine, Luether would cease to operate, and with Pervast's forces scrambling to get the mine working again, the Ruin King was vulnerable. Shard had urged Garin to strike, but he saw a different sort of opportunity—one that, if he could take advantage of it, would cement him as Luether's king apparent.

He knocked lightly on a door upstairs in the Long Dawn, heard the soft affirmation after a three-count, and pushed through. Warm, oppressive air filled the room, and he caught a variety of scents ranging from ointments and tinctures to blood and sweat. One thing in particular struck his nose, but his mind was racing with too many things to pause and linger upon it.

"Garin, what troubles?" Ovelia eased herself up from where she lay in her narrow bed, grasping a sheet over herself. Her body was a mess of bruises and bandages. Her captivity and the subsequent battle had left her more of a wreck than Alcarin.

"No no, stay," Garin said. "Rest. I'm sorry to disturb you."

Ovelia settled back onto the bed. Despite her obvious wounds, she seemed surprisingly relaxed. Garin, who had rarely seen her so at ease, found it odd and perhaps a bit unsettling.

"What passes?" she asked. "You look worse than I feel. Has something happened with Shard?"

"Coming from a blind woman, that stings less than it might." He smiled lightly for a heartbeat, but it fell away. He eased himself into a seat. "I've need of your...your advice. Normally, I'd ask Biaza, but Red Jeggs is still questioning her after the Fersi misstep. You understand."

Ovelia nodded. They both knew that Summer Lives had to consider the very real possibility that Biaza had known of Fersi's impending betrayal. If she was working with Garin's enemies, it could prove a disaster. The woman had expressed bewilderment when Garin returned to the Long Dawn and had several of his closest agents remove her by force to a safehouse not unlike the one under which he'd questioned Davargorn. Her interrogation would go on several hours.

"I feel...unmoored, without her," Garin said. "She was the one I confided in."

"Please," Ovelia said. "Speak your mind. You can always talk to me."

"I know," Garin said. "I...I value that. More than I can say." He had a momentary impulse to flee the room rather than speak of the matter, but finally he slumped back in his chair at her bedside. "The idea has been advanced that I...Luther is all but won, but in order to secure it..."

Ovelia took his hand and met his eye. "Garin. It's me. Speak."

He drew his flask of nyssa from his tunic and took a swig, then gave a great sigh. He offered her some, but she returned a declining wave.

"It's been suggested that in order to unite the Luethaar, I must marry," he said. "A queen to harden my Blood, and an heir to preserve my throne." He sighed and touched his fingers to his temples. "You see, of course, the problem." When there came no reply, he looked up. "Lady Dracaris?"

Ovelia's attention seemed to have wandered. She was, even now, gazing toward the wall as though she might see through its stones. Very strange, but she'd had a long, trying day.

"Apologies, prince." Ovelia shook herself and smiled. "A consort. Is that all? You worried me for a moment."

Garin frowned deeply. "I cannot marry. Who would I marry?"

"Alcarin, for one," Ovelia said, still a little removed. "Aye, he is younger than you, but surely it wouldn't be the first time a Luethaar master bound his squire."

"No, but it would be the first time a Ravalis man has wed another man."

"Oh." Ovelia's expression fell. "I had not even considered that. In the north, matches between men and men or women and women are commonplace, and no Vangryur would think poorly of it."

"But we are not in Tar Vangr," Garin said.

"Surely your family cannot reach you here," Ovelia said. "And even if it could, if you are King of the Summerlands, surely their opinion no longer matters."

"My cousin and I disagree, it's true, but that's not it," Garin said. "My family loathes the very thought of what I am, even after they have lived in Tar Vangr these twenty summers gone. The rest of Luether is far more set in the way of man and woman than your homeland. From old, we are commanded to mate like bulls and heifers, and never shall a bull touch another bull but in violence. No." He pounded his fist on the arm of his chair, drawing Ovelia's full attention. "If I am to marry, I must have a queen—one who will give me heirs."

Ovelia's face had cleared, and she looked upon him with full focus now. "The king can marry whomever he wishes," she said.

"I am not the king—not yet." Desperate fury filled Garin's eyes. "And even if I should ascend, I will remain king only because the people allow it. I will be their savior—strong, handsome, and charming. But the moment their shining prince takes a man to his bed, he has spat upon their traditions. The instant he shows himself for what he is, he becomes no longer a man, but a disgusting abomination."

"Surely you do not believe that," Ovelia said. "After all this time, you—"

He wanted to deny it, but Fersi's words rang out in his memory, strengthening the darkness that coiled inside him. The self-hatred he thought he had shed since Tar Vangr boiled within. He could tell that Ovelia sensed it, and it angered her.

He opened his mouth to speak, but at that moment the sound of water rushing through old pipes resounded through the room, and the door to the small mercycloset off Ovelia's chamber opened. Vilaer Vultara stood framed in the door, a blanket wrapped around her slim body for modesty and warmth. The candlelight reflected a smudge of something white on her nose, but it might have been a trick of perspective. Garin stared at her, and she stared right back, both of them startled. Ovelia as well looked startled, as though she'd quite forgotten about the nude woman in her chambers.

"Apologies," Garin and Vilaer said at the same time. Garin grinned sheepishly and Vilaer shifted her weight between her feet. Ovelia looked mortified and touched at her nose seemingly subconsciously.

"Perhaps I'd best go," the Vultara princess said, wiping her face with the towel.

"Perhaps you'd better," Ovelia said, even as Garin said, "No, stay."

Another awkward silence fell among them, but Garin broke it with a laugh. "A thousand apologies, my Lady Vultara," he said. "Lady Dracaris and I were simply discussing a political alliance."

"A marriage, you mean." Vilaer made to sit beside Ovelia, but the woman's forbidding look cut her off. Instead, she crossed the room and sat before the mirror, arranging the blanket as carefully and casually as at a state revel. "If you are to reclaim the throne, you must marry. I agree."

"Exactly right," Garin said. "I should welcome your advice as well, Lady Vultara. You know Luether as well as I do. Perhaps you have an opinion on how to proceed?"

Ovelia glanced at Vilaer sidelong. If she had seemed distracted when Garin entered before, Ovelia had regained all of her focus now. She seemed just as distrustful and cautious as ever.

"I don't think we should be discussing this just now," Ovelia said.

"Nonsense!" Garin ignored Ovelia's pointed, disapproving look. "I see my Lady Warder trusts you quite…intimately, Lady Vultara."

"So it would seem." Vilaer cast Ovelia a cool, suggestive look, and Garin saw something very rare on Ovelia's face: an embarrassed flush. "You have caught us in an odd moment, but this is pressing. You've consulted your other advisors, I imagine?"

"We've talked about it for some time," Garin said. " 'Twas Red Jeggs's idea, if you can believe that. Leave it to that oaf to dream up a way to appeal to Luether's 'grand traditions.' He suggested I 'pick a wide-hipped lass and put a son in her right off, with or without a crown.' Neblen suggested I marry a smart girl—to make up for me, whatever that means. Biaza agreed—when she was still here—and Corvus too. I think he'd be especially pleased to see me with a woman." He looked at his hands. "I've spoken with Shard as well."

"You asked her before you brought this to me?" Ovelia asked. "You barely know her."

"We've only met recently," Garin said. "But I've known her for many years. Probably I know her better than you. Though—" He grinned sheepishly. "I suppose I fantasized about her as a man."

Ovelia looked displeased, but let it pass. "You know what I will ask next," she said softly.

"About Allie." Garin felt the breath flow out of him, and he felt a dozen summers older in a single moment. "Allie opposed it, of course, but…Old *Gods*, Ovelia."

"Of course," Ovelia said. "You cannot turn your back upon love."

"Can I not?" he asked. "How can I even be considering this? I cannot—I cannot think of a day spent without Allie. A night with some other…" He shook his head. "I cannot do it."

"Well, that is simple," Vilaer said. "Tell me of this 'Allie.' What is she, low-born? Without Blood? So keep her as a lover. Many in your Blood have done far more scandalous things. Freeing you up to marry for politics, if only we could find a suitable bride. Let me think—" She smiled indulgently, then frowned. "Why do you look at me in that way?"

Ovelia's face fell, and Garin abruptly understood why. Vilaer did not know his secret. But now she would.

"You don't—" Vilaer's eyes widened. "You mean your squire. That boy. I had heard rumors, but I never believed…" She pressed her hand over her mouth. "A *man*."

"Is it so difficult to imagine?" Garin asked. "You lay with Ovelia, did you not?"

"Yes, but—" Vilaer said. "I thought you meant a mistress—someone unsuitable. But a man?" She shook her head. "Luether would never accept that. None would follow you. No."

"Your highness," Ovelia said, her tone warning. She started to rise from the bed.

"No, it passes well." Garin waved away Ovelia's intervention and looked to Vilaer directly. "Highness, you say nothing I've not said to myself a thousand times. But I cannot lie. I will love as I must." He closed his fist. "Alcarin is my best friend and true love."

"No." Vilaer's face had deepened to a purple tone. "I cannot listen to this. You were our chance—*my* chance—to redeem this city! To fix my Blood's mistakes and cast out the barbarians. And now you will sacrifice that for a boy's infatuation?"

"Vilaer." There was no gentleness to Ovelia's words now. "*Stop.*"

"No, Lady Dracaris," she said, but the sharp word had broken her concentration. "Prince Garin, I meant to suggest you marry *me*—your claim, my connections, an unbroken line of succession—but I—I have to think." Hurriedly, she plucked up garments and pushed out of the chamber. "Pass well."

Ovelia uttered a deep sigh, and Garin saw the pain writ on her face.

"It passes well enough," Garin said. "She is old Luethaar Blood. Such things disturb her, and if her good soul grew angry, imagine how the rest of Luether will react." He sighed. "Though you got her in bed with you. Repressed urges, perhaps?"

Ovelia shook her head. "It doesn't matter," she said. "Only the right path matters."

"The right path." Garin leaned his head back and gazed at the ceiling. "If only it were so simple."

"Perhaps it is." Ovelia's hand touched his, and he looked down at her. She was looking him in the eye, her cloudy gaze surprisingly direct. "Vilaer may have grown flustered and stormed out, but she was not wrong. Marry for politics—marry Vilaer, if it's advantageous—but love for yourself."

"Keep Alcarin as what? A bed-slave? A serving boy for…*extra* services?" He shook his head. "But the risk. The danger."

"No," Ovelia said, the word firm. "No one tells the king who to love."

Garin considered this a moment, and he could feel the darkness draining away, replaced gradually by first relief, then resolve.

"You," he said.

"Me." Ovelia shrugged. "Surely you do not mean for *me* to pick a mate for your throne. I know little enough of Luether's politics. If you'll not marry Vilaer, at least consult her. Narfire, ask Shard. She can advise you better—"

"That's not what I mean." The idea bloomed in him so bright it drove away the doubting darkness. "You and I have fought so long and so hard together. The Luethaar have seen us. Firehair the Fury, Bloodbreaker of a Thousand Bloods, Shield of the Summer Prince. They sing your praises louder than mine."

"Almost as loudly," Ovelia said. "But no, I'll not tell you who to marry. I am your Shield, sire—not your master. And—"

He touched her lips, stopping her words.

"You," Garin said. "I'll marry *you*."

Ovelia's eyes widened. "But your Highness—"

Garin shook his head. "You have stood by me," he said. "You have bled for me. I have seen your strength and your spirit. I know the darkness of your past, and how you have transcended it. I trust you more than anyone in this ruined world or any other. You are the best person I know." He took her hands in his. "If you agree, I will marry you. Tonight. Now."

Ovelia's unseeing eyes blinked. "Yes," she said.

ACT FIVE: MARTYRS

Twelve years previous—The Bottom Shred—Luether, 970 Sorcerus Annis

THE LAD WORKED THE crowd with the smooth sort of confidence few but veteran warriors could claim, stalking from table to table with a swaying lilt that drew speculative eyes. Grease enhanced the corded muscles of his belly and sides under his red vest, and his lithe body was toned to perfection. His fingers traced the arms and shoulders of the patrons, searching, as though he could feel their hearts at a touch. He was sex on two perfect legs, and he made it rather hard for the Fox of Luether to concentrate.

"Ay!" the man sitting at the greasy bar shouted. "Who I need to stab to get a brew?"

Garin Ravalis suppressed a chuckle. The man's outburst made it less likely the tender would even acknowledge him, much less bring him the ale he wanted. He nursed his own tankard, knowing full well he'd not get another any time soon.

As an establishment, the Bottom Shred prided itself on its poor service.

Founded shortly after the fall of Luether from the ruins of a manor belonging to some Low-City upstart Blood, the Shred catered primarily to the rough-and-tumble set of Luethaar society. Tough dockhands mingled with embittered soldiers and foul-smelling beggars who had managed to scrounge up the coin. Brawls commonly settled bar tabs, and lewd acts took place in open view of all. In a way, the Bottom Shred presented a microcosm of Luether itself: battered, bruised, but still striving, full of people hardened through salt spray and bloodshed. Garin might have loved it, had he not come here with a task.

The doors opened and that very task walked through, flanked by two escorts. The one on the left wore forbidding armor fused so seamlessly with hooks and spikes Garin could not tell where armor and skin met. She wore no weapon—with all those blades, she probably needed none. The one on the right wore no armor, but he looked all the more intimidating for the two additional arms that sprouted from his shoulders and ended in long, spindly hands with the wrong number of fingers. The wiry things looked like a mocking caricature of plumes on a soldier's helmet until they started moving

259

on their own. Garin had heard legends of men so warped and deformed in the wilds of the World of Ruin as to have extra limbs or bodies, but he had never seen one. By contrast, General Tarras—Fire in the Steel, he was called—seemed mundane, though his muscular build made him easily twice the width of any man Garin had ever met.

Their presence immediately drew the attention of all, and why not? They were Children of Ruin.

Like most taverns in Low-City, the Bottom Shred occasionally catered—grudgingly—to the Children of Ruin. The barbarians remained mostly in High-City and descended only to hunt. Pervast had long ago decreed that any Luethaar who struck a Child of Ruin would pay for the act with the offending limb, but he made no such opposite imposition. Anyone marked by Ruin could and often did slay whatever Luethaar he or she wanted, lowborn or high, rich or poor. Thousands had died in the first season after the fall, and thousands died every year since over real or perceived slights.

The general swept his gaze over the gathered patrons, who all but competed to be the first to look away. Meeting his gaze could be interpreted as a challenge, and the muscle he'd brought along looked eager for some brawling.

After six summers of barbarian rule, Luether hovered just on the edge of total collapse. When Garin's father had loosed the Narfire in a vain attempt to defend the city, thousands of barbarians had perished but the flames had gutted Luether of its moral strength. The Mines of Tuerine had kept the city afloat, but economic isolation had all but destroyed its once great wealth. It had fallen into a ruin of slums and hovels, where good folk cowered from the sun and Ruin-scarred madmen held sway. Garin longed to reawaken his people—to restore Luether to the glory it had known in his youth. He waged his war alone, as he had for five summers, but he would find a way—

"Hail," said a voice soft and smooth as fresh silk. It was the lad Garin had been watching across the common room. "What do you fancy, handsome one?"

"Ah." Garin strained to look away from the young man's beautiful features and over his shoulder. "I'm waiting for someone—"

"I can see that." The lad laid his hand on the inside of Garin's left leg. "I'd say someone's come. Or will, soon enough."

Garin smiled at that. "You're very forward," he said.

"I know what I like," the lad said. "And I know what *you* like. Tell me I'm wrong."

"Oh, you're not wrong." A couple patrons had looked over toward them with interest. Garin pulled the cowl lower over his face and took a draught of his sour ale. "Far from wrong," he said. "It just so happens I'm here to meet another gentleman, one far less handsome and charming than yourself."

The lad's eyes flicked to the center of the common room, where General Tarras and his barbarians had brow-beaten a pair of dour patrons into vacating a table. The four-armed one sat heavily, making the chair groan, and roared for ale. His demand would actually be answered, Garin suspected. The general sat as well, taking his ease like a king, while the one in the barbed armor stood over him like a protective gargoyle.

"Those bleeders?" he asked. "They don't seem like your speed."

"And what do you know about my speed?" Garin asked.

"Look at them." The young man smiled wide. "They aren't at all like me."

Again, Garin had to smile, and he shook his head in bemusement. "What's your name, boy?"

"Alcarin." Flames lit in the young man's eyes. "Though you can call me Allie—everyone else does. And I'm not a boy."

"Oh?" Garin asked. "This is what, your fifteenth summer?"

"Sixteenth." The word was sharp on his tongue. "But I haven't been a boy since Luether fell."

"I suppose none of us have." Garin drained the last of his ale. "Still, I cannot involve you in my business of tonight. Perhaps later—" He blinked. The lad had vanished.

Alcarin made his swaying way across the common room without so much as a backward glance. He strode right up to the general, laid himself in the man's lap, and kissed him full on the lips. That, more than the arrival of the barbarians or their domineering manner, shocked the common room. The Bottom Shred had a reputation for all manner of sex for sale, but most Luethaar did not look kindly on the act of one man kissing another. More than this, though, the sheer boldness of the gesture seemed impossible outside of a bard's tale, and so no one moved—not the patrons, not the general's bodyguards, and not even Tarras himself. The general seemed startled but more than vaguely pleased. Alcarin held the kiss, pressing himself hard into the burly man, and Garin saw the glint of steel at the edge of his sleeve.

"Burn me," Garin said, reaching for his caster.

Alcarin palmed a knife and stabbed it into the general's throat, sending blood spraying up toward the ceiling. General Tarras shoved the gorgeous boy back and toppled backward in the rickety chair, choking and gurgling blood. Lifeblood smeared across his face, Alcarin danced back in perfect balance. Stunned, the woman with all the blades and spikes grabbed for the ailing general and the metal screeched against the thick leather of his hauberk and hooked into his skin. Four-Arms barreled up from his seat, roaring like a beast, and lunged for Alcarin. The lad managed to slip free, and even slashed a bright streak across one of those spindly arms as he went. The barbarian's blood bloomed thick and sickly orange in the smoky candlelight. One of his big, meaty hands closed around Alcarin's wrist—

A thunderous *crack* split the chamber, and Garin's casterbolt exploded into Four-Arms with enough force to send him staggering back.

Then the common room exploded into chaos. Patrons drew weapons, smashed chairs into each other, or waded in with fists flying. More cracks of discharging casters exploded against Garin's ears as he scurried toward the center of the melee. Four-Arms roared over and over like a wounded boar, a casterbolt jutting from his chest, and smashed aside grubby men and women with his flailing. He picked one man up in his big hands, transferred him to his surprisingly strong shoulder arms, and hurled him out the nearest shuttered window, making it explode open to the murky night beyond. Garin couldn't even see the woman with the barbed armor. He kept low and moved swiftly, not engaging with any combatant.

"Allie," he said sharply. "Allie!"

A hand pawed at his ankle and Garin instinctively pulled away. Alcarin's bright eyes gleamed up at him from beneath a draped table. He ducked in to join the lad, who smiled impishly.

"What have you done?" Garin asked sharply. "Did I ask you to—?"

Alcarin seized the prince's cheeks and locked their lips together. The kiss was warm and strong, lingering as the battle raged. It was their first, but Garin knew in that moment it would not be their last.

It might have gone on, but then the drapery over the table pulled aside, and the barbarian with the nightmare armor leered at them, her grimace revealing teeth that were too long and too sharp for a mortal mouth. She loosed a sound like that of a pouncing snake and grasped at them with one clawed gauntlet. Alcarin sucked in a breath, but Garin had already taken a bright pink capsule from his belt. He kissed the lad again and hurled the capsule right in the woman's face.

The capsule exploded in a pink cloud that filled the space under the table and boiled out from under it like smoke. The barbarian gasped, coughed, and looked at Garin with a bewildered look that turned into dizzy euphoria. She tumbled back on her hindquarters and sat, stupefied, until one of the brawlers smashed a fist into her face. The man yelped in pain and cradled his knuckles, which had split open against her helmet.

Garin broke the kiss only after the fumes had spread outward—to stop them both from breathing them, of course. Then he took Alcarin by the hand and pulled him toward the nearest exit from the tavern. They scurried through the unfolding, faltering melee. As the pink smoke spread, the brawlers lost some of their coordination, staggering and flailing blindly at their opponents without much heart. Even Four-Arms was looking around, confused—the arms sprouting from his shoulders waved madly in the air, fingers splayed like fans. The battle became more of a wild dance: less effective and just as violent.

They broke out into the warm darkness of Luether's Low-City, with its oppressive haze and filthy streets. They'd caught some of the fumes, of course, and it made Garin heady and Alcarin giddy. He sniffed at the air, drawing in the smell of salt water mingled with the aroma of charring meat. Also…

"Come," he said, drawing Alcarin toward the barn attached to the tavern. He kicked the door, which shuddered but did not open.

"How romantic," Alcarin said. "Rescue the lad in distress, then whisk him away to a barn."

"Is that what you did with me?" Garin kicked again, but the door held.

"Absolutely it is." Alcarin looked through the barn window. "A dismal place for a tryst."

"Feel the air lightening?" Garin asked. "The drop in pressure indicates rain. And we don't want to be outside when that happens."

"Why didn't you say so?" Gently, Alcarin pushed Garin's hands aside and fiddled with the latch. "There's a trick to it."

Garin heard the fighting in the tavern escalate, and Four-Arms's roars sounded like thunder in the street. Soon he would be searching for them, and more Children of Ruin could arrive at any moment.

The latch clicked open, and Alcarin pulled the door wide with a creak. He slipped in, and Garin followed and shut the door just before shadows passed by at the mouth of the alley. He set down his uncharged caster and reached for his belt, fingering a maelstrom explosive. He didn't want to use the horrid thing, but he would not hesitate if he needed it. Alcarin was staring at the device, fascinated.

The Children of Ruin passed them by without pause and instead rushed into the Bottom Shred with weapons drawn.

"I suppose old Bram won't want me back now," Alcarin said. "After I caused all this."

"More like *I* caused this," Garin said. "Well, that was a failure—a spectacular one, but not the way I intended to handle that at all."

"What do you mean?" Alcarin asked. "Is there another way to treat with these savages?"

"Assassination wasn't my goal, here," Garin said. "I meant to acquire information. Secrets. Names. Places. But instead, you sparked a brawl, and put who knows how many Luethaar in danger."

"Low-City folk can take care of themselves." Alcarin crossed his arms. "Acquire information? The general would sooner gut you than confide in you. What was your plan?"

"To seduce him and find out what he knew," Garin said. "I do that often. We've met on several occasions. He was there looking for me, actually."

"Oh." Alcarin's eyes widened. "Well, how was I to know?"

"You could have listened—" Garin shrugged. He'd meant to rebuke the young man, but instead he found himself on the defensive. It might have galled him, but Alcarin's beauty made it amusing instead. He uttered a helpless sigh. "The general was a terrible man, I agree, and his death will help my quest, but not as much as his secrets would have. Though I suppose it might not have worked, since he brought new enforcers with him. He might have been onto me. So perhaps you saved my life. Thanks?"

At first, Alcarin looked confused, but Garin could see his sharp mind racing to catch up. Then his eyes sparkled. "Quest?" he asked. "I knew it! You're the Fox of Luether! Destined to overthrow Pervast."

"Trying, anyway." Garin shrugged. "I hope that isn't a problem for you."

"Quite the opposite." Alcarin took his hands. "Take me as your squire. Teach me. Let me help you." His expression turned determined. "The Children have all but destroyed my city. I have nothing left. Show me how to fight them. *Please.*"

Garin hardly had to consider. How could he say no to this beautiful boy?

"I have to tell you," Garin said. "This path will probably kill me, and if you follow me, you're destined for a horrid death of your own. A noble one, but a certain one as well."

Alcarin considered. "Will there be plenty of sex involved before the death bit?"

Garin grinned. "Absolutely there will."

Alcarin smiled wide, dazzling Garin with his beauty. "Then let's get started."

"The deal is struck and sealed. Martyrs together we shall be." Garin kissed him. "Squire."

"Master," Alcarin said. "What do we do first?"

"This." They kissed again, and tumbled together into the hay.

TWENTY-SEVEN

The flames had no heat this time, but she knew they would eventually burn her. They always had.

Ovelia stood in a dark cavern, separated from the roiling inferno by an invisible wall delicate as the skin of a soap bubble. She could have broken the barrier open with a touch, but instead she waited, watching the fires. They were dancing and moving, forming shapes that she had never seen before.

Eventually, the flames resolved themselves into a vaguely humanoid form whose face hid in the cacophony of silver fire but whom she nonetheless recognized: Lenalin.

In the way of dreams, Ovelia screamed silently, and the figure did not notice her. She reached forward and placed her hands on the invisible wall, which felt oddly cool to the touch. Always before in the dream, the wall had ruptured at the slightest pressure, but this time it resisted her like thick glass. Ovelia shoved on it, to no effect, then hammered her palms on the wall, breaking the skin and smearing blood through the air. The barrier would not give, and finally she sank down, heaving, and rested her head against the wall.

"Sister."

She looked up, and there was Lenalin gazing back, her face a rictus of scars and burns. She hardly resembled a vestige of herself, and yet Ovelia would know her face despite a thousand disfigurements and deaths. She wept tears of joy to see Lenalin again, and bitterness at her fate.

"I failed you," Ovelia said. "I—"

Then Lenalin reached through the wall and laid her hands on either side of Ovelia's cheeks. Their eyes met, and Ovelia felt a burning in her head as though Lenalin's gaze had become fire. The princess opened her mouth to speak, and what came out was flame and pain.

"You abandon me," Lenalin said. "You do not love me. You love another."

"No, I—"

As the world slowed, the wall shattered all around them and a thousand shards of dark glass cut into her, rending her flesh from her bones. Then the wave of heat struck, and she felt her body burning away even as Lenalin's grasp grew tighter.

She could not even scream.

～

L ADY DRACARIS?" GARIN ASKED as they bounced along. When no reply came, he leaned across the intervening space in the shadowed interior of the carriage. "Ovelia."

The woman leaned against the wall of the carriage near the window, light flowing along her skin as they passed the flickering street lamps of Low-City. With the blindfold, it became difficult to tell at times if Ovelia slumbered, and Garin only knew it now because she twitched occasionally as though in a dream. A sad, distant expression painted her face, and she looked as though she might weep at any moment. Seeing her thus made him profoundly uneasy, and also a bit jealous.

"How can she sleep at a time like this?" For his part, it was all Garin could do not to burst out of the carriage in his mania. He contented himself with drumming his fingers on his legs.

"Oh, leave her be." Alcarin shifted uneasily next to him. "The poor woman's barely slept in days. It's not her fault you don't *need* to."

"True enough." Garin chuckled. He'd waked Alcarin a dozen times in the last two nights alone with earnest entreaties to listen to his new ideas about the next moves in their war against Pervast. Garin never seemed to need much sleep, unless the darkness had him in its grasp. And after this night, he knew, that would never happen again.

It was working.

Luether had not functioned as a city since the fall of Tuerine, and that time had proven truly costly for Pervast. Reports came in hourly of allies abandoning the Ruin King, asserting their own control of their assets or openly pledging themselves to Garin. Then, over the last day, word of Garin's confrontation with the late Captain Fersi had spread throughout the city. That he had extended a hand of friendship toward a known enemy, one who had attempted to slay him, and that he had suffered a wound to that very hand…such a story carried weight in Luether. The city had reached a tipping point, and word of Garin's marriage would provide the needed impetus to bring Pervast crashing down.

"We are so close," Garin said. "When my cousin marches in three days' time, he'll find a peaceful city awaiting him, with me sitting upon the throne."

"You think so?" Alcarin sat, arms folded, slumped back into the seat across from him.

"Absolutely," Garin said. "Among the Mine ceasing, the merchant lords deserting him, and the loss of Princess Vilaer, Pervast's claim on the throne has all but broken, while my star has ascended. And after tonight—with the last heiress of the Blood Dracaris at my side, restoring the power and majesty of Luether—it will be a simple matter to convince him to step down."

"You'll *convince* him." Alcarin shifted to look away. "Because that went so well last time."

"True." Garin flexed his splinted hand, feeling the kinetic magic he'd woven into the silver fibers convulse and sizzle. "If I'm to rule the city of smiths, it makes sense that I am part artifice, does it not?"

Alcarin looked anything but amused. He was looking at Garin with eyes that gleamed in the play of light and shadow as the carriage made its way up the street. Even for one practiced in the art of reading people, Garin had never been the best at knowing his squire's mind at a glance. It was one of many reasons he'd enlisted him. But the way Alcarin sat and spoke now, even a child could tell how he felt.

"You are angry," Garin said.

"You're burning *right* I'm angry," Alcarin said.

Garin glanced at Ovelia and looked down at his folded hands in his lap. "You know this is how it must be, Allie," he said. "To be a viable king to Luether, I must have a wife, one who can give me heirs." He put his hand on Alcarin's knee. "It changes nothing between us. No one will tell the king who he—"

"No." Alcarin wrenched his leg away. "It's not that."

"But—" Garin stumbled over his words. "What is it, then? Talk to me."

"You are such an idiot." Alcarin shook his head. "This whole task—your quest to save Luether. Before, you could maintain perspective, but now, with your cousin's impending march…you've taken too many risks. Made too many uncertain alliances. You're not considering your own safety."

"I can't imagine what you mean," Garin said.

"Vilaer Vultara? She is heir to the traitors who handed Luether to Pervast in the first place. How can you trust her?"

"Vilaer wants to drive out the barbarians as much as any of us," Garin said. "They have brutalized and murdered their way through her Blood, all the way to her. You saw her sister take her own life in despair. Vilaer has more than proven herself. And besides—" He inclined his head toward the snoozing Ovelia. "Lady Dracaris trusts her."

"Enough to rut her, perhaps," Alcarin said. "But Vilaer is only one of your many blind spots. You forged an alliance with Shard the Pirate Queen, who has been killing our countrymen for decades. You can't even see her face to know if she lies to you. How can you trust a lawless woman who'd sooner gut you and gird herself in your guts than smile?"

"Colorful as your description may be," Garin said. "I know what Shard wants. She'll not betray me—at least not until she gets it." He crossed his arms. "Who else will you question? Captain Fersi? Yes, I would have allied with him, past differences aside, but he is dead, and I have his fleet."

"And what of Biaza?" Alcarin asked. "She spoke against you and cost you a third of our best operatives, including Svista."

"We've already spoken of that," Garin said. "Svista and her men have been replaced."

"With people whose loyalty I do not know," Alcarin said. "By the Fire, Garin, why won't you *listen* to me?"

"I cannot please everyone. I cannot be everyone's ally," Garin said. "This is the path I have chosen, and I will walk it to its end. Approve or not, I do not care, but you *will* accept it."

Alcarin gazed at him for a long time, his eyes both sad and furious. Then he hung his head. "Yes, my master," he said.

Garin gave him a gentle smile. "You worry too much."

"And you," Alcarin said, "not nearly enough."

Their words trailed away and they sat in silence for a time.

"Do you ever—" Alcarin started, then fell silent once more.

"Do I ever what?" Garin asked.

"Wish we could go back," Alcarin said. "Back to before this all happened. Before Summer Lives. Before we had this war. Back when it was but us."

Garin wanted to say that he did—that he thought of it all the time—but that seemed like it would hurt Alcarin all the more. He shook his head. "We have to move forward, not backward," he said.

Alcarin nodded.

A hand rattled lightly on the metal door of the carriage, and Lis's face appeared in the window. After the assault on Fersi's floating armada, Garin had offered her a substantial reward, but she'd asked only to continue serving him. Now she followed him everywhere, and he welcomed the extra eyes.

"We've arrived," she said.

Garin smiled and clapped the door in reply. Lis disappeared back atop the carriage.

The sound made Ovelia stir, and she blinked her unseeing eyes. "Soon?" she asked.

Garin nodded. "Soon."

Alcarin looked away and said nothing.

~

The carriage pulled through the crumbling gates of Aertem's Temple, the ironshod wheels scrabbling and scraping over the uneven path. The place lay in rubble and ruin from its collapse the previous season, and the scavengers had only just finished picking it clean. The ancient halls and spiraling towers had fallen to merely heaps of stone, and all that remained of the place was a small bubble at the center of what had once been a vast hall of worship. At its core stood a dusty gray stone which seemed to glint like moving shadow in the moonlight.

It was to this spot that the carriage hastened and discharged its passengers. Among a few other carriages waited a small crowd of folk draped in gray and black cloaks against prying eyes. It struck Garin as odd and not a little tragic that such a ritual had to be conducted by moonlight and in secret, but he well understood necessity.

When Ovelia stepped out of the carriage into the warm Luether night, her cloak fell open to expose a gleaming swath of glowing red silk. Garin closed her cloak once more, and Ovelia's expression grew distant. She seemed far, far away.

"Pass well?" Garin asked, suddenly concerned.

"Yes," Ovelia said. "This place—I have memories of it. Not good ones."

"Well," Garin said. "Let us hope this night will pass better."

Not many had gathered here, but their import to Summer Lives and to Luether in general could not be overstated. Corvus stood ready, fully armored and leaning on his sheathed sword like a staff. Neblen crouched at his side, clad in something that must have been a dress at one time, until her anxious fingers had started to pick it apart and restitch it. Red Jeggs formed a forbidding mountain at the edge of the clearing, ready for any threat. Biaza had come too, nodding with matronly approval at Garin. Her presence meant Red Jeggs had found nothing of any suspicion during her interrogation, and Garin was glad of that. It meant more than he had expected, to find himself surrounded by his friends.

Vilaer Vultara stood tall and serene, like the queen she should have been, and refused to meet Garin's eye. Doubtless, she held some hesitation about him, but it would pass. She did cast a longing gaze at Ovelia, however, who did not return a look of any kind. Whether Ovelia ignored Vilaer out of uncertainty or her blindness had interfered, Garin could not say.

Beside Vilaer stood Lady Shard, draped in her customary black silks. The woman affected excellent composure as the situation demanded, but she raised a hand to stifle a cough as Garin and Ovelia walked past. A crack in her impenetrable vaneer, and a reminder that Shard was not to be ignored.

Ovelia paused. "Again, you come to bear witness, Shard?"

"That I do, dear one," she said. "That I do."

Garin led Ovelia onward. They stepped into the middle of the small clearing, in the group of people, and Garin drew a triangular vial from his belt. This concoction he'd crafted specifically for this moment, and he hoped it served. He unstoppered the potion, releasing a smell of berries warmed in the sunlight, and poured its contents over the stone in the center of the clearing. The stone beneath seemed to catch fire from within: it started as a core of warmth which spread outward until a rosy-pink glow suffused the entire block.

Broken and battered as the Dawnstone was, it had lost none of its magic. It needed only that little touch to reawaken it. As the magic melted into the stone and radiated forth, Ovelia caught her breath.

"Beautiful, is it?" Garin asked.

Ovelia nodded. "I wish you could see it as I do."

Garin smiled.

They stood together, man and woman, amongst their fellow conspirators and heroes, and touched the Dawnstone together. Warm power rose through Garin, and he could see it rise up Ovelia's arm as well. The power completed a circuit through their linked hands and Garin could suddenly feel everything that was in Ovelia, and she in him.

They were one, for just that moment, and the world spiraled around them.

TWENTY-EIGHT

IN THE EARLY HOURS, they took a lift to High-City, and the carriage bore them to the long-abandoned fortress Vultara.

"A royal suite for a royal wedding night." Vilaer had bowed deeply. "My gift for my new king."

The princess had long assured them they would be safe there, and indeed the Summer Lives agents set to watch her reported that she had lived there quite without incident since Tuerine. Wherever Pervast had gone into hiding, he must have abandoned this place long ago, and Garin assured her no one would look for them here. Even so, the unlit halls crawled with Summer Lives agents, keeping a low profile so as not to attract undue attention from outside.

There was little time for a tour before Vilaer ushered Ovelia and Garin to the lord's chamber at the top of the highest tower, but Ovelia collected impressions of the place. She basked in the silent hollow of soaring halls and heard the history resonating through the stones beneath her feet. She trailed her fingers along the stone and felt the wind passing over the crenellations. The holdfast stood on the very edge of the north end of High-City, with literally nothing beneath it but empty air all the way down thousands of paces to the crashing rocks below. This place had seen so much death and violence, but after this night it would mark the beginning of a new path: one of peace and mercy.

They stood together, husband and wife, in the cramped room at the top of the last tower. Long since picked clean of its former opulence, the chamber was nonetheless kingly in size and purpose. Heavy curtains had kept the room cool during the day, but throughout the night they had kept out the cold air that might have refreshed the chamber. Sweat coated Ovelia's skin, and her dress felt uncomfortably tight. The blood of summer beat in her veins to match the icy chill of winter, but she had never felt comfortable in her ancestral home. Many times this season, she had longed to return to the blissful cool of Tar Vangr, rather than humid Luether. And yet, just now, she wanted to be nowhere other than where she was.

"I—" Garin said, just as Ovelia moved away from him.

"Sorry," she said. "I just—here."

She pulled open the thick curtains and sighed in relief at the cool breeze that wafted through. It let her think more clearly, and she would need ice in her veins for what was expected of her. Fortunately, the sweetsoul Red Jeggs had inadvertently given her—and the powder she'd shared with Vilaer as they lay in bed together not two hours before—helped with that.

The sweetsoul was a key medicine to treat pain, of which Ovelia had much, and so it had seemed perfectly natural that Vilaer would offer her some. She should have refused, but she'd inhaled her first hit before she realized what was happening. For her part, Vilaer had seemed to need it to muster her own courage. She and the Vultara princess had consumed an entire pouch of the chemic together, and Ovelia might have passed a lovely night indeed had not duty intervened. She wondered if she had dreamed all this, or if it had truly come to pass.

Regardless, they were alone now, she and Garin, and the tension hung between them like a veil. The world seemed hazy and relaxed, and she felt capable of anything. This felt distantly wrong, but she had sworn a vow to aid him long ago, and she would do what she had to. If he had some sweetsoul himself, that might make this all easier, but how could she offer him that? Certainly not without revealing that she had broken her own abstinence, and then his nerve might break entirely.

After a moment to compose herself, Ovelia turned back to Garin. His confidence seemed to have faltered, and he looked as awkward as an untouched boy. This she could understand, and she did not envy him. This task would prove much harder for him than for her.

"We don't have to do this, Garin," she said.

"Yes we do, and we both know it." He blew out a long sigh. "If the ancient customs must be respected, then let them be respected. And I…I shall need an heir. At least the hope of one." He rested his fists on the side table and shook his head. "We've come this far."

Ovelia could not dispute that logic. Garin made no move to do anything about it, though—just stood and stared down at his hands. Ovelia would have work to do this night.

She began with the unnecessary tangle of ties and ribbons that held her gown to her still sore body. At least the sweetsoul diminished the ache. Garin looked away, making no move to help.

"You know," he said. "It is an old tradition among my people to recover the bloodied sheet after a wedding night and create some manner of garment for the bride to wear. Sometimes it is merely a kerchief or a skirt, but sometimes the bedding yields a dress. And that's thought to be good luck, if you can believe it. The more one bleeds, the more one is esteemed. Ha." He shook his head and took another drink. "In case you ever wondered why red was a Ravalis color."

Old Gods forfend. Ovelia resolved never to wear such a thing. "It is not my course, Garin—and I am no virgin to bleed on your sheets."

"No, of course not." He sighed. "Such childish things we think matter."

They sat together in silence, the moment stretching awkwardly between them.

"Have you ever made love to a woman before?" Ovelia asked at length.

"No. Though I've rutted a few." He gave a mirthless laugh. "Didn't fancy it, and I was never very good at it."

Ovelia nodded. She well understood the urge to deny oneself—to try desperately to fit into what was expected. She'd spent decades lying about who and what she wanted. The heart, in her experience, was stronger than the body, and both were far mightier than the mind. Ovelia's body had nothing Garin wanted, but she would not let that stop her.

"Shall I summon Alcarin?" she asked. The squire had made his antipathy quite clear over the past days, and Ovelia did not relish his company. But this night was not about her.

"What?" That caught Garin by surprise, and made him smile. "No, I think the only one more uncomfortable with this situation than me is him." His expression drooped into a sad frown, and irony tinged his voice. "He left during the wedding. Off to drink himself senseless, no doubt. In fact—" He uncorked a beaker of bright green liquor and poured himself a generous portion, which he downed in one gulp. "This helps. A concoction I mixed myself, nyssa and a few herbs for…standing to attention."

Ovelia certainly understood. Sex was relatively easy for a man, but it had its own pressures. She had the sweetsoul to help her, and it would help hide her doubt. If he saw uncertainty in her, it would shatter his resolve.

From behind him, Ovelia put her hands on either of Garin's shoulders. He flinched under her fingers, and she could feel the tension in his hard muscles. She worked his shoulders, slowly at first, then harder as he relaxed into her. She worked up to his neck, tracing the edges of his vertebrae one by one. His lustrous crimson hair was just starting to thin, and she could feel irritated spots where he'd been scratching his scalp to redness.

"Close your eyes, my king," she said. "You're safe."

Garin tensed again, but he did as she asked, and she let her shift slip to the ground so that she stood naked behind him. She could feel his trembling uncertainty, and she molded herself to him like a soft blanket. Hesitantly, his body responded to hers, but she could feel his anxiety and hesitation. Garin *knew* Ovelia was not what he wanted, but he was trying hard to open himself to it. Doubt coiled in her chest, but she did her best to overlook it. What she

273

and Garin were doing was wrong, but greater people had done worse things for a crown.

She slipped her hands lower down his back, and he responded with a relieved exhalation. The last year of near constant battle and anxiety had worked knots into his muscles so tangled they begged for a knife. Ovelia worked to loosen him up, and though she could not ease all his tension, she made him breathe easier. She would be invisible and focus only upon him.

"Blood of my Summer-Fathers, that's good," Garin said.

She said nothing, only worked at his lower back until he groaned aloud. She worked her way around his soft-fleshed sides, up to his chest, where she undid two buttons of his tunic so she could slip a hand inside and feel his body. At the same time, she pressed herself against his back, willing the touch to be welcome, rather than awkward. The man was no pinnacle of might, but Ovelia could feel the strength beneath his skin. She caressed his chest with one hand, while with the other she made her way down, pushing buttons open with the pressure. His stomach stretched under her fingers, and she felt a little spark of desire for the man for the first time. It unsettled her.

As Garin stood trembling, she reached down the slope of his belly and slid her hand into his trousers. The hair felt coarse and moist with nervous sweat. And when she touched his half-hard...

"Nnhh!" Garin made a strangled cry and wrenched away from her.

Ovelia pulled a blanket up to her chest, but the illusion was broken. Her feminine body did not repel him, exactly, but neither did it excite him. He looked away, embarrassed. She wrapped the blanket around herself and folded it over to keep it closed.

"No, no, I—I cannot do this." Garin pulled away and crossed his arms protectively over his chest. "I know what my duty demands, but I..." He sat on the bed and shook his head sadly. "I'm so selfish. This is not fair to you. I'm sorry I cannot want you as you should be wanted, or love you as you should be loved. I am not the Lord of Tears." Then he looked up, his face flushed. "I did not mean to—"

"No. No, it's all right." The reminder stung Ovelia, but not for the reason Garin expected. She clasped her robe tight about her body, unexpectedly self-conscious. "In many ways, the way you are looking at me right now is not unlike the way Regel does."

"Oh?" Garin was intrigued. "I always thought him a man who knew well how to love a woman."

"Yes." *Perhaps too well and too much*, she thought. "But that is not what I mean."

Ovelia crossed to the window and looked out over the gray, lapping sea. To her, it felt like an unending sheet of darkness, beneath which brightly colored creatures of fiery magic churned and thrashed. Somewhere out there, she could feel Regel staring at the same darkness, and she suspected he recognized the danger that lurked there as well. She wondered where he was and whether he breathed still. But she knew he didn't think the same of her—or anything of her. She was not his princess, after all.

"Regel and I." Ovelia shook her head. "I am not myself to him, but someone he loves far more."

"You mean Lenalin." Garin's eyes widened. "When you are together, he sees you as her. Old Gods, that's why you dyed your hair. To seduce him with memories of what could have been."

Had been. Ovelia knew Regel had lain with his princess at least once, but that secret was not hers to share, and Garin had enough on his mind. She began to see what he needed.

Ovelia moved to the desk, touched her fingers to her tongue, and extinguished the candles.

"We all long for things we sometimes cannot have, and have to find what we want in what lies before us," she said. "For the Lord of Tears, it was his lost princess. For your cousin Paeter, it was me."

"You and Paeter," Garin said. "I never knew that."

"But you are not surprised."

She recognized Garin's easy breath and heard his slow heartbeat. It made sense to him. She had felt that way herself once, when Regel spoke of Lenalin, and the secret they had shared together. Garin felt the same churning emptiness of desire Ovelia had known that night. Both men had lost loves: Regel had Lenalin, and Garin had Paeter. That confirmed for Ovelia exactly what she needed to do, though it pained her to do so. The blurry summer moon seemed as hot as the sun through the window. It put fire in her blood, and she would need that. She pulled her hair back and tied it loosely around itself.

"Yes." She extinguished the last of the candles and collected her breath in the near darkness. "It was an arrangement of mutual benefit." Her voice deepened. "The whore wanted something from me, and I took what I wanted from her."

Garin looked confused. "What are you saying—?"

Ovelia stepped across and backhanded the king across the face. Utterly surprised, Garin staggered back and fell to one knee. Completely shocked, he looked up at her towering over him.

"You are not a king but a worthless weakling." Ovelia spoke in Paeter's strong baritone. She turned away and crossed her arms. "I say you are a child, too afraid to take what is yours by rights."

Garin's voice wavered. "I am not a child."

Ovelia glanced over her shoulder. "Did you speak, child?"

He looked down at his balled fists. "I am *not* a child."

"Claim what you will, but you and I both know the truth," she said. "My own cousin. Too afraid of what others think to stand on his own. If not a child, then a coward."

Ovelia reached up to ready a strike, but Garin's responding intake of breath made her hesitate. If she beat the fight out of him, then this was all for naught. The moment strummed like a taut chord.

"Not a child." Garin climbed to his feet. "A man. A king."

The air between them crackled, and it was all Ovelia could do to breathe and meet Garin's eye. Regel had looked at her that way: not seeing her, but seeing someone he wanted.

"Then prove it," she said.

He moved faster than she could have expected. Blind, she did not see his left hand move, but she sensed his attack before he launched it. Another night, she might have caught his hand, twisted his arm, and left him with broken bones, but this night demanded a perfect performance. She blocked the attack lazily and held his hand an inch from her face, her strength matched to his.

Garin's eyes were on fire as they burned at her face. Words boiled behind his lips.

Ovelia opened her mouth to speak, but he leaned in and kissed her hard. She felt teeth. They wrestled for a moment, muscles straining, and she let him shove her down onto the bed. Her hand went to the crest of the blanket wrapped around her body, but Garin slapped her hand away. He looped one hand around her head, fingers woven through her red hair, and drew her up into a sitting position before him, her head level with his chest. His eyes never left her face: her eyes, her nose, her mouth. Particularly her mouth. He ran his thumb over her lips and pressed it between her teeth.

"No, cousin." He thrust his trousers down. "I prefer you clad for this."

Ovelia understood. She slipped off the bed and down to her knees.

TWENTY-NINE

As the night wore on, Alcarin drained the last of his heavy ale and waved for another. When no reply came, he murmured in consternation and looked for a server to signal. No such luck. Half the scantily clad lads and maids who carried drinks in this place were engaged in one form of prostitution or another, and the other half ignored him in favor of louder, more boisterous patrons who would break something were they not appeased. It was, after all, the Bottom Shred.

Alcarin could not say exactly what had drawn him back here. He'd not set foot in his old tavern in so long—not since Garin had drawn him up out of anonymity to join his great quest. He still remembered how Garin had looked that night: young, dashing, heroic. Some of that had faded over the long summers, but he remained vital and charismatic and just as foolish as ever. And Alcarin loved him just as much tonight as he had that first night, even if he had lost him this night.

It took four ales for Alcarin to admit to himself that Garin had left him. Their leavetaking had stretched as they had grown apart, finding more divisions between them than unions. Aye, Garin yet remained, physically speaking: they had sex on a regular basis, but it had gone from enthusiastic rutting and genuine lovemaking to rote repetition. The more Alcarin sat with Garin, the more he became aware that the prince had moved past him—looking to the future rather than the past or even the present. He loved Alcarin, yes, but he loved Luether far more.

And yet, Alcarin had managed to convince himself that his doubts had no foundation. He'd dared to believe that he and his shining Fox Prince would spend their lives together. They would redeem Luether together and rule the city as king and consort, damn tradition and public opinion. Tonight had proved, once and forever, that Alcarin's fantastic dream had been just that—fantasy.

"Ho, ho!" Red Jeggs's massive body collapsed onto the stool beside him at the bar, making the metal groan. He set two tankards down. "I've not seen you in here, boy, but I know what brings you."

"Oh?" Alcarin eyed the ale, suddenly thirsty again. "What's that?"

Red Jeggs leaned in as though to speak in confidence, but all but shouted anyway. "Your lover giving it to mine," he said. "I've half a mind to try *you* out this night. Would you like that, fancy lad?"

"How very…flattering." Alcarin turned up his nostrils at Red Jeggs's breath. The man stooped very low in his cups. "You're not to my taste."

That made Red Jeggs laugh uproariously, a sound Alcarin thought held some relief. Of course the man had to assert his dominance, even over Alcarin. "Rather be rutting a woman anyway," he said. "Not that red-headed whore, though."

Alcarin thought immediately to correct him, but instead he took a long draught of his ale. Red Jeggs was clinging to his manhood by a thin thread, because of Ovelia. First, the woman defeated him at their first meeting, so he became her lover to convince himself he was yet lord over her. Then she dismissed him publicly, which he'd likely been able to brush off as flirtation. Then she'd left him for another woman, which he'd seemed pleased with… until he realized they had no intention inviting him into their bed. And now, she'd married the Prince of Luether, leaving Red Jeggs forever behind. Red Jeggs, the pinnacle of the Luethaar *man*, could not understand these things.

For the first time, Alcarin saw through Red Jeggs's tough exterior to the tormented creature beneath and understood him. The man was a boisterous, arrogant, conceited wretch, but Alcarin pitied him all the same. "Rut her, then," he said.

Red Jeggs brightened. "Rut her good and bloody."

That was mostly the liquor talking. Alcarin did not blame Ovelia for Garin's wayward path—that had started long before he'd ever met her. Her presence had accelerated it, though, and she made a convenient target for his ire.

"To whores and inconstant lovers!" Red Jeggs grimaced. "May they contract the pox and burn in the rain!"

"How colorful," Alcarin said.

They clanked tankards together and drained them.

Red Jeggs waved for a second round.

Ovelia awoke some hours later, muscles sore from the vigor of Garin's desire. She tasted him in her mouth and felt warm from his seed inside her. None since Paeter had savaged her quite as he had, and Ovelia knew it had not been for her own sake. Garin had had much to work through that night, and even more to prove. She wondered if he would ever have had the chance without her.

The prince—king, she corrected herself—lay apart from her, spent and sleeping fitfully, curled up as far from her as possible on the bed. The glamour she had woven to become Paeter Ravalis for a night had lasted only so long, and now Garin's body wanted nothing to do with her. Every so often, he whimpered in his sleep, saying nothing she could understand. It would not do to linger—for him or for her—and so she climbed to her feet. She felt shaky—a combination of the soreness she was just starting to feel and the sweetsoul that had not quite worn off. Taking her time, she drew on her night gown and slipped out of the room.

Loyal Corvus stood outside the door, as alert and watchful as ever, and they exchanged a friendly nod. On some level, Corvus understood this marriage was a political arrangement, but Ovelia suspected it pleased him to see his beloved king fulfilling what Luether saw as a man's duty. As she passed on silently, she hoped the rest of Luether would feel the same.

The crumbling fortress of Vultara was an unfamiliar place to Ovelia, devoid of life and dangers that might have triggered the shadows she followed. She didn't even need Draca any more—not for simple movement. Her senses let her move unhindered, but she still trailed her fingers along the wall for guidance. The old stones of the Blood Vultara filled her mind with shadows of their own: tales of a thousand summers of heat, blood, and sex. If she spent too long listening, she'd become giddy.

She came upon the great hall, through which a wind billowed from the two balconies: one overlooking Luether, the other revealing nothing but water and sky meeting at a series of nigh impassable cliffs across the bay. Luether's natural archipelago made it difficult to reach for a powerful navy, and even a small force could delay them in those cliffs. This throne room surveyed both Luether's key resource—its people—and its most potent defense at once. Ovelia could feel the power in this place.

As if to cap off the feeling, a throne stood on a raised dais in the center, turned at the moment toward the bay balcony. It surprised her to find such a thing, but then even the lords of Thinbloods in Tar Vangr affected such airs of royalty. Why not the Vultara, who had stood second only to the Ravalis in power and influence? She could tell by exploring with her fingers that the throne was a thing of beauty: cunningly crafted of gears and pistons, more a machine than a piece of furniture. She wondered if it could move on its own—if it would rise and dance when a true king of Luether sat upon it.

"Magnificent, is it not?" a woman's quiet voice asked from behind her. "The actual throne of Luether. That magnificent seat has accommodated hundreds of Ravalis asses. *Thousands*."

Only when the woman spoke did Ovelia realize she was not alone. The woman stood out on the balcony across from the throne, looking out into the night. "Shard," Ovelia said. "I did not hear you."

"Ironic, isn't it?" Shard asked. "Pervast gave that thing as a gift to Blood Vultara after the Fall. They had wanted to rule, after all, so he gave them the throne—after he threw all their male heirs from High-City or burned them alive." She chuckled. "I can't imagine how Vilaer even looks at it."

"What passes?" Ovelia crossed her arms. "Why are you here?"

The pirate queen turned from the night and considered Ovelia. Unmoving and without hostile intent, Lady Shard floated in and out of her awareness indistinctly. She made only a little sound and existed mostly as a smell. Beneath the sweaty stink of piracy, Ovelia smelled a faint scent as of roses the morning after a rain. It was so startling that Ovelia had to focus upon it, but as soon as she did it flitted out of her awareness as if it had never existed.

"Always so suspicious, dear one," Shard said. "What have I done to deserve such suspicion?"

"All that you do is suspicious," Ovelia said. "And do not call me that."

"As you wish." Shard stepped toward her, and Ovelia immediately stepped away, shifting into a defensive stance. The pirate queen paused. "I mean you no harm, Lady Dracaris," she said.

"That I know," Ovelia said. "I did not give you leave to touch me."

"Apologies," Shard said. "You look cold. One should not wander these halls unadorned."

"Perhaps." Indeed, Ovelia shivered in the altitude. Down in Low-City, it seemed so hot all the time, but at the pinnacle of Luether, here against the waning night, her thin shift did her no favors.

"And you are a Queen now," Shard said. "You should have a proper mantle."

Her unseen hands draped something around Ovelia's shoulders—a cloak that held off the night's unexpected chill. Then she stepped back to admire Ovelia, for a long moment. The shadows roiled, speaking of dangers to unfold or darker secrets. Ovelia felt suddenly uneasy under the woman's scrutiny.

"What?" Ovelia asked.

Shard stepped to her and seized Ovelia's face between her hands. Taken by surprise just as utterly as Garin only hours before, Ovelia went taut and her hands curled into impotent claws. The moment burned into her mind, and all other considerations fell away. Shard leaned close, as though to kiss her through her veil, and Ovelia could feel her hot breath on her cheeks.

Finally, Shard leaned away and released her. "You smell of man," she said. "Come back to me another night, Queen Ravalis, when your heart and body are your own."

Then Lady Shard—Queen of the Cutting Winds, and Empress of the Endless Seas—went away, leaving Ovelia standing, dumbfounded and trembling.

THIRTY

THE WOMAN GASPED, EYES going as wide as the wound in her chest. She sank to the ground, twisting onto her back around the curved blade. The steel slipped from her and dripped blood in the ruddy moonlight. Davargorn put a foot on her twitching body and held the blade up for her companions to see.

"So," he said as blood dripped onto the muddy cobblestones. "Which of you dies next?"

In the filthy Low-City alley, three blades of Summer stood arrayed like the points of a trident held out before him. They were the three of them traitors to Summer Lives, come this night to protect a conspiracy to overthrow Garin Ravalis and undo all his efforts.

Under other circumstances, Davargorn might have joined them in that, but Alistra had insisted. She was his master now, whether he admitted it to himself or not.

For the past days, he and Alistra had scoured Summer Lives for traitors, cutting off potential threats before they could present themselves. And now, this night, they had finally come across the leaders of the conspiracy. Right through the door these burners protected, in fact.

The bald man with the mace on the left was thick and stocky, his features weathered over much pain and hardship. The woman in the middle had clipped ears to go along with her twin swords, and her dark eyes glittered with anger and not a little fear. The third—another man, this one with a thick red beard and a huge belly—hefted his smith's hammer in trembling hands. The woman shuddering into a corpse under his boot made four.

Davargorn analyzed them each with his warrior's intuition, guessing their likely steps and the weaknesses in their styles. If they came at him together, they could overwhelm him. But the speed with which he'd dispatched his first assailant had done its work, and now the three traitors were too intimidated to do as they should. They shifted uneasily in their protective positions in front of the door of tarnished, pitted metal on the wall of the building behind them. The fat one with the beard eased back toward the door, taking one hand from his hammer to touch the latch, but Clip-Ears hissed a rebuke at him. The fat one he would kill last, simply because the man would avoid facing him as long as possible. Bald-Mace would probably come at him first, with his mace that exuded a faint whine in his hands, then Clip-Ears if she was smart.

Davargorn had killed many men and women over the course of his short, violent life—a substantial minority of them so far this year—and these three would prove no different.

"You are fools," Davargorn said. "Your king even now beds his queen, Pervast is on the verge of collapse, and you are plotting to overthrow him? Do you have the slightest idea what this city needs?"

Not that he particularly cared, either way. He wanted Garin Ravalis dead as much as any of these would-be assassins, but *his* would be the blade that spilled the blood of Summer, not theirs.

The irony that he risked his life nightly to protect a man he wanted nothing more than to slay had indeed occurred to him, but Davargorn tried not to dwell on it.

The attack came suddenly and as he had guessed it would unfold. Bald-Mace lunged forward with surprising speed and brought his mace whistling around at eye level. Davargorn leaned away and ducked, letting the mace sweep just over his head, but the man twisted his hips and brought the weapon arcing back around to slam into his left shoulder with a sizzling pop. A glancing blow, but a shock of pain ripped down Davargorn's arm, followed by numbness. That was the sound he had heard—a faint, thaumaturgical charge that sent a jolt of magic through anything it struck. He pedaled back on his mismatched feet, warding the man off with his falcat more than attempting to counter.

"Get 'em, Kratch!" the stocky man by the door shouted. He gestured with his hammer once or twice, but still hesitated to join the actual fighting.

The woman with the clipped ears hissed a curse at him. "Aid or shut up, Dulle!"

She lunged in, slashing two wide tears through Davargorn's cloak as he threw himself aside. Unfortunately, she drove him right into the reach of Kratch's mace, and the weapon smashed into Davargorn's bad leg. The limb went numb, and he would have fallen if not for the wall behind him. The woman's two swords came at him again, and he managed to knock one aside but the other cut a hot line across his arm. His shoulder crunched back against the wall and he hissed in pain.

"Well struck, Felid!" Dulle said, shaking his hammer. He hesitated to join the fray, however, for which Davargorn was glad.

The woman—Felid—came at him again, one sword stabbing at his chest even as the other thrust toward his gut. Davargorn managed to bat aside the one, but the second would have run him through had he not drawn his second falcat in a rising sweep that knocked her staggering back. He didn't have the chance to pursue her, though, for Kratch was heading his way again, mace high.

Where the *Fire* was Alistra? This was going badly.

Bald Kratch shot forward, much faster than his size suggested, and smashed his mace into the wall as Davargorn flinched his head out of the way. The old mud brick caved in with little resistance, leaving a crater, and Davargorn's skull ached in sympathy. He slashed at the man with his falcat, making him back off and stumble over the corpse on the ground. Davargorn readied himself to lunge, but Felid stepped in behind him and cut open his back with two expert slashes of her swords. Then she bounced back out just as quickly, before he could counter. Somehow, they'd worked their way onto either side of him. How he missed his razor-edged cloak—that would have given one or both of them a nasty surprise.

The battle had turned quickly, but that only made Davargorn angry, not afraid. How dare these gutter-slaves think they could challenge him. He, who had faced some of the greatest warriors the World of Ruin had ever known, including the Frostburn himself. This was not how he died, alone in a grimy alley, pecked to death by carrion birds. He swore it.

The mace came swishing through the air at him again, and Davargorn swept up his arm to knock it aside. Fortunately, his vambrace deflected the head of the mace, so its vile enchantment could not touch his skin. He felt the shock through the metal, though, making his forearm erupt in tingling bristles from elbow to wrist. At least the mace had not caved in his face. His already bad leg barely supported him as he staggered between opponents, foiling their attacks mostly by slashing at them until they backed off.

He needed a breath to tap into his healing magic and restore full mobility, but Kratch and Felid kept up their assault without pause. He ducked and wheeled around his mace and slapped aside her thrusts, keeping in constant motion, looking for an escape. He could keep them at bay—fighting one long enough to focus on the other—but in a few breaths he would tire, or else Dulle would muster his courage and join the melee. Then, Davargorn would fall quickly enough.

Finally the moment came. He feinted right, drawing Kratch's mace in that direction, and turned to engage Felid. Her twin swords dripped with his blood as she stalked toward him, one blade high and the other low. She hesitated a little when he whirled toward her, both swords ready, and that gave Davargorn the opportunity he needed. He slammed his forward sword into her defense with enough force to make her hands ring with pain. It did little but anger her, but that was his aim. As she barreled forward with a counter, he caught both her swords with his two blades, held them wide, and roared as he kicked her in the chest with his good foot. Felid staggered back, caught off guard.

He made to follow her for a killing blow, but his club foot and half-numbed leg would not support him. Even as he toppled forward, Davargorn hacked both swords wildly down at Felid's retreating body. One hit nothing but air while the other slit open the tough, boiled leather of her hauberk and blood bloomed in the night. The smell and her cry of pain comforted him as he slammed, face-first, into the filthy cobblestones. He lost his breath and one of his falcata, jarred loose from his half-numb hand. He couldn't worry about that now—he had to move, otherwise…

Kretch's mace came rushing toward his head, and Davargorn pulled aside just in time to save his skull. The hard metal clipped his brow, which broke open to spew blood in his eyes, across his face, and onto the cobblestones. Little bits of stone and mud bounced up in the wake of the strike. Davargorn kicked out at Kretch's leg, which put the man off balance long enough to foil another attack.

Davargorn forced himself to one knee, just in time to see Dulle lumbering toward him, hammer raised. A fine time for the fat man to find his courage. At the same time, Kretch had recovered his footing and Felid stood, pressing one hand to her wound while the other clutched one of her swords. All three of them at once, then.

Again, he cursed Alistra for putting him in this position. Where was that spiteful woman?

Abruptly, a loud metallic crunch sounded through the alley, and all eyes went to the corroded door, which ground open against the rough stones. Her wiry body framed in the doorway, Alistra gazed out at Davargorn with her gleaming yellow wolf eyes. How she had got into the building without anyone's notice, he couldn't begin to guess. She wore a wry smile on her angular face.

"There you are," she said, her tone such as one might use when speaking to a child. "Have you passed a pleasant moment with your little friends?" She noted the crumpled body of the agent Davargorn had slain and her smile only widened. "I see you've played a bit rough."

The three warriors tensed, ready to assault her as a newcomer to the fight, but a woman's voice sounded from the hazy darkness of the room. "Attend me," she said to the warders. "We're moving now."

Davargorn caught a glimpse of a vaguely familiar scarred face in the darkness, but he did not know the woman's name. He collected his swords while the three filed past Alistra into the chamber, though he found it odd she did nothing to stay them. When he took a step toward the building, she shook her head firmly at him, then closed the door behind her.

"We're not—" he began, but Alistra was walking away. He had to hurry, limping, to catch up with her.

They made their way through the cobbled streets of Low-City Luether without speaking. Even ragged and covered in blood—only some of it his own—Davargorn drew little attention from the passersby. At most, a curious glance or two followed them a few paces, but he discouraged any would-be thief or ruffian. As they walked, his magic worked to repair his damaged body, making his limp gradually smoother and slighter until only the keenest eye might notice it. Dust clung to their boots and the early morning air hung with pitch from the fires that had burned all night. Alistra wore a veil to keep her breath clear, but Davargorn had no such protection and was huffing before they'd gone two blocks.

"Do you not know how to fight multiple opponents?" Alistra asked. "You were lashing out at them one by one, not using them against each other as you should. *Such* a disappointment."

As they walked, the urge rose in Davargorn to stop Alistra and roar at her in his confusion, but he suppressed it until they had gone well away from the flophouse where the traitors made their plot. No one seemed to be on the street, so he pulled her into a darkened alley. It smelled of rotten meat and defecation, with a shambles of broken crates that littered the back of a burned out warehouse. Davargorn sensed no one else nearby, and he was certain they'd acquired no tail. He held Alistra up against the wall and stared up at her, confused anger garbling the words he would speak. She simply looked at him.

"Yes?" she asked at length, her tone patient.

"What—" Davargorn paused. He released her shoulders and stood before her, breathing heavily. "What came to pass there? Were they not the schemers we sought?"

"Oh, they certainly were," Alistra said.

Davargorn was stunned. "And yet—and yet we did nothing?"

"I wouldn't say nothing," Alistra said. "You killed one of them, did you not? And wounded another? I suspect Svista is rather put out with you at the moment."

Davargorn might have healed, but he still felt the tingling, phantom pain from his wounds. "I bled for you," he said.

"You bled for *you*," Alistra said. "*I* instructed you to take stock of the conspirators' defenses. You took it upon yourself to attack the warders, and any wounds that you suffered are your own responsibility. Because of your incompetence, mostly." She laid her hands over the rents in his battle leathers, feeling at his muscular frame. "You seem well enough to me. Hmm." Her hands drifted around to cup his backside. "Very well."

Davargorn pushed free of her—not because he flinched from her touch, but because he knew when she was distracting him. And he would not be swayed so easily.

"We have spent a season ending threats to the Fox of Luether before they strike," he said. "How long have we searched for that particular set of conspirators? And you simply let them go?"

"There is nothing simple about what has passed here tonight," Alistra said. "Matters will pass quickly now, and all that we have built—you, me, Garin, Ovelia, the conspirators, even Pervast—will come rushing together in the shadows. At this point, it is all a matter of choosing where we will stand."

"And where is that?" Davargorn asked.

Alistra smiled. "For the moment, right here." She put her hand on his chest. "You and me. Here." She took his other hand and clasped it tight. "Together."

Davargorn narrowed his eyes warily. "What does that mean?"

Her smiled widened. "My foolish, foolish lad," she said. "You really have no idea how you feel, let alone how *I* might feel."

Davargorn had no reply to that. He scowled and started to pull away, but she clasped his hand tighter to restrain him. She wet her lips.

"Kiss me," she said.

His unease turned to tingling desire, and he leaned in to press his lips to hers. She drew back, slightly, putting their faces in line.

"Not *there*," she said. "Do what I showed you."

"Here?" He looked over both shoulders at the miserable alley spread around them, filled with spoor and fetid trash and other muck he didn't want to identify. "Now?"

"Right here." She slipped a hand down to unbutton her shirt down to her navel and below. "Right now." She pressed her hips against his. "Unless you're afraid."

He felt abruptly self-conscious—she so beautiful, he so ugly, out in the open together where any could happen upon them. His face felt sticky, and he realized he still had blood on it. He reached up to wipe it away, but she caught his wrist.

"I prefer it that way," she said.

Then she kissed his lips, his nose, his forehead, and the top of his head, all the while gently pressing him downward.

He did as she asked, kissing her neck and the slope of her collarbone. He kissed along her soft breasts and the coarser skin of her nipples, lingering on each until she shivered slightly. He sank down on a leg no longer shivering from thaumaturgical shock and kissed her belly, which had softened since her imprisonment. He kissed his way down her pubic bone to the soft down between her thighs.

"Yes." Alistra caught her breath, lips slightly parted. She smiled wide, hand on his head. "*Yes.*"

THIRTY-ONE

WHEN OVELIA AWOKE, SHE lay in the wide bed of the King of Luether, feeling warm and entirely, terribly sober. Her body felt awful: a combination of pain from the previous day's captivity and the night's exertions, and the agony in her head and stomach aching for sweetsoul. She lay for a moment, collecting herself. Warm sunlight drifted in through the open window, and the drapes lapped against the edge of the bed. Much as it had cost her, Garin's seemingly mad goal of reclaiming Luether by peaceful means seemed finally possible.

"A good morn, queen-to-be." Garin sat in a comfortable chair by the bed, fully dressed and freshly shaved. She could smell the soap on him and sense his awakened enthusiasm. "I've been up two hours now, reading, pacing, and finally watching you sleep. I find it rather soothing, to see such a powerful creature at her ease."

"Flatterer." Ovelia smiled blithely. "I'd call that an attempt to woo me, but I know better."

"Indeed." He chuckled. "I may lack the drive to romance you, my queen, but you cannot say I am not skilled in that art. I can cuddle and kiss and embrace like the tenderest of lovers."

"Perhaps—" Ovelia bit her lip. "Perhaps not just now."

Tempting as that sounded, it was a new level of intimacy between them she did not feel entirely comfortable sharing. For whatever reason, she could not shake the memory of Lady Shard, of all people: giving her that cloak and then all but kissing her. It had passed the oddest night she could well imagine.

"I understand entirely," Garin said. "As an alternative, would you like, perhaps, a foot massage?"

"That seems only fair, considering."

"Considering what you have given me?" Garin snapped his fingers. "It is but the first of many retributive gifts. But first!" He pointed to the sideboard. "A drink this fine morn."

Ovelia nodded at what seemed a sensible and, perhaps, necessary suggestion. The great weight of the previous night hung between them, but somehow Garin's exuberance made it seem far away and invisible. He did not have to speak of it, and neither did she. All could return to how it had once been: the two of them, fighting side by side, to reclaim this city from Ruin.

Even so, she felt oddly conflicted. True, she had aided Garin in accomplishing this part of his quest, but she had done so in part by deceiving him. She had pretended to be his cousin, yes, but before that, she had relapsed into her sweetsoul haze. The chemic had been so powerful after a season of withdrawal…would she have acted differently had she not consumed it? The question unsettled her. She hoped wedding Garin would prove the right choice—for him, for herself, and for Luether.

The truth was on the tip of her tongue. She felt like she was keeping secrets from him—things he needed to know. But would they help or harm?

There was some sort of commotion out in the hall, which barely radiated through the thick doors. Only without her sight did Ovelia even notice the dim voices echoing through the stone. She felt almost as though she held Draca and it was warning her, though the blade rested on the table five paces across the chamber. She glanced at Draca curiously, and tiny flames licked at the blade.

"Wait." Curious, Ovelia rose and made her way toward it.

"What is it?" Garin paused in lacing up his coat.

Ovelia put her fingers around the hilt of the scabbarded sword and the flames roared into life.

Abruptly, one of the double doors shattered open under a heavy boot, and three warriors poured into the chamber, weapons raised. They wore roughspun woolens, tattered half-cloaks, and mismatched patchwork armor, but they carried weapons of cold hard steel. They had belted corroded plates over their boiled leather and donned greaves and pauldrons of low quality and haphazard construction. Ovelia smelled the fresh blood and mud smeared across their clothes and faces: the mark of Children of Ruin.

Draca's shadows showed her who approached and how to move, and she trusted them.

Garin shouted something in surprise, but Ovelia was already lunging forward. She met the first one with a pommel strike to his metal-studded face that sent him staggering back, spraying blood. As she struck, she reached out and touched the second man's chest with her free hand, marking his position for certain. As she thrust out with Draca's hilt, she put the blade perfectly in line with her thumb. She drove the blade down into the second man, shearing through his collarbone and through one of his lungs. The man dropped, gurgling, and Ovelia ripped her sword out of him in a shower of gore. As she'd seen in the shadows, the warrior she'd struck in the face rose toward her, but she raked Draca across under his chin. Blood sprayed Ovelia's face and she whirled to face the third would-be slayer.

The woman staggered back a step and lowered her axe a fraction. Ovelia could not see the woman's face, but she thought the sudden, furious attack had given her pause. Her hesitation would last only a heartbeat, so Ovelia drove forward, Draca slashing for the woman's throat. The swirling flames around Draca parted to reveal more fighting, and Ovelia realized she had miscalculated. The woman parried surprisingly well, and their blades rang against the wall—not as intimidated as Ovelia had thought, it seemed. The Children were fearless. She caught her breath.

With a roar, the third warrior threw herself at Ovelia, teeth gnashing, and knocked her back into the royal chamber. Ovelia lost her balance and they went down in a heap. Her head struck the floorboards, making the world swim, and when she tried to grasp her attacker, the woman knelt hard on her free hand. Her sword rose over Ovelia's face, point downward. Ovelia stared at Draca, searching the flames for an escape, but she saw only one thing: a blade stabbing into her throat. The barbarian roared in triumph.

A sharp whine made the room vibrate, and the woman exploded backward as though batted away with a hammer. Her arms slammed into the sides of the doorframe, crossing in front of her in a grotesque embrace, and her body bounced and rolled away down the corridor. Ovelia watched it all in a shadowy blur, her hearing swallowed in the roar of the weapon that had struck her attacker.

Garin knelt by Ovelia's side, the concussive caster smoking in his right hand, and helped Ovelia up. He was shouting in her face, panicked, but somehow his words held no meaning. She saw no more attacks in Draca's flames—they had a moment. She waved Garin off and stepped toward the bureau, still felt shaky on her feet. She set down Draca and leaned on both hands to balance herself. Blood smeared the blade and coated her hand, and she was glad she could not see it. She breathed heavily until the world came back and the ringing in her ears passed.

"—Lia!" Garin shouted from the door. "Ovelia!"

He was kneeling over Corvus, who slumped dead against the wall. A throwing dagger sprouted from his throat, his eyes had turned to glass, and blood marked dozens of wounds on his body. Even without her sight, she could tell the throat wound had come first, cutting off any cry of warning. Then they'd savaged him like animals. With the door open, she could hear the sounds of dozens of folk running elsewhere in the castle. Cries echoed down the halls, and they heard the sounds of battle. They were besieged. Terror rose in her, but she tried to crush it back down.

"You need your armor." Garin had reclaimed his warpick, which he set on the table beside Draca. "Let me help."

Ovelia nodded. If they had to fight their way free, she could hardly be expected to fight in her bare skin. Garin helped her into her steel hauberk and leather breeches. The armor was lighter than she would have liked, but she appreciated how quickly it could be secured. She listened to the dim shouting out in the hall and silently bid him hurry, but his fingers were shaking. The terror was upon him too. At their feet, the barbarian she'd stunned groaned, starting to come around. "Quickly," she said.

"Children," Garin said. "I knew this place was not secure. We never should have come here."

Ovelia pushed his uncertain hands aside. "Good enough," she said.

Garin nodded, but he seemed far away. He raised his hands to the sides of his head. "How would they know to look here? Who knew we were—"

"It does not matter," Ovelia said. "We need to get out." As she slipped into her boots, she longed for a shield. Instead, she wrapped Shard's cloak around her arm. It would have to do.

The dying barbarian asked a guttural question in a bleary voice. In reply, Ovelia plunged Draca into his chest, cutting him off. She wrenched the blade free and held out a hand. "Lead me."

Garin took her by the hand, and together they made their way down the corridor to the nearest stairwell. Boots stomped on the steps below them, and Ovelia pulled Garin back from the precipice.

"I saw a servant's stair," he said. "Back this way."

Ovelia nodded. Blind, she might have found such a route eventually, but more barbarians could fall upon them at any moment. The palace roared with battle, as Garin's soldiers sold their lives to buy them time to escape. They padded back down the cool stones, and Garin held aside a tapestry so Ovelia could climb under. The stairs were narrow and very dark, and Ovelia touched the cold walls to keep balance as Garin led her down. She could feel him trembling through his hand.

"Corvus—he's stood beside me since I was a child." Garin sounded beyond nervous and on the edge of panic. She could almost see the darkness rising within him. If it overwhelmed him now... "Someone did this to us. Someone there at the wedding. Who could have—?"

"Listen." Ovelia grasped him by the shoulders and shoved him against the wall. "We don't have time. I swear to you, those responsible for this will be punished. Do you believe me?"

He nodded limply, and she could tell he wanted to protest. She harmed him by acting in this way, but she had no choice. Better a dejected and catatonic king than a dead one.

"Anyone could have betrayed us," she said, though she had a good idea who had done it. "For now, we trust no one. Only ourselves. Understand?" He nodded. "Say you understand."

"I understand." Garin peered upward, where the sounds of booted feet grew loud, and they could hear angry voices. He licked his lips. "Onward?"

Ovelia released him, and they hurried down the steps, favoring haste over stealth. As they ran, she clutched the dark fabric of her cloak and thought back to her strange encounter with Shard the previous night. Of course the pirate queen had done this. She had never declared a clear loyalty to him or to Pervast, and she had watched almost every one of Garin's moves—even orchestrated some of them. Shard had manipulated Garin's endgame since they had first seen her in the skies over Atropis. Ovelia swore to slay the woman the next she lay eyes upon her.

But escape must come first. Protecting Garin stood above all.

The servant's stair led down to the lord's hall, which had grown warm as the morning sun rose. Garin lifted the tapestry obscuring the secret door and sucked in a sharp breath.

"You don't have to tell me," Ovelia said.

Through Draca's flames and her senses, she knew all about the fighting out in the throne room: at least a score of men and women screaming and slashing and bleeding. They battled around and over the throne of Luether, which was soaked in blood spatter and spittle. Something had activated it, and it whirred and clicked with its own gears and mechanisms.

Ovelia could not make out details, but she knew the battle was gruesome and all but lost. The main stair lay on the other side of the chamber, and it was their only way out.

Ovelia heard triumphant shouts above and could feel the vibrations of boots on the spiral staircase. If they were to move, it had to be now. She clutched Garin's hand hard.

"When we go in," she said. "We stay low and move fast. Don't engage any of them. Follow my lead, step where I step. Do not even look to the side."

"No," Garin said. "We have to stay. We have to help them."

"Your warriors are sacrificing themselves for you," Ovelia said. "Would you spit upon that?"

He hung his head in defeat. "I—" he said. "I never wanted—"

"I know." Ovelia leaned her forehead against his. "Follow me, my king. I am your shield."

Hesitantly, he nodded. "You are my shield."

Ovelia reached down to his recharging weapon and aimed it at the tapestry.

Then she covered her ears. He sucked in a breath and squeezed the trigger.

A wave of force blasted the tapestry free of the wall and sent three Children of Ruin flying away from the hidden entrance. Ovelia ran right through the gap, Draca blazing in her hand. She cut down one barbarian who stared at her, dazed and deafened in the blast, and snaked Draca around to knock aside an incoming spear. She whirled the black cloak, catching a seeking sword. Shadows swirled and she rammed Draca through the chest of a second man, braced on the hilt and pommel, and launched a kick to the chest that sent a barbarian woman staggering back, her twin axes clattering to the floor from nerveless hands.

There were so many, but she knew no fear. She could not.

"Go!" Ovelia cried over her shoulder to Garin. "Run!"

Shadows poured from Draca, but she did not need to look at them. She *felt* them. *Knew* what would happen before it did, rather than merely seeing it. The blade became an extension of her arm as she cut and sliced and whirled and tore a path through the Children of Ruin. She could have rallied Garin's agents, but only for a valiant death. They had to flee while they had the chance.

It was then she realized the king had not followed her. "Garin?"

The Fox of Luether stepped out into Ovelia's bloody wake and discharged his cannon into a knot of barbarians who had crowded around a fallen Luethaar woman, spears raised. The brutes went flying away, and Garin ran to the woman, but another Child of Ruin rose in his path. She had steel spikes woven into her hair and scalp. That one earned a warpick to the chest for her trouble, but she pressed forward despite the wound and shoved Garin into the wall.

"Garin!" Ovelia sensed three barbarians coming for her, and she slashed to keep them back.

The spiky-haired barbarian raised a knife to plunge into the king's throat, but Garin reached up and caught it through the palm of his thaumaturgical hand. Power surged, and the woman screamed in pain as fire engulfed her head, biting at her greasy hair. She released Garin to slump against the wall. Gritting his teeth, he pulled the knife free just in time to ward off two hissing barbarians.

"I'm coming!" Sweat pouring down her face, Ovelia wheeled around a barbarian and ran her through the small of her back. A shadowy hulk clipped her cheek with a studded fist, sending blood and spittle flying, but she had known the unavoidable attack was coming and twisted to mitigate the harm. She caught the man's arm out wide and hacked down with Draca, severing it neatly at the elbow. As the barbarian fell screaming to the floor, aided by a strong left hook, she pushed on toward Garin.

The room was filling with surging, roaring bodies and hacking swords, axes, and heavy bludgeons. Ovelia lost count of how many she had slain, or how many coats of blood from how many dying men and women she wore. A spear wrenched away her cloak-shield and she held Draca in both hands, both a sword and a shield. Her lungs heaved and blood surged in her veins. How long could she continue—clad in steel, fighting an army single-handedly—before her body gave out entirely?

She sensed someone approaching, and looked up. She saw the woman only vaguely, but the scars across her face glowed fiercely in the shadowy world. *Svista.*

She walked casually toward Garin. In her left hand she held a double dagger—serrate blades extending from both ends of her fist like the arms of a bow—while in her right hand she held something that burned with magic. This, Ovelia could see clearly: a glass orb, cunningly wrought, within which she saw a storm of dark bits of gems and metal. Draca became a torrent of warning flames in its presence.

"Svista!" Ovelia shouted. "Help him!"

The scarred woman focused on the king as he struggled with a growing crowd of barbarians.

"You have failed this city, Garin Ravalis," Svista said. "Die with the rest of these wretches."

Then she casually tossed the crystalline object at Garin's feet. The king tried to shove a barbarian off, but succeeded only in knocking them both to the ground, his face no more than a pace from the device. It hummed and glowed brighter and brighter.

"Garin!" Ovelia screamed. She ran toward him, desperate—

The device exploded, knocking her flying.

THIRTY-TWO

A FTER DRINKING ALL NIGHT, going round for round with Red Jeggs, Alcarin found himself genuinely enjoying the big man's company. He wondered why they didn't do this more often.

"Now then!" Red Jeggs pointed around the room at the diminished crowd of patrons. Most had long since retired, and only the tired regulars remained. "I've coin to spend. Pick one of those sword-swallowing man-whores for your bed tonight, and I'll buy her for you."

"Ah," Alcarin said under his breath. "That's why."

Red Jeggs pointed to a Luethaar lad with a shock of crimson hair that flowed in a tail down his back. The hair comprised most of his wardrobe. "What about that one?" he asked. "That's a man, yes?"

"This really isn't necessary," Alcarin said.

"Oh, but it is!" Red Jeggs said. "There is nothing to take the sting out of sorrow than a woman's squeals as you ram your cock into her. Or...a man..." He paused, thinking. "You know what I mean."

"You're drunk," Alcarin said.

"Yes, but that makes it no less true." Red Jeggs hiccupped. "Now, isss—"

The word trailed into a serpentine hiss as he looked past her. Alcarin followed his gaze and he sucked in a breath. Lis swayed up to them, no longer the lanky, awkward creature Alcarin remembered. Instead, she became a predator—sensuous and lissome—drawing the gazes of every man in the tavern and many of the women. Alcarin understood what she was doing, but he was too drunk to speak.

"Well." Red Jeggs rose to confront her. "The dustling. What would you have?"

"A man." Lis gave him a sly look, and Alcarin realized for the first time that she had bright yellow eyes, like those of a wolf. "Do you know where I might find one?"

Red Jeggs threw his tankard down to shatter on the floor. "I'll show you one."

Lis inclined her head. "Finally."

She took him by the hand and led him toward the stairs. Red Jeggs flashed a woozy smile back as they headed up the steps. Alcarin looked down at his tankard. Had any of that really happened?

Someone sat on Red Jeggs's vacated stool, and Alcarin looked over, suddenly uneasy. The man had seen perhaps twenty summers, most of them of hard labor and fighting based on how well his body was built. His face was oddly distorted, and not because of the drink. One milky-white eye much exceeded the other in size, and his twisted face wore a perpetual scowl.

"Davargorn, is it?" Alcarin reached for his dagger and found the razor tip of a blade at his groin.

"I wouldn't." A smile changed Davargorn's face from ugly to something truly fearful.

The door exploded open and a horde of barbarians poured in.

❧

Ovelia blinked her way back into consciousness. Her ears rang, and the rest of the world echoed as though it were underwater. She could breathe, though, and that meant she yet lived.

The explosion seemed to have stilled the battle for a moment, as all took stock of the awesome power on display. The surviving Children of Ruin stood back, holding their weapons up before them like manic apes with branches and rocks. Ovelia saw a few Summer Lives agents, bloody and battered and barely alive, who were staring at Svista with confusion and terror. The scarred woman stood before the throne of Luether, one hand on its complex clockwork surface.

"Garin." Ovelia's voice rang hollow to her own ears. "Garin!"

He lay some paces away, covered in the burnt, shredded corpses of two of the barbarians he had been fighting. Her heart skipped as she touched his ravaged face, half of it covered in blackening blood and burns. He was…by the Fire, he was missing his left *arm*.

"You still don't recognize me, do you?" Svista ripped off her eyepatch, and her scars burned bright in Ovelia's shadowy sight. "From the Fall? The night you pretended you'd save us? But you can't save anyone, Garin Ravalis—not even yourself."

Ovelia could tell he yet breathed, if shallowly. She laid her hands on his cheeks and shook him gently, willing him to wake. Though perhaps it would be kinder to let him slumber, considering how much pain he would know upon waking.

"Let the would-be king die, Bloodbreaker." Svista stood over them, casually spinning the double-dagger through the air. She wore a second such weapon at her belt. She trailed her fingers along the throne's arm. "Luether is better served without—"

Ovelia rose with a cry and slashed Draca up at the source of the words. The blade scraped off the floor, showering crimson flames, and smashed into

Svista's hasty defense. The force of the blow sent the traitor leaping back. Their audience trembled as though struck by a fearsome wind. Svista danced aside as Ovelia staggered into the throne, exhausted and coughing blood.

"Really, Bloodbreaker." Svista held up a hand to stay the Summer Lives agents, then drew out her second double-dagger. "You've lost. Be gracious."

With a scream from deep inside her, Ovelia rushed again at Svista, flailing blindly with the sword. Draca poured forth flame, but she couldn't watch it. Her rage drowned out thought and strategy. She fought solely out of reflex, like a mortally wounded hunting dog that did not realize it was already dead. Svista deflected her again, this time casually cutting open her arm as Ovelia staggered past. Her aim was perfect, catching just under the edge of one of the steel plates. The double daggers whirled in Svista's hands like leaves in a hurricane, sending red droplets across the floor. More blood flowed, but Ovelia could hardly feel it. Her heart thudded in her head, her body on the verge of exhaustion.

"Enough of this." Svista scowled. "I would have spared you, one woman to another, but you are not worthy of mercy. You are an animal, unfit to walk the streets of this great city."

Ovelia raised Draca, but it fell from her suddenly weak fingers. Its flames dimmed, and she could no longer see well enough to read them. She could see nothing, and all her senses were failing. Her body longed to collapse and die.

"I expected more of the great Bloodbreaker," Svista said from somewhere.

Ovelia shut her sightless eyes beneath their blindfold.

And *saw*.

Svista's dagger came for her throat, and Ovelia caught her wrist. She spun, stepped just inside the woman's reach, and closed her bare hand around the dagger's shorter end. Heedless of the pain in her fingers, she drove the blade up and into Svista's throat. The scarred woman's eyes went wide and she gurgled something surprised. Her own blood flowing over her wrist, Ovelia shoved the blade up and into her brain, and let the traitor collapse backward with a thud. She watched it all, seeing without sight.

Ovelia sank to her knees, heaving. She looked sightlessly up at the ceiling. The gathered agents and Children of Ruin held back, but she could hear their murmurs. What they had just seen…She heard the word "magic" and "angel" but could not credit either. She'd simply done what had to be done. Soon their growing anxiety would boil over into violence that no amount of intimidation would stay.

It all recalled another night in another throne room, much like this one: surrounded by hostile faces, beside a king she had failed just as surely as Garin Ravalis. Ovelia raised her hands, palms open, one bleeding heavily, waiting for death to come.

Then there came a gasp, followed by labored breath. Ovelia turned, and she saw Garin struggling to move. He spat blood and breathed through crackling stones and cursed in agony but he was *alive*.

Ovelia could not get up, let alone walk, so she crawled over to him. It seemed impossible that he could have survived, but sure enough, her senses hadn't deceived her. He looked up at her with angry fire in his eyes that she could see so clearly. She touched him on the shoulder and pressed her face to his.

"I'm sorry, my king," she said. "I've failed you."

He shook his head. With the three working fingers of his ensorcelled hand, he pulled out a vial from his belt and drank. After a heartbeat, his eyes cleared and his breathing eased.

"It is I…I who have failed," Garin said, coughing. "I should have expected this—I should have understood, but…I ignored your counsel. I ignored everyone. I brought this upon us."

"Did you?" A woman's voice floated through the chamber, one that tickled Ovelia's senses. "Did you truly? I rather think you simply made one key mistake."

Ovelia cast about for the source of the words. "Vilaer," she said.

Vilaer strode into the room, resplendent in a black and green gown cut with crimson cloth so that it flashed like blood in the cascading sunlight. It burned like fire in Ovelia's world, and she could make out its colors as clearly as if she could see perfectly well.

"Run," Ovelia said. "Get—get out of here."

"My poor, poor Fox." Vilaer stood by the throne, her hand caressing its intricately crafted arm. "Do you truly not understand? Even now?"

"You." Garin's voice was ragged as he tried to sit up. "Betrayed us. Sold us to Pervast."

"No, no, you silly pervert." Vilaer laughed, a delicate sound like that of water crashing on glass, but undercut with something darker and more forbidding. "You've spent all this time maneuvering around a shadowy, unseen foe—always fearing that Pervast would strike. And you were right to fear."

She sent her skirts flaring with a practiced gesture and sat down on the throne.

"I *am* Pervast."

❧

They came with no warning. Behind the bar of the Long Dawn, Biaza's eye caught a shadow upon the threshold, and in the next breath, a dozen Children of Ruin swarmed inside. Not all the patrons of the Long Dawn were Summer Lives agents this day, but those who were reacted as quickly as they could: drawing weapons or taking cover where they could find it.

It was all too little and too slow.

A hulking man with metal spines hacked apart one man who rose against them, sword half out of its scabbard, and blood showered the common room. Horrified screams echoed and the room became a scurrying madhouse of flailing, fleeing bodies. A woman with axes for hands screeched and threw herself into their midst, flailing wildly like a living thresher machine. Two barbarians lurked at the back of the group, hurling daggers and light axes to cut down any who might have escaped.

Pervast had discovered them, and Summer Lives would die this day.

Biaza dropped behind the bar and pressed herself back against it, trembling. It was not fear that stayed her, but anger. She was no warrior—she could not fight even a single barbarian, let alone an army—but she would gladly give her life for the cause. That it would end so abruptly and so violently seemed wrong, and that made her angry. She pushed open the cupboard and drew out the double caster she kept on hand for just such an occasion. At her touch, it whined to life and began to charge.

Now," she said, urging the caster to charge faster. "Now—*now*."

Through a knot hole in the back of the cupboard, she saw Neblen leap from the window of the private viewing chamber and land on the back and shoulders of one of the barbarians. This man, who boasted goat horns curling around his head, flailed and struck at her, but Neblen drove her knives over and over into his throat. He finally sagged and she jumped off, blood sailing, and landed in a spider's crouch on one of the round tables. She was laughing madly.

The spined barbarian brought his fists crashing down on the edge of Neblen's table, sending her flying awkwardly through the air toward him. She slashed wildly and succeeded in slicing a lucky gash across his face. The barbarian hardly seemed pained, however. Without apparent effort, he caught Neblen by the arm and slammed her against him. The little knife in her other hand flashed, opening his armor and exposed flesh, but it was not enough.

With a roar, the barbarian seized Neblen's head in his powerful hand and squeezed, wrenching a muted scream from the little thief. He lifted her whole body into the air by her head, bones crackling, and slammed her face into the floor. Again he did it, and again, until her body stopped flopping. All that remained of Neblen's head was a heap of gristle, bone, and brains.

That man, Biaza decided, would die first.

The double caster buzzed at full charge. She stood and put the first bolt in the spined barbarian's back, blowing a hole through him. The axe-armed woman roared at her, and Biaza cast at her too, shattering her face.

"Summer Lives!" Biaza cried. "Luether lives!"

299

A knife came flying at her face.

~

"You—" Garin couldn't understand this. "But how?"

"Your aid, mostly," Vilaer said. "You couldn't wait to give me everything. You showed me the faces of your chief lieutenants—told me the names of your conspirators. You took me to your holdfast—even invited me to sleep there." She shuddered. "So long as I pleased that red-haired harlot, of course."

"But—" Garin fought to clear his head. The philter he'd drunk blunted the edge of the pain, but it still felt like a thousand dull knives pressed into his flesh. The stump of his left arm burned, demanding he scratch. "All this time. You've been Pervast all this time?"

Vilaer laughed aloud. "Of course not," she said. "We both of us met the first Pervast—a great, rotund waste of a man who led the barbarians into Luether. He rutted and murdered his way through my mother, aunts, and all my older sisters, and finally set on my twin and myself. Usually both at once. Ultimately, we murdered him and took his place. How long ago…" She tapped her lacquered fingers against her lips. "It must be fifteen summers now. How the time goes."

"Fifteen," Garin said, horror rising like bile in his throat. "You have tortured, murdered, and terrorized your own people for *fifteen years?*" He trembled with helpless rage. "Why?"

"One must maintain appearances," Vilaer said. "If the Winter King—or more importantly, your uncle—had come to suspect Luether of weakness, war would have befallen. I had to continue the reign of the barbarians, even if I had become their new queen. Utora and I, we opened trade with Tar Vangr. We sought to police the pirates, and we kept Shard from carving out a vast empire in the Dusk Sea."

"You and Utora," Garin said. "Then why—?"

"Why did she kill herself?" Vilaer asked. "She lost her stomach for this long ago. She'd always been the weaker. Shame." She shrugged. "But Luether needs only one queen, not two."

"How?" Ovelia asked at his side. "How did you compel the Children of Ruin to follow you?"

"We had slain their master, and that earned us their fealty. Most of them, anyway. The others—" She put out a hand, and the nearest barbarian stood ready at her side as she caressed his chiseled stomach. "Some took coin, some weapons, some prisoners to play with, but in the end, all bowed. Understand, Luether was not easy to manage, but the dumb brutes all have their…*levers* to be pulled and pushed."

She slipped her hand into the man's loincloth. He stiffened, and the look on his face was one of mindless pleasure and subservience. Garin felt sick.

"I am not alone," he said. "You won't—"

"Thank you for the reminder, Highness."

Vilaer gestured, and the gathered barbarians snapped to the assault like trained hounds. They loomed over the remaining agents of Summer Lives, who could do little but scream and perish. His people were dying, and Garin could do nothing to stop it.

A man whose arms were wrapped in chains and a woman whose hair seemed to be made of blades stepped toward Garin, but Ovelia interposed herself. Vilaer made an ugly noise in her throat.

"Not them," she said. "Not yet."

The Queen of Luether rose from the throne and floated toward them.

"Do you know why this throne room has two balconies? One to gaze out over the city and the other over the sea?" she asked as she approached. "My mother told me once, before she made a deal that led to her death, that the bay balcony served two purposes. To remind the Vultara of old of the wider world that awaited them." She stopped a few paces away and gestured. The two barbarians stepped close enough to touch Ovelia and Garin. "And so they could sit in comfort while they watched executions."

Garin felt Ovelia tense at his side, but he knew she had nothing left. "That is to be our fate, then?" he asked. "To fall, as your sister did?"

"Not yours, little Fox," Vilaer said. "You, I have further use for. Her, however."

She gestured and the barbarians seized Ovelia roughly by the upper arms. She struggled but could not loosen their grasp. They dragged her, feet smearing the blood on the stones, toward the balcony.

Ovelia muttered something hardly decipherable through her swollen lip.

Vilaer held up a hand, and the barbarians stopped. "What, whore?" She stepped around Ovelia to gaze into her bloody face. "You have a word for me?"

"Pity." Ovelia raised her chin. "You do not know yourself, and I pity you for it."

For a heartbeat, Vilaer hesitated. Her face softened and her hand trembled slightly at her side. Then she smiled hungrily. "Reserve your pity for yourself, Shield of the Summer Prince," she said. "If you truly wish to give me something, there is something I would have from you." She stepped closer, heedless of Ovelia's bloody and gory visage. "Kiss me."

Ovelia averted her face, as though—in that moment—Vilaer's face repulsed even the blind.

"Very well." Vilaer made a gesture involving opening her hand. "I'll have that armor, then."

The barbarians holding Ovelia grasped the plates of the sacred armor and ripped it, piece by piece from her body. Some of the plates refused to budge at first, and they cut them free with sharp knives. Finally, Ovelia stood naked and shivering, her body a mass of scars and bruises, but her head did not bow. She stared sightlessly at Vilaer. For his part, Garin could do nothing but watch and try not to weep. The darkness rose inside him, answering the creeping pain.

"Now," Vilaer said. "Now you can throw her into the sea."

The barbarians seized Ovelia's shoulders once more.

"Stay a moment," came a familiar voice.

Garin caught his breath to see Shard appear at the edge of the bloody chamber, her black silk seeming to soak up the gore without adverse effect. She held a bundle of some sort of cloth in her hands.

"Yes, Admiral?" Vilaer asked. "Pass with haste. I've an execution to oversee."

The pirate queen strode forward briskly. Unlike Garin, Ovelia seemed not at all surprised at her presence, as if she had expected Shard to appear. The two women exchanged a long, unseen look—one that promised a reckoning—and finally Shard laid about Ovelia's shoulders a tattered black cloak. The very garment she had worn into the chamber.

"No one should go to her death entirely unadorned," she said. "It would not be civilized."

Vilaer shrugged. The barbarians seized Ovelia once more—one grasping her legs, the other her neck—and dragged her out onto the balcony like a disobedient hound. She lay limply as one already dead. She would offer them no satisfying struggles.

"Stop," Garin said. "I'll—I'll do what you want." The barbarians lifted Ovelia up on the edge. "I'll marry you! Make you queen both of the Blood and the barbarians!"

Vilaer raised her hand once again to stay her slaves. They held Ovelia just at the edge of the open sky, hanging limp in their rough hands. She looked up at Garin, her face covered in blood and her shoulders heaving. She shook her head slightly.

"You will?" Vilaer asked. "After all that has passed between us?"

Garin swallowed and nodded. "Do what you will afterward, just don't hurt anyone else."

"Your infamous path of peace," Vilaer said, bemused. "That would be quite a triumph—the savior of Luether, the Ravalis and Vultara finally reconciled, their great feud ended."

"Think—think of it." The pain was starting to creep around the edges of

Garin's potion. His vision shook and his teeth rattled. "You can be the hero of this tale, and not its villain."

"Hmm." Vilaer put her fist to her lips. "No."

She gestured, and the barbarians shoved Ovelia over the edge. Abruptly, she vanished from Garin's field of view, tumbling away without even a scream. He gasped as though Vilaer had stabbed him in the gut. And indeed, the pain of his horrific wounds rushed in along with the darkness, threatening to swallow him.

"I *am* the hero of this tale," Vilaer said. "The hero who does what must be done."

ACT SIX: BETRAYERS

Fifteen years previous—After the Fall—Luether—967 Sorcerus Annis

THE BLADE SANK IN, and she felt its keen length scrape against a bruised rib. Her body seemed to draw in around the steel, screaming around its intrusion.

It had done the same with the six other knives the barbarian had sunk into Vilaer Vultara's body as she hung naked from the chain strung up from the ceiling of the Vultara throne room. Her bleeding wrists and bruised knees had long since ceased to hurt, but she felt every one of the daggers just as keenly as she had when they first sank home.

Her tormentor calmly drew a seventh knife from the nearby table and turned it over in his hands. The blade was small—about the size of her thumb—but the edge was so sharp it faded almost to invisibility in the dying sunlight from the balcony.

"No," Vilaer said. "Please—*no*." She used the name he'd once worn. "Jorak. Don't—"

The barbarian—his face a blank mask that betrayed not a single emotion—set the knife's point against the tip of Vilaer's nose and traced her nostril and across her cheek. She tried not to flinch as he ran the blade down over her throat and along her collarbone. He made his way to her shoulder and upper arm, then found the fleshy part beneath her armpit. There he paused and levered the blade up until it stood perpendicular to her arm.

"No," she said. "No! Don't—"

The torturer drove the knife in with one quick thrust, and Vilaer screamed as the world turned to blinding white. She squirmed and struggled, her body fighting to free itself. Some of the eight daggers he'd sunk into her body clicked together, and the sound set her teeth on edge. She coughed raggedly, panting for breath, and came up with a mewling growl.

"Be not afraid, princess," said the gluttonous heap of a man perched on the divan before her. "By my breath, Stares Coldly at Death will not slay you."

"No?" Vilaer heaved for breath. "He's certainly…trying."

Pervast laughed, making the thick rolls of fat padding his body tremble, which in turn loosed a foul waft of corruption that made Vilaer gag. At least her blood smelled fresh, not rotten. The Ruin King had grown corpulent, unable to clean himself or utter certain words—"by," "breath," any that started with that same sound—without slurring. Five summers in power, and the man had grown as large as two or three of his fellows. Why the Children of Ruin followed this hulking waste of flesh, Vilaer had no idea. And yet, he ruled this city—her beloved Luether—from the throne room of his would-be allies.

"Pain, not death," he said. "Precision is Stares Coldly's finest quality. He can leave many daggers in a body, none biting the right spots to kill. Eight, though—that is many. You should be proud."

Not for the first time, Vilaer cursed her mother for bringing this doom upon them. Vortan Vultara had been a proud woman, not content to share power over her own house with an empty-headed patriarch as her foremothers had done ever since the founding of Luether. The Blood Vultara had led a failed rebellion in those days, and the victorious Ravalis had decreed that no woman would ever hold power in Luether. And so had begun a feud that had lasted centuries and eventually seen Vultara, in its desperation to destroy the Ravalis, forge an alliance with the barbarians at the gates. And, of course, the Children had promptly betrayed them, all but slain their blood, and reduced Luether to a disgusting perversion of itself.

Had Vortan truly expected a different result?

"Princess," said Pervast. "Have eight proved too much after all?" He waved. "Refresh her."

Someone threw a bucket of filth in her face: icy water, blood, and not a little vomit. She hoped it was her own. She sputtered, coughing and trying not to swallow any of it. Her body trembled and shook, making the chains grind like bones rattling in the wind. She felt not proud but humiliated: her every vulnerability drawn to light with a scalpel, her shredded body on display for Pervast's amusement. But her will—that was not broken.

"Try for a ninth." Her eyes flicked to the barbarian called Stares Coldly at Death. "I am unafraid."

The barbarian met her gaze levelly with his corpse eyes, and she thought she saw something there. Something like respect, perhaps? She could not say for certain.

Pervast pursed his slimy lips, displeased to have Vilaer undermine his victory. He raised one blubberous hand to stay his torturer, then snapped his fingers. Another barbarian approached—a woman whose hair seemed to be made of slim blades—and Pervast whispered in her ear. The woman nodded and headed toward the servant's stair.

"Another fresh...idea?" Vilaer asked. "Sending your whore for more knives, perhaps?"

305

The Ruin King smiled at her, his mouth reminding her of a pig's snout. The malevolent hunger in his eyes made her feel like heaving, but anything that came up would end up back in her face shortly thereafter. She managed to restrain herself.

Vilaer and Pervast had done this dance every so often since the fall. She spent most of her days in a cold dungeon, trying to catch enough rats to eat raw so she'd not starve. On occasion, Pervast designed new torments for her: thrusting her head under icy water over and over until she all but drowned, pressing red-hot irons against her skin, or perhaps leaving her hanging from shackles for hours at a time. Vilaer's body was a mess of scars and constantly renewed bruises, but each fresh torture felt as sharp as that first night. She was an exposed nerve, its protective flesh flensed away, and it was all she could do to keep her mind intact. Her mother's fire made her strong and stubborn, possibly too much so to survive. So far as she knew, she was the last Vultara, and she would sooner burn in the Narfire than allow a wretch like Pervast to break her. If she no longer had any power over her life, she could at least control her death.

She realized time had passed only when the door scraped back open and knife-hair reappeared, leading someone on a black leather leash. At first, she thought this some new horror Pervast would use to threaten her, but then the woman's drawn face came into view and she caught her breath.

"Sister," Vilaer said, her voice barely a whisper.

Her twin's appearance made Vilaer's heart sink. The barbarians had made some sort of effort to dress, paint, and primp Utora Vultara as a noblewoman deserved, but the disgusting parody they'd made of it only served to mock her. Her fine dark hair stood like a bloated nest of hornets atop her head, locks hanging down like limp arms from a corpse cart. She wore a threadbare green gown, worn and shredded in places to reveal sunken ribs and limbs that looked more like sticks than body parts belonging to a living body. Her bare feet shook as she limped along in the wake of her captor. Her eyes glittered out of sunken sockets and her mouth had shrunk into a thin, hard line that trembled.

"Sister!" Vilaer struggled anew. "Sister!"

Utora didn't seem to hear. She moved in a haze, like a dead woman walking. Vilaer recognized the raw tracks under her nostrils that spoke of heavy kefa snorting. Utora was a woman barely alive.

"What have you done to my sister, you repulsive filth?" Vilaer asked.

A knife flicked out between Stares Coldly's fingers and he put it under her chin, silencing her as surely as a blow to the gut. Pervast raised a hand to stay him.

"No need for a ninth blade," the Ruin King said. "I want her awake to watch."

Vilaer gritted her teeth and pulled at the shackles overhead. She felt skin tearing from her wrist and blood ran down her filthy arms. "Don't you touch her!"

Pervast chuckled, making his huge belly jiggle like a skin of wine. "Tell that to her," he said. "Your lovely twin lives to please me. Do you not, Utora?"

Utora smiled without mirth, and her teeth were the sickly yellow of a sweetsoul addict. She strode to Pervast and caressed his bulging belly. She sighed with something like desire, and it made Vilaer want to vomit. "What have you done to my sister?" she demanded.

"I have showered affection upon her," Pervast said, taking her leash from the barbarian with blades for hair. "Since Ruin's Rise, she has known the finest luxuries Luether can offer—my treasured guest in these halls. Kept quiescent, in part, out of concern for your well-being. Such a noble girl. So beautiful." He held up one hand and Utora ran her cheek along it, not unlike a hound showing affection for its master. "In time, I simply could not help myself."

"What did you do to her?" Vilaer strained. "Answer me!"

"The worst thing I could have, I suppose." The Ruin King pushed Utora's face gently away, and Vilaer's twin fell to her knees, awaiting his command. He looked to Vilaer instead, and showed her a ring of gold gleaming around one of his sausage-like fingers. "I followed in the ways of your people and married her, making her Queen of the Burning City." A sickly smile split his fat face. "Just as I married your mother, and your sisters, and your brothers. Your entire family, in fact—save you two. For last."

Churning horror stirred inside Vilaer, and suddenly the burning agony of the knives seemed far away. This, she could not face. She could not…"What do you want of us?" Vilaer asked.

"A bargain, is it?" Pervast asked. "What I want of you, I already have." He drew Utora's leash taut, hauling the woman to her feet. "I want your horror. Your fear. Your despair."

He made a cutting gesture toward Utora, who immediately reached up to shrug out of her dress. It puddled around her ankles, leaving her naked and trembling before the throne. Beneath the meager coverings, her emaciated body was miraculously smooth and pure in stark contrast to the grotesquerie of the court. She barely seemed to be there, as though Pervast had sucked all the life out of her.

As she undressed, Utora stole a look back at her sister, and Vilaer saw in her eyes a terrible fear.

"I'll tear out your guts," Vilaer said. "I swear it."

"I grow weary of your sister, if you must know," Pervast said. "She is not what she once was. This will be the last time I rut her—while you watch. Enjoy it."

The Ruin King gestured down at himself. Mechanically, Utora reached for the folds of his robe. "What is the saying among your people?" Pervast asked as Utora wearily climbed atop him. "The finest pleasure—" He held out a hand, and the barbarian with the blade hair handed him a serrated knife. Utora fumbled and tried to pull away, but he grasped her throat in one meaty hand. "To rut with your lover's blood on your hands?"

He put the knife over his thumb against Utora's bulging throat. The gaunt princess gasped and tried to squirm away, but he held her tight.

"You displease me." Pervast gave Utora the ugliest glare Vilaer had ever seen. He nodded to Stares Coldly. "Put the ninth blade in."

"No—" Utora wavered on her feet. "You swore you'd not hurt her. You swore if I —"

"And you believed me."

He slapped Utora with such force she slid off him onto the floor. Her head smashed into the stone and she lay gasping and dizzy. Pervast pushed himself to his feet, blade loose in his hand. Vilaer watched as her sister struggled to crawl away.

No.

Blood welled around her wrist and her bones crackled, but Vilaer hardly felt it. Teeth on edge, Vilaer wrenched hard, her thumb snapped, and she ripped free of the left shackle. She hit the floor with bruising force, and the heavy chain snaked down toward her right hand. She closed her right hand around the blood-slick dagger sticking out of her left side and pulled. The blade slid out and blood trickled over her skin. She looked up through blood and tears at Pervast, his face wide in a rictus of surprise.

"Ward me!" he cried, throwing up his fat hands. "Ward me!"

Vilaer coiled her legs under her and sprang at Pervast, roaring like a beast finally loosed from a cage. The chain connected to the ceiling went taut, wrenching back her right arm, and she slipped midway through her leap. Worse, she landed on a dagger, and it sank in deeper. She ended up kneeling before Pervast, blood flowing freely onto the stones of the throne room. Stares Coldly at Death came to stand beside her, a silent specter and reminder of her helplessness.

The Ruin King shook with a fit of deep, mocking laughter. He had found his ease once more, secure in his power over her. "If you want a taste, princess—" He threw wide his arms, displaying his engorged manhood for all to see. "You've but to *beg*."

Slowly, Vilaer stood and turned to Stares Coldly. "This blade came out," she said, offering him the knife. "Put it back, would you?"

Pervast laughed loud and long, and with every slurred chuckle, Vilaer hardened herself.

Stares Coldly must have seen Vilaer's resolve, for he nodded and closed Vilaer's fingers more tightly around the dagger. Then he grasped her right wrist and fit a tiny key into the shackle. He clicked it open, then pulled the iron from around Vilaer's wrist.

"What passes?" Pervast's wide, stupid face looked perplexed.

With a wild cry, Vilaer rushed past Stares Coldly and tackled Pervast back into his throne. She plunged the knife to the hilt in the Ruin King's massive gut, just below the valley that led to his navel. He stared at her, his bloodshot eyes wide and his wet lips smacking.

"I promised you," she said.

Vilaer wrenched the blade up and across, and blood and entrails spewed around her. She screamed and laughed and plunged the blade home again and again, splashing her face with gore. Something inside her broke, and she couldn't have stopped herself even had she wanted to.

Silently, the Children of Ruin watched as Vilaer tore and ripped their master apart. Then—one by one—they sank to one knee and inclined their heads.

When she was done—when the thing beneath her hardly resembled a man any more—Vilaer finally looked up from her gruesome work. She noted the barbarians bowing, but that hardly surprised her. Instead, she realized that she was free, and she could look out at her beloved city.

The city that had destroyed itself and her.

"Sister?" Utora said, shaking on the floor. "Sister?"

Vilaer shook her head. She felt far apart from herself. A new body, reborn without the soul that Pervast had ripped away. She had no city. No sister. No mother.

No mother but Ruin.

Slowly, Vilaer climbed off Pervast and headed out to the balcony. Heat rose from the city below, but it had none of the sweet smell of Luether's haze. Instead, it stank of offal and sewage—of moldering pitch and scalded wood. A nightmare lay before her: a burned corpse of Luether, blackened and criss-crossed with burning scars.

"No," the Ruin Queen said with a smile. "This cannot stand."

THIRTY-THREE

Midsummer's Eve—High-City, Luether

FROM UP ON THE balcony overlooking the city, Vilaer Vultara had always liked listening to the city cooking late in the day. It made her feel powerful, as though the World of Ruin itself conspired to keep Luether under her heel. Idly, she leaned on the banister separating her from the great city spread out below and inhaled deeply of the rancid smell. It struck her nostrils with the sickly-sweet reek of rotting flesh, bodily waste, and decaying wood. The monstrous stench had revolted her at first, but in time she'd come to love it. Possibly the very same day she had torn Pervast apart and Utora had helped her hurl his bloated body off the balcony. She admired how the city always seemed to come back around to itself.

Luether was a city of circles.

The latter half of the day brought Luether's true, sweltering heat. As the sun began its descent from its midday zenith, all the fire it had lashed against the city throughout the morning settled in Luether's furrows and niches, where it festered and combined with the loosed Narfire to turn the city to an oven for its oppressed people. Tempers rose with the heat, and bloodshed inevitably followed. By dusk, Luether had all but lost its mind every day, and only after a night spent in drinking and fighting would the cycle begin again.

The effect crept upon locals gradually enough that they grew accustomed to it and barely noticed, with one particular exception: after a rain. The liquid fire from the skies came rarely to Luether in summer and was widely considered an ill-omen, not the least because of the *sound* it produced. The clouds had opened up around midday, chasing most inside to escape the scalding rain, leaving pools of murky water that turned to metallic-smelling steam. The city sizzled in the heat, like a slab of meat left too long on a greasy rack.

Luether was *her* city. Every rotted rooftop, lice-infested whorehouse, and shit-stained street corner belonged to her. Every hapless fool who crossed the wrong bloodthirsty wretch and ended up disemboweled in the square owed her allegiance. Every raging monstrosity of gears and blades that roamed Luether served her will.

Alas, it would not last forever, especially not if the path Garin had laid out

310

before her proved as fruitful as he believed it would. The time would soon come to drive out the barbarians and rebuild Luether. Perhaps she could appeal to King Lan in Tar Vangr: sell him a story about his brother's revolution succeeding in deposing Pervast and breaking the power of the barbarians, even if Garin himself had perished in the attempt. Lan had been laughably easy to allure and captivate as a boy, and she couldn't imagine he'd grown wiser with age. She could even present herself as the lone survivor of her house, who had risen to aid Garin in slaying Pervast and somehow clung to power.

There would be a certain amount of truth to that claim, but Vilaer was not the sort to gamble. She much preferred to palm cards and set up her own victories. If only her guest would be more…pliable.

"Enough of this." She wiped away the sweat of her brow with one blood-soaked forearm, leaving a crimson smear against her dark skin. "Prisoners don't break themselves."

She strode back into the throne room, where Garin screamed anew as her attendants tightened the clamp on his already warped pectoral muscle. Between his severed left arm and scarred face, he looked less a man than a hunk of meat in a butcher's shop. His left chest had become an oozing sore where one of them—the dead-eyed ravager called, appropriately, Stares Coldly at Death—had cut away the nipple and stretched out the flesh with a vice. Blood and pus oozed out to drip on the floor, and Garin panted and gasped in dizzying pain. The second barbarian, She Draws Blood—a woman twice Vilaer's size—slowly caressed Garin's breastbone with the rusty, bladed fingers of her left hand, opening slits in his skin to let blood run in rivulets over his heaving chest.

"This bloodless revolution of yours." Vilaer swept her hand around the room, indicating the gory stains on the walls and stone floors. She'd had the bodies removed—mostly hurled off the balcony.

Vilaer held up a hand to stay both of the barbarians, and they backed away to leave Garin hanging before her on a set of rings looped through the flesh of his back.

"Is it truly such a difficult thing I ask of you?" She cupped Garin's chin in her hand. "I only need your signature and a mark on a scrap of paper, transferring your claim to me. It's not as though I want you to rut me." She clutched him between the legs and poured, "Not even a bit."

Garin let out a garbled chuckle. "If I loved women, you'd be the last one I'd rut," he said. "After the Hag, spiky-fingers over there, and your dead burning *sister*."

At the mention of Utora, Vilaer stepped forward and seized the troublesome prince by the throat. "Slur my sister's name again, you little monster, and I will make you *beg* to rut me."

Garin stared up at Vilaer with his one good eye. "At least…" he said. "At least Utora…had the courage…to reject this horror you've become."

It took more effort to control herself than it would to murder him. It would have been easy to stab him over and over just as she had Pervast. The master barbarian had been thrice Garin's size and weight, however: she suspected the squelching would be less satisfying.

"We all become horrors," she said, glancing at Stares Coldly. "This one here—do you recognize him? He served you, once, and betrayed you. Now he serves me." She thought hard. "I've forgotten his old name. But I suppose it matters little, does it my pet?"

Stares Coldly nodded, making not a sound.

Vilaer traced her fingers under Garin's jawline. "You could serve me too, Garin," she said. "My sister was always fond of you. Perhaps—"

He looked up at, defiance in his diminished face, and she knew that more torture would be required to break this one. She relished the challenge.

"Your Majesty," said a polite voice.

With an impressive show of will, Vilaer took her hands from Garin's throat and looked up. "Oh it's you," she said. "What do you want?"

Lady Shard swept into the room, her black robe trailing through the vast tracks of dried blood that still made the place smell like a charnel house. Her face hid behind her black veil, but her body language betrayed a touch of unease. Good. Garin looked up reproachfully at her through his one good eye.

"I've come to speak with you regarding the disposition of my fleet," Shard said. "I must say—"

Vilaer stepped away from her entertainment of the day and wiped her hands together to get some of the blood off. "You mean *my* fleet," she said. "Unless you've forgotten our bargain, *Admiral?*"

The pirate queen fell silent for a heartbeat, then nodded. "*Your* fleet," she said. "As instructed I've dispatched orders to position ships throughout the cliffs, rather than keep a distant watch."

"Yes," Vilaer said. "Until we resolve this internal matter, we cannot afford to waste our ships on useless forays over the Dusk Sea. One never knows if they'll turn pirate and never return. We'll keep them close during these first seasons of our alliance." She looked to She Draws Blood and spoke in the rough barbarian tongue: "And we're holding the hostages as I instructed? Undamaged and unspoiled?"

The woman nodded and sneered at Shard. Imprisoning the first mate of each skyship would keep the pirates from turning on Vilaer. She held

Shard's own mate—the big Aeldad woman, who had taken three barbarians to incapacitate her—as collateral to keep her admiral in line. There was no sense letting Shard betray her as she had Garin. For her part, the pirate queen received the news impassively.

Garin coughed, and Vilaer realized she'd almost forgotten he was there. He was looking at Shard with intense resentment. "Should've..." he said. "Should've just given you...what you wanted."

Lady Shard stood very still, staring at him. Vilaer thought she was holding her breath.

Vilaer perked up. "What does he mean, Shard?"

"I could not say, Queen Vultara." The pirate queen drew up to her full height. "The ramblings of a dying man hardly warrant your credence."

"*Hek...*" Garin said, stumbling over words. "I promised her *Hekatomb*."

"I see." Vilaer scrutinized Shard. "A secret pact between you?"

"A deal I offered, but he refused," Shard said. "It is a dead matter that came to no end. Must I share everything with you, Majesty?"

Vilaer started to answer in the affirmative, but thought better of it. Shard sought only to provoke her, and she would not rise to the bait. "Are there other secrets you keep from me?" Vilaer asked. "Think carefully before you answer."

Shard raised her fingers to her chin as though in thought. "Yes, though not of my own doing."

Vilaer balked, and her two barbarian escorts went instantly alert. She controlled her temper with an effort. "What does that mean?"

"You interrupted me earlier," Shard said. "I bring important news."

"What?" Vilaer scoffed. "What could you possibly have to tell me—?"

"We're under attack," Shard said.

At that moment, the floor beneath them shook, and a massive explosion lit up the sky outside the palace. Vilaer rushed to the balcony overlooking the Dusk Sea, and saw a column of smoke rising from the manorhouses that jutted from the rocky cliffs north and south of her vantage point. Two skyships, both hovering upon serrate rings of gleaming steel, fired volley after punishing volley of cannon and heavy casterbolts into the rock-mounted holdfasts. Vilaer could hardly breathe as she watched the burning wreckage of buildings tumbling from the cliffs and into the bay.

"Explain this!" Vilaer rounded on Shard. "Your ships were supposed to be guarding the passes to the city!"

"And they are woefully unprepared for a massive invasion force, which is exactly what comes." Shard sounded entirely too calm, considering.

"They are *cowards*," Vilaer said. "They should be giving their lives to slow invaders in the passes while we muster a defense!"

"They are pragmatists, and you control them through threat of force, not through loyalty," Shard said. "Had they scouted north as I suggested and you ignored, we might have had some warning. As it passes—"

Another blast shook the palace, and dust and shards of stone rained down from the ceiling. Vilaer's heart thudded in her chest fit to tear its way free. Even had she known of the attack earlier, she'd never prosecuted a war or defended Luether. And so focused had she been on Garin's revolution that the sudden assault took her off-guard. She didn't know what to do.

Garin made a bemused sound that turned into a cough. "Cousin Lan," he said. "He came early."

Vilaer recognized the blue and red markings on the skyships, as well as the banners they flew.

"So the Blood Ravalis finally returns to claim its birthright," Shard said softly.

"Hold her!" The barbarians seized Shard by either arm, and Vilaer thrust a finger in her face. "You knew this would come to pass! That was part of your pact with him. He would give you protection from this invasion, and in return you would let them destroy Luether."

Regal and unassuming despite the brutes holding her arms, Shard nodded toward Garin. "Look upon him," she said. "Does he look like a man who can protect anyone?"

"Shut up!" Vilaer gestured, and Stares Coldly at Death drove Shard to her knees, blade at her throat. "I should kill you now, Admiral—you and all your treacherous pirates! You have doomed us all!"

The hail of fire continued to fall outside, and Vilaer chanced a look. She saw more ships on the emerging through the cliffs on the far side of the bay, all of them shining with the colors of the Ravalis.

"You." Vilaer lifted Garin's chin. "You, at least, *knew* of this attack. You know what Lan plans to do. And you must have a plan to escape his wrath." She cupped his cheeks and forced him to meet her gaze. "Were you to meet him? Announce that you had succeeded, and welcome his army as Luether's king? Answer me!"

Garin shook his head. "He…coming anyway," he said. "Didn't trust me. Never trusted me. Wants me dead as much as you. You think…he will show mercy to a Vultara?" He grinned at her, dribbling blood. "You're rutted, good and bloody."

The stink of Luether swept through the throne room, but now it mingled with smoke and burning flesh. She had not smelled something quite like this since the day of Luether's fall. All that she had worked and wept for, sweated and bled for, *murdered* for—all of it would come undone.

"Not yet," she said at length. "Not *yet*."

She gestured to her attendants, and to the ruined body of Garin.

"Bring them," she said. "We are not beaten yet."

"Where?" Garin retched as She Draws Blood lowered him down by the ropes. "There is nowhere you can…" He gasped as he fell to the floor. "Nowhere you can hide from this."

Garin stared at the bay balcony. At first, Vilaer thought he watched the advancing fleet, but ultimately she realized his eyes fell lower, toward the broken stone where he'd last seen Ovelia Dracaris. Understanding his anguish made Vilaer feel stronger.

"Not hiding," Vilaer said. "*Fighting*."

She wrenched Garin's head up by the hair, making him gurgle in pain.

"We're going to awaken *Hekatomb*."

THIRTY-FOUR

FROM THE SHADOW OF the door leading into the common room of the Long Dawn, Davargorn watched as Alistra moved sinuously behind the bar, her hand trailing along the half-full shelves. The battle in the tavern had rooted all life from the place, destroyed most of the doors and windows, and shattered many of the bottles of spirits and wines that lined the wall. Alistra made a thoughtful purring sound as she searched. A wide dagger jutted out of the wall, dripping with blood.

Her oddly domestic activity seemed particularly strange in a house of such death. The Children of Ruin had done their job well, leaving not a single patron alive. Davargorn eyed the corpses she'd had him pile against the far wall, near the entrance to the shuttered private chamber. Doing so left the floor mostly bare, though the bloodstains and marks of violence remained. The place hardly seemed fit for habitation any longer, but at least it offered shelter from the war raging in the streets outside. Alistra wore a slim black robe, loose in the dank heat of the Summerlands, and nothing beneath. By contrast, Davargorn had donned a suit of boiled leather for the day's work. The mad courage of the woman made his head hurt, his heart race, and his cock strain against his breeches. Even after she'd betrayed him and tortured him, he still couldn't say whether he wanted to kill her or rut her. Both.

"What passes here?" he asked. "Why do we wait?"

"Patience," Alistra said. "Almost—ah." She gave a little hop, then knelt down to hoist up a limp, bloody arm behind the bar. "You missed one, it seems."

Davargorn checked the locks on the private chamber—sealed—then crossed the room and hauled the offending corpse away. He dimly recognized the aging woman by face if not name. She had taken a blade to the throat with such force that it left her head attached by only a thin strip of flesh. He cradled her head so she might at least have some dignity in death.

"Ah. Perfect." Alistra pulled a silvery bottle down from the shelves and uncorked it. She took a swig, grimaced, then poured its contents over her hands. She brushed off the blood that coated her wrists, then pooled more in her palms to clean her face. The day had been a bloody one thus far.

The brunt of Lan's assault had fallen upon High-City, leaving Low-City comparatively unscathed, but the arrival of the Vangryur had thrown the people into chaos. Luethaar fought barbarian in the streets with rusty blades

316

and tools hardly designed for warfare, and corpses littered the cobbled roads. Davargorn and Alistra had killed more than a few people to get this far, then taken refuge in the hollowed-out tavern to watch the chaos rise like a pot left too long unattended, boiling over into madness. It was a revolution, albeit not the bloodless one Garin had intended. Alistra assured Davargorn that it would likely fail on its own, but it occupied the barbarians and—more importantly—distracted from *them*.

Someone pounded on the locked doors to the private chamber, and Davargorn slammed his fist on the doors in response. No further knocks came.

"What passes here?" he asked again. "Is not our quest accomplished?"

"Not remotely." Alistra selected another bottle, uncorked it with her teeth, and spat the cork out into the common room. "We do what my brother told us to do: ensure little cousin Garin succeeds."

Davargorn furrowed his brow and gestured around the ruined tavern. "Summer Lives is broken. Your cousin is surely dead at the hands of one of the many traitors he enlisted. Even now, your brother already descends upon Luether, and yet you say there is more to accomplish?"

"There is." Alistra took a deep draught from the liquor and smiled. "You're forgetting one agent in all your summation."

"Ovelia Dracaris." Davargorn's guts churned. "Surely she is dead."

"You think so, or you hope so?" Alistra slid over the bar and sat on it, hugging her knees to her chest. She looked at him coquettishly. "Should I be jealous?"

Davargorn scowled. "Not at all."

"Hmm." Alistra spread her legs wide on the bar. "Come here and show me."

Davargorn didn't need to be told twice. He strode toward her, unlacing his breeches.

As the war raged outside the battered tavern and the world crumbled around them, they rutted like animals, grunting and cursing and crying out in their shared lust.

The foundations of Luether quaked and cinders rained down from the sky. Half a dozen heavy skyships floated over the bay, loosing scores of smaller craft that swarmed like enraged hornets to blast apart buildings and decimate the Summer City's defenders. The barbarians launched ships of their own: rickety, clanking things soldered together from rusted out carriages and ancient war machines long since past their fighting best. The skyships of Summer droned angrily amongst the attacking fleet, cut down almost instantly against the superior maneuverability and firepower of the comparatively young northern craft. Hunks of metal and burning corpses plummeted from the sky and splashed down into the water.

The Ravalis fleet might have swept to a swift victory, but as the vanguard drew close to Luether it met a wall of heavy casterbolts and cannonfire that sent ship after ship tumbling down into the bay. What the Children of Ruin lacked in skyships, they more than made up in mounted and personal weaponry. Ballistae mounted in the red cliffs beside the city tracked would-be invaders and cast bolt after bolt of deadly energy in their path. Most casts went wild, but enough found their marks to slow the advance.

Far below the embattled city, blood and filth seeped into the bay. The black water lapped gently at the roots of the mountain, deceptively calm when juxtaposed against the twisted bodies that rotted on the stones. Two score corpses had recently tumbled from the heights of Luether, most striking the stones or water with enough force to splatter apart like softened pumpkins. Corpses gaped up at the burning sun with endless screams or bloody eyes, reaching up skeletal hands that would never find aid.

A woman lay on her back among them, gazing up at the blazing sky, her body surprisingly whole considering her long fall. Her left arm hooked across her chest as if to hold something tightly, while her right arm hung from the rock, fingers half curled around the hilt of a sword long taken from her. Blood-matted rags scantily covered her bruised and bloody frame. A tattered black cloak hung over the rock, sodden with gore and murky sea water. The sun had chapped her skin over the long day, particularly around her scarred eyes.

The water stirred as something moved below the surface. In a moment, one of the corpses near her left foot slid slowly away, only to vanish into the gentle tide. Muted sounds of crunching and sucking rose from the water, as of something eating.

Then a sticky black tentacle slid from the waves, wrapped daintily around her boot, and *pulled*.

Hitting the oily water shocked Ovelia to a disoriented wakefulness, and she flailed for something to hold. She saw only flashes of light and blurs in the sky above, and then she was under, filth rushing into her parched throat. She could see the ravenous beast before her: a churning, bulbous mass of rogue magic. She caught something solid above, then kicked hard at the tentacle pulling her down. The creature, surprised, lost its grip for a heartbeat, and Ovelia hauled herself back to the surface.

She broke into the air and gasped. By chance, her hand had fallen on the hilt of a jagged sword scabbarded at the belt of a broken corpse. She'd half drawn it in her struggle, and the steel glinted dully beneath dried splotches of blood caked onto the blade. Her blood, perhaps. So much blood. The jagged rocks of the bay had become a charnel pit of corpses and gore from shattered bodies. Blood and flesh had burst in gobbets all around her, splintery bones stood up like the broken limbs of fallen trees, and entrails festooned the rocks like sea kelp washed onto shore.

She was alive. How could she have survived such a fall?

Then the creature collected itself, grasped Ovelia's ankle tighter, and pulled thrice as hard. It had done so idly before—almost lazily and without intention—but now it exerted a strength upon her she'd never felt from a mortal creature. Ovelia barely had time to wrench the blade free and suck in a breath before the tentacle hauled her under. It pulsated and rippled like a swollen skin filled nigh to bursting with bubbling, steaming water.

She knew the beast then: it was the same monster she had glimpsed from the prow of the *Avenger*—a bright spot of magic in a world of shadow far below— and it was the same beast that had devoured Captain Fersi. She had heard the tales of leviathan and kraken in the Dusk Sea, but always thought them mere sailors' fancy. Now she understood that the tales far undercut the truth.

The creature pulled her deeper. It should have blinded her, had she relied upon her actual eyes, but instead she could see it perfectly. The mass of churning black magic loomed below her, impossibly bright against her shadowy world. Fighting the water resistance, she hacked at the tentacle that held her leg and it parted surprisingly easily. The creature reared, coalescing for a heartbeat, then grew half a dozen tentacles to grasp at her. She fended them off as best she could, thrashing to make her hard to grab. One tentacle enwrapped her leg, and she hacked into it with the sword, feeling the edge bite shallowly into her thigh. Another tentacle slithered around her throat, and she brought the sword up to saw at it, hardly caring if she cut herself.

Like a trapped animal, Ovelia fought with strength born of desperation, but she knew she was lost. She had neither the strength nor the power to escape, and her awareness had started to tremble without air in her lungs. She was only a pace below the surface, but she could not fight her way to it. She saw a line of white light appear in the mass of darkness that was the creature, which parted like a mouth. The tentacles drew her toward it.

Of a sudden, a huge shard of steel crashed into the sea just above them, and Ovelia felt it like a hammer striking her all over in one blow. It jarred her loose from the creature, which she dimly saw reel back from the offending shrapnel. She couldn't quite tell, but she thought the falling debris had stabbed into the beast, which dragging it down under the weight. Without breath, her world seemed far away and fading, but with her last ounce of strength she kicked up toward what she thought was the surface.

Ovelia burst into the open air and sucked breath into her lungs in huge gasps. Flames rose around her: the water was on fire from leaking fuel of the crashed skyship. A thunderous roar shook the bay, making her ears hurt. Heaving, Ovelia made herself swim back toward the shore. At least, she hoped so: she was alone and blind in a place she'd never been, and all around her was death and fire and blinding light. She might have been swimming out into the bay, never to return.

Fortunately, her hand struck a rock with bruising force, and she hauled herself back with shaking arms onto the stones at the shore. She heaved the sword, gummy with kraken blood, onto the stones. There she lay, wet and exhausted and trembling, as war raged in the city above her.

All Ovelia wanted to do was lie back and sleep. Her body hovered on the verge of collapse, every muscle numb or trembling with exhaustion. She craved sweetsoul, not just to assuage the hunger but to hide the pain. The adrenaline pouring through her had given her enough strength to get to shore, but it was fading fast. She had to be done. What else could she do?

"Garin," she said.

She still had a vow to fulfill.

Ovelia pushed herself to her feet. She stood, the wind stirring the tattered black cloak around her shoulders, and gazed up at the display of flashing lights in the sky. She stooped, unbuckled the swordbelt from the dead man who'd lent her his jagged blade, and secured it around her waist. Then she looked up at the nearest access to Low-City: a nearly sheer slope that rose twenty paces to an unused dock. From up there, she could hear men and women screaming and the clash of blades.

She started to climb.

THIRTY-FIVE

THE HOURS OF THE climb were the hardest of Ovelia's life.

The height was not great, but the conditions made it all but impossible. Blind, she had to grope for handholds and prod the stone with her bare feet for edges that might support her weight. A sighted climber could have inspected the rock face and charted a route up, one replete with handholds that avoided overhangs and impossible stretches. Without her sight, she had to guess and hope that her chosen path wouldn't end in smooth stone or empty air. The howling wind deafened her, enough to blur the sounds of battle but not to drown the thunder of her heart beating in her head. She felt naked and helpless, lashed against the rock like a corpse caught in a storm.

Halfway up, the jagged sword slipped out of the borrowed scabbard and clattered to the stones far below. She paused, the sea winds cutting her trembling body, and considered heading back down for the weapon. At length, she resumed the climb.

After what seemed like hours, Ovelia's bloody, dusty fingers reached over a parapet and fell on smooth, perpendicular stone. The battle grew louder, and she could see shadows writhing amongst the smoke. When she pulled herself up, upper arms and shoulders straining to their limit, she looked out onto a sea of madness.

Low-City stewed like bloody water set too long to simmer until it finally boils over in a crimson flood. Houses burned, loosing thick, greasy black plumes up into the rancid air. Men and women screamed in panic and rage and slaughtered one another in the streets. The noise fairly deafened anyone nearby. Naked steel whined against thick iron shields and the crack of casters sounded like clinking glass against the massive explosions that sounded just overhead. Mage-glass showered down, cutting unsuspecting folk apart into bloody pulp.

Into this chaos, Ovelia hauled herself, blind and exhausted. She levered herself up, rolled over the parapet, and fell in the filthy street with a shock. The grime plastered to her skin felt noxious and smelled worse, but she had to keep moving. Windows shattered down the block, and doors grunted and caved in under hobnailed boots. She shivered to hear the screams of the wounded and choked wails of the dying. Her heart ached but she had to focus on her own path. She half-crawled, half-limped across the street and took shelter behind a burning hut, where she huddled against the wall and hunched down to catch her breath in quick, ragged gasps. Every breath was toxic with blood, smoke, and awful fumes.

Something exploded just to her left. She felt the force before she heard the sound—the terrible shriek of metal and stone, the roar of flame—and it sent her hurtling through the wall of a nearby hovel. She lay amongst the debris, stones clattering off her, and tried to catch her breath. A painful ring filled her ears, like a bell caught on one shrieking high note, never to stop.

Embracing herself tightly, Ovelia focused on appraising her condition. Her muscles shook badly, and she wondered if her back, arms, and legs would ever unclench. Her hands and feet itched, raw and vulnerable. Her limbs tingled where the sea creature's tentacles had enwrapped them, and she saw faint pulsing magic: shaped like bruises and of a similar deep purple color. Nothing she could do about that. The ringing in her ears had diminished. Ovelia found no other injuries, but her bones felt fragile and her body on the verge of collapse. She'd pushed herself beyond her capabilities but had to keep moving.

Garin needed her.

Muscles screaming at her, she got up, climbed out of the burning hovel, and pressed on.

She thought she recognized the shadows of buildings well enough to place herself: the Long Dawn stood just a little along this road. Walking there would have proved a simple matter if not for the fighting in the streets, but this alley connected with the route Alcarin had showed her. If she remembered it well enough, she could avoid the embattled main road.

As Ovelia ambled, glass and loose wood crunched underfoot, making her wince at every step. When Vilaer had stripped her armor, Ovelia had thought only of her own humiliation and vulnerability. She hadn't even imagined the punishment it would inflict on her feet, feeling every single broken chip of stone or shard of glass. Worse still, because she couldn't see the offending debris before she stepped on it. It was slow going, but she concentrated on putting one foot before the other. Buildings burned around her, chunks of rock cratered the cobblestones, and at one point, another explosion knocked her staggering aside. She steadied herself on a filthy wall, wincing at the second chime in her ears. She wiped her runny nose and inhaled the overly flowered reek of the meat shop across from the Long Dawn. She had made it.

Unfortunately, the brawl in street made the entrance seem a league away.

The street ahead of her boasted at least a dozen combatants, mostly Low-City Luethaar fighting Children of Ruin or each other. Ovelia could not intervene: even had she managed to keep the jagged sword, she felt in no condition to fend off an attacker. She hunched behind cover as the combatants hacked at one another, grunting and cursing. Only death awaited her if she took so much as a step out of the concealing shadows.

Then she heard it: a low rhythmic *click-click-click* that grew louder and closer. She opened her mouth to shout a warning, but an explosion of fire magic overhead drowned her out.

Then the street thresher burst upon the melee, its gore-strewn teeth churning as it roared through the street. Thankfully, Ovelia saw only the angry red magic driving the monstrosity on, but she could *hear* its work well enough. She heard the crunch of bones, the shearing of flesh, and the wet splats of discarded limbs striking the buildings and cobblestones. A man's hand and part of his arm slapped against the wall by her head and blood spattered her face. She turned away, praying to the Narfire the thaumaturgical beast turned down the street. Her stomach churned.

It did, finally, plowing destruction elsewhere. Ovelia vomited onto the muddy stones and hugged herself until the shaking subsided. She felt something sharp next to her left knee: the severed hand had arrived holding a long dagger, which was better than nothing. She pried the weapon from the dead fingers, wiped its smeared hilt and blade on her black cloak, and padded across the street in the thresher's wake. As she had hoped, the automaton left no survivors to trouble her, and her path lay clear to the Long Dawn. She reached the threshold and put her hand on the gnarled rail.

Something crunched under her step, and pain exploded up from her left foot. Ovelia almost fell but managed to keep herself up with one hand on the ground. She felt at her foot and her fingers found a hunk of mage-glass that must have fallen from above jutting from the meat of her foot. She tugged it out easily enough, but copious blood coated her fingers thereafter. Ovelia made a face, but she had no one to complain to. She limped up to the porch, jolts of pain arcing up her leg with each step.

She touched the door, expecting to find it locked, but it swung easily into the shadowy interior of the tavern. That put Ovelia immediately on her guard, and she raised the dagger before her like a sword. The room seemed empty but with her blindness she could not be certain. It reeked of blood and sweat, and she thought she detected a faint, sweeter smell beneath the stench of death.

"Biaza?" she asked. "Alcarin?"

Ovelia heard a muffled thump from the raised private booth: something pounding the inside of the shutters, she thought.

Something moved behind the bar—a bottle clinking against another—and she turned. Ovelia did not move toward the source of the sound, however: somehow she knew to defend herself against an attack from the opposite direction, and she stepped toward the noise and stooped low. She ducked a sword that slashed through the air where her throat had been and staggered back toward the door. A frustrated hiss of air cut her off, and she danced aside as a blade shot past and stabbed into the door jam. Ovelia tried the latch anyway, but found it stuck. Without a better option, she whirled and fell into a defensive stance.

Her attacker snaked toward her, limping in a familiar, curious pattern. He moved cautiously, seemingly unnerved after her inexplicable dodge. She recognized Tithian Davargorn by the coursing blue light that limned his bones through his flesh, pulsing brightly in her world of shadows. His face as well she could dimly perceive, attesting to his hostile intent—and the hooked falcat in his hand.

"How?" he asked. "How does a blind woman elude me?"

Ovelia wished she knew. She didn't even have Draca's shadows to guide her. "You do not frighten me, boy," she said, hoping she believed him. "Stand aside."

"No," he said. "She promised me a hundred-count, and I intend to use all hundred."

"She?"

Then Davargorn was on her, falcat flashing for her throat. She managed to catch his sword on the long knife, deflecting the slash harmlessly high, but the force of his cut knocked the blade ringing from her hands. She stumbled away, cut foot screaming in agony, and plucked up a stool to keep him at bay. Davargorn cut at her, but she caught the falcat in the legs of the stool and twisted it out of his hand.

The slayer cursed and fell back a step, his mismatched eyes glowing with rage. Another weapon appeared in his hand, one so powerfully ensorcelled that it practically burned Ovelia's unseeing eyes. It looked as though he'd drawn a bloody red star of light.

"Vhaerynn's dagger," Ovelia said. "You took that from Garin's study. You—this was your plan all along. Join Summer Lives only to betray us?"

He lunged at her, and she barely caught his arm in both hands, holding the dagger a scant thumb's breadth from her cheek. She knew the danger of that fell blade: even if she had never seen it enact its horrific powers, she could somehow see it clearly in her mind. A single scratch of that golden steel and she would perish in terrible pain.

And so they fought, muscle to muscle, Davargorn's cold against Ovelia's panic. He drove the blade down and she pushed it away with all her nigh-extinguished might, locking the weapon between them. She was far the stronger, but while she'd spent hours emptying her strength, Davargorn was all but fresh. He put both arms to the task of driving the blade in, and it was slowly sinking toward her face. She could not hold him back forever.

Ovelia took a chance.

She dropped one hand from his arms, and slammed her fist into his ribs. He wore boiled leather, but that would only muffle a punch, not stop it. Davargorn grunted at the impact, and she felt his body shiver. He still pressed down, but his strength had lessened. She hit him again and again, and finally his strength all but vanished. He drew back the blade and attempted some sort of flourish, but Ovelia had expected that. She put both feet under his chest and launched him back to dance awkwardly onto one of the tables. There he crouched, blade held wide, while Ovelia struggled to her feet.

"What madness passes?" she asked. "The city is at war. Luether burns around you. And you stay to fight *me?*" She shook her head. "Do you hate me that much?"

"You," Davargorn said. "Semana. Regel. The Ravalis. *Every* Ravalis."

"Well, not *every* Ravalis," someone said from behind the bar. Perched atop it, Ovelia thought. "Some of us you love quite vigorously, Tithian."

Ovelia could not see the speaker—not even the shadowy outline she detected around most people. She moved so quietly that she might as well not have existed. And that gave Ovelia the clue she needed to identify her. "Lis," she said.

"*Alistra,* rather," she said, stepping closer. "Alistra Ravalis, sister to King Lan, cousin to Prince Garin." She paused a moment. "You don't seem surprised."

"Should I be?" Ovelia shrugged. She knew only a little of Demetrus's notorious, mad daughter. She'd seen Alistra only once, during Lenalin's first visit to Luether, and then only at a distance. She'd heard that the Ravalis locked her up shortly afterward, and nothing of her since. "Why do you pass here? I'd assumed you'd long since died in the dark."

"Alas, no," Alistra said. "My father might have hated me, but blood is blood. In time, I proved useful, and my horrid little brother set me loose like a hound to hunt down and slay his enemies."

"Me," Ovelia said.

"Garin, actually," Alistra said. "You were just the lure for my pet, there. Lan promised he'd get to kill you if he accompanied us to Luether. Oh how he *loathes* you."

325

Davargorn made a threatening sound in his throat. He grew more substantial in Ovelia's shadowy world, and she could practically see his lust to kill her. Had she held Draca, she suspected it would have shown her dying a dozen grisly deaths at the lad's gnarled hands.

"Hold no worries, though," Alistra said. "He will attack only when I loose him."

She had moved closer, Ovelia realized, because a blade reached across and laid itself on the hollow between Ovelia's neck and shoulder. She could see neither the weapon nor the one holding it, and she did her best to remain calm.

"You said 'us,' no?" Ovelia glanced at the burning crimson magic in Davargorn's hand. "You mean Vhaerynn. That's why your hound carries that dagger."

"Reasoned that out so quickly, did you?" Alistra asked. "I see your mind is your finest feature. Though I'm told these are spectacular as well." A cool, strong hand cupped one of Ovelia's breasts, then squeezed the other. "Hmm."

Ovelia raised her chin. "So you are Lan's dog, and Davargorn is yours." She nodded at the enraged slayer. "Why stay him? Even without your blade at my throat, I am all but defenseless and bleeding. And before, on Fersi's ship—I was helpless then as well. Why not do what you came to do?"

She could not see it, but Ovelia could practically hear Alistra smile widely. "Because blood is blood," she said, turning the sword over so that Ovelia felt its sharp edge briefly, then the cold flat of the other side. "And I hear congratulations are in order."

A sharp-edged hole appeared in Ovelia's gut, sucking breath and blood from the rest of her body. "Garin," she said. "Why?"

"Your husband is the only one of my Blood who ever loved me," Alistra said. "The rest of Ravalis insulted me, spat on me, ignored me, or locked me away, and they will all pay for their crimes against me. But Garin was ever my friend, perverse little coward that he is."

"And yet you came to Luether to slay Garin," Ovelia said.

"Did I?" Alistra asked.

At first, Ovelia didn't understand. Then it dawned on her. "No, you did not," she said. "You came to overthrow Luether, just as he did. But instead of joining him openly, you aided him against Pervast from the shadows, playing them against each other to the death—leaving only you to unite the broken city." She clenched her fists. "You want to rule in his place."

"Just so," Alistra said. "With one correction: had Garin's quest succeeded, and he ascended to the throne, I would have gladly knelt at his feet and followed him. But that is not what has passed. A shame, but blood is blood, and a Ravalis must rule Luether."

Davargorn loosed a low growl, like an angry dog, but Alistra snapped her fingers to silence him.

"You would choose your Blood over Garin?" Ovelia asked. "You claimed to hate them. That you would punish them for their crimes against you."

"Oh I do, and I will." Alistra said. "But your man-loving husband is not blameless in my broken life. I gave everything to aid Garin once, and he did nothing in return. I consider his fall and my inaction the discharge of our debt."

"You will not help him?"

"No," Alistra said. "But you might."

"What do you mean?"

"Pervast is coming here—you and Garin have seen to that, by showing her my cousin's little war machine in the catacombs," she said. "I suspect they'll arrive any moment now. So you have a choice to make, and quickly. Will you aid him, or will you attempt to punish me for my own choice?"

"I cannot do both, I suppose," Ovelia said.

"I said *attempt*," Alistra said. "Even if you do manage to overcome me and my dog, you will be in no condition to fight Pervast and her minions. Let me go unmolested, and you might have a chance."

"Look at me," Ovelia said. "I am nigh-dead already."

"My cousin is such a clever little chemic," Alistra said. "I'm sure you could find something here to aid you. But if you have to fight now?" She made a series of sharp clicking noises against her teeth. "The odds lengthen against you."

She was right, of course. If Alistra left her in peace, Ovelia might find a potion like the one Garin had taken, which had let him speak and move despite horrific injuries. But that meant turning her back on Alistra's crimes. Perhaps...

"Time to choose," Alistra said.

"Come with me," Ovelia asked. "You do not have to do this. You can be better than this."

"Perhaps," Alistra said. The blade lifted from Ovelia's shoulder. "Farewell, Prince's Shield. May Ruin turn her gaze from your steps."

"Wait—" Ovelia lunged to catch Alistra, but the woman eluded her. Pain raged from her foot, and she collapsed to one knee. Her guts felt like expelling themselves, and she barely held them in.

"Tithian," Alistra said.

The glowing slayer stood over Ovelia, burning with rage and magic. He kept his silence but she could read his thoughts in his glare. Finally, he moved away, reclaimed his fallen sword, and walked out of the Long Dawn. Unseen, Alistra followed behind him.

"You have your duty, and I have mine," she said from the door. "Ours is a horrid, disgusting Blood, but it is mine. And I will not forsake it."

Then she was gone, leaving Ovelia dizzy and coughing on the common room floor.

~

They made it halfway to the lift back to High-City before Davargorn stopped, unable to take one more step. He stood beneath a frayed awning on the porch of a building that had once been a café of some sort. Lightning and shrapnel rained down around them, and a nearby building erupted in flame. Between cobbled streets strewn with rubble and spattered with blood to torn bodies hanging amongst twisted machinery thrown down from the battle, the already damaged city had become an even harsher caricature of itself. The devastation was enough to cause even a hardened veteran to panic. Through that maze of death and horror they made their way, but ultimately Davargorn could not continue for another purpose—one that had nothing to do with his nerves.

Alistra paused, realizing that he no longer followed her, and looked back. Her expression mingled lust, disappointment, and understanding all in one look. "You need to go back," she said.

He nodded.

She stepped toward him, her black robe flowing around her muscular legs like smoke. Embers drifted over her shoulders, sticking to her bald head like the hair Davargorn had watched Lan burn away. *Fearless* was his word for her, and *invincible*. Now, at the height of her power, as the city crumbled to rubble and ashes around Alistra, it seemed impossible that Davargorn might deny her anything. And yet.

"Ovelia Dracaris." Alistra shook her head. "Does your hatred mean so much to you?"

"It does." Davargorn nodded once more.

"More than me."

She had not needed to ask. She knew the truth, even if Davargorn himself could not have answered. He shrugged. "This is my choice," he said. "I swore I would slay that woman, and I must."

Alistra raised her chin and looked at him for the first time with something like respect. "Then here we part ways," she said. "I will not say I expected more of you, for it would be a lie. *Hoped*, perhaps, but—ah. Burn it all."

She grasped Davargorn roughly by the shoulders and pressed her lips to his. They kissed roughly, and he could feel her teeth on his lips and on his tongue.

Her clawed hands scratched at the leather of his hauberk and she wrapped one leg around his waist. When she pulled away at length, she shoved him hard enough that he fell on his hindquarters in the dust and grime. She stood over him, her expression turned to one of unbridled rage.

"You have made your choice," she said. "I do not think you will survive this, but even if you do, do not seek me out. We are ended, you and I." Alistra disappeared into the smoke.

Davargorn nodded. He had expected no less.

He climbed to his feet and checked the falcat sheathed at his right hip, balanced against Vhaerynn's dagger sheathed on his left. Then he picked his way back down the embattled street.

THIRTY-SIX

THE WORLD SHOOK, AND awareness rushed back in. Ovelia realized she must have slept, and she had no way of knowing how long. The common room stood empty so far as she could tell, and she wondered what had woke her. Her body felt thick, swollen to bursting with bloody sludge that gurgled deep inside for release. Ovelia vomited onto the floorboards, and at least her insides stopped hurting quite as much. Every inch of her skin felt chapped or abraded or both, her muscles had become wet sacks of flour, and her body wanted nothing more than to go back to sleep in her own sick.

Ovelia might have done so, but a heavy blow made the world shake. She scrambled back against the wall, like a sick child terrified of a noise, and cast her muddy senses around the common room.

The sound came again—three pounding bursts this time—and this time Ovelia ascertained its origin: the opposite side of the wall against which she leaned. She sat near the doors to the raised, private chamber, and something pounded on the doors from inside. Shakily and with the aid of the wall, she climbed to her feet and felt at the handles, which were secured with a cold length of metal pipe. Whoever was locked in there, at least they could not get at her.

The doors caved outward slightly under another heavy blow, and she heard an angry grunt from within—one that stayed her. She opened her mouth, then thought better of it. No one would hear her.

Again the doors shook, and Ovelia replied with a swat of her own. There was a pause, then a muffled voice asked a question. She put both hands against the door and leaned against it for a moment to catch her breath, then felt at the pipe stuck through the handles. The bashing had wedged it particularly tight, almost fusing it into the wood at one end, but she managed to wrench it free with the last of her strength. She stepped back, let the pipe clatter to the floor, and slumped down to one knee, breathing hard.

The doors burst open, admitting two amorphous figures she nonetheless knew well. One was big and filled with hot, red rage, while the other was wiry and filled with cold fury. A pair of muscular arms crushed her into a burly chest. Ovelia could hardly breathe, but for the first time in what felt like days, she actually felt safe.

"By the Fire, wench, you look horrid." Red Jeggs held her away long enough to look her over. "What's happened? Where are your clothes?" Then he pulled her back to himself.

Ovelia shook her head. It was too much, and there was no time. "Coming," she said. "Pervast—"

"Leave off," said Alcarin, who stepped up behind Red Jeggs. "Can't you see she's wounded?"

The hulking warrior's embrace suddenly grew tentative—surprisingly gentle, as though Ovelia had become a glass sculpture that could fall and shatter on the floor. Another day, she might have corrected him, but not this day. Indeed, she wondered if she fell whether she would be able to rise again. Alcarin took her from Red Jeggs, and she leaned on his slim shoulder.

"What do you need?" Red Jeggs asked Alcarin.

"Garin's study," Alcarin said. "False stone behind the headboard. Satchel. Bring it. Quickly."

Red Jeggs grunted in reply and was gone. Alcarin helped Ovelia to a nearby bench, where she sat against the wall and heaved for breath. Each time she coughed, Ovelia felt two distinct stabbing pains in her chest. At least she could see Alcarin well enough—he'd always been easy for her to see, but usually she'd had Draca at hand. Now he seemed almost clearer without the lost sword.

"How bad?" Ovelia asked.

"Not good, certainly," Alcarin said. "I can only see surface damage. That foot is bad—almost black. You're covered in bruises. You need half a dozen curatives: a stypic, maybe some sweetsoul—"

"*No*," Ovelia insisted, even though every part of her craved the poison.

For once, Alcarin did not argue with her. "Tell me how you feel," he said. "What hurts?"

"Everything."

"I wager it does," Alcarin said. "Garin hides a healing pack for emergencies. The barbarians that torched the Dawn probably looted his room, but they wouldn't have found that." He sounded like he was trying to convince both of them.

"Did...did you fight them?" Ovelia asked.

Alcarin shook his head, which she could dimly see. "No," he said. "They struck before we got here. I saw the bodies—Biaza. Neblen. A score of others." He growled in frustration and anger.

"How long?" Ovelia asked.

"Just this morn." Alcarin prodded her bleeding foot, making Ovelia wince. "Lis and that ugly slayer...they brought us and locked us in that room. Never said a word."

"This is Alistra's play," Ovelia said. "She knew Vilaer would come here for *Hekatomb*. She left you here to help me stop her."

331

"Vilaer?" Alcarin frowned as he worked. "What does she have to do with this?"

"She's Pervast," Ovelia said. "It's…it's hard to explain, but—"

"No." Alcarin put a finger to her lips. "That makes a foolish sort of sense. I knew we shouldn't have trusted her, but Garin…" He uttered a curse. "No sense worrying about it just now. What did you do to this foot? Is this—is this *mage-glass*? You walked here barefoot?"

Ovelia offered a non-committal shrug. "I had no choice."

Alcarin nodded. He understood. "You took a risk opening those doors. If we'd been Children—"

"I knew it was you," Ovelia said. "Red Jeggs has a…memorable grunt."

Alcarin loosed a short burst of laughter that seemed terribly out of place, but Ovelia welcomed it. Then she coughed, and blood leaked over her lips. The mirth died immediately, and she could feel Alcarin's sudden fear.

"You're bleeding inside," he said. "Burn it all, where's Jeggs?" He shouted back down the corridor, then growled in frustration. He laid his hand on Ovelia's forehead. "Was it too much to ask for you to bring Garin with you? He'd know exactly what to do."

"Garin," Ovelia managed to say. "I have…have to tell you…"

"Gird up and wait for Jeggs," Alcarin said. "You've come this far—wait a bit longer."

"I'm…I'm sorry," Ovelia said.

"It's not for you. If you talk yourself to death before aid arrives, then I'll never know." Alcarin looked away. "Just one thing," he said. "Is he alive?"

"I don't know," she said. "I…I think so."

Alcarin's eyes blazed like stars in her vision. "Then there's hope," he said. "The rest can wait."

The world started to blur as they waited, seeming to float around her. Everything seemed lighter, and the pain eased. Alcarin shouted again, though Ovelia couldn't say if he directed the harsh words at Jeggs or at her.

Sitting there with Alcarin, Ovelia found herself more comfortable than she could remember ever feeling. In the back of her mind, a woman's voice urged her to speak up—to tell Alcarin something—but she couldn't keep track of what had passed. She could just…

～

The world burned around her, but it brought her no pain. Rather, she felt only comforting warmth that lulled her as she knelt in the dark chamber. Before her, she glimpsed the wall of silver fire raging just out of reach, and she realized for the first time that she was home. This was where she was meant to be: after her long journey, she had well earned this rest.

A figure emerged from the inferno: a woman clad in black flames from head to foot, crisping away at the fringes into gray and finally silver. The flames were consuming her, Ovelia realized, and it made her distantly sad. The woman stood over her and burned.

"So you will surrender," the woman said. "You do not have the strength to go on."

"All is lost, Lena," she said. "There is nothing—"

Suddenly, the woman tore back her hood, sending a halo of silvery-blonde hair tumbling around her head. It flicked away into flame at the ends. The princess's eyes blazed down at Ovelia. "Do you love me no longer?" The words cut Ovelia to the bone. "Will you abandon me?"

Ovelia felt tears in her eyes. "Please," she said. "Do not ask this of me. I can do no more."

Lenalin extended a hand toward her, and Ovelia found herself reaching for the black-sheathed fingers. If only she could touch her beloved, she knew she would be free. Their fingers almost touched.

"Wake up," Lenalin said.

"What?"

The black-wrapped hand seized Ovelia's wrist with a grip like steel. The other hand caught her other wrist and the princess wrenched her arms unnaturally up, where she transferred the grip into the same hand. Pain exploded through Ovelia's body, and the flames were suddenly hot all around her. Lenalin's face had become a skull and her eyes vanished into infinite darkness.

"Wake," she said, her free hand cupping Ovelia's chin. "Up."

THIRTY-SEVEN

W AKE UP!"

Ovelia's eyes went wide, and she thought for a second that she saw a woman made of fire holding her arms against the wall. She realized, belatedly, that it was Alcarin who was shouting in her face, urging her to drink the vial he pressed to her lips. She saw everything—her allies, her attackers, the common room of the Long Dawn. She saw without seeing. She had no time to question how, nor anyone to ask.

"Ovelia!" Alcarin cried. "We need you! We need—"

Past the lad, Ovelia saw shadowy forms weaving and dancing in battle: two barbarians expertly cutting apart Red Jeggs as he stood against both of them. He roared and fought on with impressive strength and stamina, but Ovelia could tell at a glance that he could not triumph. Beyond them, four others stepped into the doorway: Vilaer, Lady Shard, another barbarian escort, and a bloody mess Ovelia immediately recognized as Garin. She would know his shadow anywhere.

"By the Fire." Alcarin shook at the sight of his master. "Garin!"

Unexpectedly, Alcarin released her and rushed into the fray, leaving Ovelia to slump to the side. She bobbled the vial, which plinked off the wall and rolled onto the stained floorboards. She lurched for it, but her clumsy fingers only knocked it rolling. The pain was transcendent. Chunks of her body felt like they would separate from each other, leaving her a broken mess on the floor.

Out in the common room, Red Jeggs had downed one of his attackers and roared in pain and fury as his axe hacked at the Child of Ruin that Vilaer had called Stares Coldly at Death. The barbarian slipped nimbly around the man's mighty blows, moving more like a snake than a man. He eluded each attack fiercely, reaching out with almost casual ease to cut open the big man's arm or his back. Soon enough, Red Jeggs collapsed to one knee under the blood loss, and the axe skittered from his nerveless hands. The barbarian strolled in easy circles around him, holding him down under the weight of those dead eyes.

Foot exploding in pain under her, Ovelia slipped down to the floor and swept her trembling fingers around for the vial. She had seen Garin use such chemics before, and if it could revive her even for a few moments, she might be able to turn the battle. She felt a wet spot where it was spilling out, and caught the tiny vial. When she raised it to her lips, however, her fingers shook badly she could not drink what was left in the vial. She cursed by the Narfire.

Alcarin fared little better. Fighting in a whirling, lunging hurricane, She Draws Blood warded off his sword with her clawed fingers and long blade-hair. Whenever Alcarin came close to breaking through her ceaseless offense, she slashed open his arm with half a dozen tiny cuts as casually as running her fingers through a stream. Soon, his sleeve was soaked in red, as befitted her name. Alcarin kept crying out for Garin, and Ovelia thought it was the only reason he kept moving at all.

Finally, Ovelia popped the stopper off the vial and downed it in a single go. It hit her tongue with a sharp, bitter tang and filled her stomach with angry fire. She coughed so hard she expected to expel her guts on the spot. Through force of will, she suppressed the urge to vomit, fighting to keep the chemic down. She could feel it working inside her, washing the pain away slowly. So slowly.

Sweetsoul. By the Fire, she wanted sweetsoul. Needed it so very, very badly.

Across the room, Vilaer stood in her blood-spattered gown, arms crossed, with a triumphant smirk on her face. And at her side stood Lady Shard, her black cloak hanging lifelessly from her angular body. Belted at the veiled woman's waist, Ovelia perceived Draca, its shadows too far to be of any use. At their feet, Garin drooled blood onto the floor. He was dying, just as Ovelia was.

"Get up," she told herself, or was that Lenalin's voice? "Get. *Up.*"

"Come." Vilaer shoved the bloody mass of Garin toward the back of the common room. "My warders will dispense with this rabble." When Shard hesitated, the Queen of Luether looked back with irritation. "*Now.*"

The pirate queen was staring at Ovelia, and somehow she lent strength through that gaze. Or else the chemic was doing its work. Red Jeggs's axe lay close to hand, and Ovelia reached for it.

A casterbolt exploded into the floor, shattering the haft of the axe and nearly taking her fingers with it. That cast should have destroyed her hand, but somehow she'd known to flinch at the last instant.

Ovelia looked up. Tithian Davargorn strode through the chamber, smoking caster in one hand and heavily ensorcelled golden dagger in the other. She Draws Blood turned, startled at his sudden arrival, and hissed a challenge at him. Davargorn smoothly eluded her slashing talons and raked the golden dagger across her upper arm, turning it to gray mold. The corruption spread across her like wood burning to ash, and she crumbled to nothing over a gasping Alcarin. The other barbarian stayed back, sparing Red Jeggs a killing blow while he watched.

"Bloodbreaker!" Davargorn roared.

He would not be swayed or slowed. He was death—Ovelia's and that of anyone who stood in his way. Ovelia saw no escape, and yet her mind was calm. She knew without knowing what would come to pass, and opened her hand wide toward Davargorn.

The ugly lad smiled disjointedly. "Die begging me if you like, whore," he said. "You still die—"

Metal skittered across the floorboards in a wave of sparks and smoke and Ovelia snatched Draca just in time to plunge it up into Davargorn's belly. The lad jerked taut, mismatched eyes wide in surprise.

"What?" Vilaer rounded on the pirate queen. "*You?*"

"Yes." Shard rose from where she had slid the sword to Ovelia. As she moved, she drew a curved dagger from under her robes and pointed it at Vilaer. "Me."

She stepped toward Vilaer and Garin, but Stares Coldly disengaged from his stalking circle and moved to intercept her. The Ruin Queen gave Shard a withering look and gestured to her warder to kill the woman. Then Vilaer hurried toward the back of the tavern, Garin in tow.

Davargorn fought off his shock and snarled at Ovelia, blood running down from his mouth. He slashed at her ineffectually with the golden dagger; the sword kept him at too great a distance. The deadly magic of the blade snapped and sparked off Draca's crossbar, just a thumb's breadth from Ovelia's blood-slick hand.

"Kill you," he said. "Kill you!"

Davargorn unleashed a sucking roar and forced himself further down the blade toward Ovelia, blood welling around him. She caught his wrist, but in her weakened state she could hardly hold him back for long. The blade angled toward her arm, where just the tiniest cut would prove fatal. She gritted her teeth and put all her strength against him. The curative was helping, but not fast enough.

Then Alcarin was there, seizing Davargorn about the shoulders. He pulled back on the slayer's arm, giving Ovelia that extra bit of strength she needed. She twisted the golden dagger out of line and let it stab into the floor beside her even as she drove Draca upward, into, and through Davargorn. The slayer's eyes bugged and he sagged around the blade, blood bubbling out around its length. The fight went out of Davargorn's body, the dagger clattered from his hand, and he collapsed against Ovelia in a grotesque caricature of a child upon its mother's breast.

For a moment, Ovelia lay stunned, unable to do anything but cradle the boy's body atop her. Then she realized Alcarin was shouting at her. Shard had engaged the barbarian, and they wove an elaborate dance of steel and blood around each other. Alcarin himself, bleeding from a dozen wounds, hardly seemed able to stand. He pointed toward the entrance to the tunnels, where Vilaer must have taken Garin.

Toward *Hekatomb*.

"Go!" Alcarin was saying. "Go!"

Get up, Ovelia told herself.

She did.

THIRTY-EIGHT

The tunnels under the Long Dawn fell away into their own world beneath the city, but it was one that could not truly escape the chaos above. Distant explosions shook the sewers, and more than once Ovelia had to catch her footing to keep upright. The huddled folk in their filthy cloaks scattered in all directions, like birds fleeing a hound that bursts into their midst. In one hand, Ovelia held the blood-slick Draca, while the other traced the dark stone with weak fingers. The heat of the sewers was oppressive, making her want to shed the tattered cloak Shard had given her. Ovelia kept it, somehow sure it would prove not only useful but necessary.

Navigating the sewers was much easier now that she could see once more, even if she could not explain how. The world flashed before her sightless eyes, fleeting and emphasizing those things that most mattered: threats, hazards, and opportunities. More than once, she ducked into an alcove or hollow of stone just as a group of barbarians thundered past. The invasion had come in earnest, it seemed, and everywhere the sounds of fighting drowned out the cries of the wounded and terrified.

It occurred to Ovelia to wonder how she knew intuitively when would-be dangers arose, but she had to focus on Vilaer and Garin. Through Draca's magic, she had seen *Hekatomb* in a way Garin didn't even understand it. Its destructive potential far exceeded anything the World of Ruin had ever known. If Vilaer activated and controlled that sort of weapon…

There, she saw the concealed door to Garin's workshop, slightly ajar and waiting.

Ovelia strode forward, then hesitated as something sweet caught her nose. There it was, placed on a stone walkway beside a river of sewer filth: a leathern pouch, its drawstring slackened to open it wide. She didn't need to taste the contents to know them. *Sweetsoul.* A whole pouch of it, like the one she and Vilaer had consumed as they lay in bed together.

Immediately, Ovelia's world stopped. Her body *yearned* for it, with a need that threatened to pull her apart. It all came rushing back: her doubts, her fears, her self-hatred. She wanted to throw herself down and consume all of it in one rush. She wanted to drown herself in the sewer. She wanted—

She must have been staring down at the sweetsoul for some time, because she was no longer alone. Half a dozen huddled figures had appeared in the nearby sewer, seemingly from side passages and holes in the stone. Their faces were gaunt and stretched, eyes deeply shadowed, and their mouths lacked most of their teeth—all signs of sweetsoul addiction. They pulled up short, watching her with glassy eyes from the shadows, their bodies trembling with longing. Ovelia realized she was holding the pouch in her free hand, balanced atop her palm. She held Draca loosely in her other hand, and it must have been the simmering flames that kept the hungry wretches at bay. If she dropped the sword, they would fall upon her like a swarm, consuming it and her with equal abandon.

Ovelia turned her wrist, slowly letting the powder slide from the pouch and onto her hand. She almost thought she could taste it through her skin, which grew almost painfully hot on contact. A shudder passed through her body and she tried hard to suppress it. It was so beautiful—so delicious. It promised fulfillment and pleasure beyond all imagining. She forgot everything: why she had come this way—what drew her on. She forgot the world itself.

Then she heard a cry of pain from somewhere in the tunnels up ahead, and she recognized Garin's voice. It grounded her, drawing her back to the world from which the sweetsoul had lured her.

She realized the sewer folk had approached closer, lurking just beyond her reach. She hefted Draca, which burned with warning shadows, and they fell back with a chorus of hisses and gibbering pleas. She had bought herself a moment, but she knew their desire would soon overcome their fear of her blade and they would come for her.

Through sheer force of will, Ovelia cast the sweetsoul down, letting it shower across the stone floor and into the flowing muck of the sewer. The silvery white rain was beautiful and terrible, and Ovelia felt a hollow pang to see it. Even as it fell, she turned her face and moved on, unable to bear the sight.

She paused on the threshold to Garin's workshop as a terrible sound caught her ear. Behind her, the sewer folk had fallen upon the mess on the disgusting floor and floating on the flow of refuse. In desperation, their grayish tongues lapped at the powder, and a couple drank the sewer water.

Ovelia turned away, her stomach churning.

ᖰ

As dust rained from the cavern ceiling above, *Hekatomb* floated among the rising fumes of the Narfire below, a purring engine of destruction waiting to be given its lead. Thaumaturgical magic flowed around its graceful lines and crackled around its masthead. Now that she had regained her vision somehow, she could perceive the figure: an angel neither male nor female but a perfect, sinuous union of the two. Its sword, flamed like Draca, stabbed forward with enough strength to pierce stone or steel.

339

Vilaer stood on the stone dock before the figurehead, flicking blood onto the ship from a wavy dagger in her hand. Garin knelt at her feet, and if he had not been all but dead before, he looked it now. Stripped to his waist, his skin had gone the white of spoiled cream. Furious red gashes covered his face, chest, and neck—none of them deep enough to kill, all more than sufficient to torment any sane man. Clearly, Vilaer wanted each cut to hurt—to delay killing Garin as long as possible. Each droplet of blood struck Hekatomb's prow and crackled with lightning, empowering the skyship. The ritual required only a moment, but Vilaer had taken her time, savoring every tiny sensation of her impending victory.

On the ruins of Garin's face, Ovelia expected to see terror or pain but instead found a tragic sort of resolution. This would be his fate, and he could not change it.

Ovelia, on the other hand, knew that *she* could.

"Pervast!" she cried.

Vilaer looked up from her gory work. Her blood-spattered expression went from annoyance to amusement to delight. "Fitting," she said. "That you should be here to see this."

Ovelia stepped forward, and Vilaer raised a caster to point at her. Only five paces separated them, and Vilaer could hardly miss at such a range. Ovelia lowered Draca but did not relinquish the sword.

"You planned this," Ovelia said. "From the beginning?"

"It is amusing." Vilaer smiled. "It was pure chance that when Garin came to Tuerine, I was observing the barbarians at work, and I saw an opportunity."

The Ruin Queen stepped toward Ovelia, cutting the distance between them to just over three paces. Behind her, Garin sighed and slumped onto his haunches.

"Those wounds." Ovelia nodded to Vilaer's bare arms, livid with mostly healed cuts from the wounds upon her at the Mines of Tuerine. "You inflicted those on yourself. To sway his sympathies."

"To stir his heart," Vilaer said. "At first, I only wanted to undermine and destroy him, but I realized that his new path, to unite barbarians and Luethaar? It is wisdom."

"But only with you beside him," Ovelia said. "As queen—rescued from the horrors of Pervast."

"A beautiful tale, no? Too bad it was not to be." Vilaer sighed. "The would-be king turned out to be a perversion of nature, and I could not suffer such a...*thing* to touch me." She shuddered. "I will do much for my city, but there are depths to which even I cannot stoop."

340

"But not mine, it seems." Ovelia shook her head at the insanity. "You would lie with me—a woman—and yet condemn him?" She pointed to Garin. "Do you have no love in your heart?"

Vilaer stood up to her full height and a disgusted scowl twisted her face. "Stupid, blind whore," she said. "I never loved *you*. I only shared your bed because I had a use for you—to win Garin's trust by rutting my way to yours." She hefted the caster. "No longer."

"Who are you trying to convince?" Ovelia asked. "Me, or yourself?"

"What?" The caster shook in Vilaer's hands. "You are as much a perversion as the Fox. Every second you touched me *disgusted* me. I will carry your stench to the end of my days."

"I am sorry you feel that way." Ovelia raised her chin and hefted Draca like a shield. The flames boiled forth, warning of her coming, unavoidable death. At such a range, she could not dodge the bolt that Vilaer would cast. Then the flames stopped, their purpose fulfilled. "And I forgive you."

"*You* forgive *me?*" Vilaer squeezed the caster's trigger. "I will spit on your corpse."

A mighty *crack* split the air, resounding around the chamber. The bolt sailed toward Ovelia's heart, and time itself seemed to stretch to a halt. Ovelia's hair wafted in Narfire-stirred air, and she breathed in. She watched its flight, seeing the world as it truly passed.

She snapped Draca across and cut the casterbolt from the air.

A fragment of metal rang off the stone at Ovelia's feet, and a shard of casterbolt imbedded itself in the wall. She felt where it had cut along her arm, leaving a deep scratch in her skin. She breathed out a low, peaceful sigh. She set Draca down, and it glimmered dully on the stone. She had no further need of it just now.

"What?" Vilaer asked, her eyes wide. She lowered the caster, and it clattered to the floor. "I don't—" She coughed, and blood flowed over her lips. She touched her stomach, where most of the casterbolt had lodged itself. "I don't understand—"

The Vultara princess faltered, and Ovelia caught her before she collapsed to the floor. She cradled Vilaer's body in her arms and cupped her head in her hands. The Ruin Queen felt so small and fragile.

"Pass well," Ovelia said, her voice shaking. She touched Vilaer's forehead. "Pass well."

Vilaer looked bewildered, heaving for breath that came only in spurts of blood. There was no anger or madness in her eyes now—only pain and sorrow. "Utora," she said, growing pale. "Sister—"

Then Vilaer coughed and died.

Ovelia held her a moment longer. Tears streamed down her face, but she could not credit them. She hugged Vilaer's corpse to her chest.

"You…" Garin managed to sit up, and his cough sent red into the air. "You are crying."

Ovelia shook her head at him. "I don't know why," she said. "She was a traitor. A murderer. A butcher of your people. She hated me and you—hated the world. Why would I mourn her?"

"No."

Lady Shard stepped out of the darkness behind them, her black cloak swirling in the rising heat of the Narfire. She held Vhaerynn's golden dagger in her hand—a war trophy and a threat.

"You do not mourn her," Shard said to Ovelia. "You mourn *yourself*."

Ovelia wanted to reply, but she could not think of the words. Instead she merely laid Vilaer down and stooped to reclaim Draca. The sword gleamed, its shadows restless.

Alcarin appeared from behind Shard, looking haggard and bruised but whole. His eyes widened when he saw the bloody ruin of Garin, and he staggered past Ovelia to throw his arms around his master.

"Don't—" Garin coughed. "Don't look at me. I'm hideous."

"You burning idiot," Alcarin said, covering Garin's face with kisses. "You were always hideous."

The Fox of Luether chuckled dryly and leaned his head against Alcarin's shoulder. It might have been sweet, had Ovelia not known what would befall. Garin had lost too much blood, and the only reason he lived now was the curative potions Vilaer had stuffed down his throat. When those wore off…

Her heart lightened even as tears welled in her eyes, Ovelia turned back toward Shard. "You—"

A battered form loomed out of the tunnel, curved sword raised high and gleaming over Shard's unsuspecting back.

Without hesitation, Ovelia drew back and hurled Draca end over end to bloom in Davargorn's chest. The slayer faltered, the sword tumbling from his hands, and Ovelia met him in a rush. She hit him with a leaping left hook that should have shattered his jaw, but he managed to turn enough to catch it on the shoulder. She bounced to her feet and led in with a right cross, but Davargorn's club foot shot out and hit her square in the chest, knocking her staggering back. The two of them, battered and exhausted, circled one another, only two paces separating them. Ovelia's burning sword studded Davargorn's chest like a hot poker thrust through a burning log.

"You," Davargorn said. "I left her for you. I'll be burned before I let you live."

Ovelia wondered if he meant Semana or Alistra. Both, probably. "You left her for *you*," she said, holding out a staying hand behind her toward Shard. "And you won't be 'letting' me do anything."

"No?" Davargorn put his hands on the hilt of Draca and wrenched it out. Blood poured forth, but Ovelia could see his magic restoring his flesh. He hefted the sword. "We'll see."

Ovelia smiled slightly. She had already seen it.

He came at her, Draca hacking a fiery swath down through the air. Grasping the fringes of her cloak, Ovelia twisted inside his slash, letting Draca miss her head close enough to slice free a trail of red hairs. She wrapped one arm back around his neck, plastering the cloak to Davargorn's body. He flailed and drove forward, just as she had foreseen, and she whirled around him to draw the cloak tight, locking his arms against his body. She let loose the cloak, leaving him enwrapped and blinded, and moved around him so that he was between her and the edge of the cliff.

Draca slashed wildly at her, but she caught the hilt in one hand and slammed her free fist into the lad's wrist, breaking his grip. Ovelia tossed Draca down and crouched, putting all her weight into her legs. With an expulsion of breath, she exploded upward and slammed into Davaragorn, making him stagger against the fiery void. Ovelia breathed a sigh that was almost sad.

He fought to keep his balance, teetered on the edge, then toppled out over the pit. Ovelia watched him go, his body burning with power as it sought to reknit itself even as he fell to his doom.

Then Ovelia saw another magic rise in the cloak: a bright azure as of a summer sky. As if with a mind of its own, the cloak spread wide like wings and floated on the rising fumes of the Narfire, carrying the limp Davargorn gently downward. Ovelia stared, unable to believe it, until a boiling column of smoke made her recoil. When she looked again, Davargorn had vanished into the smoke and flame.

The cloak. That was how she had survived the fall from High-City. It must have caught her, even senseless, and set her down gently beside the waves. Shard had given her that cloak only the night before.

"You." She turned to Shard, who knelt beside Garin, hand pressed to his wounds. "You saved me. Why?"

"Time presses on." The pirate queen cradled the shuddering prince of Luether, where Alcarin held him. "If you have final words to share, you should do so."

Ovelia knelt beside them and laid her fingers on Garin's cheeks. He coughed more than he breathed, he shook like a terrified child in Shard's arms, and words crept from his mouth in broken whispers. "*Hek—*" he said. "*Hekatomb—*"

"Yes." Ovelia put her forehead against his. "I'll finish what you started. I'll sink it. No fear—"

"If—" Garin coughed up black blood and shook his head dimly. He panted for breath now, his whole body shaking. "If you choose. Or...or you *use* it."

"Garin," Ovelia said. "But you said—"

"Burn what I...what I said." Garin spat up blood over his chin and chest. "I trust you. *Both* of you." He gestured weakly to Shard. "You will save...save Luether. Save...every...one..."

"I...I will."

Ovelia felt Shard tense at her back. Then the pirate queen nodded her assent.

"*We* will," she said. "Both of us."

Garin smiled, his expression distant and wan. "Allie," he said. "You were... every..."

Then his eyes shivered and glazed over. His lungs gave a muted heave, and then a last sigh rattled from his throat.

"Garin?" Alcarin's voice broke. "Gar—?"

He looked up at Ovelia, who shook her head. Alcarin buried his face in Garin's chest and wept.

Ovelia rose and looked at the beautiful instrument of destruction that floated before her. The ceiling of the cavern was collapsing—*Hekatomb* would be destroyed in moments anyway. The great silver rings surrounding the skyship hummed, floating just below and all on a single plane. The skyship was ready for launch, empowered by the Blood of Summer and almost visibly quaking for a chance to wreak ruin upon the invading army, the barbaric usurpers, or the innocent Luethaar of the city. Perhaps all three. It was a weapon, just like Draca or Vhaerynn's golden dagger—it could be wielded by any hand to any end, and only that would give it purpose and meaning.

I am a weapon, Mask had once told Ovelia.

Only now did she understand what the sorcerer had meant.

"You want to destroy it," Shard said at her side.

Ovelia nodded. "I *must* destroy it," she said.

"There is no *must*, dear one," Shard said. "Only what can be done and what cannot. We choose among those things." She touched Ovelia's hand. "What do you choose?"

Ovelia thought for a moment. Her vision had grown dim once more, as though the uncertainty of the future discolored it. She could see only shadows before her, and the fiery power of the *Hekatomb*. She could hear Alcarin weeping over his dead master—her husband and her friend. She could not see Shard, but she could feel the woman's powerful determination.

She squeezed Shard's hand.

THIRTY-NINE

CLAD IN HIS SHINING war armor, Lan Ravalis the Golden King sat upon his throne affixed to the *Avenger*'s command chambers. Captain Hyldir had been kind enough to bequeath the skyship to him—not that she'd had a choice—but since it was still tied to her, she insisted on accompanying him into battle as his second. He might have preferred to throw her into the Dusk Sea as an accomplice to his cousin's treachery, but for now he needed her. After this day, he suspected that would no longer be the case.

Luether was falling easily and efficiently. The armies of Tar Vangr had flown and sailed south in force, blessed with fair winds and surprise. Whatever Garin had been about this last season, his activities had certainly distracted Pervast, leaving the barbarians disorganized and undermanned to repel the invasion. The outer defenses had crumbled first. After that first panicked hour, foot soldiers and war machines rolled through the streets of Low-City and seized the lifts, and smaller skyships dropped Ironclads into High-City to sweep up opposition there. The *Avenger* floated above it all, golden rings buzzing excitedly as they turned in time with the main cannon. The city would fall by dusk.

"Keep firing," Lan said. "Do not relent until all opposition lies in waste."

The crew of the *Avenger* hastened to relay his commands to the various firing teams. Lan had not wanted to destroy Luether had it been preventable, but Lan could not deny a little thrill to watch the destroyed buildings crumble under the blasts of the cannon. Better to destroy and rebuild the homeland of his Blood, cleansing it after the infestation of Ruin-born vermin. If he killed any Luethaar remaining in the city, so be it. He would accomplish what his father never could, whatever the cost.

He wished Vhaerynn had returned with a report, but this would suffice regardless.

When he first heard the rumble, he thought it perhaps cannon fire from another skyship, or that a war machine had found a weapons cache somewhere in the city. He looked out the windows but saw no massive explosion to account for the sound.

"Captain," he said to a pale-faced Hyldir. "What was that?"

She shook her head. "I'm not certain, your Majesty," she said. "The city— it appears to be shaking. We're receiving reports of widespread tremors."

"Fly closer," Lan said.

"Closer? Is that—?" Hyldir swallowed hard when Lan gave her a murderous glare. "Immediately, your Majesty."

Directed by the rings, the *Avenger* fell back and downward through the smoky air until it hovered just outside Low-City and a few hundred feet up. All of Luether trembled, from the spiraling towers to High-City to the foundation forges below. As he watched, cracks ran through the streets and split open buildings just below them. They swept up the support columns that held up the mage-glass of High-City and dislodged a horse-sized chunk of rock that flew at the *Avenger*. It bounced off the golden rings, making the skyship shake and buck.

"What is—?" Lan's eyes widened.

Rising out of a massive courtyard in the city, shattering stone out of its path, was a monstrous war machine of some sort—a *skyship*, he realized. Its silver rings cut the stone out of the way in efficient scything motions, toppling soldiers and war machines alike in its path. It rose, ripping free of the ground like a birthing calf out of a dying heifer. And it came out firing, discharging half a hundred heavy casters and cannon to destroy Ironclad after Ironclad and scatter invading units like so many insects. The ship looked brand new, its metal shining with a dazzling bright luster.

"Majesty, the fleet reports attack on all sides," Hyldir said. "Ships flying the black flag of Shard!"

"Wake the seeing stone!" Lan barked.

The captain swept a hand over the mage-engine control station, and an image of the massive skyship's bridge shimmered to life before them. Standing at the controls was a woman in a full black cloak and veil—Lady Shard, he thought. He had heard her tales, though he had never seen her. And beside her, clad more in dust and blood than clothes, but with her fiery red hair shining in the sunlight...

"*Dracaris!*" Lan's groin roared in pain, and he clutched himself. "Attack! Attack! Kill that ship!"

Hyldir obeyed, and the *Avenger* shot forward, all weapons firing. Most of the casterbolts reflected off the spinning silver rings of the great skyship, though a few penetrated to scar the deck. One even landed close to the bridge, making Ovelia step back slightly. Lan snarled in triumph.

Then Lady Shard raised her hand and pointed directly at the seeing stone sensor. The image blurred and broke apart.

"What?" Lan asked. "What passes?"

"Some sort of disruption field," Hyldir said. "And...she's charging her main! Full retreat!"

"No!" Lan cried. "Stay and fight! *Kill* her!"

Through the window, he saw the angelic figurehead of the mighty skyship crackle with crimson energy. Lightning and smoke surged around it, making its sword glow fiery red.

"Brace!" Hyldir shouted, her voice amplified throughout the skyship. "Brace! Brace!"

A beam of crimson light shot out of the figurehead on the skyship and slammed into the Avenger. It cut right through the protective rings, which broke apart and flew in all directions with shattering force. Massive gold smashed through buildings on all sides, and one section of ring ended up in its own crater in a nearby mountain. The blast cut into the Avenger herself, and Lan watched in horror as the top deck buckled and ripped up into the air. Then they were falling, sliding to the side and down.

Lan heard Hyldir screaming about an impending impact, but he could not understand. He had planned for all of this. He—

The *Avenger* smashed into the ground in a thunderous cloud of smoke and dust.

~

Ovelia watched the devastation as she and Shard rose into the sky in the *Hekatomb*. The invading armies had been repulsed, and Shard's skyships were even now dispatching the rest of Tar Vangr's skyships. Ovelia saw most had been taken more or less intact, but many small, flailing bodies were thrown from the sides as the pirates purged those who would not surrender command. The *Avenger*, Tar Vangr's flagship, lay in smoldering ruin on Luether's south hill, where they had knocked it out of the sky.

But the city was saved, the war ended even as it began.

"You knew this would happen," Ovelia said, wind challenging her words.

"I planned for this possibility, yes," Shard said. "My own army held in reserve until the signal. And this"—she swept her hand around to indicate the *Hekatomb*—"was quite the signal."

Ovelia hung her head. "I should have destroyed this monstrosity."

"Perhaps." Shard glanced at her, face hidden behind the black veil. "But thousands are alive who might have died this day because of you. That is not nothing, dear one."

"I'm not sure it is enough."

They watched the smoke rise from Luether in silence for a moment. Shard steered the *Hekatomb* with an easy, relaxed posture. They climbed to cleaner air, and Ovelia breathed in the peace and calm. The World of Ruin seemed so much less hostile at this distance.

"What passes now?" Ovelia asked.

Shard spoke without looking at her. "What do you mean?"

"To Luether. To me." Ovelia touched the pirate queen's hand. "To us."

"Us?" Lady Shard turned to face her. "Lia—"

"*Us*," Ovelia said. "Did you think I would not know?"

She reached up and took the edges of Shard's veil. The woman trembled but did not resist as Ovelia drew the veil up and away, exposing the pirate queen's face to the air.

"Do not—do not look at me, Tall Sister." Shard looked away. "I am ashamed."

"Be not ashamed," Ovelia said. "We are the people we choose to be, Lena."

Ovelia laid her hands on the woman's cheeks and kissed her.

～

The sun had set before Lan jerked awake again, suspended almost upside down against the wall of the *Avenger* command cabin. At first, he did not recognize his surroundings, but he had only to hear the groan of metal and screams of the dying to start to remember. He hung along the floor, but the world was sideways. What had passed?

On the floor of the cabin, Hyldir lay before and below him, eyes protruding from her face, blood trickling from her mouth. He thought her rude to stare so—as though she wanted him—until he realized the lower half of her body lay crushed under a heavy metal bulkhead.

"Help?" he asked experimentally.

No reply.

Lan tried to move and cursed. His armor might have cushioned him during the crash, but he was still trapped under his broken throne. If he hadn't insisted on bringing the burning thing, this might not have come to pass. He pulled at his pinned leg, which only made him dizzy. The king felt at his head, and his hand came away sticky with blood.

"Burning Dracaris," he said, flicking the blood away to hit the cabin wall near the captain's body. "She did this. All of this. I'll—"

Metal groaned, and his leg came suddenly free, dumping him unceremoniously down to the wall of the cabin. He landed halfway onto Hyldir's body, which buckled under him with a grotesque squish and crackle.

He refused to look, feeling his gorge rise.

His blood trembled on the wall of the cabin. At first, Lan thought another tremor had passed through Luether, but he felt nothing. The blood moved on its own, as though driven by an internal pressure. A quaking, ancient hand emerged from the pool, followed by an arm.

"Vhaerynn?" he asked.

The necromancer emerged before him, trembling and gaunt. He looked older than Lan had ever seen him—older than any living creature he had ever seen. Skin barely concealed his bones, and his face was a blackened skull. He looked to be in pain, and his drooling face wore a look of constant, unimaginable horror. Around his neck he wore a barbed chain, from which brackish, sickly blood leaked.

"What—what has passed with you, man?" Lan asked.

"I have," came a woman's voice.

Behind Vhaerynn rose another body out of the blood. This one was a woman, powerfully built and clad in blood-smeared silks turned to wet rags by the journey. She had very short red hair and very dark skin, visible even despite all the blood. Somehow, being covered in gore made not a bit of difference to her, for she smiled all the wider. She held a chain, which attached at the other end to Vhaerynn's collar.

"Hail, brother," Alistra said, stretching and flicking blood from her hands. "I, Queen of Luether, have come to discuss terms of our peace."

"Our peace?" Lan clasped his hands on the arms of the command chair hard enough to dent the metal. "You dare?"

"Your surrender, then." Alistra smiled. "And yes. I *do* dare."

THE NAMED AND MARKED OF RUIN

Ravalis, the Blood of Summer ("Summer Lasts a Day"): Outlander Rulers of Tar Vangr, City of Winter

Cassian Ravalis (892–961): Last King of Luether (City of Summer), elder brother to Demetrus, father to Garin, perished in fall of Luether.

Demetrus Ravalis (894–981): Former King of Tar Vangr, younger brother to Cassian, father to Strevon, Paeter, Alistra, Lan and others. Slain Ruin's Night before 982 in Tar Vangr.

Ansa Ravalis nô Dorane (889–938): Wife to Demetrus Ravalis, perished birthing daughter Alistra.

Anthien Ravalis nô Vultara (916–961): Mistress and eventually second wife to Demetrus Ravalis, perished in the fall of Luether.

Toblius Ravalis (910–present): Younger half-brother to Cassian and Demetrus, husband to Alcha Varas.

Strevon Ravalis (930–961): The Hawk of Luether, first son of Demetrus, perished in the fall of Luether.

Paeter Ravalis (933–976): The Jackal of Luether, second son of Demetrus, husband to Lenalin Denerre, father to Darak and Semana, slain under mysterious circumstances.

Nameless (935–937): Third son of Demetrus, perished nameless.

Alistra (938–present?): The Spider of Luether, only daughter of Demetrus, imprisoned in the tunnels for unknown crimes.

Dorian Ravalis (940–961): The Wolf of Luether, son to Demetrus, perished in the fall of Luether.

Garin Ravalis (943–present): The Fox of Luether, former crown-prince of Luether, only son of Cassian.

Alcarin Summer (954–present): Smallborn squire to Garin.

King Lan Ravalis (944–present): King of Tar Vangr, the Eunuch King, the Bear of Luether, son of Demetrus, husband to Laegra.

Laegra Ravalis nô Vargaen (940–present): Daughter of house Vargaen, neglected wife to Lan.

Alcha Ravalis nô Varas (930–present): Wife to Toblius, wed after Fall of Luether.

Boulis Ravalis (948–present): The Hound of Luether, son of Toblius.

Tolus Ravalis (951–present): The Falcon of Luether, son of Toblius.

Vhaerynn the Necromancer (unknown–present): Blood sorcerer and vizier to Demetrus.

Denerre, the Blood of Winter ("Justice In the Storm"): Former Rulers of Tar Vangr, all but extinct

Aritana Denerre (885–932): Former ruler of Tar Vangr (910-932), youngest ruler of Tar Vangr in centuries, mother to Mortiun and Orbrin.

Moritun Denerre (911–936): Former ruler of Tar Vangr (932-936), elder brother to Orbrin, perished suddenly and unexpectedly in battle.

Orbrin Denerre (916–976): The Winter King, former ruler of Tar Vangr (r. 936-976), father to Althar and Lenalin and a third nameless child, perished at the hands of Ovelia the Bloodbreaker.

Matir Thorass (914–961): Wife to Moritun, political bond to Orbrin, mother to Althar and Lenalin and a third nameless child, perished in the fall of Luether.

Althar Denerre (937–955): Former Crown Prince of Denerre, perished in a duel.

Nameless (938–942): Second son of Denerre, perished in the cradle without a name.

Lenalin Denerre (940–966): Wife to Lan Ravalis, perished under mysterious circumstances.

Darak Ravalis nô Denerre (961–971?): Son to Lan Ravalis and Lenalin Denerre, exiled to Ruin for treason at a young age, presumed dead.

Semana Denerre nô Ravalis (963–present): Last Heir of Winter, daughter to Lan and Lenalin, master to Tithian. Faked death in 976 and took up the mantle of Mask.

Tithian Davargorn (963–present?): Smallborn Winterblood pageboy, then squire to Semana. Faked death in 976 and became loyal servant of Semana.

Dracaris, the Blood of the Dragon ("Eternal, Unyielding"): Treacherous Sworn Shields to Denerre

Norlest Dracaris (917–961): Sworn Shield to Orbrin, father to Ovelia, perished in the fall of Luether.

Aniset Winter (922-942): Smallborn mother to Ovelia, perished in childbirth.

Ovelia Dracaris the Bloodbreaker (942–present?): Sworn Shield to Lenalin, slew the Winter King in 976, mortally injured in the assault on the Summer King Demetrus in 981.

The Circle of Tears ("Ever Weep, Ever Watch"): A consortium of Spies in Tar Vangr

Regel the Oathbreaker (936–present): The Lord of Tears, formerly the Frostburn, Shadow of the Winter King, sworn slayer in service to Orbrin Denerre, current spymaster of the Circle of Tears.

Serris (960–981): Smallborn squire to Regel, First of Tears. Slain Ruin's Night 981.

Erim (961–present): Smallborn thief, occasional lover to Serris, bastard son of a Dolvrath noble.

Vidia (946–present): Smallborn baker.

Nacacia (957–present): Smallborn warrior.

Daren (955–present): Smallborn warrior.

Krystir (955–present): Smallborn spy.

Meron (940–981): Soldier, bastard son of a Vortusk noble, slain by Ravalis soldiers.

Sarelle (979–present): Child of Serris.

Court of Pervast, Ruin King

Pervast (unknown–present): Child of Ruin, ruler of Fallen Luether, City of Pyres.

Utora Vultara (943–present): Current consort to Pervast, twin sister to Vilaer.

Vilaer Vultara (943–present): Twin sister to Utora.

Stares Coldly at Death (unknown–present): Child of Ruin, male.

She Draws Blood (unknown–present): Child of Ruin, female.

Summer Lives: A rebellious insurgency in Luether dedicated to overthrowing Pervast.

Biaza (932–present): Quartermaster and second in command.

Red Jeggs (946–present): Armsmaster, braggart.

Neblen (960–present): Beggar, thief, and rumor-monger.

Corvus (932–present): Ravalis soldier turned ruffian.

Others

Shard (unknown–present): Skyship pirate lord, captain of the Reaver, self-proclaimed Emperor of the Dusk Sea.

Aeldad (unknown–present): Free Islander skyship pirate, first mate of Shard.

Hyldir (940–present): winterborn captain of the Avenger.

www.ingramcontent.com/pod-product-compliance
Lightning Source LLC
Chambersburg PA
CBHW031103030726
47496CB00002BA/356